Twelve Sundays

A Novel Based on True Events

Connie Dixon

Enjoy my first novel.

Connie Dixon

12/2016

ARCHWAY
PUBLISHING

Archway Publishing books may be ordered through booksellers or by contacting:

Archway Publishing
1663 Liberty Drive
Bloomington, IN 47403
www.archwaypublishing.com
1 (888) 242-5904

ISBN: 978-1-4808-3994-6 (sc)
ISBN: 978-1-4808-3995-3 (hc)
ISBN: 978-1-4808-3996-0 (e)

Library of Congress Control Number: 2016919015

Print information available on the last page.

Archway Publishing rev. date: 11/22/2016

I dedicate this book to my twin brother, Kenneth Dixon. I'm thankful I had the opportunity to spend the last twelve Sundays visiting you while you passed. You taught me that even though we were twins, we had different childhood memories and experiences. We were always connected, even when we were apart. I feel you every day and know you are watching from above, smiling. I always said I wanted to write a book, but I didn't know it would be a novel with much of your story thrown in. I know you would love it. I love you, my twin!

Acknowledgments

I want to thank Roger Mack for being the first person to believe in me writing this book. Thank you for being my editor and reader in the beginning. You gave me confidence by taking the time to read whatever I sent you and give me good feedback. Also, thank you for keeping LouLou during all those weekends when I went to the cabin to write.

Bernice Savell, you were one of the first people I told about writing this book. Your support has been tremendous. Thank you for your guidance and for the time we shared through this endeavor.

I have to thank the person who told me I had to share the story of how my brother died: Michael White, my friend and longtime client. I'm glad I shared with you my experience with my brother before he passed.

Juli Bouchillon, thank you for believing and supporting me through this journey since the beginning.

My dear friend, Honey Secunda, thank you for helping me find that wonderful cabin in the mountains. It was my catalyst for finishing my book.

Julius "Buddy" Hicks, thank you from the bottom of my heart for allowing me to use your cabin all those weekends to hibernate and write. It was the perfect spot. Thank you for your hospitality and kindness.

Thank you, Missy Bridgers, for offering your home for me to hibernate and write pushing me to get my book finished. I enjoyed writing in your Palm Beach home.

To my mom, thanks for understanding that I had to make my book an exciting and adventurous novel. Thanks for understanding that your character in the book is not you. I can't wait for you to read what I did with the story of my twin and your son's life.

Thank you to my own son, Evan. When I told you about my book, you were amazed and thrilled. You gave me hope and the desire to complete it. You have been a great soundboard and supporter. I love you!

Finally, thank you, Candi Cross, for turning my story into a book with your invaluable, creative editing and organizational skills.

Chapter 1

It was a misty, dark morning as Seela drove on the twelfth Sunday to see her dying twin brother, Sam. She sipped fiercely on her morning courage cocktail of vodka and orange juice from a tall tumbler. The radio blared Creedence Clearwater Revival, one of Sam's favorites, as Seela drove and thought about his life and how horrible it had been these last few months to watch him die in this awful situation—locked up and dying in the crazy judicial system. Through it all, somehow, Seela had discovered true love and connection with the family she had left long ago.

Seela reflected on the past week. Her heart's emotions had been ripped out and then put back together as one great puzzle. Seela's speedometer was pressed all the way to the right as she drove fearlessly down the highway. "Oh shit! I'd better slow down, or else I'll never make it to see Sam," she said nervously.

As Seela crested over a small hill on the highway, black clouds stretched across the wide, luminous sky. In the blink of an eye, the clouds quickly started to separate into three sections of sunlit tunnels. The sun's rays parted the gloomy clouds as if beams of heaven were tugging Sam's soul up into sky. It was a glorious eternal sight through Seela's hazy, tearful eyes. She pulled over to the side of the highway and pressed her forehead against the windshield.

Seela prayed aloud. "Dear Lord, if this is a sign you are taking my twin brother from me today, please let his soul rise up to you and my family who are already in heaven. Please, Lord, let him go fishing again with Dad and Granddaddy. I know they have been waiting for him.

Thank you, God, for sending him back to me. I've learned as much as Sam has learned in these twelve weeks." Seela looked up to the sky one more time before pulling back onto the highway. "When Sam makes it to you all, give me a sign, okay?" Seela smiled with tears rolling down her face as she drove on toward the state prison, gulping her vodka and orange juice cocktail.

Chapter 2

Three months ago, it had been a typical Friday in Seela's hair salon. The place brimmed with clients waiting for their weekly styles like kids waiting to see Santa Claus. Seela, the owner of the salon, appeared to be heading into surgery rather than hairstyling as she rushed through her salon with latex gloves on, careful not to touch anything but hair desperate for coloring. Her golden-brown hair squirreled around on top of her head as if she were going to the beach. Seela was a fit, petite woman with a beautiful smile that would have warmed a broken heater.

She blew her bangs away from her face while yelling to her assistant. "Dee! Do you have a timer for Ms. Lourdes? I need Kathy shampooed, and then you can get Ms. Lourdes. Put her under the dryer with conditioner."

Seela winked at Dee to let her know she was behind with her clients, and Dee winked back. After working together for years, Seela and Dee had their signs and signals down better than any coaching staff. Dee, a tall woman with a radiant presence of golden-honey skin and a flawless complexion thanks to her mixed nationality, was always on standby to make Seela happy.

Loud noises flowed over from next door, where contractors were hurriedly working to get Seela's other dream project completed—an art gallery filled with Seela's paintings and those of local artists.

"Sorry for all the noise today!" shouted Seela while blow-drying a mass of hair. "The contractors are supposed to be working at night, but now that they're behind, they're working days just to catch up. I didn't know how hard this remodeling was going to be. I thought, *Hang art, and be done with it,* but it hasn't been that simple, Kathy."

Kathy replied, "I don't know how you do it, Seela. All day long, you're styling hair, and you still have time to start another business. I know this new venture will be a success."

Seela placed the blow-dryer back in the holder while combing Kathy's hair before spraying it. She looked at Kathy in the mirror, beaming. "Well, there you go. You look like a million bucks!"

Kathy smiled as she looked at her hair with the handheld mirror. Her hair was coiffed to perfection and saturated with enough hair spray to hold it for a week. "Seela, you did it again!" Kathy exclaimed. "It looks fabulous!"

Kathy stood and walked to the front of the salon as Seela followed. Smiling strangely, Dee approached Seela, speaking as softly as she could. "Meet me in your office. Your mamaw is on the phone."

Seela froze, as she hadn't heard from anyone on the island in a long time.

Seela told the receptionist Kathy's total for the day and then reached around to hug Kathy. "It was so great to see you, Kathy. Maybe next week, you won't have to endure this drilling and hammering. The contractors should be painting by then. Hopefully, the smell of hair color will drown out the paint odor and keep all my clients from getting sick."

Kathy replied, "Honey, I told you it will be worth it soon! I know you are real happy. I can't wait for the grand opening. Don't be surprised if I bring a crowd of ladies." Kathy hugged Seela while slipping an envelope into the front pocket of the apron draped around Seela's neck. She whispered, "Sugar, take this as a donation to help your new art gallery. We are all happy you have made our sweet little town your home. You have been nothing but a ray of sunshine since the first time you walked into my husband's bank for that loan for this little ole nugget of a gold mine. What would we women do if we didn't have you?"

Knowing her hair was perfect, Kathy left the salon with a proud southern swagger. She walked toward her driver, who was waiting in the parking lot with the back door of her Bentley open for her.

On the way back to her office, Seela yelled out to Ms. Lourdes, "Go ahead and take a seat in my chair! I'll be right there, Ms. L. Can I bring you a glass of white wine, or would you rather have a hot tea today?"

Ms. Lourdes replied, "Glass of white today, dahlin'. I feel like I need to relax a little more. The dryer with conditioner was doing the trick, so why not make it better?" Ms. Lourdes glanced at the lady in the styling chair across from her, smiling politely. In no time, a salon assistant appeared with her wine.

Seela stood at the door, observing Dee with her hands in the air while Mamaw spoke on the other end. Seela had been so wrapped up with the art gallery construction that she hadn't thought of her mom and grandmother in some time. Relieving Dee of the duty, Seela took the phone from her. "Mamaw? Mamaw, is that you?"

"Seela, there's your sweet voice! I've been trying to find your number for months now. I had a list of numbers that dated back twenty years, I think." Mamaw sat on the other end of the phone with her top teeth plate out of her mouth. Her head was wrapped with a turban as old as Seela, and she was dressed in a mismatch of clothes, with a kitchen hand towel draped around her neck for warmth. She sat in her remote wheelchair, holding her twenty-year-old cordless phone, which had an antenna as long as her arm.

Seela's shoulders shrunk down as she listened to her grandmother talk. Her eyes filled with tears. Dee remained seated, anxiously awaiting any big news.

Seela became incensed. "Mamaw, where *is* Mom? Is she all right? Why didn't she give you my number?"

"That's why I'm calling you. Your mother has gone crazy ever since your brother got real sick. She lives down there in that little house and never comes up here to check on me."

Seela could picture Mamaw grinning with her gums and no teeth. Her heart felt heavy. "Mamaw, is there anyone helping you at all? How long has it been since you last saw Mom?"

Mamaw replied sheepishly, "I don't know. I know it's been awhile. I've marked over a month of days on the calendar. It's not a 2000 calendar, but it's got the same amount of days for the month. I know it's been a whole month when I have to turn to the next page. That's why I'm calling you. You are coming, right? I need you to get here quick! I don't know what to do!"

Seela, frustrated, looked at Dee with a confused expression while holding the phone to her chest. Her eyes welled with tears. She knew her family needed her now. She'd have to leave her personal sanctuary behind for a little while. "Yes, Mamaw. I'll be there tomorrow by lunch," Seela whispered. "I love you, Mamaw."

Seela hung up the phone, holding her head down. Dee handed her a tissue while placing her hand on Seela's forearm. "Girl, I don't know what is going on, but whatever it is, you know I've got your back. I will do whatever it takes to keep everything rolling smoothly while you go check on your mamaw and your mama. Take a day off, and drive down. I'll take care of everything."

Dee wrapped her long arms around Seela to give her the comfort she needed. Seela melted into her longtime friend. "I'm so lucky I have you, Dee. I can tell you, though, that this isn't going to be just a day project. Something tells me there is a lot more to this trip than just visiting for a day."

Dee rose from Seela's desk. "You get on out of here. I'll finish Ms. Lourdes's hair. I'll tell her you had an emergency you had to take care of." Dee picked up the hairbrush on Seela's desk and persisted. "I've got this. You get on!" Dee popped Seela on the arm lightly.

Upon arriving home, Seela rushed to her bedroom to start packing. She tried on outfit after outfit for her homecoming, only to come to the conclusion that jeans, T-shirts, and shorts were all that this trip required. Finally, after getting her suitcase packed, Seela thought maybe she should add one dress just in case. She walked back into her closet to find something suitable. Standing with a blank face, she forgot what she had come into the closet for. Then, on the top shelf, Seela spotted her grandmother's seafoam-green scarf. Her grandfather had bought it for her grandmother years ago. Seela wrapped the scarf around her neck, sniffing for any residual scent of her grandmother. She smiled while tossing it into her canvas overnight bag.

Seela prepared to call Dee the next morning and give her all the notes she had jotted down the night before. She'd always thought the only reason she'd ever return to her grandmother's home would be for a family member's funeral. Whose? When? Seela's heart leaped at the chance of spending time with Mamaw, who had raised her, but at the same time, she feared what she would be walking into after the four-hour drive to the little town she had left as soon as she'd graduated high school.

Seela called Dee while sitting in her office in a soft white T-shirt, rolled-up jeans, and her favorite pair of flip-flops. Just when she was preparing to leave a long-winded voice mail, Dee answered in a bubbly voice. "Yes, I know to call you if I have questions about color formulas and the hot contractors next door. I know where the cash goes. This week is going to be easy peasy, lemon squeezy! We'll all be fine here. You just take care of yourself driving today. You got good music to listen to? Grab some of those old CDs you used to mix up for your beach trips. Get down there, and get things straightened out, so you can get your sweet little butt back here for your grand opening!"

Seela smiled as she closed her eyes, fantasizing about the grand gala she had been meticulously planning. "Oh yes, the grand opening. But for now, I don't know what to expect. I am really concerned for my mom and my grandmother's well-being. No use expecting the worst, I suppose." Seela lingered on the phone, gaining strength from Dee as she thought about what lay ahead.

"Seela, my mind and heart are with you today. Everything's going to be all right. It always is. Isn't that what you always tell me?"

Seela smiled and said, "Yes, you are right, Dee. It always works out. I gotta run and look for some of those crazy CDs to take for my ride down. Good music always cheers me up."

Dee chuckled. "I love you, Seela. You're the best to me! You know that? You're the one who gives me inspiration. I'm so glad you decided to land in our little town. Ms. Kathy is right. You've brought nuttin' but a constant ray of sunshine here. Hell, I bet if you took a vote, this whole town would agree."

They exchanged their long, sentimental good-byes before Seela grabbed a bundle of CDs and headed out.

Chapter 3

Seela drove with her sunroof open and her stereo turned up as loud as she could stand it. The narrow, bumpy roads were the same as she remembered from traveling on them as a child. She stopped at a gas station that appeared just as outdated as it had when she'd left eighteen years ago. She wondered how the ancient pumps still operated. Suddenly, a young boy ran out from behind the station as Seela approached the entrance. His bare feet looked as if they had brown soles painted on the bottom with red clay. His overalls hung on him with one strap broken, hanging down long enough for him to trip over. Although he was obese, he was quick on his feet. His hair was as black as coal, reminding Seela of her granddaddy's when he was that young.

He wasted no time in speaking to Seela. "Hey, lady, I need a quarter to buy me an ice cream sammich. Will you give me one?" His accent was so country that Seela chuckled. Seela could tell the child had Down's syndrome, but he appeared to be high functioning. She smiled at him and asked his name just to hear him speak once again. The boy smiled proudly with his front tooth missing and said, "My name is Chester Johnson, but they call me Chubby."

Trying not to spill anything, Seela reached into her overstuffed purse as she stumbled to the sidewalk. Chester trotted close to her, determined to catch anything before it hit the red clay ground.

"Do you want me to hold that for you?" asked Chester.

Seela looked at his hands, seeing nothing but dirt-covered paws and fingernails. Smiling, she replied, "No, thank you, honey. I got it." She found a loose dollar and quickly handed it to the plump lad. Chester's

eyes grew to the size of half dollars, and the buckle on his overalls
jingled as he bounced happily. Seela quickly stepped back so Chester
would not reach out to touch her clean white T-shirt.

"Well, Chester, it was certainly a pleasure to meet you today. I hope
you enjoy your ice cream." Seela winked at him before heading into the
tiny station.

Chester jumped up onto the sidewalk and pushed the door open.
He shouted, "You can call me Chubby, 'cause that's what everybody else
do! I'll get the door for you! Do you want me to wash yer winders for
you while yer inside?"

Seela slipped past Chester, trying not to inhale his sweaty boy smell,
which was slowly permeating the space around her. "Honey, that's quite
all right. You go on. Get your ice cream, and enjoy it." Seela softly spoke
to him while winking at the same time.

"I can't," said Chester. "The ice cream man won't come till later
on today. My pa makes me work out here till the ice cream man comes.
Then I get to eat my ice cream on my walk home over yonder." Chester
pointed down the road toward a dirt drive leading to a worn-down
house with dilapidated cars littering the front yard like sculptures. Seela
smiled candidly at Chester, feeling sorry for him after seeing the only
life he knew.

Chester stood in front of the store, watching Seela get into her
shiny car, which stood out in the little town of Fairplay, Georgia, a rural
town with a population of 1,500 located just outside her hometown of
St. Simons Island. Chester looked as if he had just met a movie star. He
yelled out to Seela, "Hey! Do you live around here?"

Seela popped her head out of the window. "No, honey, I don't. I'm
just coming to visit some family on the island."

Chester ran up to her car and leaned his large head into Seela's
passenger window. "My pa takes me over the bridge to fish on Sundays
on the island. I just wish he would take me to the beach sometimes. He
says we have to catch our dinner, and the beach is for ole, lazy people."

Seela smiled sadly, reaching into her purse. She gave Chester a
business card. "Honey, if your pa will let you go with me to the beach

one day while I'm here, you call me at that number on my card. I'll take you anytime he will let you go. Do you have a swimsuit?"

Chester jumped up and down with excitement, shouting, "I've never been swimming, ma'am!" His rosacea-covered cheeks lit up like a Christmas tree. He looked down at her card, staring hard, before turning his face to Seela. "What if my pa won't let me go?"

Seela responded, "Don't worry about that. I think I'll be able to persuade him. You just call me, okay?"

Seela drove off while watching Chester in her rearview mirror. He stood like a stone statue while studying her card. He wore a quizzical, sad expression, as if wondering if he would ever see this mysterious woman again.

The drive across the bridge was breathtaking. Seela reminisced about her childhood and how hard it had been to grow up on the island as a biracial person with wealthy small-town blue bloods. She wondered how many of them still resided there and if anything had changed.

Seela pulled onto the dirt road that led to her grandmother's house. Childhood memories flashed through Seela's mind. She recalled walking to catch the bus and her shoes becoming muddy by the time she got to her bus stop. She'd always carried an extra pair to change into so the children wouldn't make fun of her wet, muddy ones. "Less fortunate"— that was what her family was, according to Mamaw, compared to those of old plantation money.

Seela steered her car through the swampy trees dominating the road to her grandmother's house. She was bewildered to see that everything was overgrown or dead all around the property. Before stepping out of her car, Seela paused for the unknown. Seela tried wheeling her suitcase down the broken driveway. After struggling, she picked her weathered suitcase up and carried it to her grandmother's carport. To Seela's surprise as she approached the door, there sat her mamaw, waiting with a big, toothless grin. Seela stopped to evaluate her grandmother's appearance. Seela's grandmother looked nothing like what she remembered with her false teeth missing from her mouth, her mismatched clothes, a dish towel draped around her neck like a mink stole, and her hair standing up all over.

From her electric wheelchair at the door, waiting patiently for Seela to come in, she exclaimed, "I'm so glad you came! Your mom is gone crazy, and your twin is dying. I can't take it anymore. You need to help them. I'll have a stroke if you want me to. You know I know how to have one of those! Just look at me now—stuck in this wheelchair because of the last one. Seela, you need to help me with what is going on here. I haven't seen your mom in three months. She's gone crazy, knowing your twin is dying in that prison. She's blaming herself, I do believe. It's killing my heart, Seels. I think she's gonna die with him. She's been down there since he was brought here to the island facility. She was going to see him once a week. I do believe it's killin' her, Seela. That's why I called you. You're the only one who can help this awful situation!"

Seela didn't have a chance to respond as they made their way to the kitchen, as Mamaw continued venting, happy to have someone near her with ears. Seela sat down at the kitchen table gazing at all of the untouched sea of memories she had forgotten. The same pictures that had been plastered on the fridge seventeen years ago were still there, telling the same memories, only with faded colors. Mamaw wheeled around the kitchen, hoping Seela would offer to cook something.

"Mamaw, let me fix us something to eat. I'm sure Mavvie has brought you some food since Mom has been holed up. She is checking on you, right? I smell her sage in here."

Seela smiled at her grandmother, knowing she didn't believe in her sister's healing abilities and modalities—including the use of sage.

Mamaw grinned, showing her shiny red gums. "You still burn that smelly stuff, Seela?"

"Yes, I do, Mamaw, and I don't want to hear your beliefs on it, okay?"

Mamaw retracted. "No, no, it's okay, Seela. I understand your beliefs and Mavvie's. I finally respect it. You know, it's kind of grown on me all these years. She does help me when I get sick. I haven't been to a doctor in years."

Realizing she would be continually shocked on this trip, Seela replied, "That's not good, Mamaw. You always need a checkup. Let me look and see what Mavvie has left here in your kitchen." Seela opened the pantry and spotted the same fabric holder that had held the plastic grocery bags when she was a young child. Wooden shelves from the 1950s were stacked with jars of pickled peppers and fig preserves. She didn't want to know how long ago they had been stocked. Seela grabbed a jar of figs and a bag of flour out of the pantry. "How 'bout I make some fluffy biscuits? We can pour these delicious fig preserves over them, along with a fried egg—just like Granddaddy used to do it."

Mamaw smiled widely. "Do you remember how to make cathead biscuits, Seela?"

"Of course I do, Mamaw. I make them at least once a week. Still my favorite! I still remember the day you taught me how to make them. I think there was more flour on the kitchen floor and counters than in my biscuits. I thought they were going to look like real cat heads. You kept telling me they were some good-looking catheads."

Seela and Mamaw laughed heartily together. Seela leaned down and hugged her grandmother from behind in her wheelchair. "I've missed you, Mamaw. I'm sorry I haven't seen you in a while." Seela caught the whiff of a soured dish rag and recoiled. "Mamaw, what is that around your neck?"

Mamaw reached for the dish towel. "It's my neck warmer. I just throw it round my neck when I get the chills."

"Oh good Lord, that thing has mildew growing on it, Mamaw! You have asthma. You want to kill yourself?"

Mamaw replied, "I thought I smelled something this morning but couldn't figure it out! I kept checking my shirt, thinking it was time for a change."

Seela went to her suitcase and retrieved the scarf she had brought from her home. She gently wrapped it around Mamaw's neck. "My spirit guides told me to bring this scarf. Now I know why!"

Mamaw studied it and said, "Your granddaddy gave this to me

years ago. I remember the day he brought it home to me. How come you have it?"

"You gave it to me years ago for good luck, Mamaw."

"I did? Well, I don't remember, so can I have it back?"

Seela chuckled. "Of course. Please just promise me you won't wear any more dish rags!"

Mamaw crossed her heart like a little girl.

"So, Mamaw, who is helping you since Mom hasn't been up here?"

Mamaw said, "No one but Mavvie. She checks on me once a day when she's not busy working her witchcraft on people." Mamaw scratched her head with her crippled hands. Her hair stood straight up like a rooster's feathers as she pulled her hands back down, causing Seela to laugh. They enjoyed the meal without words for a few minutes. Seela needed to take in all of this information being thrown at her. All she wanted was a stiff drink. Seela watched her grandmother sop up the preserves with a biscuit. The juice from the preserves dripped down the sides of her wrinkled, leathery old hands.

"Whoo, Seela, I do believe these are the best biscuits I've had in a long time. They're so fluffy and light, just the way I like them!"

Seela beamed. "Just the way you taught me." Seela pushed her chair back, folded her napkin, and placed it on her plate. "Now, Mamaw, let's talk about Sam. What is going on with him?"

"It's a big mess, and I think he's dying, but I can't get an answer from your mom. She told me awhile back Sam has liver cancer. The prison system sent him up to the state prison because he's so sick he keeps going in and out of the hospital with his liver. You know he got that hepatitis C, and it's killin' him. But something funny's going on now. He always called me every day, saying he love me, and a week ago, he stopped calling. That's why I called you. You got to find out what's going on. Sam got one of those fancy phones last year in there from one of his guard friends. He used to send me pictures and videos on his phone. I ain't got one since last Tuesday. Here—you can see for yourself. He don't look so good. He's been getting thinner and thinner in the past few months. You would never know you two are twins, Seela!"

Seela replied, "When did you learn to use an iPhone?"

"When your mom left me up here with it and hasn't returned. Sam started calling it, and I figured out how to answer it. He told me how to use some things on it. It's the only way I could stay in touch with him."

"I'm calling the prison in the morning and demanding to see him," Seela said sternly. "I need to see what's going on. Someone has to take charge."

"I knew you would get to the bottom of this, Seela," Mamaw said with pride. "Are you going down to get your mom to come out?"

Seela stared out the window, thinking about how long it had been since she had seen or talked to her mom. "I don't know if I should tonight, Mamaw. Let me see what's going on with Sam in the morning." Seela reached across the table and covered her grandmother's hands with hers to reassure her that she was no longer alone and helpless.

Seela took her things to the bedroom she'd grown up in, which was still decorated in floral pink-and-blue wallpaper. When she sat down quickly on the four-poster bed, dust flew into the air. Seela jumped up, realizing her room had probably not been touched for years. She immediately removed the bedspread and sheets while patting the mattress to see how much dust flew free.

"Yuck," Seela whispered while coughing on stagnant air. She immediately took the sheets out to the laundry shed. While loading the machine, she looked out the old blurred window pane above the washer. Seela saw her mother's shadow move across the tiny cottage window. She stopped, waiting for the shadow to reappear, but it never did. Seela stared at the window, wondering how long she should wait before paying a visit to her mother. Just then, the lights went out.

Seela walked back to Mamaw's house, carefully positioning each step so as not to trip over yard art and overgrown plants and flowers. It was like a minefield. Just as she got close to the house, a raccoon darted out from under the porch. He quickly sprinted across the yard with an empty tuna can clutched in his mouth. Seela shrieked loudly, running to the house.

"What startled you, Seela? You look like you saw a big ole bear out there!" Mamaw chuckled. "Was some swamp animal chasing you?" Her eyes grew big as she waited to hear what Seela reported.

"No, it was just a nasty raccoon that had gotten in yall's trash. He had an empty can of tuna in his mouth!"

"Oh, Seela, they won't hurt you. You not afraid of a little raccoon, are you?"

Seela responded, "Oh no, Mamaw, it just startled me." Seela grabbed a paper towel. She wiped the swampy mist that had coated her face and neck like a layer of cellophane. "Whew, I had forgotten how this island has its own air down here. I know why you used to say you could cut it with a butter knife."

"Did you see your mom when you went to the laundry room?" Mamaw asked.

Seela replied, "I saw her shadow, and then the lights went out. I don't think she saw me. She probably thought I was Mavvie in the laundry, if she saw anyone. I'll visit her tomorrow after I see about Sam. Mamaw, do you think I should help you get a shower before bed?" Seela hoped her grandmother would agree. She knew it had been quite a while since water had touched the poor woman's body.

Mamaw paused and then said, "Tomorrow, Seels. I'm too tired tonight. I'm also too excited with you here. It feels like Christmas Eve, Seels. I don't know if I'll be able to sleep a wink tonight just basking in the glory of having you here with me once again."

Seela leaned down and draped her arms over her grandmother from behind. "Oh, Mamaw, I'm so glad I'm here with you too." Mamaw's hair was like a Brillo pad in color and texture. When Seela stood back up, her grandmother's hair pressed down in the middle where Seela had laid her head. Seela laughed.

"What you laughing about?" said Mamaw, looking confused. Seela reached for a hand mirror on the side table that contained anything and everything Mamaw would need. She held it in front of Mamaw, who chuckled. Her round belly jiggled up and down. "That's enough to make a crying baby laugh, Seels. I promise I'll let you bathe me tomorrow and get me smelling good like you."

Seela pulled Mamaw's straw-textured hair back up to make it look normal. Seela was thankful her hair was more like her father's soft, silky hair, which could be shaped and shifted into various dos she had been taught as a stylist.

Mamaw wheeled down the hall, stopping at Seela's room. "Every night, my routine is the same. Before I go to bed, I stop here at your room and pretend that you are still living here and your granddaddy is in his chair. You are getting ready for bed, and I'm getting ready to tuck you in. I sit here, say my prayers, and say good night to you. I then go on to my room and get myself to bed while saying good night to Edward. I fold down his side of the bed as if he's coming in after the news."

At these words, Seela cried silently while Mamaw stared into Seela's room. Once Mamaw backed her head out of the room, Seela wiped the tears from her face with her white T-shirt, covering the shirt with mascara.

Seela spoke with a crackled voice. "Mamaw, why don't I get some clean sheets out of linen closet, and we'll make my bed together like old times?"

Mamaw smiled at the little gesture that held so much joy for her in an instant. "Go get the softest sheets you can find, Seels!"

Seela grabbed a heap of pink sheets that were decades old and trotted down the hall back to her room, shouting, "Look what I found, Mamaw—my favorite sheets!"

After she made the bed, Seela lay down across the fitted sheet, sniffing, as she had when she was a young girl. Mamaw wheeled over to the side of the bed, pressing her nostrils tightly against the sheets with her. "Well, they don't smell like they did when you were little. I haven't used the clothesline since my stroke. Maybe you can wash my sheets and put them on the line for me?"

Seela smiled as she stood up from the bed. "You bet, Mamaw. I'll do towels too. I do love the fresh outdoor smell. What a great childhood memory."

Seela and Mamaw finished making the bed and then sat for a few more minutes in silence. After mutually yawning, they parted for the night with a kiss. Seela couldn't stand to see her grandmother in such a reckless state physically, but she promised that would all change with her help in the morning. Seela went to the bathroom to wash her face. While looking for her toothbrush, she realized she had forgotten to bring toothpaste. Seela looked in her grandparents' medicine cabinet and snickered. Every item must have been at least thirty years old. She pulled out a bottle of Merthiolate, which wasn't on the market any longer. *Antique mosquito bite burner*, Seela thought, and she resolved to take it home with her.

Chapter 4

Seela tried hard to go to sleep, but after tossing and turning for an hour, she decided to forget battling with insomnia and have a cup of tea. Seela walked into the kitchen to start a pot of water. She stood at the kitchen sink, filling the teapot and staring out the window into the swampy backyard. All of a sudden, Seela saw someone leap across the yard. Seela put the teapot down and turned on the outside light. Mavvie stopped in her tracks with a big stick in her hand.

"Hey, Mavvie. It's me—Seela. Don't be afraid!"

Mavvie's eyes grew to the size of silver dollars. The whites were so big that they made her skin look even darker. Her headdress made her appear six feet tall. Mavvie ran quickly across the yard toward Seela. She spoke in her broken Baton Rouge accent. "Oh my, Seela. When did you get here, my love? Your mamaw said you were coming. I saged the house and your room as soon as I heard." Mavvie grabbed Seela and squeezed her tightly, whispering, "It's okay now. You have work to do. Soon you will be soaring like an eagle like you are supposed to, Seela. It's time!"

Seela huffed sarcastically. "I thought I was done here on this island, Mavvie.

Mavvie caressed Seela's face with her soft, oily hands. "Baby, it's okay. Your twin needs you now. You have to help him leave this world. He will be better on the other side. You know he's been tortured here all his life. It's time. We have to help him know God and help him not be afraid. I feel his sadness of dying. You are the only one who can teach him not to be afraid. You have to teach him to let go so that he doesn't suffer anymore."

The thought of losing her twin forever finally hit home as she melted into her worldly great-aunt. Seela felt her stomach tighten, and her throat close up. She snorted, trying to catch her breath. Mavvie gently pushed Seela's head down, massaging her back, urging her to focus on her breath. Seela's body lifted gradually as she regained her composure with Mavvie's healing touch.

"Mavvie, how am I going to do this? I have to go to the prison tomorrow to see my twin brother after seventeen years. He has never stopped loving me. I left him and everyone else behind. I feel horrible now when I see my grandmother in the condition she's in. I haven't been here to help. Was that selfish of me? Was it selfish that I wanted to have a better life? You told me it was the best thing for me. I believed you. I've had a normal life, a successful life, but damn, this right here is my family that I left, and now look!" Seela threw her hands into the air, pointing toward her grandmother's house. She paced back and forth, raising her voice as if it were noon instead of midnight. Then there was silence. Even the cicadas seemed to be listening to Seela's plight. Wildlife waited for Seela's next outburst.

Mavvie grabbed Seela's hand and steered her to her home. "Let's make tea. It will make you feel better. We can even put you on the table and do some work before you go tomorrow."

Seela's eyes lit up. They skipped excitedly toward the door like little girls going to the hairdresser with their mother for the first time. "I want to get on the table. Forget the tea. I need to make sure I'm ready for tomorrow. You know Sam will come up in the session—he always does. I need to know: Are you up for it this late at night, Mavvie?"

Mavvie caressed and kissed Seela's face. "Anything for you, my love. I knew this was coming."

"Of course you did. What was I thinking?" Seela smiled and popped her forehead with her hand.

They walked into Mavvie's shack of a house. On the outside, it appeared to be an old wooden house. The inside was a richly decorated Zen world that made Seela feel euphoric and divine. Beautiful organic fabrics and stones the size of furniture illuminated the room. An amalgamation of colors made the room shine, and giant, glowing amethysts sat all around.

"I've missed this place, Mavvie. I know you've worked on me through the telephone and letters, but there is nothing like being in this room. I think it reminds me of a little piece of heaven." Seela walked around, touching the items and remembering her childhood. Mavvie lit a sage stick and swirled its power around the room, softly chanting.

"Go now. Lie down on my table. I'll be there in a minute. I'm being told I need some tools for this session."

Seela approached the table and stood for a second, inhaling the strong sage scent floating through the air. Once she placed her body flat on Mavvie's working table, she saw that Mavvie had painted the ceiling to look like the night sky. "You have a night sky now. It's so beautiful!" she shouted.

Mavvie stepped closer and whispered, "It's time for our session now. I'll tell you about my sky another time." She shook what appeared to be an old straw broom over Seela.

Seela closed her eyes, waiting patiently for images to appear on the movie screen of her mind. She languished in a trance of meditation before shadows of skulls flew by rapidly. At one point, Seela flinched at the appearance of a flying, screaming skull face that was on fire with its teeth coming right at her. Seela felt someone squeeze her leg, causing her to open her eyes. Mavvie stood over Seela's core, holding a leather string with two cymbals clinking back and forth loudly. Seela squeezed her eyes shut so as not to disrupt the session.

When the noise stopped, Seela felt Mavvie's heavy breath at the top of her head. Mavvie whispered, "Are you okay? You can sit up when you are ready."

Seela sat up, looking wildly at Mavvie. "So much was coming at me, Mavvie. I couldn't make out who or what it was. I saw this screaming skull on fire. It freaked me out!" Her childlike description didn't seem to do the sight justice.

Mavvie's eyes bugged out like giant gumballs. "I know you will figure out what came to you, Seela. Just pay attention to what you saw, and it will appear again."

"I don't want it to appear again, Mavvie! It was scary. I'm not kidding when I say it looked freaky and on fire."

Mavvie held her cymbals in front of Seela. "Your father was here in our session tonight. He told me to hold this over your core, where you are connected to your twin. This is all I did." Mavvie held the string in front of Seela with her fingers at each end and the cymbals hanging down. The cymbals made no noise. Mavvie then hit the symbols and continued. "When I held these over your core, they immediately started clanging back and forth by themselves. This work had to be done before you go see Sam tomorrow." Mavvie moved around the room, looking for something. "That's strange. I know I put my security stone here to give you for your visit in the morning. It's been moved. I will find it. Someone's playing with me right now." Mavvie scanned the room as if it were full of spirits playing hide-and-seek with the object.

Spent from the powerful session, the women parted for the evening. Seela skipped energetically up to her grandmother's house, as if she had gotten her battery recharged. She tiptoed into the carport, hoping she wouldn't wake her grandmother. A fat feral cat darted across the yard, scaring the living daylights out of Seela. There were all kinds of animals everywhere on the property, running wildly.

Seela crept down the hallway and quietly peeked into Mamaw's room. To her surprise, her grandmother was not in her bed. She cautiously walked toward the kitchen, where she found Mamaw eating a cake doughnut and drinking a small glass of orange juice in the dark. Seela turned the light switch on.

Mamaw grinned with a mouthful of doughnut. "I'm eating my midnight snack. It's what I do every night."

"Oh my. Are you supposed to have something sugary this late at night with your diabetes? Aren't you still taking insulin twice a day?" Seela hated to treat an elderly woman like a child, but someone obviously needed to take control.

After savoring the cake doughnut, Mamaw replied, "Yes, honey. I've been doing this for years—way before your granddaddy died. If this is what kills me, so be it. I'm ready to go anyway."

Seela shook her head and kissed her grandmother good night for the second time on this seemingly endless night. Her duties were not over. Suddenly, she realized she hadn't called Dee.

Like teenagers, she and Dee shared tidbits of their day for nearly two hours before yawning and blowing kisses over the phone.

Chapter 5

Seela woke to the smell of percolated coffee and the sound of an old mixer grinding. She quickly dressed in her robe and slippers. As she turned the corner while coming into the kitchen, she ran into Mavvie, who was dressed in a long white muumuu. Her hair was tied high with a colorful scarf, and she held an unidentifiable drink.

"I make these smoothies for your mamaw now. I think it's what keeps her sugar level down. She doesn't know what I put in it, but she thinks it tastes good." The liquid was the color of green swamp water. The tall drink smelled like freshly cut grass. Mavvie poured Seela a small amount in a Dixie cup.

Seela examined it as if it were the castor oil her grandmother used to give her. Mavvie pushed the cup toward Seela's mouth. Seela tossed it back like a shot of tequila. Her eyes grew big. "Wow! That tastes like banana but smells like grass."

"Have I ever given you something you didn't like, my Seelie?"

Seela thought for a second. "No, but I'm sure you've told me something I didn't like!" Seela embraced Mavvie, ready to face the day. "What a way for me to wake up, seeing you first this morning, Mavvie. Where is Mamaw?"

"Go check the bathroom, Seela. I haven't heard a peep from her this morning. I've been in here for a while."

Seela hurried down the hall and tapped on her grandmother's bathroom door. Mamaw called out to her. "Honey, I think I have a mess in here. Can you come in and help me?"

Seela took a deep breath as she opened the bathroom door. Her grandmother sat naked on the commode with shit all down her legs. "Oh good Lord! What happened, Mamaw?" Seeing her so helpless broke Seela's heart.

"I tried to make it, but sometimes it just doesn't happen. I've been trying to clean myself for the past thirty minutes, but these baby wipes just aren't getting it."

Seela turned on the bathtub faucet, and Mamaw gasped. "No, Seelie. I can't get in there!"

"Why not, Mamaw? You have a seat right here that you can sit on. I'll shower you off gently."

Mamaw stared as if Seela were asking her to jump out of an airplane. "Seela, ever since those people in the rehabilitation center hung me up in that net in the air and hosed me down, I have a fear of the shower and of the bath."

After a few minutes, Seela coaxed her grandmother into complying. Seela helped Mamaw stand. "Okay, Mamaw, you can do this." After getting her in the tub, Seela gently sprayed her grandmother with water. All at once, tissue flew out from all parts of Mamaw's body into the air. Seela stared in bewilderment. Mamaw had stuffed tissue everywhere that might sweat or where skin touched skin. Seela didn't know whether to laugh or cry at the sight. "Mamaw, how often do you change your tissues?"

Her grandmother sat on the bathtub bench with her eyes closed, slouched over. Her breasts were so large that they touched her knees. It seemed to Seela that the water was foreign to her.

"How does it feel, Mamaw?"

"You were right, Seelie. This feels wonderful!" she exclaimed as her round belly shook vigorously. "Ain't I a sight, honey? It's a wonder I don't have rust on my ankles. I do try to wash with a cloth every day, though—best I can do."

"It's all right, Mamaw. We're going to get you smelling so good the folks in town will smell you!"

Mamaw spoke sternly. "We don't want that. I don't want anything to do with those folks from town. A bunch of snooty hooties they all are!"

After an hour of cleaning and pampering Mamaw, Seela proceeded to get in touch with the prison about Sam. She called several times, speaking to numerous people who didn't have answers. Finally, she received a call with solid information.

"Hi, Miss Seela Black. This is Officer Jordan. I'm handling your brother's case. I have gotten your *many* messages today. I wanted to call you to inform you that your brother has been admitted to the hospital on the island with maximum security."

Hospital with maximum security. Seela chewed on the words, trying to decipher the meaning as it related to her brother. "Is he going to be okay? When did he go there? Can I go see him?"

"We are waiting to hear about his condition. Yes, you can go there. You may not be able to see him. He is in intensive care on a secured floor for prisoners. I'll give you the number to call. They will be able to give you more information on Mr. Sam Black."

Seela thanked the nonchalant officer and called the hospital. She waited for what seemed like forever after the nurse asked her to hold the line. Another gentleman got on the phone, speaking to Seela in a more definitive voice.

"This is Officer Smith. If you want to come down here, you are allowed a one-hour visit with your brother between one and two o'clock today."

"Yes, sir, Mr. Smith. I'll be there at one to see my brother. Can you tell me what's going on with him?"

Officer Smith replied, "All I can tell you is that he's in intensive care, ma'am. I'll be here to escort you in when you arrive."

Seela hung up the phone. She stood in silence for a moment, sensing doom. Seela decided not to say anything to her grandmother. She got dressed, preparing for her drive to the hospital. She and Mavvie exchanged all-knowing glances.

Before Seela walked out the door, Mavvie ran to her. "Step back, baby. I need to sage all over you before you walk into that hospital. Be sure to wrap yourself with white light when you walk through those doors. Stay focused on what you are there for, not the other people around you." Mavvie placed her security stone in Seela's right hand. "Put this in your pocket."

The rickety wooden screen door slammed behind Seela as she jumped into her car. She hooked her phone to Bluetooth in order to call Dee. In a rapid stream, she informed Dee about dealing with her grandmother's bathroom ordeal that morning. She then explained Sam's situation—being locked up in a prison hospital with a deteriorating liver due to hepatitis C. "Dee, I just know that because he's a prisoner of the state, they haven't given him the appropriate medicine or treatment to help him."

Dee ached for her friend and boss. Seela was her world. "I think I need to just get in my car and come on down there, Seels. I can help you. We can close the shop for a few days. This is some heavy shit for you to deal with."

"In all seriousness, I am scared to death of what I will find when I see Sam, but it makes me feel so much better to know you are keeping my world up there intact."

Dee reluctantly agreed to stay put, knowing she probably wouldn't for long.

Seela realized she had missed her turn from the swampy island, cursing to Dee at the same time. "I'd better hang up, Dee, so I don't get lost. Besides, my phone connection isn't that good either."

"Kiss-kiss!" Dee managed to say before the phone went dead.

Chapter 6

Seela drove on the narrow two-lane bridge that crossed over the beautiful blue water, thinking about Sam and the tortured life he lived. Seela got to the end of the road and glanced over at the old gas station, searching for Chester. Red fog swirled through the lot so thickly that she could barely see the ancient gas pumps. As the dust settled after a large truck drove away, Chester appeared with a big smile. He waved anxiously at Seela as she pulled into the parking lot. He hustled over as fast as he could with his flat clubfeet. With each step, it looked as if Chester were walking on hot coals. His belly shook while his arms flopped around his large body. He tried to get to Seela's white BMW as quickly as possible.

Standing at the car window, Chester said, "Are you leaving the island now? I've been waiting to see you today."

"Well, I guess you got what you were waiting for, Chester. I'm not leaving yet. I'm going to be on the island for a little while. I'm on my way to the Brunswick Hospital. When I come back this afternoon, I'll stop by to see you again. I'm sure I'll be ready for something cold to drink. Maybe I'll buy you your favorite ice cream. How does that sound, Chester?"

His face colored with happiness. "We'll have ice cream together, okay?" He glowed at the thought of seeing her again and sharing a sugary treat.

Seela nodded, waving good-bye as she left Chester. There was something about Chester that drew her to him, whether it was sympathy, a motherly instinct, or just plain amusement.

As Seela pulled into the hospital parking lot, she could feel her heartbeat quickening. Then she thought of Mavvie and the stone in her pocket. It gave her a sense of security.

She would try to remember not to look anyone in the eye, as Mavvie had instructed, so as not to carry back negative energy.

Seela wound her way through the parking garage and entered the busy hospital. She focused on getting to the special floor where her brother was being held. A large, beautiful black nurse with a caramel complexion made eye contact with a hint of familiarity. "Are you needing to be escorted to floor number five? I just got a call that someone needs to be taken up there. What's your name, ma'am?"

As Seela stated her name, the nurse smiled warmly and scooted her chair back. She grabbed a ring of keys while motioning for Seela to follow her to the elevator located down the hallway. Seela felt weak in the knees as she walked with the nurse, smelling sick hospital smells in the sterile hallway. A feeling of nausea threatened to overwhelm her. The nurse inserted a key into the elevator door, as if it were a special elevator. Seela stepped into the elevator and turned back to the nurse standing in the hallway. "Push floor number five, ma'am. There will be someone waiting for you when the elevator doors open."

Seela hit the number-five button on the elevator, trying to focus on her breathing. She wished Mavvie could have accompanied her. Once the door opened on the fifth floor, a muscular man with a stunning smile greeted her. Seela felt a warm glowing feeling in her stomach as she tried to speak. She had not experienced this emotion or energy in some time and was not sure how to handle it. As a result, Seela suddenly fumbled with herself and her purse as she stepped out of the elevator.

"I'm Seela Black. I'm here to see my brother, Sam Black, who was brought here last night."

The handsome dark-skinned officer with the electrifying smile spoke politely. "Yes, ma'am, I'm Officer Quinton. I'm here to escort you to the emergency ICU. Your brother is there."

Seela gasped. "What has happened to my brother?"

"I'm not at liberty to say at this time. I'm just here to make sure you are escorted to the proper place and not left unattended while on this floor. This floor is nothing but incarcerated inmates. You will see officers at all ports of these hallways." Officer Quinton escorted Seela to a glass-encased room, where Sam laid lifeless on a gurney with his eyes bulging out. His body was blown up as if he were about to bust open. Tubes sprouted out from machines and into Sam's swollen skin. Two huge officers stood at the end of Sam's gurney, guarding him like a grand star. Seela quickly ran to Sam's side. Tears flowed like a river from her eyes. She talked to Sam, but he didn't move. She suddenly realized he was in coma. A tall, slender woman walked into the room and placed her hand gently on Seela's shoulder. "I'm so sorry. I'm Dr. Gutka, and I saved your brother's life last night."

Seela prayed voraciously to her god and spirits to protect her brother as if this were the end of his life. Seela could feel the vibration in the room, and she felt as if her brother had already left his body. He looked dead lying there.

The doctor spoke with a kind voice. "He was airlifted here from the prison he was stationed at. He had sustained a considerable amount of blood loss. He is still in highly critical condition. We won't know for a couple days if he is going to pull through. We have him in a medically induced coma so his body can try to heal some. All we can do now is give him time and rest. We will watch closely over him to see if he can make it through this. As I mentioned before, he lost a lot of blood."

Dr. Gutka awkwardly embraced Seela to try to console her as the TV blared with football play-offs. The two officers stared mechanically, as if they weren't in a dying man's periphery, cheering for their favorite football team of choice. Seela pulled away from Dr. Gutka with anger rising within.

"Get the hell out of this room right now! My brother is lying here blown up like a dead whale on a beach, and you two are standing there like we're in a football stadium!"

The officers waited for the doctor to speak and take control.

As the doctor nudged them to leave, Officer Quinton peered in. "Is something wrong?" He had heard Seela shouting. Dr. Gutka motioned for him to step into the room. Seela was relieved when she heard Dr.

Gutka ask Mr. Quinton to stick around and escort Seela out. She didn't know why, but any presence would have been better than the two assholes who didn't care about her beloved twin's suffering.

Officer Quinton brought Seela a chair so she could sit by her brother's side. Seela cried, praying over her brother for what seemed an eternity. Her face was black with mascara running in trails down her cheeks. Her hands were shaking terribly, as she, being Sam's twin, was feeling his pain. Seela sat crying and praying over Sam as two hours passed.

Officer Quinton's warm hand touched Seela's shoulder. "Ms. Black, visiting hours were over a half hour ago. Can I escort you to your car now? You can come back tomorrow. I'll see if I can get you a special four-hour visit. I've got some pull here." He winked at Seela, which brought a hint of comfort to her.

Seela kissed Sam's swollen hands and blown-up face as his eyes continued to stare into space. She turned to Officer Quinton. He reached for her, as she looked as if she were about to crumple to the floor. Seela started to heave in tears. The officer held her as she cried. "I didn't know he was this sick," she said. "I can't believe my eyes."

Officer Quinton reached over to the tray table to get a tissue for Seela. She wiped her face, trying to gather her emotions for the drive back to Mamaw's. She dreaded describing this scene to her mother, grandmother, and Mavvie.

They walked slowly as Officer Quinton told Seela that he had met her brother the last time he had been stationed at the hospital. "That Sam isn't a bad guy, just addicted." The two had gotten acquainted over a bet on a Falcons versus Saints game. Officer Quinton was from Louisiana, which made him partial to the Saints. Sam wanted his prize to be Super Bubble bubble gum if he won. With this, Seela relaxed, laughing and remembering that Sam's favorite gum as a kid was Super Bubble, while hers was Bazooka.

"Did you lose the bet?" she asked the officer.

"No, ma'am! Saints won that game, though barely."

"Well, what in the world could my brother give you for winning?" Seela chuckled.

"Let's just say he gave me a nugget, Seela."

She stopped in the hallway, turning toward Officer Quinton, who was so handsome she could barely look him in the eye. "What's a nugget?" she asked.

"Well now, that's between me and your brother. Don't worry, though. I got Mr. Sam Black some Super Bubble, and that entire day, every time I came by his room to check on him, he was chewing like a cow chewing its cud."

Officer Quinton escorted Seela to her car and opened the door like a perfect gentleman. "Really nice car, Ms. Black."

"Thank you. I sort of like it myself," Seela replied, smiling bashfully. "I'll be back tomorrow. What are the times for visiting?"

Officer Quinton leaned down so he could see Seela's face while he spoke. "I'm going to get special visitation rights for you, Ms. Black. Call the front desk tomorrow morning, and ask for the fifth-floor desk. Then ask for me. I'll let you know what time to come, and like I said, I'll get you a four-hour pass." Officer Quinton smiled broadly with his electrifying smile while holding her eyes.

Seela backed out of the parking spot and headed out of the garage. Many thoughts and emotions raced through her body as she wound down five levels to the parking attendant's booth.

Chapter 7

The roads were wet now because it had rained while Seela was inside the hospital. Seela drove slowly in a daze, trying to grasp what had just happened. How would she tell her mom and grandmother of Sam's horrific condition? It was beyond her worst projections.

She drove past Chester's gas station, not thinking about the ice cream she had promised him earlier. Then, with the memory, she slammed on her brakes. She looked in her rearview mirror, and there Chester stood, anticipating her next move. Seela turned the car around and whirled into the lot next to him.

Seela rolled her window down. "I'm so sorry, honey! I almost forgot to stop. I had a horrible visit at the hospital today. I don't think I'm up for ice cream." Seela handed Chester a five-dollar bill and said, "Buy yourself as much as this will get you. I'll see you tomorrow before I go back to the hospital. We'll share one then."

Chester looked painfully sad as he stared at the money in his hand. "Um, Ms. Seela, you gave me too much money. Ice cream only cost fifty cents."

"Well, you sure will have a lot of ice cream then!" Seela shouted, trying to feign enthusiasm, when all she wanted to do was curl up with a strong drink and sob.

With his crossed eye focusing intensely on Seela, Chester smiled through his puffy lips. Chester was a heavy boy, but his limbs and features were uncharacteristically small. He stepped back so Seela could drive away.

As Seela pulled into the driveway, she spotted Mavvie at the end of the yard with a long, twisted stick. A white silk cloth tied to the top of the stick waved about in the breeze as Mavvie chanted ritualistic sayings. Seela pulled to the side of the driveway and opened her car door to get out. Mavvie waved at Seela and put her finger over her mouth to let Seela know not to speak. Seela tiptoed out to Mavvie, reaching for her hand. Mavvie and Seela stood while Mavvie, almost in tears, prayed in her own language. Seela had no clue what she was saying, but she felt the healing words flowing out of Mavvie's mouth. As Mavvie finished praying, she handed the stick to Seela. The flag stopped flying high and fell to the side of the stick. Mavvie, dressed in white, with her black hair flowing loosely down her back, opened her eyes and frowned sadly.

"You saw him, didn't you?"

Seela replied, "Yes, Mavvie, and it was horrible. I don't know what has happened, but he is in an induced coma. Sam is blown up like an elephant. His eyes were bulging open out of his head. His hands were blown up so huge. I couldn't stop crying, Mavvie. Thank goodness this nice prison officer was there and very helpful to me. I went crazy when I saw Sam like that. I went ballistic on the two officers in Sam's room. I just couldn't control myself. Now I have to go back tomorrow at a set time. Sam needs me right now, and I can't be with him." Seela caved into her beautiful great-aunt, who squeezed her like a pillow.

"You have to go through this, my Seelie. It's a part of your path. You will be okay because you have me to guide you."

Seela and Mavvie walked to Mamaw's house hand in hand. When they stepped through the kitchen door, they found Mamaw standing by the kitchen sink with a walker. Seela had no idea she could still walk. "Mamaw, I thought you were bound to your wheelchair." Seela hurried over to help her.

Mamaw spit water out of her mouth into the sink while speaking with a scratchy voice. "Of course I can walk, Seelie! I just choose to use the chair because your old mamaw is wobbly!" Mamaw chuckled. Seela hugged her tightly with her head resting on top of her grandmother's.

Mavvie turned to head out of the house without any parting words. "Where are you going, Mavvie?" Seela asked.

"I've had a long day, Seelie. It's time for us all to get some rest tonight. You have a big day tomorrow." The women exchanged nods, sharing the same unspoken sentiment about not telling Mamaw anything just yet.

After Seela helped her grandmother lie down to read her Bible verse for the night, she went outside to call Dee. Seela dialed Dee's number while sitting on the tattered backyard swing.

Dee answered, instantly speaking before Seela could say a word. "Girl, I was just going to call you! I've been worried all day, thinking about what's going on down there. How is Sam? Did you see him today? I'm still here at the salon, closing out the register from the day."

"Dee, it's awful! He's in ICU at the state hospital, and I don't know if he's going to make it. He's in a coma right now, and I don't know why. His eyes were open, but he wasn't moving. He was blown up like an embalmed person! I don't know what has happened, but it doesn't look good. I'll go back tomorrow to see if I can find out any further information about what is happening with him. I couldn't get up the nerve to tell Mamaw. I haven't even spoken to my mom since I've been here."

Dee's voice tightened. "Seela, you must speak to your mother. She needs to know you are there. Don't hesitate. Go now."

Seela sighed. "I don't think so, Dee. I left here years ago, and she feels like I disowned her. She's been angry with me for a long time. I know I haven't shared everything with you about my family, but please try to understand. It's not as easy as knocking on her door and being let in with open arms."

Dee couldn't stand to hear her friend in so much pain. "Seela, do you want me to come down? I can close the salon for a few days and come be with you. I feel like you need me." Dee began pulling up client information on the computer as she talked to Seela. She made a note for the receptionist to move bookings a week out.

Seela hesitated and then declined. "I need you to stay at the salon. My request has not changed since yesterday, Dee. I'll call you tomorrow after I see Sam. I'll have more information by then." Seela laid down on the swing, looking into the clear dark sky. "Dee, thank you for being my best friend and salon partner. I do believe God sent you to me. I honestly don't know what I would do if I didn't have you in my life."

Dee kept Seela on the phone for a few minutes, sharing funny jokes while bustling through the salon, getting ready to close it for a week. Damned if she would leave her friend alone in whatever swampland her grandmother lived in or on. Besides, Dee's curiosity was getting the best of her. She wanted to learn more about Seela's family once and for all.

Chapter 8

The next morning, Seela woke up to find her grandmother already out of bed. They had fallen asleep together after talking and giggling long into the night. Seela could smell coffee as she left her grandmother's room. After she combed her hair and rinsed her face, Seela went to the kitchen, where Mavvie and Mamaw sat, frowning.

"Is everything okay?"

Mavvie looked at Seela with a worried face. "I told my sister what is going on with Sam."

Mamaw glared at the kitchen floor as if she saw a bug crawling toward her. Seela made her way over to her side to comfort her.

"Don't look so sad, Mamaw. It's going to be okay. What does Mavvie always tell us?

Everything will be okay. It always is and always will be."

"I just don't want Sam to suffer anymore, Seela. He's had a horrible life with his addiction to drugs, spending most of his life locked up instead of being free and happy. I know he's got to move on to the next world. This one here has not been kind to him."

Seela leaned her head on her grandmother's. "I know, Mamaw. His life has been tormented, and I've got to be the one who helps him through this. Mavvie said I'm the only one to do it."

"Yes," said Mavvie. "You are the one who will teach Sam about forgiveness and about God before he leaves this earth. Only you, his twin, can do that for him. Only you can make him understand the spiritual life that is ahead of him. He will listen to you. Just because you may have moved away from him, Seela, Sam has never left you.

He asks about you every day of his life. You two are connected from within here." Mavvie put her fist to Seela's stomach. "You were made as one, and then your souls split. You will always be connected to Sam no matter what. Even when he leaves you here on earth, your twin will follow and protect you until your soul is reunited with him once again."

With that, Seela stood up sternly. "I'm going to call the hospital to see if I can go there this morning. I need answers. I'm going to talk to the doctor who treated Sam."

Seela used the rotary phone hanging on the kitchen wall, which had a cord that extended farther than the room's width. *My, how times have changed*, she thought, contemplating having to trade in her iPhone for this lump of plastic and wires for daily use again. Seela asked for the fifth floor and Officer Quinton, as he had instructed. Once he came to the phone, Seela felt herself light up inside like the flame of a freshly lit candle.

"Hi, Ms. Seela Black. How are you doing? I got you visitation today from twelve until four o'clock. I'll meet you downstairs, if that works for you."

"Yes, Officer Quinton. I'll be there, waiting anxiously!" she replied, and she hung up without saying good-bye. She turned around to report the news to Mavvie and Mamaw. "I can see Sam from noon to four today. Hopefully, he will be awake so he will know I'm there for him. Mamaw, I need a hot tea with your makings. Can you do that for me before I see Sam?"

Mamaw wasted no time in using her walker to make it to the stove. "Your mamoo is going to make you the best tea ever! You still like two sugars?"

"You'd better make it one. Sugar is not my friend these days."

Mavvie stood up and said, "Sugar is no one's friend. You should both use honey." Mavvie smiled elegantly at the women as she pranced out the back door. "I'll see you when you get back, Seela. Today you will try to speak with your mom too. She knows you are here."

Seela looked surprised by Mavvie's stern words. "Of course I'll try to see her. I just don't know if she will want to see me. Why doesn't anyone get that?" Seela stood at the end of the kitchen island, waiting to hear Mavvie's response, which never came.

Mamaw handed Seela her tea. The two of them sat at the kitchen table, watching the wildlife out her window. "Your granddaddy sure did love sitting here in the morning, watching the birds."

Seela smiled, cupping the delicious hot tea her grandmother had made. "Every time I see cardinals and blue jays, I think of Granddaddy. He would sit on Sunday mornings, drinking his coffee, telling me how many redbirds he had counted. I would always say he was counting the same bird over and over. He would laugh at me and tell me no, he could tell the difference in all of them by the way they flew. The funny thing is that I believed him!" Seela and her grandmother smiled fondly as they reminisced.

While Seela was getting ready to visit Sam, Dee was busy back at the salon, getting ready to close shop and head down to the island. Dee called Ms. Kathy from Seela's oversized desk. "Good morning, Ms. Kathy. It's Dee. Do you have a minute to talk?"

Ms. Kathy loved talking on the phone, so she settled right in on the other end. "Sure, sugar! Are you calling about my appointment this week?"

"As a matter of fact, I am. Seela has had some stuff come up with her family down south. She probably won't be back until maybe next week, and I am going down there today. I need to reschedule everyone for the following week. I know that won't work for you, so another girl will shampoo and set your hair. Will that be all right?"

"Sure, honey!" Ms. Kathy shouted. "That will be quite all right. I hope everything is okay with my sweet Seela. She never talks about her family much. Is it something I should be praying for?"

"Yes, Ms. Kathy, please pray hard for Seela's family. I'll tell you about it next week when I see you again."

Dee hung up the phone with their best—and richest—client and hurried through the salon, checking twice for any outstanding items.

Her plan had to go smoothly so Seela wouldn't be angry about Dee going against her orders. She closed the wooden and glass door, pressing her face against the glass as if she had forgotten something.

"Good-bye, salon. I'll see you next week. It feels funny locking you up this time, almost like we are closing shop. But don't you worry. We'll be back next week and back to our busy selves!" Dee declared, chuckling at herself.

Dee strolled down the street, thinking about how she had met Seela—divine intervention. Eager to get to her friend, she picked up the pace to her apartment on a side street. Dee ran up the steps to the cute wooden porch lined with flowering clay pots. As she stepped up to the top step of her floral porch, Dee saw an envelope in the crack of the door.

"Who would be leaving an envelope on my door?" Dee said aloud. She put her backpack down and quickly opened the envelope before unlocking her red front door. It contained a note and five crisp one-hundred-dollar bills. Dee's eyes grew as big as golf balls. "Holy shit! What in the world?"

The letter read,

My dear Dee,

I'm saddened to hear Seela is going through some trouble with her family. I want you to take this money and use it for your expenses while you are gone. I know how your finances are, and of all people, you cannot afford to take time off without pay. I love you two ladies and am here for you both as long as I'm alive. Keep me posted on how things are going, and I'll keep praying for all.

Much love,
Ms. Kathy

Dee stuffed the money into her back hip wallet. "Thank you, Ms. Kathy!" Dee shouted as if Ms. Kathy were nearby to hear.

Dee packed her suitcase and looked online to map out her route to Seela's grandmother's house. She noted the address on an envelope she'd found, from a letter Seela had received from her aunt Mavvie. Dee threw her suitcase into the back of her pickup truck, which Ms. Kathy had given her after her wealthy husband had passed away—no cash, no strings attached. It was just a kind and much-needed gift.

The southern morning dew was already taking a toll. Dee turned her headlights on the brightest setting. The air conditioner didn't work, nor did her stereo. Dee wore her headphones, listening to hip-hop tunes on her iPod as she meandered her way to Seela's grandmother's home. She smiled happily, knowing she would be with Seela soon.

Chapter 9

Seela finished getting dressed, determined to not only speak with her mother but also persuade her to go to the hospital with her.

"I don't think she will be able to go, Seela. Your mom is real sick too. She's been sick for a year now. I don't know what it is, but a few months ago, when she locked herself in the little house, she was starting to throw up a lot. You need to know the truth. Both your brother and your mother may not be here much longer."

Seela paused at her grandmother's words. It was all too much to withstand over the course of a few days. She thought of the salon and her art gallery, and part of her wanted to run back to it all. However, she had to be strong for Sam. Seela marched to the window, surveying her mother's cottage like a spy. The blinds were closed tightly.

Mamaw wheeled herself close to Seela, and they peered out the window together. "She's not awake. She stays up all hours in the night and sleeps all day now. She got her days mixed all up, I do believe."

Seela resolved to deal with her mother later and straightened up the house. She made a sandwich for her grandmother and left it in the fridge. Mamaw smiled at the thought of having food already prepared.

"Did you cut the crust off, Seelie, like I used to do for you? You know my gums don't chew food up." She laughed and coughed simultaneously.

Seela ran to her side and tapped her back softly. "Of course I cut the crust off. That's what you taught me to do. Are you okay, Mamaw?" She waited for Mamaw to recover from the coughing spell. Seela grabbed her purse, which now contained only a driver's license, money, and lipstick so as not to delay her entry through security at the hospital.

On her way to surprise Seela, Dee melted against the escalating heat. "Whew, it sure is swampy back here. How in the world do you decide to live this far from civilization with just the wildlife among you out here?" Dee said out loud. She had never driven in such thick, swampy woods before. The weeping willows and mimosa trees were so thick she couldn't see the sky in some places as she drove down the dirt road.

Dee turned into Mamaw's drive, where she noticed a tall wooden stick standing in the ground with a white cloth flying high in the sky. "Must be a welcome sign!" Dee drove down the rocky driveway toward the little wood-framed house. She passed Mavvie's house, wondering if it was Mavvie's. She had heard many stories about Mavvie's spiritual ways. Dee knew Seela did some spiritual work also. Dee pulled up to the empty carport and parked her truck next to an even older truck. She looked toward the back screen door and instantly saw Seela's grandmother sitting in her scooter chair, holding a shotgun. Mamaw was glaring at Dee as if she were going to shoot her with it.

Afraid for her life but feeling silly at the same time, Dee rolled her window down, peeping out her head. "Hey there, Mamaw. I'm Dee, Seela's assistant—and best friend."

As soon as Mamaw heard the name Dee, she dropped the gun to the floor and scrambled to get the screen door open. Her caution turned to joy, as if she had been told Jesus appeared. "Aw, honey! I've heard so much about you. Hurry—get over here, and give me a hug! Seela didn't tell me you were coming. I wouldn't have scared you like that. You know, I'm just an old, crazy woman having to protect myself and my property. I'll pop 'em in the ass with this here gun. I don't want to kill anybody, but I for sure will slow them down."

Dee's eyes bulged with surprise at Seela's grandmother's skin color. Seela had never told Dee her grandmother was a black woman. Seela had the skin of an ivory-colored rose. All Dee could do was smile. Dee towered over Mamaw. She finally composed herself enough to inform her of the surprise visit for Seela.

They sat at Mamaw's kitchen table, exchanging stories over sugar-free cookies and tea for what seemed like hours until Mavvie knocked once on the back door before entering. She studied Dee from head to toe, smiling brightly. Both women oozed sensuality, casting a stark contrast to Mamaw, who was slouched and disheveled in the electric scooter, grinning with no teeth.

Dee stood up quickly, holding her hand out to Mavvie. "It's so nice to meet you, Ms. Mavvie. I've heard so much about you. You are even more beautiful in person than pictures Seelie has around her house. Mamaw, that goes for you too."

Mavvie extended her body to hug Dee instead of shaking her hand. "Come here! What a beautiful light and soul you have."

Dee felt warmth as Mavvie closed in on her. The scent emanating from Mavvie made Dee feel peaceful and calm. She stood tall, looking down at Mavvie. "I feel I've been touched by an angel. I definitely want to visit your home, Mavvie. I get what Seels talks about now." Dee kind of shook herself, as if she'd been electrocuted with good feelings and love all at once.

Seela passed the gas station slowly, not seeing Chester out waiting for her. She wondered if he was okay or if he had already forgotten her. She didn't know all the symptoms of Down's syndrome. Seela watched through her rearview mirror as long as she could see the station behind her. Soon it faded into nothing but a mirage.

Seela pulled into the parking garage of the hospital. As she made her way to the entrance, she saw Officer Quinton at the door. He smiled while holding the door open for her. "I just came down, thinking you would be coming in. I wanted to escort you to Mr. Sam's room. I heard the doctor talking about bringing Sam out of the coma. Maybe you will be able to be with him when he wakes up."

Seela shrieked with delight, as if she had just won the lottery. "Really? That soon? He looked so bad yesterday! I can't wait to talk with him."

Officer Quinton touched Seela's back with a firm, comforting hand. He seemed to have a protective quality emanating from his gorgeous, chiseled body. She found herself wondering about his relationship status and then snapped back to the present—her dying brother.

"I don't know how to thank you for being so helpful to me, Officer Quinton. This is so devastating now, knowing what's going on with my twin. It's driving me crazy, knowing that I have no control over it. He is a prisoner of the state of Georgia, and they could care less about his health and well-being."

Officer Quinton displayed a perfect smile that could have warmed a broken heater. "Ms. Seela, Sam is going to be so surprised to see you if he wakes up. I've heard stories about you. You are one person that man loves and idolizes. You may not know it, but your twin has been watching after you all your life. At least that's what he always told me."

They walked in silence down the freshly mopped hospital hallway. Stealing glances, Officer Quinton attempted to admire Seela's beauty without being noticed. Seela sized up the officer and felt fire in her face.

"Okay, Ms. Seela Black, this is where I'll leave you with your twin," the officer said. He left her at Sam's hospital room, which was guarded by two officers. One reached for the door handle and motioned for her to enter.

Seela stepped lightly inside. Sam appeared to be much more peaceful than he had been the previous day. Seela touched his swollen hand, stroking it tenderly. A nurse entered and asked who she was.

"I'm his twin sister. Are you going to bring him out of his coma today?"

"We are going to try," the nurse said. "Hopefully, you will be able to help. You just need to talk softly to him. He will hear you. You being his twin, I'm sure he'll wake up as soon as he hears your voice. The doctor will be in shortly. I understand Mr. Black has been sedated for a couple of days."

Seela wasted no time in trying to cull information from the nurse.

"Nurse, I don't understand what has happened to him to put him in this condition. My grandmother told me he has liver cancer along with Hep-C, but why would he be sedated like this?"

The nurse looked confused herself. "I'm not sure, Ms. Black. I was just assigned to your brother today. I can try to get answers for you, though."

"Please, Nurse. I would like to know his health history and why he ended up here. His sentence in prison is light. I don't understand why the prison would not release him to die at home."

"I understand," replied the dumbfounded nurse. "You just keep talking to Mr. Black, because we have taken him off of the medication that keeps him sedated, so eventually, he will wake up." She left as quietly as she had appeared.

Seela turned to Sam, whispering softly in his ear. "I'm so sorry this has happened to you, my brother. I love you so much, and I apologize for leaving you. I will never leave you again. You need to wake up and see my crazy, sad face right now. You need to make me smile. You hear me?" Seela reached across Sam's body, resting her head on his chest.

Suddenly, Sam's body moved. Seela jumped back, looking down at his face. Sam moved his head back and forth before opening his eyes. When his eyes popped open, they fixed on Seela. He started shaking his head vigorously, as if he wanted to be transported elsewhere or have another set of circumstances. He tried to speak, but his voice was crackly.

"Don't try to talk yet, Sam. You have been in a coma for the past two days. You are just now coming out. I'm here for you."

Sam surveyed Seela as if taking in her face for the first time. "Seela, how did you know?"

Seela reached down, caressing Sam's dry, cracked face. He looked old enough to be her father instead of her brother.

"The doctor told me you died, and they brought you back to life. Did you see anything, Sam? You know how I think and what I believe." Seela wanted him to report something profound, something beyond the here and now.

"Yes, Seels, I was fishing with Dad and Granddaddy. We were in a boat, and they were drunker than hell. It was crazy, Sis. We were drinking wine!" Sam exclaimed excitedly.

"Wine? Dad and Granddaddy always drank whiskey."

"I know," said Sam, "but we had to because that was all we had. Then Granddaddy stood up in the boat and said, 'Boy, come on!'" Sam looked discouraged. "I didn't go. I just sat there in the boat while Granddaddy walked away. And now I wake up to see you, Seels! Holy shit!" Sam tried to move his feet, realizing they were shackled to the bed. "I'm still in fuckin' prison!

I thought you being here beside me meant I was free!"

Seela reached down under his cover to check out her brother's cuffed ankles. She hadn't known that the hospital had Sam shackled to the bed. She tried not to show her shock and outrage as Sam huffed. "What the fuck do they think I'm going to do? Jump up and run out of here?"

Sam cried and spoke through clenched teeth. "I hate you seeing me like this, Sis! I must look like a chained-up beast. You know, I'm the one who protects you, and now I can't."

Seela looked at Sam with confusion. She rationalized that the medication was making him talk like this since her brother had been incarcerated most of his adult life with no logical way to watch after her.

Officer Quinton walked into Sam's hospital room with a look of having horrible news himself. "They just radioed to me that your visit is up, Ms. Black. I'm so sorry it can't be for a longer time, but I have to abide by my orders."

Seela didn't want to leave Sam so soon and wondered what the hell was going on. "I'm finding out how I can get you out of here and take you home. I'll be damned if you stay in here any longer!" she said.

Sam smirked at Seela, knowing her mission would not be that easy. "Twin, I don't want you to worry about me. I'll be okay, as I always am," Sam said, as he winked at Officer Quinton. "You here, Quinton—I know you'll be watching after me, right?"

Officer Quinton nodded before stepping out of the room briefly to allow the siblings to say good-bye. Seela caressed her brother, feeling his pain and sorrow. "Sam, I can't bear to see you like this. The fact that I can't help you is breaking my heart. This is just not right. I'm calling tomorrow to see about getting you home."

Sam turned his head back and forth, as if he were getting agitated with Seela. "Seels, they aren't going to release me. I'm a prisoner of the fucking state."

Seela couldn't comprehend that. "Sam, you only have a year remaining on your sentence. Why wouldn't they release you to me while you're in this condition? We can take care of you at home, and it will be less for the state to pay."

Sam frowned. "I'm telling you, Seels. Ain't no one going to release me."

Seela smoothed out Sam's bedsheets as if she were tucking him in for the night. "Well, Brother, we will see about that." She kissed his cheek and forehead while squeezing his hand tightly. Before exiting the room in tears, Seela whispered, "Your twin is here now, and I'm not going anywhere. You hear me? I'm sorry I haven't been here, but I can promise you I'm never leaving you again."

Sam smiled for the first time since his eyes had opened. "Seels, you never left me. I've always had you. Baby, if I didn't have you, I wouldn't be me! We're twins!" Sam held his hand up with his index and middle fingers crossed, showing Seela the sign he'd always used when they were children.

Seela kissed Sam again and hurried out to meet Officer Quinton. "You know my brother pretty well it seems," she said.

Officer Quinton looked as if he had been caught reaching for a cookie without asking. He shrugged while remaining silent.

Seela pressed on. "Okay, you don't have to disclose anything right now, but I do know my brother, and I can tell you guys have far more of a relationship than you being his guard."

"Ms. Black, please don't start assuming anything. Your brother has a long road to tow on getting better. That should be your number-one priority."

"Don't worry, Mr. Quinton. My brother is my priority, and you'd better believe I'm going to get him out of here and home, where we can take care of him. This is just crazy. He's not a hard-core criminal; he's a drug addict. Now he's dying, and I refuse to let him die in prison."

At the hospital exit, Seela shook Officer Quinton's hand and walked to her car. Officer Quinton chased her with his eyes until she was no longer in his sight.

Chapter 10

Seela took her time returning to Mamaw's house. She first pulled into the gas station, where Chester stood waiting, as if she had called with a specific appointment time.

"I've been waiting for you, Ms. Seela," he said. "My pa said you would be coming to see me today."

Seela frowned. "I'm sorry, honey. I haven't spoken to your pa. I wonder why he told you that."

Chester shrugged, thankful to see Seela again.

"Where is your pa, and what is his name? I would like to speak with him and ask if I can take you to the beach sometime."

Chester pointed toward the gas station door. "Um, his name is Mr. Johnson. His first name is Bill," he said with a lisp.

As Seela entered the old gas station, Bill stood up from his half-broken chair behind the counter. "What can I help you with today, ma'am?" His face was weathered like an old pair of shoes that had been worn every day for years.

With Chester trailing behind her, Seela stepped toward the counter, knowing how awkward this situation might have been in any other part of the country, but this was the rural South, and she sensed a deep loneliness in Chester that she felt compelled to ease. "Hi. My name is Seela Black, and I have chatted with your son a few times. He's a very special young man. I was wondering if you would allow him to come visit with me on the island. He said he's never been to the beach, and I would love to take him." *There. I did my duty.*

Bill smirked at both of them. "Chubby tell you he wants to go to the beach? I take him fishing all the time. That boy won't like the beach. The beach is for sissies!"

Seela dismissed the man's opinion, which paired well with his antiquated gas station. "I see, but if you don't mind, I would like to take Chester."

Chester stared at the floor, almost unable to contain his excitement at the attention being paid to him. His father sighed. "Boy, this here lady says you want to go to the beach. Is that right?"

Chester shrugged while smiling, at which his father chuckled and threw his hands into the air. "If you want to go on down to the beach, then you have at it. I'll bet you come back and tell me you like fishing better!"

Seela promised she would pick up Chester the following day at three o'clock for their beach adventure, and she scurried toward the door. Chester ran behind her, barreling his big body into her from behind. "I will be here waiting for you, Ms. Seela!"

"It's a date, Chester. I'll see you tomorrow."

Seela pulled into her grandmother's drive, passing the white cloth still flying high on Mavvie's wooden stick. Then she spotted Dee's truck parked next to her granddaddy's dilapidated pickup. It took a few moments for the unexpected visit to set in. Her friend had closed the salon and come to be with her despite her wishes. Seela was excited for the familiar company, though.

Dee opened the back door and sprang out to greet Seela. "Honey, I guess I'm a great surprise to you today! Just like your black grandmother was to me." Dee smiled sarcastically.

Seela jumped out of the car and hugged Dee, squeezing her tightly. "I'm so happy to see you, Dee, you crazy girl! How did you find my grandmother's home? Why didn't you tell me you were coming? What did you do about the salon?"

Dee stood firmly, addressing all the questions she had anticipated. "Everything is taken care of. I closed the salon for a few days, and if I had insisted on coming, you probably would still demanded I stay at salon. Now I'm here, and it looks like it's a good thing." Dee put her arm around Seela's small shoulders, steering Seela toward the house.

Seela leaned her head on Dee as they reached the carport. "I'm really glad you are here, and yes, my family is black!" The women wailed as they entered the back door.

Mamaw wheeled around to peek her head in. "Seela, you didn't tell me Dee was our color. She's tall and pretty too!" Mamaw sat in her electric chair with her clean dish towel around her neck and her hair sticking straight up like the feathers of a rooster running in the wind. She pushed her button on the arm handle of her scooter, approaching Dee to size her up once again.

"Jeez, we're all people here. What's all the biz about color talk?" Seela snapped, glad to be surrounded by love after seeing her sick brother shackled to a hospital bed.

"All right, all right," Dee replied. "Now, you need to tell me what's going on with your brother. Mamaw was just telling me a little when you pulled up." Dee looked back at Mamaw. "Can I call you Mamaw, or would you prefer I call you by your name?"

Mamaw grinned proudly. "You better call me Mamaw, because that's all I answer to." She reached for Dee's hand. "You work for my Seels, and she loves you. I can tell, so that makes you family."

"Seels, where did you get your green eyes? This house is full of nuttin' but brownies. I believe you may be the milkman's daughter."

Seela sighed. "I'm the only one in the family with green eyes, but believe me, I am a true Black family member!"

Mamaw turned her electric wheelchair and rode over to Seela's side. She clutched Seela's arm and caressed her as if she were a newborn baby. "Yes, you are a true Black, my Seels! You're just like your granddaddy in many ways. Determined and self-driven people, you two are."

Seela kissed her grandmother's cheek while motioning for Dee to step outside for some swamp air and a chat about Sam. They headed for the backyard garden area, where Seela attempted to make a comfortable seat for Dee, but all the furniture was either broken or covered in dust so thick that they couldn't tell the color of anything. She laughed as she dusted a wooden chair off.

"Can you believe this, Dee? I don't even know what is really happening, but I'm trying to keep it together for my grandmother. I really think Sam is dying, Dee. This is going to kill her and my mom. I think Sam has been their life since my granddaddy passed. Hell, I haven't even seen Mom since I've been here for the past three days. I don't know what is happening with her, because I've spent all my time trying to find out about Sam. He looks like death, Dee!"

Dee absorbed Seela's pain and reached to hold her. The rickety chair Dee was sitting in fell apart, causing her to fall to the ground. They laughed hysterically until tears flowed down their faces. Seela jumped down onto the ground with Dee, nestling next to her, looking into the beautiful cornflower-blue sky. The clouds were puffy and white.

Seela said dreamily, "Did you ever look at clouds and try to see faces or objects when you were a kid? My brother and I did many times when we were little. We would lie out here in this same backyard and see who could see the most. It only counted if the other could see what you saw."

Dee squeezed Seela's hand and replied, "Let's play it now, Seels. I see a few things as I'm looking up. Damn, this is some beautiful sky today!"

Seela and Dee lay there for at least an hour, giggling like ten-year-old girls and pointing up at the sky, showing each other what they saw in white clouds that spread sporadically over them.

Later, Mavvie glided into Mamaw's back kitchen door swiftly with her flowing white dress and scarves flying behind her. "Sister, where is my Seels? I need to speak with her."

Mamaw looked out the window, where she could see Seela and Dee lying on the ground. "I don't know what the heck they doing, but they been lying out there for a long time now. I'm getting hungry." She smiled her toothless grin while her sister snickered at her rooster hair.

Mavvie ran quickly out the back door, as if she hadn't heard a word her sister said. She ran through the grass, holding her dress up so as not to trip on it. She yelled, "Seela, honey, I need you to come to my house right now! I feel a presence, and I need you with me."

Dee sat up quickly with her eyes as big as saucers. "A presence of what? What kind of voodoo do you ladies do?" she said.

Seela jumped up quickly to her feet. "I'm coming, Mavvie. Dee, go check on Mamaw, and I'll be back shortly."

Seela grabbed Mavvie's hand as they sprinted like two happy girls through the yard to Mavvie's house. Dee observed them cautiously, wondering what presence lurked.

Chapter 11

Mavvie and Seela gathered in the healing room. Seela lit specific candles around the room as Mavvie swirled sage in every corner. She chanted in a language that Seela was familiar with but could never fully grasp.

"Mavvie, who do you feel is here with us?" Seela whispered.

Mavvie looked deeply into Seela's eyes. "I feel a strange, bad energy. We need to clean the air, and then we will meditate to see what has come forth for us."

Seela sat on her favorite pillow on the floor. It was velvet with a deep purple color. Mavvie finished saging and placed the burning stick on a shiny pewter platter. Ashes were all around the plate. She sat in front of Seela as they clasped hands. Mavvie took a deep breath and then went into deep meditative breathing. Seela followed suit. They meditated for at least fifteen minutes until Mavvie broke the silence with her strong Cajun accent. "I had good things come forth. You did as well, right, Seels?"

Seela agreed. She felt a sense of relaxation and renewal that didn't indicate the bad energy that Mavvie had prepared her for. "Sam came forth, and I feel he will pass soon, but he let me know he has always been with me and always will be. He said not to worry, for I have a lot of angels watching over me. I do feel I have angels with me, and he gave me confirmation. I can't wait to go see him tomorrow now that he is awake."

Mavvie nodded. "Seela, he is passing soon, and what came forth for me is that you have to help him know God before he passes. You have to show him what love is, because that is what God is." Tears filled

Mavvie's eyes. She cupped Seela's face. "You have a purpose, my sweet baby. You have to help your twin cross over to our wonderful place beyond here." Mavvie raised her hands up to the ceiling as if it were the universe beyond.

Seela looked up to see the shimmering painted scene. "Mavvie, you have done such a wonderful job on your ceiling. It makes me feel so peaceful." Seela fell back onto her pillow and lay there, gazing.

Mavvie stood up and reached for her symbols. "Stay there, my love. I want to hold these over your core to make sure you are staying fine-tuned to everything that is going on and what is going to happen."

Seela remained still. Mavvie's symbols started clashing together as she held them over Seela's stomach. Seela was amazed to see the symbols moving without assistance. She closed her eyes. She could feel Mavvie's breath and hear her heartbeat above her head. Seela felt as if someone or something were squeezing the calf of her leg. Minutes later, the symbols stopped. Mavvie walked to her side.

"You can open your eyes now, Seela."

Seela opened her eyes and appeared to be confused. "Mavvie, it was the strangest thing. I felt someone, who I thought was you, squeezing my leg, but at the same time, I felt you at the top of my head."

Mavvie's expression was serious. "We had visitors today, Seels. I felt your father strongly and someone else, but I couldn't figure out who that person was. Did you see anything in your mind?"

"Yes, I did," said Seela. "I thought I saw a woman walking back and forth with something in her hands. I can't figure out what she was holding, Mavvie. It had to be important."

"You will figure it out, and you let me know as soon as you do." Mavvie took Seela's hands, squeezing them tightly. "Now, you go see about your friend Dee. There is no telling what my kooky sister has her doing."

Seela and Mavvie parted as Seela headed through the weeded yard back to her grandmother's house. All of a sudden, she heard what sounded like a motorcycle coming down the road. Seela stopped to see who it could be. Dust flew and morphed into a cloud in front of her. Seela squinted as she held her hand over her brow. Chester appeared, riding an off-road vehicle with three wheels. It was tattooed with stickers. Chester's goggles were strapped tightly around his fat face. His smile was so contagiously sweet that Seela couldn't help but grin from ear to ear. Chester stopped abruptly in front of Seela. He pulled his helmet and goggles off his sweaty, wet head.

"Hi, Ms. Seela Black. My pa told me where you lived, so I came to see you. I miss you." Chester stood as proudly as he could, as if he were coming to court Seela and ask for her hand in marriage. He wiped his forehead with his arm, which caused red dirt to smear across his face.

Shaking her head in disbelief and amusement, Seela motioned for Chester to follow her to the house to get cleaned up. "This place is full of surprises!" she shouted to no one.

She and Chester trotted to Mamaw's house. Chester followed Seela with determination, as if he never wanted her out of his sight again. Seela opened the carport screen door, and there stood her grandmother at the kitchen sink. "We have a visitor, Mamaw."

Mamaw spat water into the kitchen sink before turning to sit back down in her scooter chair. Chester ran over as if he could help her, but Mamaw plopped down quickly. "Good Lord, I did a plop! That won't be good for my back later." Mamaw turned her chair on and moved the control so that the chair would face Chester.

Chester stepped back so as not to get run over. "I like your chair."

Happy to have an innocent child in the house again, Mamaw beamed. "You want to take it for a ride? I'll let you. It goes pretty fast."

Chester chuckled. "I have a motorcycle outside. It goes real fast. My uncle give it to me. It has three wheels, not two." He held up three fingers for reinforcement.

"Chester, I hope you weren't on main roads coming over here. I don't think it is legal to drive your three-wheeler on the roads," Seela said while wiping his face with a washcloth.

Dee popped in after giving herself a tour of Mamaw's home. "What's all the hoopla?" Dee fixed her eyes on Chester and held out her hand. "Hi. I'm Dee. And who might you be, handsome fellow?"

Seela put her arm around Chester, introducing him. "I met him a few days ago on my way here. His father owns the town gas station."

Chester held out his pudgy hand to shake Dee's. "I love Ms. Seela Black. You her friend? She's my friend now too!" Chester smiled, showing off his two front rabbit teeth.

Dee laughed heartily at all the action, watching Seela scrub Chester's face vigorously. "Well, Chester, you are one lucky guy to have Ms. Seela as your friend. She is one great friend to have."

When Seela offered to feed him, Chester could hardly believe his luck. Mamaw wheeled over to Chester and reached for his hand. "Come, Chester. Let's go see what we have to eat. I've been hungry for a while, and nobody here is doing anything about it. You and I goin' in here to fix us something!"

"I like PBJs," said Chester.

"Well, you are in luck, Chester. Mamaw always have peanut butter and two or three kinds of jelly in my kitchen. I like peanut butter and banana sandwiches."

"Um, I never had one of those. Can I try one with you?"

Knowing exactly how her grandmother liked them, Seela insisted on preparing the sandwiches for everyone. Chester instantly sat at the kitchen table and placed a paper napkin in his shirt. He observed the three women with elation. He had lost his mother years ago and didn't have other women in his life. "Can I have milk too?"

"Seela, give the first sandwich to Chester," Mamaw said. "I believe he real hungry." She slid her sleeve of sugar-free cookies over to Chester. "You take a few of these too." Chester reached for the cookies, counted out three, and placed them on his napkin, smiling at Mamaw for their shared secret.

Seela placed the plates in front of Dee, her grandmother, and Chester. "Here you go, just like Mamaw likes it." The crusts were cut perfectly off, and the sandwiches were in four small squares.

Chester ate two squares before Mamaw or Dee could even get a bite in. "It's yummy!"

"After lunch, you will need to head back home, Chester. I don't want you to be out at dusk riding your three-wheeler. That could be dangerous," said Seela. "Tomorrow after I see Sam, I'll take you to the beach."

"I want to go with you two. I'll teach you how to bodysurf!" exclaimed Dee.

Seela looked at Dee as if she had three heads. "You know how to bodysurf? Now, I've got to see this in action. I bet you look like an orca coming on shore in a wave." The women roared. Chester joined in, not wanting to be left out.

After dinner, Seela helped Chester get his protective gear on. Dee stood in the front living room window alongside Mamaw, watching Seela with Chester. "Seela's really taken to this here Chester. I've never seen her be so attentive to a child. Especially someone she just met."

"He special, Dee. That's what Seels is attracted to. He has bright light, and she doesn't even realize it right now. Chester said he loved Seela already. He's only known her for three days. He really do love her, Dee. He was being truthful. Their lights have connected. You watch my words, Dee. You hear me?"

"What are your words to watch, Mamaw?"

Mamaw looked up at Dee with irritation. "I told you, Dee. Bright lights! They connected the first time they met. Seela will always be there for Chester now. Those are the words you watch. You got it?"

"Yes, ma'am," Dee obediently replied.

Wanting nothing more than to relax now, Seela returned inside to get Dee settled. As Dee walked down the hallway, she inspected all the framed photos lining the walls. "Whew, Seels! Look at all the black folks hanging out with the white folk. You sure did keep a good secret."

"I didn't keep a secret, Dee. I just didn't tell you that my mother is black. Can we just agree that skin color is nothing and that it's your heart that matters?"

Determined to put the subject of color—and everything else—to rest for the day, Seela made up a bed for Dee in the room adjacent to hers. She then kissed her friend good night.

Chapter 12

The next morning, Dee woke to Seela shouting at someone on the phone. Buttoning up her pajamas and throwing her hair up, she ran to Seela's room and popped her head in without a knock.

Seela slammed the iPhone onto the nightstand and turned to Dee. "The hospital just told me they shipped Sam to a prison hospital two hours away from here. I can't see him today. They said I have to wait until he is processed there before I can go visit him. I feel so sick right now. He is probably thinking I've left him and am not going to help him. I've got to find out the number to this facility and see what is really going on."

Dee poured Seela a cup of coffee from the old percolator as they settled at the kitchen table. "I will look up the number, Seela. Give me the name of the place where they sent Sam." Dee picked up her phone. "I'll just Google the damn place." She didn't realize that Internet service was spotty along the bayou.

Seela sat with a look of shock on her face, as if she had been told Sam was already dead. "I can't believe this is happening, Dee. I feel like he is so afraid right now, and it's killing my heart. I'm going to call Officer Quinton. I bet he has answers for me." Seela jumped up and grabbed the old olive-green rotary wall phone.

Dee chuckled, watching Seela read Officer Quinton's number off of her cell phone. "Girl, why you using that old phone? Just hit his name and call him on your phone."

Seela turned to Dee with confidence. "I have only talked to him from this number, so I know he will know who I am if I call from

Mamaw's phone." She winked at Dee and smiled. "He may not answer if he doesn't recognize my number."

"I feel like I have gone back in time here, but yes, that makes sense," Dee said. "I'm going to go see if Mamaw wants me to help her get up this morning. I think she's still sleeping."

Seela blew her a kiss, grateful to have such a dear friend in the middle of this chaos. As if on cue, Officer Quinton answered the phone. "Good morning, Ms. Black. I was expecting your call. I just heard the news this morning myself. I'm actually shocked they moved him so fast."

"I can't believe it either. How could they do that? He seemed so sick yesterday."

"I really don't know, Ms. Black. I do know that he is in a state correctional institution hospital. He did not get sent back to where he was. Sam will have to be processed before you can see him. That may take a few days or so."

Seela sank down into the kitchen chair with a crushed spirit. "I feel so bad for Sam, Officer Quinton. He probably doesn't even know what's going on. I told him I was taking him out of the hospital to our home."

Officer Quinton paused before saying, "I'll call you as soon as I hear something, Ms. Black."

"Please call me Seela. I'm not used to being called by my last name. Makes me sound like an old hen!"

The officer chuckled with relief. "Well, in that case, please call me Joseph." Seela could feel her heart perk up a little at the sound of his first name. "Seela, it will be okay. Your brother knows the system and what they can do with him. He is a prisoner of the state. There will be a lot of strings to be pulled to get him released."

"I don't understand all this. He only has a year left on his sentence, and he is dying!"

"Sometimes laws can cause the problems that you are experiencing now. I promise you I will investigate and call you as soon as I know something."

Feeling reassured by Officer Joseph Quinton, Seela replied that she would be waiting for his call.

Seela sipped on her coffee for a few minutes until Dee reappeared to find out the latest news. "Joseph said he would find out more information on Sam and get back to me."

"Who the hell is Joseph?" Dee said.

"Officer Quinton. He told me his name is Joseph and said I could call him by his first name," Seela said with a hopeful expression. Dee's eyes twinkled with curiosity as she left Seela to be alone with her thoughts.

Dee set out to meet Seela's mom without notifying the others. She couldn't stand all the mystery surrounding this family. She made her way to Catherine's door and knocked. "Good afternoon, Ms. Black. I'm Dee, your daughter's assistant and friend. Can I come in and meet you?" she said through the door. There was silence. "Hello! Are you in there?"

The doorknob turned, and the door opened a crack. Dee's eyes grew big. Seela's mother looked nothing like what she had imagined. She was tall like Dee and looked as if she hadn't done anything with herself in a long time. Her clothes were covered in paint, and her hair stood up like Mamaw's rooster hair, only with a younger texture.

She scanned Dee and said, "How come you are here, and where is Seela?"

"Ms. Black, Seela is here in your mom's house. She been here a few days, trying to see about Sam. You know he's real sick, don't you?"

To Dee's surprise, Seela's mother turned to shut the door. Dee pushed so that she couldn't. "Why don't you want to talk to me? Don't you want to know about Sam?"

"I know Sam is sick. He's been sick for a long time." She gave Dee an evil face. "You go back home and leave us alone here." This time, she slammed the door before Dee could respond.

Dee stood there in shock and confusion before making her way back to Mamaw's house. When Seela asked Dee where she had gone, Dee paused before responding, "I went down to meet your mom. I do believe that was a big surprise for her and for me. She wasn't too happy to meet me, and from what I gathered from the few words she said to me, she doesn't care that we are here, Seela."

Seela could feel herself getting incensed by her mother's ways. "Dee, I haven't even tried to see her yet. She hates me for leaving everyone here years ago. She is a very bitter woman."

Dee chewed on this new information. Your mom appeared to know more than we do about Sam. "It was almost like she was hiding something and doesn't want you to know. I think you should try to see her now."

Chapter 13

Seela stopped as she reached her mother's porch. The smell of marijuana slithered through her front door. Seela knocked three times softly. There was no answer. Seela shouted, "Mama, I know you are in there! Will you please come open the door?" Seela waited patiently, peeking in through the peephole to see if her mother was standing at the door. A moment later, the door opened a small crack.

Catherine squinted tightly, and then her eyes grew large, as if a ghost had appeared. "Well, that woman was right. You are here on our property. Who you down here to see, Seela? You left us a long time ago."

Seela frowned with sadness and embarrassment. "I know, Mama, but I'm here now, and I'm not leaving, so will you let me in your house?"

"No, not now, Seels. It's a mess! I'll clean up, and you can come back tonight. We will talk then. I need to rest. My body's not doing so well these days. You seen Sam yet, Seela? He's been real sick. I haven't heard from him in days."

Seela began to tell her mother what she knew about Sam, but the door was shutting. "Please, Mama, listen to me a minute."

"Seels, I need to rest. We will talk tonight." With that, the door closed. Her mother was hidden from the world again.

With the increasing heat and humidity of the day, Seela rubbed her sweaty forehead in annoyance. She returned to Mamaw's house to find Dee on the phone with Joseph. Sensing Seela's irritation, Dee handed the phone to her without informing Joseph.

"Hello, Joseph. Please tell me you found out some good news," said Seela.

"I'm not sure if it's good news, Seela, but at least you will know where he is. You will be able to see Sam this coming Sunday for a five-hour visit," replied Joseph, feeling glad he could be of service to such a beautiful woman.

"Five hours sounds great, but where is he? Where have they put him?"

"When you go see Sam, he is in a state prison hospital. You will be taken inside the facility where all the inmates are. So I suggest you be very calm through your entire visit so that you are not escorted out. This visit will not be like your hospital visits."

As Seela began to cry, Dee rushed to be by her side.

"Joseph, I will follow your lead. I appreciate you letting me know," Seela said, wiping the tears from her face. "If you are ever on the swamp side of the island, give us a call and come meet Sam's mother and grandmother."

Dee waited patiently as Seela hung up the olive-green rotary phone. "I can't see Sam until this Sunday," Seela said. "He's back in a state prison facility that has a hospital floor that will take care of him until he passes or I can get him home here to die."

Dee reached her arms out to hug Seela. Seela walked into Dee's long, lean arms. Dee embraced her as if she were a wrapped-up newborn baby as she cried. Once Seela gained her composure, they made a plan to follow each other home and return together on Saturday. Mamaw was crushed to see the women go, but she knew Seela would be back to tend to her dying brother. After they said a long good-bye to Mavvie, who handed Seela a lush amethyst stone for safety on their journey, the women were off.

Chapter 14

That night, as Seela settled back into the comforts of her own home, she was simultaneously glad and sad for the solitude. She missed her grandmother wheeling around and making her laugh. She also contemplated her new connections with Chester and Joseph. *A police officer! Really, Seela,* she mused. Were they just there as entertainment along the bayou while she managed Sam's situation, or could either or both be much more? She wondered as she drifted into a deep sleep.

The next morning, Seela woke to someone pounding on her front door. She tossed and turned in disarray, forgetting where she was. Then she heard Ms. Kathy's voice and hurriedly got dressed, wondering why in the world Ms. Kathy was on her doorstep. She looked out the peephole to be sure. *Yep, Ms. Kathy.* Seela opened the door.

"Is everything okay, Kathy? How did you know I came back?"

"Everything is okay, sugar. I was just checking on you. I wanted to make sure you and your family are okay. You know I worry about you like you were my own!" Kathy exclaimed while handing Seela a bouquet of fresh-cut flowers. She was dressed meticulously like a rich middle-aged southern woman, sporting an Easter egg–pink suit, strappy heels, jewels, and dramatic makeup. "I had my gardener cut you some fresh, pretty flowers to welcome you back."

"Please, Ms. Kathy, come right on in, and I'll make you some coffee," Seela said, smoothing down her night T-shirt.

"No, sugar. Thank you anyway. George is driving me around town to get my errands done, so I must be going. I'll see you at the salon. My hair has been missing you terribly. Just look at this rat's nest in the back."

Kathy pointed to the back of her head as she walked off of Seela's front porch. "You may find a mouse or two in there!"

Seela giggled. "Ms. Kathy, you are too funny! I'll see you tomorrow with hair bells on."

Inspired by the surprise visit from her favorite client, Seela got dressed quickly and headed to the art gallery to see the progress the construction workers had made. They were working feverishly on mixing corrugated metal panels with the brick walls and delicate light fixtures that Seela had requested for an ultrachic, contemporary design. She couldn't believe how splendid the place looked. It was already beyond the vision board she had created from art and architecture magazine photo spreads she loved. Eager to get her approval, the contractor walked over to Seela, holding a nail gun.

"Ms. Black, it's good to see you back. What do you think? It's looking good, huh? We should be done in a few weeks. Just in time for your grand opening!"

"Henry, I am totally blown away. You've refurbished the old brick to perfection. I can't wait to see the place filled with paintings. Thank you from the bottom of my heart! I see that you guys didn't need me as a chaperone this week after all." Seela chuckled. She was filled with excitement and then alarm. "Oh my gosh, that reminds me. I have to get in touch with the other local artists! I need to get a count of how many artists and how many paintings I'm going to have for my grand opening night."

Indifferent to art talk, the contractor politely excused himself and went back to work.

Seela took one last look around the space before heading to the salon. Dee was working like a honeybee making honey on a honeycomb. She grinned from ear to ear when she saw Seela.

"Well, if that ain't a sight for a sore eye. It's so great to see you back, blessing us with your great light and beauty, Seels! It's just not the same without you here." The women hugged long and hard, as if they hadn't seen each other in decades.

"It feels so good to be back to work, Dee," said Seela. She inhaled the aromas of the salon. "It smells like home here. I am so thankful for all I have. My salon and soon my art gallery. It's everything I've ever wanted. Have you seen it, Dee? Oh my goodness, it's going to be beautiful."

Dee strolled over to the window and peeked out at Seela's new project. "Seela, what are you going to name it?"

Seela sighed. "I need to get clear on that like yesterday. I have to notify all the artists, and I've just been calling it 'the new gallery next to the salon.' All this stuff going on with Sam has turned it all upside down. I wish he could be here for the opening. Wouldn't that be so marvelous?" Seela knew this was a fantasy that would never come true. Instead, she had to help him get right with God and cross over. The weight of it all brought tears to her eyes for the umpteenth time.

"You've got this, Seela!" Dee said. "Do not break down here. We will be going down in four days, and you'll see Sam before you know it. Let's take care of the clients this week. You give me a sign if you need anything. Remember, four days."

Seela straightened up. "You're right. Let's get down to business. And, Dee, if it comes up, I'm going to tell the clients Sam is in hospice. Will you go along with my story? I just can't talk about the truth right now. It's too painful."

Dee kept her voice low as the receptionist turned up the music in the salon. "These women here don't need to know nothing you don't want them to. Your family business is private. You and me, girl. Let's get this day started."

As they parted ways in the bustling salon, Seela heard a howl. "Whew wee! If that isn't the best sight I've seen in over a week. My fabulous hairstylist." Ms. Kathy sashayed through the salon with a bouquet of hydrangeas from her garden, neatly arranged with a bright blue ribbon. The woman obviously loved growing and sharing her flowers. She handed the bouquet to Dee and embraced Seela. "Time to get prettied up! I hope you like these blue ones. I know everything going on right now is hard, but you just think happy—think flowers—and everything will be okay. You got me, sugar?"

Dee and Seela nodded and laughed as Ms. Kathy, not waiting for a response, swayed her hips back and forth as she walked to the dressing room to put on a smock. On the way, she asked the shampoo assistant for a cup of coffee with cream. "And please, no sweetener. I like it the color of Dee."

Enjoying Ms. Kathy's southern charm, Dee smiled and shook her head in fondness. "It's so good to see you today, Ms. Kathy. Let me say that you are just what we needed in here to start our week."

After Seela finished Ms. Kathy's hair, she realized she hadn't discussed her family situation at all. Asking no questions, Ms. Kathy monopolized the whole conversation to keep Seela from having to talk about Sam.

Chapter 15

On Friday, eager to see about Sam's condition, Dee and Seela headed down to Mamaw's. "This sure is a nice ride, Seels. I spend so little time in a car that I forget how nice they can be." Dee rubbed the leather across the dash as if it were a brand-new leather purse. "Dang, Seels, you even got wood grain in here. I feel like I'm back in your living room."

Seela popped Dee on the arm. "Stop it, Dee. My car is not that nice. It's at least eight years old. Besides, all these cars have this interior." Seela thought about her friend's beat-up truck with no air conditioner, no radio, no leather, and definitely no wood grain. Neither of them had purchased their current automobiles. Seela had just lucked out first. "Okay, I do love it. If it weren't for Ms. Kathy, I wouldn't have it. I'm so happy she didn't like it and decided to get a new car. I'll drive it until the wheels fall off."

"You know, that woman is an angel in our town. When she gave me that truck, I was in shock for days. It's old, but I do love it." Dee chuckled.

"Dee, we are lucky to have her. I think she loves us like family. You know, this week, she didn't even ask me about Sam. It was almost like she knew everything and didn't have to ask. It was strange, but at the same time, I was thankful she didn't mention it."

"That is weird, Seels. Ms. Kathy is always the one who wants to know everything you did over the weekend. I can't believe she didn't ask one question about Sam."

They pulled onto Mamaw's dusty road. "Well, I guess no rain here this week. This road is dustier than a torn bag of flour," Seela said, leaning forward with her head against the windshield. "It's so thick I can't even see where the road is."

Dee looked with her head close to the windshield, as if she could help Seela drive. "Girl, I can't see a damn thing. Maybe we should stop and let the dust settle a minute. We can walk from here if you want."

Seela gawked at Dee as if she were crazy. "I'm not walking. I got this. We will just drive straight and hope nothing runs out in front of us."

"Hopefully your voodoo aunt won't be running around here with her white stick," Dee said.

"She's not voodoo, Dee. Spiritual is the work. She'll wash your mouth out for saying that," Seela joked.

"You'd better not tell her I said it then. I don't want her to do any voodoo on me," Dee quipped, waving her hands in the air and then holding them up as if she were hanging herself with her tongue hanging out. Seela and Dee laughed so hard they didn't realize they were now in front of her grandmother, who was sitting in the drive in her scooter wheelchair, waiting for the pair.

Mamaw shouted, "I've been sitting out here for an hour, burning up while waiting on you to get here! Where you been? I thought you said you would be here after work."

Seela greeted her grandmother while Dee grabbed their suitcases. "It took us three and a half hours to drive here, Mamaw," Dee said. "The way your granddaughter speeds, we made it in good time, actually."

Mamaw's face softened. "I wasn't thinking straight. I'm glad y'all are here now. Come on in. I have a surprise for both of you."

They walked through Mamaw's back door, stepping into what smelled like an Italian kitchen. The aromas of fresh tomatoes, garlic, herbs, and spices dominated the air.

"Wow, Mamaw. Did you cook this?" Seela lifted the lid on the pot of boiling spaghetti sauce. She sniffed lightly so as not to burn her nostrils. "This was always my favorite when I was little, Dee. Come smell. It's the best!"

Dee hurried to the stove. "Mamaw, what have you done? It smells amazing up in here." Dee leaned her tall frame over Seela. "Honey, this is some good-smelling sauce. You would think Mamma Mia from Sicily had been here. What got into you Mamaw? How did you stand and make this sauce?"

All of the sudden, Chester appeared from the hallway. "Hey!" he said in his thick-tongued voice. He was dressed in clothes that were not his. Spaghetti sauce ran down the front of his shirt. Chester walked over to Seela and rested his head on her shoulder as he hugged her from the side. "I've missed you, Ms. Seela. I come see Mamaw at night on my three-wheeler. I wait for Pa to fall asleep after he eats and drinks his beer. He doesn't know I'm gone."

Mamaw turned her scooter on and rode over to Chester. "He been here every evening since you been gone, Seela. Chubby and I been doing a lot around here. He's been a ray of sunshine for me this past week. Wait until you see the backyard. Chubby already cleaned all the dead shrubbery out for me. You can see the bird feeders now from the kitchen window, like when you were a child."

Chester stood like a proud rooster with his chest puffed out. "Yep! Mamaw and I been working. I help her, and then we have dinner before I go home. She makes biscuits for me. I like biscuits with butter and honey. Yep! That's what she makes me." He smiled at Mamaw with such love that it was as if she had been his grandmother forever.

"Wow, I am so happy you two have gotten to be buddies," Seela replied. "I hope your pa knows and approves of you riding that far on the island from your house at night."

Chester looked at Seela with concern, fearing that she didn't approve. "He's sleeping, and I wake him up when I get home. He and I go to bed when I wake him up. He doesn't know I went anywhere. It's okay, though."

"No, Chester, it's not okay. Your pa should know where you are. He could wake up and get upset when he realizes you aren't there. I can't allow you to do that anymore without telling him. Okay?" Seela attempted to be stern. The truth was that she didn't want the man to ban his son from spending time with them. She had only introduced herself to Mr. Johnson the other day.

Chester shifted as if he were about to weep. "Please don't tell him, Ms. Seela. I won't do it anymore. I promise. He will be mad at me and put me on restriction. Please don't say anything to my pa."

Mamaw pulled her chair next to him and held on to his shirt. "Don't you worry, honey. Ms. Seela won't say anything to your pa. I'll whoop her ass if she does." Mamaw laughed with her toothless grin, causing her belly to shake and her chest to start wheezing. "You hear me, Seels? You ain't saying anything about Chubby coming here."

Seela sighed. "Okay, but you have to be safe driving over here, Chester. I'll worry about you at night, knowing you are out on this island, riding that three-wheeler. Besides, aren't you afraid of driving through the woods in the dark?"

"I'm tough, and I have a light on the front of my three-wheeler. I'm not 'fraid of the dark. A lot comes out at night, and I like seeing the creatures."

Tired of the discussion, Mamaw wheeled over to the stove, where bubbles of sauce popped in the huge old pot. "Chubby, you need to come check on your special spaghetti sauce you've made for Seela and Dee." She then glanced at Seela and Dee to gauge their expressions. As planned, they were both surprised.

Chester ambled over to the stove. "I got this, Mamaw. I know what to do." He stirred the sauce slowly with a wooden spoon. He then turned his boiling noodles off and put a lid on them. He turned back around to face the women. "Mamaw taught me how to make spaghetti, and I wanted to surprise you with dinner. She taught me how to cook a lot this week. I love her!"

Seela teared up at the bond that Chester and her grandmother had formed while she was away. She urged him to call his father to ask if he could stay over. Chester decided to hand her his cell phone instead. Seela swiftly persuaded Chester's father to allow him to spend the night. She thought he seemed rather nonchalant about permitting his son to stay overnight with three strange adults, but perhaps he never got much of a break from his son.

The four of them sat around the backyard table, sharing their wonderful spaghetti dinner. They talked and laughed until the nightly wildlife went to sleep. Seela made Chester's bed and then sat with him as he nestled in. Chester smiled with love pouring out of his heart while Seela tucked his sheet in tightly around him.

"That tickles!" Chester shouted.

"I'm sorry, Chester. This is what my mamaw used to do to me when I was little."

Chester lit up. "I like it, Ms. Seela. It feels good."

Seela smiled and rested her head on Chester's bed, beside his body. "I'm glad you are here, Chester, and if you need me, I'm one door away, okay?"

Chester winked at Seela and said, "I'll be okay, Ms. Seela. I'm happy I'm spending the night with you and Mamaw. I love you bofe."

Seela smiled at Chester while wiping his hair off of his forehead. "You've made my night. You get some rest, and I'll see you in the funny papers."

Chester looked confused. "What is the funny papers, Ms. Seela?"

"It's your dreams you have at night. Maybe I'll be in them, Chester." Seela walked out the door as she turned his light switch off. The nightlight glowing by the nightstand made a golden halo around Chester's head. He rolled onto his side in comfort, loving the smell of the sheets and feather pillows. Seela watched Chester, wondering if he would wake and be scared.

Chapter 16

Seela woke to her alarm blaring and sat up to see that it was 7:00 a.m. She threw on a robe and ran to Chester's room. He was sound asleep, snoring loudly. Seela melted while watching him sleep. He was content there with three protective women.

Seela made coffee while starting breakfast for everyone. She couldn't wait to visit Sam and anxiously waited for a call from Joseph to give her the green light. Chester walked into the kitchen with puffy eyes and crusty lips. He smiled at Seela with his usual crooked smile. "Good morning, Ms. Seela. I slept good!" He scratched his head, his hair in disarray. "It smells good in here—like bacon. I like bacon."

"That's great to know, Chester, because in this house, it's mandatory you like bacon, especially mine. Come over here, and try a strip." Chester walked quickly to Seela, reaching for a hot piece of bacon. "Be careful, Chester. Don't burn your tongue. I know you will love my famous sugar bacon. I learned it from my one and only mamaw."

Chester smiled as he took a bite. "It's good! It's the best bacon I've ever had." He ate it as if he would never get another piece, savoring the last morsel.

"Do you like pancakes, Chester, or would you rather have eggs this morning?"

Chester had never been given choices for breakfast or any other meal. Having options seemed to confuse him. "I like everything, Ms. Seela."

"Okay, then we will have eggs and pancakes, Chester. Let's wake Mamaw up and see what she would like this morning."

Chester walked slowly down the hall to Mamaw's room. As he reached her door, he saw her sitting on the side of her bed. "Ms. Seela's cooking breakfast for us. You getting up now?" he asked bashfully.

At the thought of a full breakfast, Mamaw beamed at Chester. "Hey, honey. Come on in here. Help me get up off this bed. Boy, am I ever ready for breakfast. Seela makin' cathead biscuits?"

Chester was baffled. "What's cathead biscuits, Mamaw?"

"They're the size of a cat's head and as fluffy as a cat's hair! I taught Seels how to make them when she was younger than you."

"I want a cathead too," said Chester.

Chester helped Mamaw get in her scooter, and the pair made their way back to the kitchen to partake in the goodies Seela was cooking.

"It sure does smell good in here, just like when your granddaddy was alive and cooking. You learned well, Seels. I can't wait to taste what you got cooking in here," Mamaw said.

Seela bustled around, preparing everything. "I have sausage gravy with cathead biscuits just the way you like them. Chester, you just wait until you taste one. Y'all take a seat."

Chester pulled the table back so that Mamaw could push her electric scooter up to the end of the table, where Seela had already placed her grandmother's medicine with a spoonful of applesauce.

"Thank you, Seels, for fixin' my drugs up here. I could have done it. I see you remember I like applesauce with my pills. Bring some applesauce over for Chester. He likes it too," Mamaw said.

Chester felt so cared for he could hardly contain himself. "Yes, ma'am, I do!" said Chester.

Mamaw smiled with a mouthful of applesauce and said, "Yes, you are like Mikey. You'll pretty much eat anything, as I've found out this past week." They both laughed as they finished their applesauce. Chester licked his spoon dry.

While they were enjoying breakfast, Dee strolled in from outside. "Whew, it smells good up in here. I guess it's breakfast time at the Blacks'."

"Dee, where have you been? I thought you were still sleeping," Seela said.

"I got up early because I couldn't sleep. I just came from visiting your mama."

Seela sighed and paused. "She let you in her house?"

"Well, not without some coercing. She's one tough cookie to break."

Mamaw chuckled with her mouth full of food. "All I got to say is that you are one persistent cookie if you got her to let you in, especially since she doesn't know you."

Dee appeared to be proud and boastful while Seela eyed her cautiously and continued eating. "I sat and started talking to her through the door. I guess she got tired of me sitting out there, so she let me in— but only to the front room. I'll tell you one thing: her place smells strong like paint and turpentine. I see where you get your artist talent from now, Seels. Your mom has some really nice paintings hanging down there in that little place of hers. Have you seen any of her work lately?"

Seela vigorously shook her head. "Of course not, Dee. I haven't seen my mom in years."

Mamaw turned her scooter on and wheeled to the front window to look out at her daughter's place. "She been down there painting for months. That's how Cat deal with her depression and illness."

Chester remained at the table as if he weren't listening to anything they were saying. He kept eating his biscuit, sopping up every last bit of the sausage gravy he could get off his plate. Mamaw's kitchen wall phone rang, startling Seela and her grandmother. The only one without food in her mouth, Dee sprang to answer the old-timey phone.

"Good morning. This is Dee speaking. Whom do I have the pleasure of speaking with this lovely morning?" She winked at everyone at the kitchen table. "Ah, Officer Joseph Quinton. Oh yes, you may speak to Ms. Seela Black."

At the sound of his name, Seela's stomach did flip-flops inside of her body. Seela didn't know if the butterflies revolved around impending news about Sam or knowing she would hear Joseph's voice.

"Hi, Ms. Seela. I have good news for you. The prison is going to let you visit Sam tomorrow from ten o'clock until three o'clock. You will be escorted into the prison by an officer guard, and you will then be taken to Mr. Sam's room. Please only bring your identification. You will go through security, and you would not want to be denied the opportunity to see Sam."

Seela's eyes filled with tears. "You mean I can't see him today, Joseph?"

"No, ma'am. They will only allow you to come on Sunday. Their visiting schedule on Saturdays is busy for other inmates. They have a full house in the prison cafeteria, where the inmates visit their families. The guards are too busy with that to be able to help you get inside with a sick prisoner who needs round-the-clock care. Remember not to wear a jacket either."

Seela sighed. "Okay, I guess I'll take what time I can get. Is there any way you can get a message to him that I'll be there tomorrow?"

"I'll try, Ms. Seela. I'm not at that facility, so I'll have to make a few calls and determine who I know there. I promise you I'll do my best."

"So that means I won't see you tomorrow then?"

"No, ma'am, you won't. I'll tell you what I'll do. I'll come by your grandmother's house to see how Sam is doing after your visit with him. How does that sound? I would be curious myself to hear how he is."

Seela's face lit up like a flickering Christmas tree. "That would be fabulous, Joseph. I'll call you when I get back home." Seela hung the phone back on the wall while turning to her waiting audience.

"Well, tell us, Seels," Dee said. "Do you get to see Sam today?" Dee looked at Seela with big eyes, as if she were waiting on Seela to give her a giant piece of cake.

"No, they won't let me see Sam until ten o'clock tomorrow morning. I get five hours with him then." Seela teared up as she spoke. "I feel sick to my stomach in thinking that Sam believes I'm just not seeing him and am not concerned about him. I need to lie down, guys. Is that okay with you all? I can clean the kitchen later."

"Hell no. You ain't cleaning anything, Seels," Dee said. "Chubby and I got this. You go lie your pretty self down. We will see you in a little while."

Chester jumped up from the kitchen table and started to help Dee clean the kitchen. "I know how to clean. I do it at home for my pa. He's messy," said Chester in his thick country accent. "I love you, Ms. Seela."

Seela walked over to Chester and squeezed him. "I love you too. I'm so glad you are here with us. I just need to lie down and get rid of these yucky feelings I have right now. You probably should go home and see your pa. I know he will be wondering where you are today."

"Okay, but can I come back later if my pa will let me?" Chester looked sad. He didn't ever want to leave the house of these women.

"Of course, Chester. You are welcome anytime. You just need to clear it with your pa. Okay?" Seela kissed Chester on his forehead before adjourning to her bedroom.

Seela stretched across the bed sideways. Tears filled her eyes as she tried hard not to cry. She could feel Sam's pain and heartache. Seela softly sang one of Sam's favorite songs by an oldie but goodie, Dobie Gray. She hoped singing it would calm her insides, which were trembling with emotions. *"Beginning to think that I'm wasting time. Don't understand the things I do. The world outside looks so unkind. Lord, that's why I'm counting on you to carry me through."*

Seela wiped her tears and sat up on the side of her bed. Dee was standing at her bedroom door with tears rolling down her smooth cinnamon-colored skin. "Dee, I didn't know you were there. Come lie down beside me." Seela patted the bed beside her body.

Dee jumped onto the bed, causing it to squeak loudly. "Oh shit, did I just break your bed, Seels? I didn't know you liked that song. It's one of my all-time favorites."

"It's Sam's too," Seela replied. "He always sang that song and Creedence Clearwater Revival's 'Have You Ever Seen the Rain?'"

"I love that song too," said Dee. "He's got good taste in music, Seela."

"He always loved to sing. That was the one thing that made Sam happy."

Chapter 17

Saturday went by slowly. Mamaw seemed to be sad and was watching movies on Lifetime. She didn't want to eat and kept asking if it were time to go to bed. She wanted Sunday to come so Seela could see Sam and gather new information. Mamaw felt old and helpless.

Seela visited Mavvie while Dee attempted to see Cat again. This time, Cat would not let Dee in. Dee sat patiently outside by the door, talking against the wood barrier. "Seela's going to see Sam tomorrow. He's been shipped to an institutionalized state prison two hours southwest of here that has a hospital floor. We will find out more about his condition then. If you want, I'll come tell you when I hear something. Or would you rather Seela come tell you?"

There was silence. Then Cat's door opened, causing Dee to fall backward. "Oh shit!" Dee hit her head against the door as she tried to catch herself as she tumbled over to the side.

Cat looked at Dee as if she were a klutz. "Get up from there. Why you sitting on the ground? Seela's going to see Sam tomorrow, huh? She better be prepared. He not the same anymore. He act crazy on the phone with me the last few months. I don't know what drugs he was on, but they made him say crazy stuff to me."

Dee walked into Cat's dwelling, prepared for the strong smell of turpentine this time.

Not used to strangers being in her home, Cat opened a window. "I keep my paintbrushes stored in turpentine cleaner when I'm not painting." Cat then shut the door to the room where she stored all of her paintings. Dee assumed Cat didn't want her to see the art.

"What kind of painting do you like to do? You know, Seela likes painting with oils too. I recognize the smell in here. She said she gets her artistic abilities from you. She's very proud of that, Ms. Cat."

"Until I get to know you better, call me Ms. Black," she replied stoically. Cat's weathered, leathery skin signaled a rough life. Her small brown eyes swirled with stories from her past. She walked over to an old recliner and plopped down. "So, Ms. Dee, tell me a little about yourself. You been working with Seels awhile now. I knew about you before you ever met Seela. You probably don't even know how you got to meet my Seela. Do you?"

Dee paused. Perhaps the woman had been sniffing turpentine too long. Of course she could remember meeting Seela. She brushed off Cat's words and let the moment pass.

"You just wait till Seela sees Sam," Cat said. "He may tell her before he dies all the stuff he done from inside that god-awful prison he been in pretty much all his adulthood. That's why he don't care about being locked up. Hopefully he will tell her."

Dee wondered if Cat were telling the truth or just plain crazy. It seemed there was a lot to learn about Seela and Sam. As if the suspense had gotten the best of her, Dee stood abruptly. "Well, I guess I best be going to check on Mamaw. She's been worried about you, Ms. Black. I'll let her know you doing all right. Does that sound okay?"

"You tell her what you want. She knows where I'm at. You best be going. I feel I need to take a nap."

Dee meandered back to Mamaw's house, contemplating what Cat had said to her. It was almost as if Cat were talking in code and leaving Dee to figure out her meaning. Dee stopped before getting to the carport and sat down in a swing hanging between two large weeping willows. The wind blew just enough for the twigs to swish together. It made such a nice sound that Dee closed her eyes to think. Her mind floated to the women's prison years ago. She had tried to forget that life after meeting Seela and finding inner peace and happiness. Maybe Cat knew about the time she had done. Seela approached Dee quietly. Dee jumped when Seela spoke her name.

"Oh girl, you just scared the living shit out of me. You know there's all kinds of critters living in these parts."

Seela laughed. "How did it go visiting my mom? Did she let you in her house?"

"As a matter of fact, she did, and we actually had a conversation. I can't tell you exactly what it was about, because it was almost like she was speaking in code. She was trying to tell me something important, and you bet your bottom dollar I will find out exactly what."

Just then, they heard Chester's three-wheeler and saw him coming down the road with dust and white smoke following. He stopped in front of the swing and pulled his old sticker-covered helmet off. His hair stood up everywhere. "Hey! My pa said I could come over for two hours." Chester held two fingers up. "I missed you today."

Seela jumped up from the swing and immediately started wiping Chester's face with the bottom of her shirt. "Oh, honey, let's go inside and get all this dirt off of you." Chester stood proudly while Seela wiped his face. He loved the attention.

The night was quiet. They sat in the living room, sharing stories about Seela and Sam when they were little, along with some of their grandfather's stories. Dee and Chester loved listening to Mamaw and Seela narrate.

As Seela walked Chester out to his three-wheeler, Chester stared at her thoughtfully. "Ms. Seela, I hope you see Sam tomorrow. Can I come over before you go home? I'm going to miss you again." Chester held his head down. He didn't want Seela to see the tears that filled his eyes. He wiped them before looking up again and smiling.

Seela rubbed his soft, chubby cheek. "You can come see me tomorrow, and I promise next Saturday, Dee and I will take you to the beach."

Chester's eyes grew big as he smiled even bigger. "Okay, I got a swimsuit." Seela's words seemed to have instantly wiped away Chester's sadness.

Seela stood watching Chester kick up dust until he was no longer in her sight.

Chapter 18

Starting at four o'clock in the morning, Seela woke up on the hour every hour until it was time to get up at seven. She had a restless night, knowing she was going into something she had never experienced or seen before. Her twin brother had lived a life of incarceration for most of his adulthood; it was all he knew. Seela stayed in the shower for some time, trying to ease her mind, and then got dressed.

Dee found her in the kitchen, drinking a cup of coffee and staring out the window. "Good morning, Seels. You're already dressed to go. How long you think it will take you to get there?"

"I looked on the map on my phone. I'll give myself extra time, but it should take me about an hour and a half. I'm not going to wake Mamaw up before I leave. Will you see about her, Dee? I can't deal with her emotions this morning on top of everything. I should be back here by four thirty or so. I guess we will have dinner with Mamaw, Mavvie, and Chester when I get back before we head home. Does that sound okay with you, Dee?"

Seela was sharper this morning than Dee had estimated she would be. "Heck yeah, Seels. I'll even cook dinner for everyone today. You just go be strong for Sam, and find out exactly what is going on. We will all be here, waiting to hear something."

Seela drove down the dusty road and headed off the island. When she came across the bridge, she saw Bill Johnson standing out by his gas station, staring at her car at the red light. She waved at him. He waved to her to drive over to him. Seela rolled her window down. "Good morning, Bill. How are you today?"

Bill wiped his forehead, which was already covered with sweat from the hot, swampy air that remained from sunup to sundown that time of year. "Chubby tells me you going to see your brother, Sam, today. I know Sam and want you to keep your hopes up for him. He always been good to me whenever he out here running free for the short times he had. He love my boy like you do. That three-wheeler came from Sam. Hell, who knows where it came from? But one day he pulled up, jumped off of it, and gave it to Chubby. Chubby already worn two sets of wheels out on it. It was brand spanking new! Do me a favor. Chubby loves your brother like his real uncle. He doesn't need to know the severity of Sam's condition. So up to me, I'd like to keep it that way until we know for sure what is happening with Sam."

Seela tried to contain her confusion regarding the man's connection to Sam. "Chester doesn't need to worry about something he can't do anything about. I must admit I didn't know that you guys were that close to him. Chester told me he calls my brother Uncle Sam."

Bill pointed to a metal Uncle Sam poster in red, white, and blue hanging on the outside of the gas station wall. "That's why he calls him Uncle Sam. Sam would point to Chubby and say, 'I want you,' every time before he would leave the gas station, so Chubby called him Uncle Sam." Bill smiled and tapped Seela's car door. "You best be getting to see Sam."

Seela drove off, looking back in her mirror and wondering what all Bill knew about Sam. It seemed he had deep feelings for him. Seela drove on country roads for what seemed like an eternity. She finally reached the prison entrance, which was surrounded by a tall barbed-wire fence. She drove down the long, winding road, passing some inmates out working on the grounds. Her body was so nervous that she could feel her heartbeat in her stomach. She kept her head forward, trying not to look at anyone.

As she walked up to the high gate, Seela tried talking herself out of all the nervousness she felt. When she reached the metal door at the first building, she pressed a big red button, and a loud buzz sounded. A small black woman opened a sliding window the size of a shoebox.

She spoke with a meager voice. "I need your ID, please. Fill out one of those sheets over there, and I'll be back to pick it up from you. Who are you here to see, ma'am?"

Seela leaned down to look in the tiny open window. "I'm here to see Sam Black. I have special visiting set up today from ten to three." The window closed without the lady responding to Seela. Seela filled out the paper on a clipboard and hung it by the window. She stood for a few minutes, wondering if she would get to go inside the prison to see Sam. Maybe Joseph had given her wrong information.

Then the window slid open quickly. "Ms. Black, there will be an officer coming down to escort you in as soon as we get him on walkie-talkie. I'm having a hard time reaching him. Go ahead and have a seat. Someone will be here shortly."

Seela sat for what seemed like an hour before a double metal door opened. The sun was glaring through the glass window, so when the officer walked through, Seela could hardly see his face. "Well, what a beautiful sight to see here in this place."

Seela jumped up as soon as she heard Joseph's voice. "Joseph, I thought you said you didn't work at this facility."

Joseph's smile flashed as the glare lifted. "I don't normally, but I got a phone call yesterday asking if I wanted to do high security here because of all the gangs and murders going on in here. Don't worry about Sam. He's in a separate wing with only sick inmates. He has prison nurses watching over him twenty-four hours a day. I went by and told him I was coming down to get you. I want you to be prepared, Seela. It's not like it was when you visited at the hospital. Remember, we are in a prison, and you will be locked in his room with him. If you need anything, there is a button you push, and a nurse will come unlock Sam's door and help you. The front wall of his room is glass, so you can see out onto the floor to the other sick inmates and the nurses' station in the center of the floor, just as you would see on an ICU floor at a regular hospital." Joseph explained all of this to Seela as they walked down the shiny, freshly mopped floors. His eyes were looking in all directions as if waiting for a target to pop out for him to shoot.

Joseph grabbed Seela's elbow, pulling her to a stop. "We need to take this elevator up to the fourth floor, Ms. Seela." He pushed the button on the wall after swiping his security card. "When we step off this elevator, you will then be behind the prison walls. Are you ready?"

Seela swallowed hard before speaking. She cleared her throat. "Is it going to be bad, Joseph?" Seela was visibly trembling.

Joseph smiled at Seela while touching her arm to let her know it was going to be all right. "You have nothing to worry about, Ms. Seela. You are safe on this floor as long as you stay in your brother's room. I'll come get you at the end of your visit and walk you out. Sam also said to tell you to walk straight to his room and not look into other rooms. I guess he doesn't want you to see other dying, sick men."

"Okay, I'm ready. I just want to see Sam."

They walked off the elevator and started down a long, cold hallway. The floor was so shiny that the sunlight flickering through the tiny windows made it look like a puddle of water. Inmates in white uniforms with blue stripes down the sides of their shirts and pants busily cleaned restrooms, mopping floors vigorously. The prisoners glanced at Seela, wondering why they were seeing a civilian in regular clothes inside their caged world. As soon as Officer Quinton looked at the inmates, they would turn their heads away but tell him, "Good morning."

Seela tried to keep her eyes straight ahead. She could hear other sick men moaning in pain and angry ones yelling for a nurse. Joseph stopped quickly. "Okay, Seela, there's Sam's room."

Without hesitation, Seela approached the room and spotted Sam lying there like a dead man with his stomach blown up like a nine-month-pregnant woman waiting for the delivery of her baby. His eyes were closed, so he didn't see her. Seela jumped back against the wall, covering her face as she cried. Trying not to make a sound, afraid she would be thrown out if she did, she stood there crying in her mind and soul. Joseph stepped in front of her to cover her and prevent anyone from seeing her have a meltdown. He grabbed her shoulders.

"Seela, go in there, and be strong for your twin. He needs you real bad at this point. He's been given sixty days to live. He told me this morning. You are the only one who can help him, Seela."

Seela looked up into Joseph's eyes. His face was handsome, and his eyes penetrated her flesh. She had only experienced this feeling once before in her life. Seela wiped her tears and put on a smile. "You're right, Joseph. I'll see you in five hours."

Seela tapped on the window so that Sam would see her before she went through the metal door. She didn't want the buzzer to startle him. Sam turned his head and saw Seela peeping through the glass. He yelled, "Open the fucking door right now, and let my twin in!"

Seela was startled as she turned to look at the nurses' station. One of the guard-dressed nurses smiled slightly at Seela and buzzed her in.

Sam looked horrible. Seela tried to remain calm. His coloring was pale, and his stomach was huge. His feet were so swollen he couldn't even stand on his own two feet. His lips were cracked like thirty-year-old asphalt that needed to be repaved.

"Sam, honey, I'm so sorry they brought you here. I'm trying to get you out of here and get you home so we can take care of you. I hope you didn't think I was leaving you again. They took you in the middle of the night without telling us." Seela sat beside Sam, trying to hold his hand.

Sam pulled his arm away from her with anger. "Don't try to hold my hand, Seels. I know what fucking time it is! They fucking filling me up with morphine and going to kill me in here now. You and Mom don't understand. They ain't letting me out of here. That's why they shipped me here. You see that tall black woman over there?" Sam pointed toward the nurses' station. "I call her Big Sexy. She know what time it is too. I was fucking killed in Jacks State Prison. They didn't bother to tell you that piece of info when they were letting you come see me, did they?"

"Sam, what are you talking about? You are sick with liver cancer, and your ammonia levels got so high you passed out at Jacks State Prison. That's what they told me."

Sam ripped back his bedsheet away from his swollen legs. "Well, they fucking lied to you. I was shanked, Seela. Look at all of my stitches. From my fucking asshole straight through my ball sack. I was found in a pool of blood and airlifted to Atlanta Medical. If only I could have laid there for one more fucking minute, I wouldn't be going through any more hell here on earth. If only I would have walked out of that boat with Granddaddy." Sam shook his head with tears rolling down his face. He covered himself with his faded, dingy sheet, throwing his busted knuckles up for Seela to see.

"You see this, Seels? That's where I was fighting the two shits who shanked me. One grabbed me up out of the bed, and the other put the shank to my fucking nut sack. I told him he didn't have to do it and said they could have anything in my locker, but last I remember, he said, 'No, thanks. This was special ordered.' Then the lights went out for me. I woke up to you looking over me at the hospital. This place is fucking horrible. Look what they brought me to eat." He pointed to a tray with a makeshift white-bread cheese sandwich and an orange. "They brought me two fucking things my body can't have. I'll fucking starve to death. They won't need much morphine." Sam was becoming irrational. "If I could get up out of this fucking bed, I would get somebody told." Sam rolled his head back and forth. "I can't believe this is happening. Seela, you going to have to help me now. I got money spread out everywhere. You got to get it for me, you hear? Seels, I fucked up bad this time!"

Seela looked at Sam as if he were hallucinating from the fluid that filled his body. "Sam, I don't know what you are talking about. Maybe you need to rest a minute, and then we will visit. Did they just give you a shot?"

Sam sat up as quickly as his huge torso would allow. "I'm fucking serious, Seela. I got thousands out there floating around, and I'll be damned if these people keep my money. I got a business going on inside where I was, and right now, I need your help to find out what my partner's doing in Cottonwood. He's got my cell phone, you see. He's the one who got me airlifted the first time out of there. I didn't want to leave; he had to do it. I was so sick I couldn't even get out of my own fucking bed. It got to where he couldn't protect me at certain times. Jones is his name, and when you leave here today, I want you to call him. Tell him what's going on. I need you to get something to write on so I can give you some names and numbers to call these people. They better send my goddamn money to you ASAP. Tell them I'll send somebody after their ass if they don't. You hear me, Sis?"

Seela was overwhelmed by her brother's tirade. He had been told he only had sixty days to live, and all he could think about was his money. Did he believe he was dying? Did he believe the authorities were lying? These thoughts ran ragged through Seela's head as she sat in the cold metal chair, listening to her brother talk in his broken Cajun Louisianan accent.

The door buzzer went off, startling Seela. An older woman in civilian clothes and a nurse jacket walked in the room, addressing Seela. "Hi. I'm Sam's caregiver, Ms. Lee. I'll be here with him while he goes through this process. I'll be coming to check on him three times a week, and I'll give him any emotional support I can. I've tried to explain to him what is happening, but I don't think Mr. Black has come to terms with it." Ms. Lee handed Seela a stapled packet of papers labeled, in big letters, "Palliative Care."

Sam started yelling at Ms. Lee. "You get the fuck out of my room! I told you earlier. Don't come back here to see me. I'm not fucking dying in this hellhole. You people just wait. I got contacts. When you get me a fucking wheelchair, I'll go down to the warden and get this shit taken care of. Seela, tell them I need a wheelchair. I can't even go to the fucking commode by myself."

Ms. Lee stood close to the locked metal door, as if she were afraid. At the same time, she felt sorry for Sam and his situation. Seela pushed the buzzer so the nurse would let Ms. Lee out. "Can I step outside for a minute and have a word with you, Ms. Lee? Are we allowed?"

"Yes, please. Are you his twin sister? He told me you were coming to see him."

"Yes, I am. I'm so shocked about all of this at the moment. He just told me he was shanked at Jackson, and I don't understand why they wouldn't tell us that. I saw his stitches."

"Ms. Black, I know nothing of that story. I'm a civilian volunteer, so I have nothing to do with anything that goes on in these facilities.

I feel so bad for your brother. I will try to console him when I'm here visiting, if he will allow me to."

Seela walked back into Sam's room as the door locked loudly. "Where you been, Sis?" he said. "Did you find me something to eat? You know, they have vending machines downstairs in the visiting room. I bet they let you get me something and bring it in here."

Seela was desperate to comply, as it would fill her heart to give Sam this slight pleasure. "How will I do that, Sam? I don't have any money with me."

"You got some in the car, don't you?"

"Of course I do. But I can't go out and then back in. Officer Quinton said I'm in here until three o'clock."

Sam smiled candidly at Seela. "You getting to know Officer Quinton? He a good guy, you know. He's helped me many a time. He came to see me this morning, and I kinda felt he was asking a lot of questions about you, Seels. What you think about him?" He grinned with only six teeth showing up top.

"Sam, Officer Quinton is a polite gentleman who, thank God, has helped me in seeing you."

"That ain't what I asked you, Sis. I know all that bullshit!"

A short tattooed inmate walked by Sam's glass wall, and Sam yelled, "Lil Jon, this is my twin I was telling you about! She's a lot prettier than me." Seela waved to Lil Jon and smiled. He approached the glass window. Sam mouthed, "Go get Officer Quinton." Lil Jon gave a thumbs-up, grabbed a mop and bucket, and headed down the hall and through the metal doors.

Seela watched Lil Jon and said, "What was that all about? I didn't think any of you guys could get out those locked doors. How is he going through them?"

Sam smiled at Seela. "Who told you that? Officer Quinton? No, he's right; we guys in here can't go out, but Lil Jon is a trustee. He getting out in six months, so he has a key for this floor. That's his job every day—to come down our hall to clean bathrooms and floors. He's cool."

"Why did you tell him to go get Officer Quinton?"

"Because Officer Quinton will take you downstairs to get me some food, and you can pay him back when you see him in the outside world." Sam said this as if Seela and Joseph had already set a date. Seela felt as if she were in another world. Her brother, who she'd thought would be loving, as he was in the hospital, was back to his old self, ordering people around and flipping out when things weren't going his way. Seela had locked these memories far away in her hidden closet. Sam was starting to remind her of his outrageous ways.

Suddenly, Officer Quinton tapped on the glass with his big, round metal key ring. He smiled at Seela, motioning for her to come to the door. Seela stood up and turned to Sam. "Is he taking me downstairs for you?"

Sam smiled his old shit-eating grin. "Hell yeah, he's taking you down there. I want you to get me three hamburgers, two bean burritos, a couple bags of chips, and five honey buns. No, better make it six. That way, I'll have one every morning until you come back next Sunday." He ordered his food as if Seela were a drive-through window. It broke her heart that this little food provided such excitement for her caged, dying brother.

Joseph and Seela walked slowly down the hallway. Joseph spoke quietly to Seela. "When I open the main door downstairs, you put your hand on the handle and reach for the twenty between my fingers. There are cameras everywhere but not on that door because of how it sits on the corner of the hallway."

Seela nodded. Her heart pounded so thunderously she thought the first person she came across would see it reverberating in her chest. Her hand shook when she reached for the folded twenty from Joseph's two middle fingers as he reached for the door. When the door shut behind them, Seela turned as if someone had seen what she had done. Joseph pressed Seela's back softly.

"Now, if you look to the right wall, there are vending machines where you can purchase Sam's order." Joseph chuckled. "There is a machine where you can get that twenty changed to smaller bills. Sorry— it was all I had in my wallet. That's all they allow us. Hopefully it's enough. That shit's expensive, but it's all he's got. He'll be able to order stuff from the prison grocery soon. I'm sure his money from Cottonwood has been transferred by now."

"Can I leave money for him?" asked Seela.

"No, ma'am. But you can go online and transfer to his account. I'm sure Sam will tell you how to do that before you leave today. Go get your order so you can get back up to visit with him." Joseph eyed Seela while she purchased all of Sam's requests, plus a couple packs of Starburst. She knew they'd been Sam's favorite when they were young.

"You had enough money, I see," said Joseph as they walked back to Sam's room.

"Thank you again, Joseph. I'll be glad to pay you back when I get to my car."

"No, that won't be necessary. I'm sure I owe Sam from some football bet we made. I hate that this is happening to him, Seela. He's a good guy. He just got hooked on that heroin. I've seen it ruin a few good people. This isn't the place to put them. Your brother could get what he wanted, I'm sure, during his times of being locked up."

The double doors opened. Joseph stopped to let Seela walk on by herself to Sam's room. Seela stood staring at Sam. He looked like an eighty-year-old man, lying there with his eyes closed. Tears filled her eyes again as she thought of her brother dying in these cinder block walls, trapped behind a big metal door. The buzzer went off, startling Seela and Sam. He turned quickly, trying with his weak body to raise himself up. The weight of his stomach held him down.

Seela dropped the vending machine goodies onto Sam's tray cart. She reached to put her arms under Sam to help him sit up in his bed. It was like lifting a thousand-pound barbell.

She tried twice as they both laughed like little children.

"Damn, Sis, I don't want you to hurt yourself. Fucking guard nurses, seeing you trying to help me. They supposed to be doing it." Sam yelled, "Big Sexy, get your fucking ass in here, and help me sit up, please!" Sam waved his hand at Big Sexy, who looked aggravated. She waddled to Sam's room with her big key ring to unlock the door.

"Sam, you wearing me out today. What you wantin' now?"

"Will you and another nurse come pull my fucking blown-up blimp-ass body up so I can eat some food my twin just went and got me?"

"This your twin, Sam?" Big Sexy stared at Seela. "She definitely got the looks! Sam, you cute, but your sister here is some pretty."

Sam smiled at Seela. "She's the good to my evil! Her light always shine bright. I don't know why she still love me."

Seela stood over Sam's food tray, trying to open a couple of the items so Big Sexy could microwave them for Sam at her nurses' station. She handed the burrito and one burger to her. "Do you want me to walk with you and bring them back, or will you bring them?" Seela said.

"You stay in here. I'll bring them back in a couple minutes. Sam, you good now? I'm sending Lil Jon and Ken in here to lift you. I don't want my back thrown out either!"

Within a few seconds, like vultures, Lil Jon and Ken were there to help Sam. Sam stuffed a sandwich and Starburst into their pockets while they lifted him up. He did it so smoothly that even a camera probably would not have caught Sam. After they left the room, Seela sat there and watched Sam eat the burrito as if he hadn't eaten in days.

"Why did you give your food away, Sam? That could have lasted you a few days."

"It's okay, Sis. I can't eat much. This here burrito will kill my stomach after you leave today. I'll pay for it, but I love me a bean burrito. I fell in love with burritos when you worked at that taco place back when we were in high school. Remember, you would bring me four bean burritos home at night with extra hot sauce?"

Seela had forgotten all about that time in their life. She thought of other times when she and Sam had shared as children and teens. Sam started to go off about his money again, but Seela was in a trance, thinking of childhood memories.

"Seela! You listening to me? I need you to write some stuff down on the back of that packet Ms. Lee gave you. When you get home, you need to call these fucking-ass people and have them send money orders to Mamaw's address. I'm going to give you names, numbers, and how much they owe me. You got it? You got to do this. It's not just a small amount, Sis. You can keep it when I die. I want you to write that down too. Everything I have goes to you."

Seela thought the ammonia level in his brain was causing him to talk like this. She looked down at the shiny floor to find something to focus on so Sam couldn't see her face. "Dammit, Seela. Look at me. I'm telling you the truth. Now, I'm going to tell you the whole goddamn truth. You got to believe me. I'm not making this shit up. I'm going to tell you how I have money, but you have to promise you will not hate me for what I'm about to tell you. I'm fucking dying, and I hope that you will be here for me, because you are all I have now."

"Sam, you are my twin. I'll always love you."

"Okay, let's get started with my story and then the names you have to write down to go after these people to get my money. They probably wondering why they haven't heard from me the past few weeks."

Chapter 19

Seela sat in shock, but she tried not to show it. She didn't want Sam to have an outburst.

Sam proceeded to tell Seela about the last prison he was incarcerated at. Sam told her he'd had a drug ring going with the warden and guards. The warden got a percentage, along with the guards who smuggled the drugs and phones in. He had affairs with female guards in order to get their help. Phones were brought in taped to the insides of computer monitors, and each sold for $500. In addition, Marlboro cigarettes were sold for five dollars apiece. Sam also directed a parlay gambling ring, which the guards allowed so they could have a cut of the winnings. Sam's earnings were sent through Green Dot cards bought by the prisoners' families. As he talked about it, Sam smiled with excitement, thinking of the great business he had going.

Seela sat in amazement, listening to her brother explain that he had thousands of dollars out on the streets from this mafia world he ran inside this awful prison. *No wonder he didn't mind being incarcerated all these years!* It sounded as if he loved his life and felt comfortable doing these deeds. The saddest thing Seela realized while listening to him was that his only loves on earth were heroin and money. He'd never had love long enough from a human to fill his heart. Sam's depiction of happiness via criminal activities in prison saddened her. He spoke about his crime ring as if it were a normal job. She knew she would fall to pieces as soon as she left Sam's side.

As Sam finished his story, he looked at the Big Ben clock on the wall. "Seels, we got thirty minutes before Officer Quinton come get you. I need you to get that paper sitting on the tray. That crazy Ms. Lee left her pen on the side table right there. You see it, Seels? I'm going to tell you some names and numbers. You write them down. You call these folks and tell them I need my fucking money sent to Mamaw's address now! Don't tell them I'm fucking dying here. Who knows? We might get me out of here before I die, and if that happens, we going on a fucking trip. Vegas, baby!"

Seela recorded the information. Then Sam noted the dollar amount each person owed him. Sam was not kidding—he had thousands of dollars out there.

"Now, write this down on another sheet of paper: 'I, Samuel Black, leave all my money and possessions to Seela Black, my twin sister.' Let me sign the paper, Seels." Seela got up and leaned over for Sam to sign his name. He was so weak he could hardly write. "Now, you get Officer Quinton to sign it too, so everybody know you had a witness."

Seela stood up, folding the paper small to fit in her hand. "Okay, I got it, Sam. When I come next week, I'll let you know if everyone sent your money."

"There's one more thing I want you to do. You see how horrible this place is. I need stuff to barter with these inmates to help take care of me. I haven't had a real shower since they brought me here. I need to get one of these guys to fucking help me. I need them to clean my floors when I can't make it to my toilet when I'm throwing up. You goin' to help me, Sis. Right? All you have to do is put Marlboros, candy, and bubble gum all in a ziplock baggie. Bubble gum huge in prison. I still like Laffy Taffy, so get me some of that, and I like old-school bubble gum: Double Bubble and Super Bubble. Wear large clothes, and tuck the stuff in your bra and the back of your pants. Nobody is going to check you."

Seela shrank down in the chair, knowing she would do it but would be afraid at the same time. Just then, Officer Quinton tapped on the glass.

"You got me, Sis. I watched you always, and now you get to watch over me. Isn't that some shit?"

Seela kissed him on the forehead as she tried to read between the lines that Sam always seemed to have.

She and Joseph stood for a few seconds, waving through the glass. "How was your visit, Seela?"

"Joseph, it was a lot of information for me in a short amount of time. I have to admit I'm a little overwhelmed right now. This visit was not at all what I expected. I even have homework from my sick, dying brother." She held up the papers.

"Whoa, whoa. It's against rules for you to carry anything out of here. Give me that, and I'll carry it out for you." Joseph opened the papers to see what they were. When he saw numbers, he closed the papers and shoved them in his pocket. Seela was worried he would not give them back. Joseph walked Seela to the main door. "Can I call you later and maybe come by to meet your grandmother and mom? Sam told me a lot about them. I hear that's where he gets his feistiness from. The two of them, I hear!"

"Only if you bring the papers in your pocket to me."

"Of course. I will give them to you now, Ms. Seela. That's Sam's business with you. I just didn't want you to lose them in there." Joseph winked at Seela as he closed her car door. "See you soon."

The dark feelings that had filled Seela's mind, body, and soul went out the window as soon as Joseph winked at her. Driving home, she thought about her twin's fixation on money. He couldn't spend it; he was dying in prison. Panic started to set in. How in the world had she, of all people, gotten stuck in this position?

Chapter 20

Seela passed the gas station and decided to turn back. Bill walked out to greet her as she rolled her window down. "Is Chester here? I was wondering if he would like to come over for dinner tonight before I head back home."

"He beat you to it, Ms. Black. Chubby called me from your grandmother's an hour ago. I guess she had him call to tell me he was there. I really appreciate that. I told him to be home by nine. How was Sam?" Bill stood with his hand on one hip and his left cowboy boot slid outward.

"Not good, Mr. Johnson. I'm going to do my best to get him home so we can take care of him in his last days."

Bill listened closely, as if Sam were a family member. "I'm so sorry to hear that, Ms. Seela. Your brother was always good to me as I tried to help him, even when he was on hard times. Sometimes I would let him stay out back and sleep for a couple days after he had been running hard for a while. Chubby would always keep an eye on him and get him stuff to eat and drink. Sometimes I would get a surprise and find him sleeping on an old sofa in my garage out back. He knew he was safe here."

Seela's eyes teared up. "Thank you for watching over him when you could, Mr. Johnson. I know he appreciated everything you did for him. I'll head on to the island so I can tell my mom and grandmother what is going on with Sam. I know they are waiting. Don't forget—next week I'm taking Chester to the beach!"

Seela zoomed into the drive to find Joseph sitting in the yard with Mamaw and Dee.

She stepped out of her car and wiped her hair away from her face. "How in the world did you beat me here?" Seela asked Joseph, astounded he had not called or wasted any time since they'd parted.

"I left just after you did, Seela. My shift was over, and I thought I would stop by on my way home. How did I beat you here?"

"I stopped for gas and to see about Chester. Is he here, Mamaw?"

Mamaw was so enamored with Joseph's handsome looks that she seemed to be tongue-tied. She'd pulled her scooter as close as she could get to Joseph. Without looking at Seela, Mamaw nodded. "He's watching television inside, Seela. Why don't you get us all some iced tea? Unless you want something stronger, Joseph? We got beer, liquor, and wine. Whatever suits your fancy!" Mamaw smiled flirtatiously.

Seela replied quickly without giving Joseph a chance to speak. "I'll bring a pitcher of tea out with some glasses. You like lemon, Joseph?"

"I'm good with just the tea, Ms. Seela. You need me to help you?"

"Oh no. You sit and enjoy Mamaw. See if Sam's stories match up."

Dee stood up to help Seela, but Seela gave her a familiar look, and Dee sat back down to enjoy Officer Joseph's conversation with Mamaw.

Seela entered the house and found Chester sitting on the sofa, enjoying what seemed to be his favorite show. "Hey, Chester! How are you doing today? I'm glad you are here for dinner tonight."

Chester stood quickly when he heard Seela's voice. "Hey!" Chester said in his raspy country voice. "I've been waiting on you to get home. Did you see Sam today?" Chester seemed sad, feeling Seela's emotions.

"Yes. I did see my brother today. It didn't go as I expected, but at least I got to see him, and I'll go back next Sunday."

Chester wandered over to Seela. He laid his head against Seela's chest. Chester stood still, as if listening for Seela's heartbeat. Seela caressed Chester's head. "Are you okay, Chester?" she said. "Your head feels warm." Seela pulled his head away and looked at Chester's eyes. "Are you feeling sick, Chester?"

"No, ma'am! I sometimes get hot when I sit for a while." Chester smiled crookedly.

"Would you like some iced tea with us out in the front yard, Chester?"

"Who is that outside with Mamaw and Dee?" Chester peered out the window from behind the curtain, as if he didn't want them to see him.

"It's okay, Chester. That's Officer Quinton. He's the nice man who has helped me with seeing Sam. He's known Sam for a while."

"Do you like him, Ms. Seela? Is that the man you call Yosef?"

"I think he is a nice gentleman, Chester. That's all!" Seela grabbed the old glass tea pitcher from her childhood. She handed Chester a bucket of ice. As they trekked to the front yard, Joseph stood up. Seela whispered under her breath, "Like I said, a perfect gentleman."

Chester looked over at Seela and smirked after hearing what she said. Chester could tell Seela felt bubbly over Joseph. He stared at Seela, watching her emotions spew out. Chester set the ice bucket down on the wooden split table. He held his right hand out to Joseph.

"Hi. I'm George Chester Johnson. Most people call me Chubby."

"It's nice to meet you, George Chester Johnson. What would you like me to call you?"

"Ms. Seela call me Chester."

"That sounds just fine with me. Chester it is," said Joseph.

Seela poured everyone a glass of tea and sat down beside Chester. She reached to feel his forehead again to make sure he didn't have a fever.

"Why you feeling his forehead, Seela? Is there something wrong?" said Mamaw.

"No, I thought he was warm when I got home, but he feels all right now."

Chester leaned against Seela as if he never wanted her out of his sight again. Joseph watched Seela and Chester as they sat across from him. He saw how attentive she was to Chester and how Chester felt for Seela. Suddenly, Mavvie ran out from the bushes, startling Joseph. Mavvie was dressed in her typical flowing, long white dress and had her hair tied in a sash high on top of her head. She'd vowed to wear white until Sam was "taken home," as she said. "Who do we have here?" Mavvie said, accentuating every word while sizing up Joseph.

"Mavvie, this is Joseph, whom I've told you about. He came to meet our family. Joseph knows Sam and is helping me with my visits," Seela replied.

Mavvie smiled as she stared into Joseph's eyes. "You are a handsome man, Mr. Joseph. Seela didn't tell me that!" Mavvie sat down gracefully beside Seela.

Mamaw smiled, showing her bright red gums. "Joseph, tell us how you met my grandson, Sam. How long have you known him?"

Joseph seemed to be comfortable with all of the attention. "I met Sam a couple years ago at a state prison hospital. They brought him in to have a physical due to his illness with hep C. I have to say, Mr. Sam Black is a character! He's a good guy. I hate that he got messed up with drugs. He seemed to be a Robin Hood in the place where he was, though. He always had great stories for me, and of course, if it was football season, he wanted to make a bet." Joseph laughed as he talked about Sam. "Of course, if I lost my bet, I knew to bring him Super Bubble the next day. That man would stuff four or five pieces in his mouth at one time. I would walk by his room sometime later that day, and he would be chewing it like a cow chewing cud." They all giggled hysterically, even Chester.

Seela listened attentively, watching Joseph's every move. She liked the way he held his hands as he spoke. He even crossed his leg as he sat, just as her granddaddy had. An hour later, Seela stood up and asked Joseph if he wanted to stay for dinner.

"I would love to, but I best be going, Seela. I have to be back early in the morning, and I have a few things I need to do this evening. I'll see you next weekend. If you need anything before then, please call me."

Seela's heart sank. She'd hoped Joseph would stay for dinner. "Yes, I will see you next weekend. Will you be escorting me in?" Seela envisioned trying to smuggle in all the items Sam had ordered.

"Yes, ma'am, I'll be your escort. Be there at ten o'clock sharp." Seeing Seela's relief, Joseph flashed a smile.

Mavvie stood to give Joseph a hug. She whispered in his ear, "She loves all-white flowers." Mavvie stepped back from Joseph quickly. "I'll see you again soon, Mr. Joseph?"

"Yes, ma'am, I hope so, Ms. Mavvie. It was a great pleasure to meet you all today."

Seela stood with Chester as they watched Joseph drive away. Chester looked up at Seela and smiled. "You like Mr. Yosef, don't you?"

"Yes, Chester. He is a nice gentleman."

"You already said that," said Chester.

"Okay, well, I said it again! Now, let's get dinner fixed so you can get home by your curfew."

"I want to stay again, Ms. Seela." He was wondering when they would go to the beach too.

"You are always welcome, Chester, but I believe your dad wants you home tonight. I'll tell you what. I'll pick you up on my way in next Saturday, and you can spend the entire weekend with us."

Chester's face brightened, and he smiled with every tooth showing. "Okay, I'll pack my suitcase and my Xbox!"

Chapter 21

Seela and Dee headed home late after dinner. Sensing Seela's exhaustion, Dee took the wheel gladly. "Damn, Seela, this car is a nice ride! So you going to tell me about the visit? You didn't even talk to your mother about seeing Sam."

"Because it was not a good visit, Dee. He's so angry, and I really don't believe he thinks he's dying. Do you know that he was shanked in the last place? He told me he thinks it was ordered from the warden of the private prison he came from before. He's been there for two years, dealing drugs and running a gambling parlay ring with the help of guards and the warden. That's why he didn't care if anyone came to see him. He was also doing drugs daily. He looks like death right now. There is no telling what kind of drugs were being brought in.

"At first, I thought he was making this shit up, but he pulled his sheet back and showed me his stitches. It was horrible, Dee! I swear he looks like one of those posters you see of someone who's done a lot of meth. I'm not exaggerating either. Sam being shanked has just kick-started his death. He has nothing to fight with in his body. It's just so surreal, Dee. He wants me to smuggle in bubble gum and cigarettes next Sunday. How in the world am I going to be able to do that?" Seela pulled out the papers with the information he'd provided while Dee shook her head vehemently, trying to take everything in.

"This is a list of people I have to contact. I have to instruct them to send the money they owe him to Mamaw. Can you believe my brother is locked up behind barbed wire and metal doors and still making money on the inside? This all takes me back to when we were just young teens.

Sam would take me to the local pool hall, and we would hustle drunk local men on the pool tables." Seela laughed, thinking about how Sam had taught her to help him hustle, with the two of them starting out first playing and then luring others over.

"Dee, Sam used to have me play with him first, and of course, he would play to half of his capability in shooting pool. Whatever Sam did as far as a sport, he would master. He would then have men walking up and placing dollars on the side of table to play the winner. After a couple of games, he would slowly step up his game. By the end of the night, we both would have our pockets full of crumpled one-dollar bills. He always split his winnings with me." Seela grinned, thinking about her visit with Sam earlier and realizing that her childhood memory had been just the beginning of Sam's days as a hustler but also a Robin Hood. Giving some of his winnings to his twin had made his heart full even back then.

Dee finally spoke. "You are not going to smuggle anything in, are you, Seels?"

"Dee, I don't know, but please just support me in this, whatever I do. My brother is dying, so if a pack of cigarettes, a fucking burrito, or a stick of gum will brighten up his day, so be it."

"Okay, okay! You will not get a scold out of me, but be damn careful, whatever you do. Do not risk everything you've worked so hard for, including that gallery still needing a name."

Dee pulled into Seela's drive, and they said good night, but not before Dee astounded Seela by offering to call everyone on Sam's list. Seela hesitated, not wanting her friend to get caught in the crossfire. "I'll pretend to be you and yell out some whoop ass if I have to. You good with that?" Dee's loyalty brought tears to Seela's eyes as she agreed.

The next day, when Seela arrived at the salon, a beautiful bouquet of white flowers had just been delivered. She reached for the card and opened the envelope. The note inside said, "I hope these flowers make you smile, and I hope they are as beautiful as you. Love, Joseph." Seela smiled in the waiting area, holding the card to her chest.

Dee walked in the front door quickly, as if she were late. "Oh, you scared me, Seels. What are you doing sitting there for?"

In a trance, Seela put the card down by her side. "I just got here myself, and these flowers were sitting on the counter. Guess who they are from."

"I'll take a wild guess," said Dee. "Ms. Kathy!"

"Wrong," said Seela. She handed the card to Dee as she walked to the back of the salon with the heavy bouquet. "Now, let's see where I would like to display these beautiful flowers." Seela sang the words, floating, delirious with warmth.

"Joseph!" Dee shouted while glancing at the card. "Don't be putting them in your office. I want these ladies to see that Ms. Seela got flowers from a handsome man. Whew wee! We goin' to have some fun this week with this one." Dee proceeded to walk around the salon with a feather duster, chuckling while dusting the shelves.

As the week went on, not much chatter buzzed about Sam in the salon. Dee had been right. Big gossip revolved around the flowers Seela received.

Seela worked feverishly all week so she and Dee could leave bright and early on Saturday to return to her grandmother's house. Dee spent her evenings calling the people on Sam's cash-collection list. Everyone complied easily, except for a woman named Charlie. Dee had several conversations with this woman and felt there was a lot more to her story with Sam. Dee decided to let Seela tell Sam about Charlie, and then he could decide what he wanted to do.

Sam counted down the days until Sunday, when Seela would visit and bring his goodies. He already had his posse in order. The inmates and nurses were all under his spell. The nurses had fallen in love with him, and the few inmates Sam interacted with were helping him feverishly like worker bees. Sam wasted no time in getting Lil Jon to find him a wheelchair and take him out in the yard daily to sit in the warm sun. Sometimes Sam took a drag of a cigarette from an inmate standing around. His body was filled with so much fluid he could hardly breathe, so taking a drag caused him to cough horribly. Tasting the addiction satisfied him, though.

Lil Jon pushed Sam down the hallway back to his locked floor. Sam looked up at Lil Jon and said, "I appreciate you, man. I'm going to take care of you too. You know what time it is, right? I got your back as long as you got mine. You understand?"

Lil Jon was a young, small tattooed dark-skinned man who had already grown attached to Sam. His heart bled for Sam, for he knew Sam was dying. Sam leaned in closer while pulling down on Lil Jon's white coverall. "You be straight when you get out of this hellhole. You understand me, boy? Look at me. I'm forty-six fucking years old, dying in here all caged up like a wild animal. I would give anything to go back now. I was first locked up when I was your age, so anytime you want to walk the wrong line, you think about me—Sam Black. I'll haunt your little black ass!"

They both laughed. "Yes, sir," said Lil Jon. "I got what you saying, Sam. Believe me, I think about life outside of here all the time. You better believe it. I'm walking straight and narrow. I never want to come back here."

Lil Jon helped Sam back into his bed. Before Lil Jon walked out, Sam spoke with a gravelly voice. "My twin be here in two days. She bringing us goodies, Lil Jon. When you see her leave, you come get me, okay?"

"Yes, sir, Sam. I'll do that. You want me to turn your light out now, Sam?"

"No, leave it on. I don't like dark anymore. I'm going to see it soon enough."

Lil Jon walked out, stopping past Sam's door, where Sam couldn't see him. He wiped the tears from his eyes with his shirtsleeve before he headed back to his room, carrying his mop and bucket.

Chapter 22

Saturday arrived. It was time for Seela and Dee to head back down to the island. Joseph and Seela had talked a couple of times during the week, mutually expressing their feelings for one another.

Seela pulled up to Dee's little house. Dee opened her red front door, wearing a backpack. When Dee hopped into the car, Seela chuckled. "You amaze me with all your stuff in that little backpack! I have this gigantic suitcase for two days."

"I know why you have a huge suitcase, Seels. You got that sexy hot of an officer waiting to see you! How many outfits did you bring, girl?"

"You know me too well," said Seela.

As they headed down the country road, Seela pulled out some old CDs that her brother liked. "Let's play some of Sam's music while we drive down. That sound good to you, Dee?"

Dee agreed, and once the tunes were on, Seela shared memories of Sam as a child. Some were funny, and some were sad. As Seela reflected on the details, she started to realize how Sam had ended up in prison and addicted to his drug of choice. He didn't have a father to idolize, since he didn't know much about him. In contrast, Seela had at least received endless love and stability from her grandparents. Sam had not, because he was faithfully stuck to his mother's hip. Because their mom had been so young when she'd had them, it was as if Sam and his mother had grown up together.

With these revelations, Seela reached the gas station, where Chester was waiting like a stone statue. "Well, lookee there," said Dee. "Chubby's waiting just like you said he would be—with his suitcase and Xbox." His clothes were spotless for the first time since Seela had met him.

He ambled to Seela's car as she jumped out to help him.

"How long have you been waiting for us, Chester?" asked Seela.

"Um, I don't know," said Chester. "I took a shower for you this morning and then came to wait for you outside."

Bill walked out of the gas station with the doorbells clinging back and forth behind him. "Good morning! Chubby been out here all morning waiting on you, Ms. Black."

"Please call me Seela."

"All right. You can call me Billy. That's what Sam calls me."

Chester looked up at his dad. "You know Uncle Sam is sick?"

"Sam is very sick, Chester," Seela said. "I'm going to do everything I can to get him home, and hopefully, we can prolong his life with us. Your dad said you helped Sam when he stayed here, so hopefully, you can help him again."

Seela reached for Chester's Xbox and motioned for Chester to put his suitcase in the trunk. Chester jumped into the backseat of Seela's car without even addressing his father. He was saddened by the news of Sam dying yet happy to be with Seela again. Seela tried to explain Sam's illness to Chester on the way to Mamaw's. Chester seemed to be listening, but Seela didn't know if Chester understood death.

"Um, Ms. Seela, can I go see Uncle Sam?"

Dee sat quietly during this exchange. Seela looked in her rearview mirror at Chester. "I'm so sorry, honey. No one is allowed in but his mother or his sibling, which is me."

"He my uncle," said Chester.

"Not by blood, Chester. The prison is really strict about that."

Chester looked out the window at the ocean as they crossed over it. "When we going to the beach, Ms. Seela?"

Dee chimed in. "How about we go today? Did you bring your suit?"

I did!" Chester shouted.

"I have an idea, Chester," said Seela. "You want to see if Mamaw would like to go too? I bet it's been a long time since she's been."

Chester looked confused. "Um, Ms. Seela? How will we get her scooter on the beach?"

Dee and Seela both laughed, knowing Mamaw's character. "Don't let Mamaw fool you, Chubby," said Dee. "She surprised me one day in the kitchen by walking with her walker. We can get her little heinie on the beach if she wants to go."

As they pulled down the dusty driveway, Seela spotted Mavvie burning her stick all around the exterior of her house. Mavvie waved as they passed. Mamaw sat waiting in the drive with her hair fixed, wearing matching clothes. Even Chester noticed.

"Mamaw looks good," said Chester. He opened Seela's car door before she could even turn off the car engine. Chester ran to Mamaw before the women could get to her. "Hey! Mamaw, you look bootiful. Did you go somewhere?"

"Not yet, Chester," Mamaw replied, hugging him. She then turned to Seela with determination. "I want to go see Sam. Will you take me, Seela?"

Seela knelt down beside her grandmother. "Mamaw, I don't think I can take you. I'll have to find out from Joseph if they will allow it."

"They better let me see my grandson, dammit! I have the right if he is dying! I haven't been able to cry since your granddaddy died, and this week, I've been crying every night. I got to see him, Seels."

"Okay, Mamaw, please don't cry. I'll see what I can do." Seela placed her head on her grandmother's lap as if she were a toddler. Dee and Chester both held back tears. "Let's all go inside and call Joseph. Let's see if he can work some magic so you can see Sam yourself, Mamaw."

Seela dialed his number from the house phone. She not only sweetly asked Joseph to pull strings for a visit for Mamaw but also invited him to dinner that evening. He wanted to squeal in delight but held his composure, simply saying that he would be pleased to come over. He never would have guessed that Sam Black's twin sister would have been the one to spark a flame.

The nurses were curious why Officer Quinton was so enthralled by Sam's stories and so protective of him. By now, the nurses and Sam's hospice caregiver knew what had happened to Sam. They felt horrible watching Sam die in such a miserable way. Everyone knew he'd been sent there to die speedily. As evidence, morphine had been ordered in high doses.

Sam could not be released to tell his stories. Too many people were involved in his criminal activity in the small private-owned prison, and Sam had been shanked in Jackson State Prison.

Officer Quinton entered Sam's room. "Hey, man, I got a message for you from your twin. She said she will be here at ten o'clock sharp, and she loves bubble gum—no, Super Bubble—too." Joseph looked at Sam, hoping for the answer he wanted.

"Come on, man," Sam said. "I'm fucking dying in here. At least let my sis bring me some bubble gum. You escorting her in, right?"

Joseph ran his hand over his forehead and eyes in frustration. "Man, Sam, why you got to pull your shenanigans on me? You already got everybody in here eating out of your palm. Now you asking me to do something that can jeopardize my job."

Sam sat up quickly in his bed. "Pull fucking shenanigans, my ripped-up ass! Your job is DEA, not one of these blood-sucking peon guards. You think I'm worried about your fucking black ass? You the one keeping me alive for my fucking stories, so you listen to me. My twin will be walking in here tomorrow with her bra packed, and you make sure she makes it in here safe. It will come off of her as soon as her pretty face hits my fucking hellhole of a room. Then she's fine. Nobody going to know where it came from if I get busted. Hell, I'll tell them it was my crazy-ass caregiver, Brandy Lee. We straight?" said Sam, holding out his hand for a shake.

Joseph sat still, looking into Sam's flaring eyes. He reached over and shook Sam's hand with a little bit of disgust. "We straight for now, Sam. You just be careful what you ask of Seela. That girl loves you to the bone, and I don't want her getting hurt."

"That's why I'm telling you what's going down tomorrow, so you make sure you are here to escort her in. You got it? I need a bank in here, even as I die. I got needs still. I'm a fucking crazy man. I sometimes scare my own self. I'm fucking OCD clean and can't even wipe my own fucking ass. I need cigarettes and bubble gum to get these caged-ass niggers to do what I ask. Marlboros are liquid gold, Joseph. Don't worry about these nurses up in that chicken coop either." Sam held two fingers up. "They wrapped so tight right now." Sam smiled big. "I got the power even when I'm fucking dying, Joseph. You going to see my twin tonight?"

"Yes. How did you know, Sam?"

Sam wiped his face with both of his hands and tossed them up into the air. "Joseph, you will be surprised what I know. Only time will tell you, my friend. Hopefully, God going to give me enough of it. I ask every day for a little more."

Joseph stood to leave. "We good, man. I got Seela tomorrow. Don't worry. You just be careful how far you go out in the halls. I heard you got Lil Jon wheeling you out on the yard. Bad things can happen out there, you know."

"Well, if they shank me again, let me die where I lay. Nothing scares me now. I'm fucking out of here soon anyway." Sam pretended to shoot a gun into his head.

"One last thing—Seela said your Mamaw wants to come see you. Do you want me to get a pass for her?" Joseph said.

"Are you fucking kidding me? I don't want anyone seeing me like this but my twin. I don't even want to see my mom. She can't see her son like this. My mama sick herself!"

"Calm down, Sam. I won't allow it then. How about I set you up with your counselor tomorrow after Seela's visit? You can call her from Mr. Williams's office phone. You can call her every day if you want."

Sam tried to catch his breath. Seela had already told Joseph about Sam's outbursts as soon as he disagreed with something. Joseph waited patiently for his reply.

"All right, man. That sounds good. You tell Mr. Williams today, though. I don't want any surprises tomorrow."

Chapter 23

Joseph opened Mr. Williams's door without knocking. An inmate was sitting there crying. Mr. Williams gave him a tissue. Joseph backed out of the door until the counselor escorted the inmate out. "I'll be in touch with you, James, on what the board says about your transfer."

Joseph took a seat in front of Mr. Williams's enormous desk with his legs crossed and hands clasped. "I know you have met one of your new dying inmates, Mr. Sam Black. He's been here two weeks now. And I know that man has been down here and given you his whole story, so I'm not having to go there, am I?"

Mr. Williams leaned back in his chair. "I know the whole goddamn sick story. I just want to know who the hell you really are. I've seen you too many times in Sam's room, sitting with him. What's your story? You're too well spoken to be one of these stupid, uneducated guards."

Joseph sat up stiffly. Mr. Williams had shocked him with that mouthful. He thought for a second before speaking. "I think you may have already summed me up by the way you just spoke. I'm going to tell you who I am, but you have to give me your honor on your badge that you will keep it on the down low. There are only two people who know who I am. The first is Sam, and now the second is going to be you. You see, I need someone to watch over Sam Black when I'm not here. I need to get your schedule, and I'll work mine when you are off."

"He needs to be guarded that much?" replied Mr. Williams. "Are they still out to kill him? He's already on his last breath. Do these people know his condition? That's just mortal torture, letting that fluid build up on him. If he doesn't smother to death, he's going to pop."

Joseph leaned forward against Mr. Williams's desk. "Listen to me. I'm DEA and am here investigating Sam's attempted murder. I can't let anyone know. Everyone's connected in these places—that's how he got shanked in the first place. Now, I need you to help me keep him from being shot up too much with morphine. If it's up to those nurses, they will go by their warden's orders. Sam will be dead within a few weeks. I need some time with him to make sure I learn everything I need to in order to help stop some of these corrupt private owned prisons we have here in our state. It's getting really bad with gangs working with the guards on the inside. Killings are happening left and right."

Mr. Williams took a deep breath, trying to comprehend and process the information provided by Officer Quinton. "My assumption was right. I figured that was what you were doing. I'm just glad I know now. It's been puzzling me. That Sam keeps a tight lip when he wants to. I bet you I've asked him every time he's come to my office about you. He never says anything—just that you're a nice guy and like to hear him talk shit." They both chuckled.

"Wait. You mean to tell me Sam's been coming down here and using your phone already?"

"Oh yeah, it was my mistake the first time, and now that man wheels his sick, dying ass down here at a certain time every day. He calls this one person he met in a county jail, but she's free now and lives in North Carolina. I believe he said her name is Charlie. Sounds like a stripper to me."

Chuckling over Sam's audacity, Joseph stood to shake Mr. Williams's hand. "I appreciate what you do for Sam."

"No, sir, I appreciate you coming to me to tell me who you are. I can tell my wife, who has been going crazy listening to me about you and Sam. I'll watch over Sam Black the best I can while I'm working, but you need to tell Sam not to go too far in here. The word is that people are waiting for goods from him already. That's how fast it spreads. I know he's met a few guys in the yard who are in F quadrant. They're all murderers or life-sentence men. I don't want to see him get hurt again."

"Those were my last words to him today. I already saw him myself in the yard. I think this week, he wanted cigarettes, so he's out there trying to get a puff from whoever. He's feeling a little better because he's got his caregiver hiding his medicine when she comes in. That morphine was killing him fast. If he feels pain, he knows when to take it."

"Officer Quinton, I'll see you tomorrow, I'm sure."

"I was going to ask you if Sam could call his grandmother tomorrow, but I guess you and Sam have that all worked out."

Seela sat on the beach, watching Chester and Dee play like five-year-old children in the ocean water. Her thoughts were shifting from them to Joseph. She loved sitting on the beach and watching the waves clash back and forth. Now there was something new in her life, pulling on her heartstrings in a good way. Even though her heart ached for her twin, another part of Seela swooned with vibrancy around Joseph, as if magic were being stirred in the air.

Chester ran to Seela's chair. His chafed belly shook up and down as he tried to run in the wet sand. "Ms. Seela, will you come get in the water with me and Dee? Don't you like to swim in the ocean too?"

"Chester, what do you mean by 'swim in the ocean too'?"

"Uncle Sam said he loved swimming in the ocean. He said when he caught a wave sideways, he wished it would take him down under with the ocean world sometimes. He said maybe it would be better out there." Chester turned his body and pointed toward the ocean.

"Sam told you that, Chester?"

"Yes, ma'am. Sam tell me a lot whenever I see him."

"Maybe you will tell me some time what Sam told you. That sound okay?"

"Yes, ma'am. I will. Now will you come out and play with me?"

Seela got up, dropped her wrap, and placed her hat on the top of her chair. She ran with

Chester to the ocean, where Dee was floating in from riding the waves. "Come on out, Seels! Let's show Chubby how to bodysurf. I know you know how!"

"Well, it's been awhile, but here it goes, Chester. You watch us, and then we will do it together. Okay?" Chester nodded with a big grin on his face. He squinted against the sunlight glistening down on the blue ocean water. He laughed hysterically while watching the women jump into the wave and surf up to the shoreline. They synchronized their movements perfectly. When Seela came out of the water, Chester jumped up and down with glee. He was clapping like a seal waiting for fish.

"You ready to try, Chester?" Seela said. Chester twisted his arms, moved his hips back and forth, and shifted his hands in an awkward position. This was the first time Seela had seen Chester show a side of his Down's syndrome. He was disturbed by the thought of going that far out in the water.

Seela ran quickly over to Chester to calm him down. "It's okay, honey. You don't have to do it. We just thought it would be fun for you."

"No, it won't be," said Chester. "A wave might take me down under to where Sam wants to go, and I don't want to. Don't make me do it!"

Seela hugged Chester. "You don't have to do anything you don't want to do. Always remember that."

"That's what my dad say too!" said Chester, relaxing.

"Do you want to build a humongous sand castle?" said Seela. "I brought the buckets to make a mansion. What do you say, Chester? Does that sound good?"

Chester gazed at the ocean as if questioning whether to go back into the beautiful blue water. He looked back at Seela. "Yep, let's build a big sand castle." He smiled his crooked grin.

Dee walked onto the beach while Seela and Chester played in the sand. "I've never done this before," said Chester, packing a bucket with wet sand and pounding it with a plastic shovel.

"You're doing great, Chester. You line the towers how you want them with your buckets. Let them sit for a minute, and then lift them up. I'll start a moat around them once you start placing them together. Remember, put them tightly together so you make a solid wall. Got to keep the swordsmen out. Do you know what a moat is, Chester?"

"Yes, ma'am, I do. We have to make a bridge to go over the moat—one that we can lift up so we can keep the bad guys out."

"You do know what a moat is, I see," said Seela.

"Yes, ma'am, I do," he repeated seriously as he worked feverishly on his first castle.

Dee returned with shells she had picked up along her trek. "Look what you can decorate your castle with, Chubby. Place them wherever you like."

Chester stood up to see what Dee had cupped in her hand. "Those are pretty, Dee. Can I take them home instead?"

"You can do whatever you want with them."

"Will you help me find sticks for the moat for our castle? Ms. Seela's going to pour water in our moat soon."

"I'll grab some twigs for you, Chubby. I see some right over there." Dee pointed to the sea grass that blew behind them.

"I see it," said Chester. "I can go get it." Chester barely ran with his right foot turned outward.

Seela nudged Dee. "Chester didn't want to bodysurf because at some point, my brother told him he wished a wave would take him down under, and he would live in the sea world at the bottom of the ocean."

Dee sat down beside Seela. "Oh, honey, I'm so sorry. That's a double whammy for you!"

"It just breaks my heart for both of them in different ways."

Dee reached for Seela's hand and caressed it gently. "Girl, I love you and your family. I feel like they've been mine always. And look at this young man." Dee pointed toward Chester. "He's a sweet, loving young soul we somehow have acquired, and now we're loving him. That's some good shit is all I'm saying!"

They laughed as they watched Chester struggle through the hot sand, trying to make it back to his towel quickly.

Chapter 24

Seela and Chester showered before they started their night of cooking. Chester entered the kitchen in clean clothes that looked as if they had been pressed.

"Chester, you look so handsome. Did your dad get you new clothes?"

"No, ma'am! Mamaw gave them to me. She showed me how to iron this week too."

"Chester, that's great. Where did she get the clothes from? She doesn't drive."

"Back there." Chester pointed to the room he was sleeping in. Seela walked to his room and peeked into the closet. There hung Sam's clothes. It was a small amount, but Seela knew they were his by the style of the pieces hanging.

"Is it okay, Ms. Seela?" Chester stood behind her, afraid of her reply.

"Of course. I just was confused about how Mamaw got these clothes for you. They are Uncle Sam's. I'm so glad they fit you." She turned back to the closet, reaching for a button-down shirt. "This will look great on you too, Chester."

"Do you want me to wear it now, Ms. Seela? I can change if you want me to."

"You're handsome in just what you have on."

They headed back to the kitchen, where Mamaw and Dee were sitting by the window, eyeing something intently. Chester retrieved an apron from the pantry closet and tied it around his chubby belly. He and Mamaw had a routine down.

"Your mom's down there, moving stuff around her porch. I haven't seen her outside in over a month, Seela. Have you tried talking to her since you saw Sam last week?"

"No, I haven't, Mamaw. It wasn't a great visit. Sam was mostly irrational after finding out he was dying. I'm sure Mom knows anyway. She's always had that connection with him."

"They practically grew up together," said Mamaw. "What a two they were!"

Seela walked over to the window and cranked the knob until it opened enough for her to yell out at her mom. "Watch this, Dee. I'll yell out to her, and she'll run in like a mouse." Seela yelled through the window, "Hey, Mom, you want to come up for dinner tonight? We would love to see you if you are feeling better." Seela winked at Dee. She started counting. "One. Two. Nope, didn't even make it to three. She's in the door. See? I told you!"

"Well, that may have to be a nut I crack, Seels. Why won't she have anything to do with you?"

"She's still hurt from the past, Dee. I can't harbor it. Mavvie helped me get beyond my past a long time ago."

"What kind of past, Seels? What you got going on in your past? Anything I should know about?" Dee looked at Seela suspiciously.

"Dee, I will share more of my past with you soon enough. Don't we all have them?"

Dee stood up from the kitchen table and made her way to Seela quickly. "Girl, whatever past you got is yours. My life with you is the life that started the day I met you. No need to talk about the past unless you want." The women smiled warmly at each other as Chester waited patiently by the stove with his apron and the chef hat Mamaw had given him. He looked like the Pillsbury Doughboy.

"What are we cooking, Ms. Seela?" he asked.

"Tonight we are grilling steaks, Chester. Do you like steak?" Seela had no idea what he ate at home, but she hoped Bill fed him properly sometimes, given his chunky belly that hung over his belt.

"I love steak! It's my favorite food ever. My dad only cook it twice a month. He said it's too expensive, when he can catch our food. I eat a lot of fish. I don't like it so much."

Seela and Chester chopped veggies, prepping everything for the grill. Seela thought grilling everything would make the dinner a group event for them all. She hoped Joseph would assist her too. She'd had enough time on the beach by herself to plot the evening out.

Chester ran to the back porch. "I hear Yosef's truck, Ms. Seela. You want me to go get him?"

Seela chuckled. She turned to Dee with a smile Dee had not seen much of.

"He makes you giggly, Seels. I see it. He makes you feel special, doesn't he?"

"Let's just say he makes me smile, Dee." Seela turned toward the carport and then back at Dee, winking shyly. "Yes, he does make me giggly."

Chester escorted Joseph up the drive, huffing as if he were already tired. Joseph felt sorry for the little guy, wishing he could help him exercise a little. "Ms. Seela say you are a nice gentleman. She told me twice," said Chester. "I think she like you, Yosef."

"It's okay, Chester. I think I like Ms. Seela too. Is that okay with you?"

"Yes, sir, it is," Chester said.

Seela appeared from behind the carport wall. "There you two are."

Sam turned quickly and smiled before he spoke. "It sure does smell like somebody is getting ready to grill something good up in here. You are speaking to my belly now, Ms. Seela. You know how to get to a man's heart real quick."

Chester spoke before Seela. "I helped, Mr. Yosef."

Seela hugged Chester around his shoulders and beamed. "Yes, Chester learned how to chop with a butcher knife today and helped chop all the veggies."

"Yep, I did," said Chester with his chest popped out proudly. "We having steak, potatoes, and veggies." Chester held his fingers out, counting the items they were having.

"Would you like a cold beer, Joseph?" Seela said. "We have a few different kinds. Lord knows why. It's not like anyone drinks on this land hardly ever anymore. I think my grandmother thinks she's got to have what my granddaddy always kept in the fridge when he was alive."

When they both agreed to have a beer, Chester chimed in. "I want a beer too, Ms. Seela. I like beer. My dad let me have a sip of his sometimes."

"Chester, that is what you will get from me—a sip!"

Chester looked at Joseph for solidarity, and Joseph said, "At least you tried, Chester. A sip is probably all you want anyway."

Seela returned with two beer bottles and a glass. She poured a swallow into the glass and handed it to Chester. "Here—we can all toast!" she said, holding her bottle up in the air. Chester grinned, feeling older with his own glass.

They all sat around like a family that had been formed many years ago. Inevitably, the topic of Sam came up numerous times while they enjoyed their food. The evening was exactly as Seela had envisioned it. Joseph told funny stories, even imitating how Sam talked. Seela enjoyed having Joseph in her presence. He was a fit, good-looking man, and she liked the way he talked with his hands. She loved that about him. Seela wanted to consume everything about Officer Joseph Quinton.

After dinner, Joseph stayed and helped Chester do the dishes since there was no dishwasher in Mamaw's house. Seela watched them with a smile, forgetting what tomorrow was going to bring. Seela walked Joseph out to his truck. Chester stood by the window, tucked behind the curtain so that Seela could not see him. Chester watched patiently.

"What you doing behind that curtain, Chester?" Dee said, entering the living room. Dee's large presence caused Chester to jump.

"You scared me, Dee," Chester said in his deep, raspy voice.

"You about scared me, Chester, all tucked in there behind that curtain. If I hadn't seen your shoes at the bottom, I don't know who I would have thought you were."

Chester chuckled with Dee. "I was watching Ms. Seela and Yosef. She like him a lot, doesn't she?"

"Yes, Chester, she does, but not as much as she likes you. Don't you worry—Ms. Seela will always have you in her life. That's just the way she is. She loves you already, son." Dee reached around and held Chester while he stared out at Seela.

"I love her too, Dee."

"This house is full of love! I tell you that right now. I don't know how Sam missed the love here. It just spews out everywhere. Don't you think so, Chester?"

"Yes, I do. That's why I come all the time now, Dee."

"Let's go sit down and give Ms. Seela some privacy."

Seela stood beside Joseph's truck with her arms crossed as if she were cold. "I forgot to tell you I talked to Sam this afternoon. He doesn't want to see your grandmother or your mom," said Joseph. "He said he can't handle them seeing him in this condition. I set up a phone call for him tomorrow to call your grandmother. I hope that will satisfy her."

Seela looked down at the ground. "I understand how he feels. I really don't want Mom or Mamaw to have that memory of how he looks now. He doesn't even look like my twin brother."

"If your mom wants to talk to him, I suggest you tell her to be at your grandmother's house around three thirty tomorrow. He'll call soon after your visit." Joseph touched Seela's cheek. "Thank you again for having me over for dinner, Seela. It was a wonderful evening with all of you."

Seela looked up at Joseph, hoping for a kiss.

He looked deeply into her eyes. "Are you ready for tomorrow, Seela?"

That was not what Seela had been expecting to hear. All she could think of at the moment was a wet kiss from him.

"I think I'm ready," Seela replied. "Is Sam worse?"

"No, he's actually better than he was last Sunday when you saw him. He's not on as much morphine, and that's keeping him more alert. Your visit should be a lot clearer tomorrow. I'll be there, waiting to escort you in." Joseph ran his finger down Seela's face as if he wanted to kiss her. Instead, he dropped his hand and said good night.

Seela's heart sank, but she knew the wait would be worth it.

Chapter 25

The next morning, Seela spread loose cigarettes and candy on the bed, contemplating how to organize everything in her bra. Dee knocked with two taps, peeked in, and then hurriedly made her way in, shutting the door behind her. "Holy shit, Seela. You are going through with it. Where did you get all of this? You been with me all weekend."

"Silly, I bought it back home last week. Just in case I decided to do it. Yes, I'm going through with it. I figure I've got Joseph taking me in, so as long as it's concealed, no one will know." Seela threw her hands into the air as if to say, "What the hell?"

"Did you tell Joseph you are doing this?" asked Dee.

"Heck no. I don't know him that well, and besides, he is on the right side of the law. I'm getting ready to break it today." Seela gave Dee a high five. "It is kind of exciting, if you want to know the truth. It's almost like a 'Fuck you' to the system for what they have done to my brother. I know he's done wrong things, but the system has done nothing but show him wrong and allow him to be wrong. It's so sad, Dee, the way it all works."

"I know, Seela. It's freaking scary on the inside of the criminal world! You almost can't get out if you get caught in that web for just a short time," Dee said, as if she had been there before.

Seela turned around with the cigarettes packed in her bra, holding her shirt up for Dee to see. "What do you think? Can I get any more in?" She turned slowly in a circle like a princess rotating on a pedestal.

"Damn, Seels. How many packs you got stuffed in there? Where did you get this bra?"

"It's from Mamaw. I never had boobs this big, but it kind of feels good!"

"I just want to know what they say when you walk out—or, better yet, what Joseph says!" They looked at each other.

"Shit," said Seela. "I forgot about Joseph! He has to know already that I'm pretty much a cup size smaller. Oh shit. What am I going to do, Dee?"

"Wear a summer sweater over your top, and keep your arms crossed over your boobs as you walk in. He'll never notice. Besides, they aren't *that* big." They continued to strap everything onto Seela.

"I can't believe I'm doing this, Dee. I've never been locked up in my life! Now I'm smuggling in cigarettes and candy for my brother. Who would have thought it?"

"You going to be okay, Seels, doing all of this? It can be scary. I don't care if you do have handsome Joseph with you. I know you have to be a little nervous."

"Yes, I am, but I can do it for Sam. He needs me right now." Then Seela heard Chester at the door. "Chester, are you up, honey?"

"Yes, ma'am, I just woke up."

Seela threw on a sweater, opened her bedroom door, and reached to give Chester a hug. He squeezed her back. "Did you sleep well?" she asked.

"Yes, ma'am, I did."

"Great. I have to be leaving shortly, but I bet Ms. Dee would love to cook you a good ole southern breakfast. I'll see you all this afternoon around five, before dinner. Does that sound good to you, Chester?"

"Yes, ma'am. Can I help cook breakfast since I can cook now?"

Dee led Chester into the kitchen so Seela could finish the business of reviewing the finished package in the mirror one last time before setting out for the prison.

On the way to the prison, Seela listened to old music from the late '70s on her Sirius radio. She could almost hear Sam singing all of the songs. She arrived early and sat in her car, getting more nervous by the minute as she scanned every sign around her. She saw a sign forbidding any kind of contraband: "You will be prosecuted by the law and face up to seven years in prison." The warning almost dared her to get out of the car. She sighed and made her move.

Seela approached the main prison gate. The female guard opened the small window, as before. She pushed a clipboard through the hole. "Fill this out. Who are you here to see?"

Seela's voice cracked when she tried to speak after an hour of driving and ruminating. She cleared her throat. "Sam Black," she said again, this time with a clear voice. The window closed with a slam. Seela's mind started racing, considering what consequences could be if she got caught bringing contraband into a state prison. She tried to fill out the papers, but her hand shook so much that she couldn't even write. *Get it together!* She thought of Sam and Joseph, which comforted her, and the panic subsided.

The window flew open. "Do you have your paperwork filled out? Your escort is on his way down here." This was not the same lady who'd been at the window the previous week. "I need you to take off all your jewelry and shoes. Step through that black scan door box."

Seela quickly filled out the paperwork and stood up. Her heart sank. She felt that security would sense the contraband stuffed in her bra. "Walk through there?" Seela pointed to the contraption with lights blinking.

"Yes, ma'am, walk through there after you take jewelry, shoes, and anything metal on you that you don't want going off."

Seela was so nervous now that her hand shook uncontrollably. She again silently talked to herself. Seela walked through the door, taking a deep breath. Nothing beeped. Her heart beat wildly, but she tried not to show any emotion. She turned toward the glass door and saw Joseph walking toward her. Her emotions simmered down. He flashed his beautiful smile, which filled Seela's heart every time. Comfort and safety replaced Seela's anxiety. Seela watched him come closer through the locked glass door. Then she realized that the female guard was yelling at her to get attention, but she was slow to process the message. All Seela could think was that the guard was telling her she knew what

Seela had stuffed against her body. Seela went into panic mode. Sweat started popping out on her face and chest.

"Ma'am, you need to get your shoes on. Then lock your watch and jewelry in one of those lockers where you are standing before you leave this room. Please do so now."

"Oh! Sorry." *Get a grip, you fool!* Seela complied.

The buzzer startled her when the guard pushed the button to open the heavy locked metal doors that stood between Seela and Joseph. Seela wanted to run into Joseph's arms for safety, but she could only smile as if they were strangers. They walked into the fenced wired building, exchanging basic pleasantries, and then Seela stepped through the metal robotic doors and saw Lil Jon mopping close to Sam's room.

"Good morning, Sam's twin. I can't remember your name, 'cause Sam always say 'my twin.'" Lil Jon laughed with his gold tooth shining through. "He excited you coming. I shaved him this morning after his shower. He ready to see you. That fool had me press his hospital gown."

Seela peered through Sam's window, and to her surprise, he was sitting in his wheelchair with his hair cut and his face cleanly shaven. He looked totally different from the previous Sunday. "Sam, you look so good. Look at you! You got a haircut, and you shaved." In reality, Sam's stomach was as big as that of a pregnant mother on the brink of delivery. His legs were wrapped with gauze to keep the fluid from oozing out onto his socks. His ankles were the size of elephants'. Still, he sat there happily, proud to greet his twin. Sam threw his arms out as if she were there for a party.

"Hey, Sis. You okay? You make it here safe?"

"Yes, I did. I have everything you asked for and probably more, but I want to get it off of me now. How are we going to do that?" Seela stood by his locker with Sam facing her in his wheelchair.

"Okay, this is what I want you to do, Sis. I'm watching everybody out there right now, so I want you to pull everything out and dump it in my lap. You hear me, Sis?" Sam looked serious as he spoke to Seela, as if they were breaking the code to a bomb. His head didn't move as he spoke.

Seela's heart was beating so fast she thought that if someone walked into Sam's room, he or she would hear it beating out of her body.

"Hurry up, Seels. Throw it all in my lap right now. No one is looking. I got it. Do it now." Seela reached under her shirt quickly, pulling her bra away from her body. The cigarettes fell into her brother's lap.

"Wow! Sis, how many packs you bring in? I'm loaded for the week now. Way to go!"

Sam hurriedly put the cigarettes in his locker, under a toboggan hat he wore often. "Damn, Sis, you did better than I thought you would. You don't know how that will help me while I die in this hellhole of a prison."

"Sam, I'm going to try my hardest to get you out of here."

"Sis, you ain't fucking getting me out of here. You don't know how the system works. I'm a fucking prisoner of the state, so when they found out all the stuff I had going on in the last place I was at and when my ass got shanked, they decided best keep me hushed up here until I die. It's so much fucking shit, Seels! I'm so sorry you have to see me like this. This is the last place I wanted you to see me. I've watched over you all our lives, even when I was locked up. You have no clue how I've watched you, Seels. You the only love I know. I just knew I wasn't good love for you, so I gave it to you secretly."

Seela sat listening to Sam intently. She tried to read between his lines but was having a hard time following. She didn't understand how he could have watched over her, when he'd been incarcerated for most of his adult life. It was heartbreaking to see him in such bad condition. His body was frail, and the fluid had blown his body up like a blimp. Sam had tiny splits all over his arms and legs, where the fluid was trying to break through. His ankles were the size of elephant legs. His feet were so swollen that his toes looked like fat thumbs. He couldn't wear regular socks, because his feet hurt to the touch. His caregiver, Brandy Lee, had cut the ends off all of his socks so they would feel better to Sam. It hurt Seela to look at her twin.

"Sis, stop staring at me. I know it's hard being here with me. You see why I can't let Mom or Mamaw see me like this. It would kill them both. I can't leave them with this memory. I've accepted I'm dying. I just don't want to go to hell. I lie awake at night, sitting on the side of my bed. I feel like I'm going to drown if I lie down. This fluid's so built up on my lungs that it's like I'm under water with my mouth open. It scares me. I can't die like that."

"Sam, I'm so sorry for you. You have to ask God for forgiveness and believe in him. That's all you have to do. You hear me? You have to learn how to pray."

"Fucking pray, Seela? You think God is listening to me? I haven't listened to God all my life. You think he's going to listen to my fucking dying self now?" Sam laughed maniacally.

"You better be the one praying, Sis. You know God; I don't. Maybe he'll listen to you and help your dying brother." Sam threw his head back against the headrest on his wheelchair. "Let's stop talking about all this. It's making my head hurt. I just want to sit here with you, okay?"

Seela reached to hold his hand. "Okay, Sam. Whatever you want to do."

Sam sat quietly with his eyes shut. Seela observed him. Minutes passed, and Sam sat straight up, sleeping with his mouth wide open. At one point, Seela examined his chest to make sure he was still breathing. Then he opened his eyes again. "Hey, Sis. How long was I out? I was dreaming about the time I escaped that prison at Phillips. That was some shit, wasn't it? I knew the prison was going on a lockdown for drug dealing. I wasn't getting my ass beat and then put in the hole as high as I was. Back there, we were all smoking crack! Or whatever drug we could get brought in. I had worked at the print shop that day, and when they dropped my sorry ass off at the main gate, the guard told me prison was on count, and I would have to wait for it to be over before he could let me in."

Sam laughed with his gravelly voice. "That was my ticket to get the hell out of there. Seels, I just walked slowly down the road, and as soon as I saw nobody was paying attention, I just took off into the woods. I ran like a coon being chased by an old hound dog, peeling my prison clothes off and getting down to my shorts and undershirt. It took them three days to catch me. I made it home and got my motorcycle and ran free and high for a few days. To tell you how I'm king, I didn't get any more time for escaping. I made a deal with the state and gave information about what was going on in Phillips. The officer who picked me up and drove me to a secured prison even drove me through your town and parked right in front of your salon. We sat there for a good ten minutes as he let me watch you, Seels. You were so happy, talking to your clients. It made my heart feel so good that I didn't even care what was going to happen to me."

Seela's eyes filled with tears, and her heart felt as if it were being ripped apart as she listened to her twin tell her this unknown story. How could he have been right outside her window without her knowing? "Sam, I would have come out to see you. Why didn't you have the officer come get me? It breaks my heart to hear this."

"I couldn't, Sis. I was just thankful he let me see you through the glass window. Your salon is so pretty. It looks just like you, Seels. There are so many stories I could tell you, Sis. I can't believe I've made it this long. Maybe you should write a book of the nine lives of Sam Black." They laughed together.

"I been having dreams of memories of my past, Seels. Not good ones. You think that's part of my redemption or purgatory I could be going through? I don't like sleeping now, because some of the shit I dream about scares me out of my sleep. I ain't ready to die yet, Sis! I've seen some crazy shit in this locked-up world of caged animals. That medicine they give me causes me to nod out. I try not to take it so much. I got my hospice nurse, Brandy Lee, helping me out now. She's a crazy woman, but at least she listens to me. I get her to toss my lunch meds in the trash over there." Sam pointed to a small trash can in his room.

Lil Jon strolled by Sam's glass wall with a mop in his hand. Sam waved at him to come in. Lil Jon motioned to the nurses' station, speaking to Big Sexy. "I need to get into Mr. Sam Black's room to mop. Will you buzz me in?"

Big Sexy unlocked Sam's door, rolling her large brown eyes. Lil Jon entered with a mop on the floor, swishing it around as if Sam's floor were dirty. Sam reached over into his locker and tossed two cigarettes onto his tray table. As Lil John mopped his way out of Sam's room, he reached for the cigarettes and shoved them quickly into his jumpsuit pocket. They nodded to each other. Seela sat as still as a mouse.

As soon as Sam's door locked, Seela sighed with relief. For some reason, she felt safe locked in Sam's room with him.

Sam smirked. "See, Sis? Now Lil Jon will be back like a buzzard, swarming around me, wanting more. I've got him in the palm of my hand. He will come back in a little while, and I'll get him to take me to the showers. I'll get me a good bath. That will be my pleasure today, Sis."

"I'm glad, Sam. If that's all it takes to keep these guys watching after you, then I'll bring more next week."

"You saw how easy it was, Seels. You wouldn't believe the shit that gets brought in here. These guys have wives and girlfriends bringing all kinds of shit in here. They stick fucking phones up their you-know-whats."

"No way, Sam!"

"Yes fucking way, Seela. I had a fucking iPhone in Cottonwood. My partner in there—he got it now. Did you call him, Sis?"

Seela looked straight at Sam, knowing she hadn't called him, and lied. "Yes, but no one answered the phone."

"Okay, he probably had it turned off. I used to have to hide it in the cinder block wall whenever we had shakedown or lockdown. That's probably what he be doing with it. They all probably sitting around waiting for me to come back. They don't know I've been killed and brought back here to die a second time around." Sam chuckled. His deep, wrinkled skin oozed with fluid dripping down his arms and ankles. His skin was tethered and worn. He looked like a corpse already, with a heart beating inside. "I was thinking, Seels. You know how I like to sing? Well, these boys in here who help me like to sing too. They just don't know my kind of music. I want you to bring me CCR and Hall and Oates CDs next Sunday. I want to teach them some real music."

"I can't bring CDs in here, Sam. The metal detector will go off!"

Sam laughed at Seela. "Damn, Seels. Don't you know what CDs are made of?"

Seela looked confused and felt stupid at the same time. "Well, at least I made you laugh!" Seela then tossed around names she could contact to see about getting Sam released. "I'll get a lawyer. I know they will eat this story up, Sam."

"Hell fucking no. You can't tell this story, Seela. You leave that to—I mean, you can't be calling and getting people into this story. I don't think you know the severity of this. I have friends who could be killed or even tortured who are locked up where I was."

Seela sat still, trying to take it all in. "What do you mean? Leave it to whom, Sam? Is there something you aren't telling me?"

"No, Seels. I just don't think that you realize how big this is. You would be getting in the biggest anthill that would cover your ass in thirty seconds."

Seela felt there was something missing from this crazy puzzle she was trying to put together. The hours grew close to the end of her second Sunday with Sam. It had been more meaningful than the first visit, but it still broke Seela's heart when it was time to leave.

Joseph was at Sam's window promptly at three o'clock. This time, he unlocked Sam's door and entered with a sweet swagger. Seela stood up quickly, hoping Joseph did not smell Sam's chewing gum, which he had been chewing for more than an hour. Joseph smiled at Seela while glancing at Sam. "I'm going to walk your sister out to her car, Sam. Then I'll come back and take you down to make that call to your grandmother and mom. You be ready, okay? I got you a new robe that Lil Jon will be bringing in to you. It should keep you warm. It's terry, just like you asked."

Joseph held his hand up for Sam to high-five. Sam smiled his broken smile. He slapped Joseph's hand. "You the man, Officer Joseph Quinton. I've been freezing my fucking ass off since I got here."

Seela watched Sam and saw how relaxed he was with Joseph. She was relieved to know someone was watching over her twin. Seela hugged and squeezed Sam as softly as she could. She didn't want to let him go.

Joseph escorted Seela down the cold hallway while other inmates tried to peek at Seela as she walked with Joseph out of the dark prison. The inmates watched as Seela turned out of their sight, thinking how beautiful she was in her civilian clothes. Nothing so pretty had graced the cinder block walls in a long time. Joseph and Seela approached the front gate, and Seela's lips screamed for a kiss that could not happen at that time. Joseph promised to call her later.

That promise was all she could taste for now.

Seela rushed home as if she were late for dinner. She couldn't wait to get home to talk to her mother and grandmother about Sam. Meanwhile, Sam aimed to tell them his own version of the day during his phone call from Mr. Williams's office. Joseph pushed Sam's wheelchair down the hallway while fantasizing about Sam's twin sister.

"So I see you got your sister to bring you some bubble gum today, Sam. You know that could be a big mistake if she got caught doing that."

Sam chuckled under his breath, which caused him to cough. When he caught his breath, he put his foot down to make the wheelchair stop. He motioned for Joseph to come closer so he could face him.

"You look here, motherfucker. That is my one and only gem in life. Seels is my twin. She's my diamond, and I'm the fucking chain it hangs on! You got it? You want my sister—well, that I know. The only thing is, you got me for the rest of my happy fucking life!" Sam smiled with a devilish grin. "You know what that means? You going to watch her every time she come in this shithole. You will make sure she is escorted by you. I got to have what she brings me. You got it? I'm fucking dying. It won't be long. But I will tell you that I like the fact you liking my twin. You a good guy, and my sis a beautiful woman from inside out. You do end up with her, you always remember what I said, Joseph Quinton."

Joseph smiled candidly at Sam as they reached Mr. Williams's office. When Joseph wheeled Sam into his office, Mr. Williams already had Mamaw on the phone. "Yes, Ms. Black, Sam just came into my office, and now I'm going to let you speak to him." He handed the phone to Sam, who lit up as if he could see her through the receiver.

"Hey, sassy pants," Sam said.

"Aw, Sam, it is your voice I hear. I've missed your daily calls, but at least I have Seela here now. She on her way back from seeing you, Sam?"

"Yes, Mamaw, she just left not too long ago. You okay, Mamaw? How's Mom? She there to talk to me?" he asked hopefully.

Mamaw paused before answering. "No, Sam, she not doing good either. She's been real sick the past few months. She stay down in her little house, and she don't come out much. She painting pictures, I know. I see her come out sometimes to clean her paintbrushes outside her front door. She won't even talk to Seela much."

Sam sat with a concerned face, listening to his grandmother's words, and then said, "Listen, Maw, this is what I want you to do. You listening? When Seels gets back there, you tell her to go down to Mom's front door and to tell Mom that I said to answer her damn phone in the morning. You got it, Mamaw? Can you do that for me?"

"Okay, Sam, honey. I will have Dee go down there and tell her right now. She seems to listen to Dee, Seela's assistant. I don't know why, but somehow, Dee got her to come out of her house a couple of times. You know Dee, Sam?"

"Of course I know who Dee is, Mamaw. This is Sam you talking to. I know everything. You get her to go down there then. I'll call back tomorrow morning when I get Joseph to bring me back to use Mr. Williams's phone again." Sam smirked and winked at Mr. Williams, who leaned back in his rickety wooden office chair, smiling and shaking his head at Sam. He was keenly aware that Sam had them all working out of the palm of his hand, including intelligent authority figures such as himself.

Sam's voice was weak from his busy day involving Seela's visit. Joseph pushed Sam back to his locked room. He helped Sam back into his bed and sat in the chair Seela had occupied all day.

"How did your visit go with Seela today? Did she deliver all of what you asked for?" Joseph raised his eyebrows as if Sam were actually going to tell him the truth.

Sam raised his index finger slowly to his cracked, dry lips. "You best be keeping to your business of what you are here to do, and I'll keep to my business, Joseph Quinton. We straight?" said Sam as he reached over to Joseph for a high-five shake.

"Yeah, we straight. You just be careful out in that yard out there. I know what you are doing. There are major mass murderers here. I don't want you getting shanked twice in a lifetime."

"Yeah, get on out of here, and go enjoy my fucking family, Joseph. I know what time it is, and I can smell my mamaw's kitchen right now. Have you had her corn bread yet?"

Joseph rubbed his belly and looked up at the ceiling. "Damn, Sam, I've got something else to look forward to? There ain't nothing I've had at your mamaw's that wasn't delicious. Even her tea is the best I've tasted. Does Seela cook like your mamaw, Sam?"

"You bet your bottom dollar she cooks like her grandmother. That's who raised Seela."

At that, Joseph left Sam to rest, but instead, Sam was soon yelling loudly, "Big Sexy, I need you in here now!" Sam kept pushing his buzzer button until he saw Big Sexy coming toward his locked room. She opened the door, screaming at him.

"Why in the hell do you have to press that buzzer a million times over? I heard it the first damn time, Sam! I can't get to you any faster than I can walk my fat ass over. Now, what is it that you need?" Big Sexy wiped her forehead, having worked up a sweat while running from the nurses' station to Sam's room.

"Big Sexy, I need you to find Lil Jon. Tell him to bring the other wheelchair that rolls out to the yard. I'm fucking freezing in here and want to get some sunshine on my body to heat it up. Hurry before we have count. I need to have sun on my body."

Big Sexy turned toward Sam's door. "Next time, mouth Lil Jon's name at me, Sam. That is all you wanted in making me run over here? I can read your lips, you know. Buzz me and mouth what you want, and if I can make it happen, I will." Big Sexy liked Sam because he made her feel beautiful no matter how large she was.

Within a minute, Lil Jon was at Sam's door with his other wheelchair. Big Sexy buzzed Lil Jon into Sam's room. As he helped Sam into the wheelchair, Sam tossed Marlboro cigarettes into Lil Jon's jumpsuit. "Let's go start a bizness, Lil Jon. If they say I only got sixty days, I'm going to do what I do best—wheel and deal!" Sam whispered.

As they strolled down the concrete halls, Sam began to sing to Lil Jon. *"Day after day, I'm more confused. Don't understand the things I do. Give me the beat, Lord, to free my soul! I want to get lost in your rock 'n' roll and drift away."* It was a verse from a song Sam by Dobie Gray.

Lil Jon stopped suddenly and said, "I like that song, man. It been a long time since I heard it. I like the way you sing it too."

Sam smiled. "I like real music, Lil Jon. Some of these guys in here listen to that fuckin' hard-core rap shit. They sing about all the bad things in life. I like singing about good things. Hell, that is about all I have good in me is my singing."

Lil Jon pushed Sam out into the yard, which was filled with scavenging buzzard inmates, as he called them. Some were playing ball and card games, while others were shooting the bullshit breeze. Lil Jon turned Sam toward the sun. Sam smiled graciously while leaning his head back on the old cracked headrest connected to his wheelchair. He closed his eyes and faced the sun for comfort.

Sam spoke, barely moving his lips, to Lil Jon. "I've already scaled everybody on this shit yard. Which one is the leader out here, Lil Jon? Is it the guy sitting on the picnic table to my right, or is it the guy straight ahead who's lifting weights?"

"Damn! Sam, you got quick eyes. Yeah, the big shit out here is the one sitting on the table. His name is AB, and don't ask me what it stands for. I don't mess with those guys. My time's short in here—that's the last group I need to know."

Sam smiled, keeping his eyes closed. "You got that straight, Lil Jon. I already told you I'll haunt your ass when I leave this mosh pit of hell if you don't stay straight when you get out of here."

Lil Jon hit Sam's hand as if he were putting a stamp on it. "I got you, man. I feel like you going to haunt me anyway, but it will be all right. I ain't afraid of your ass." They both laughed.

Sam sat still for about thirty minutes while keeping his eyes shut except for a slight crack in his right eye. He watched the other men like a hawk zooming in on prey. In that thirty minutes, Sam summed up everybody's routine in the yard. While Lil Jon pushed Sam back to his room, Sam explained what he wanted Lil Jon to do with the cigarettes he had given him earlier. "You find out what hall that AB be in, and you give him five cigarettes. You fucking tell him there are more where those came from. You tell him you got a guy in death ward who wants to meet him tomorrow out in the yard half an hour before count. You got it, Lil Jon?"

"Man, I told you—I don't mess with that group. That shit they do in here scares the living hell out of me. If something go wrong, my ass is theirs! And I don't mean just for a beating, Sam."

Sam put his foot down to stop the wheelchair. "Look here, boy. I might be dying in here, but I'm not going to let anything happen to you. You fucking hear? You don't have to do anything but relay my message. Okay? You don't have to get involved any other way. I'm getting ready to make everyone know I was goddamn king in the prison I was in before, and I'll be king in here when my time comes for me to die."

Lil Jon nodded as if he understood everything Sam was saying. "Okay, Sam, I'll get the cigarettes and message to him this afternoon after we have head count."

Lil Jon got Sam back to his room and settled him in his other wheelchair. "You want anything before I leave?"

"Yeah," said Sam. "Reach in my locker, and hand me three pieces of bubble gum. You keep one for yourself, boy. Toss me two."

"Thanks," said Lil Jon as he pitched two pieces of bubble gum into Sam's lap. Lil Jon put his piece in his front pocket for later, when he returned to his room. "That will be my dessert tonight after grub."

Sam tossed both pieces into his mouth while leaning his head on the back of his hard foam pillow. "I'll see you tomorrow, Lil Jon. I'm tired now. I think I'll lie here and rest my dying ass."

"Yeah, man, I'll be here first thing when they let me out of my hall for work duty. Also, I got you, man. Don't worry. I'll get your message to AB about the cigs. You want a shower and shave before your meeting out in the yard tomorrow?"

"You damn straight I want a shower and shave. I want one every day until I die, motherfucker," Sam joked.

Lil Jon skipped down the hall, knowing he was going to enjoy the bubble gum after dinner. He remembered AB just before he turned toward his hall. He took a left turn and headed toward AB's hall. Just before reaching the hall, he heard men laughing. Lil Jon stopped to look in the rec room and saw AB laughing with another inmate.

"Hey, man, you guys hear about this new dying inmate we got up on the third floor?" Lil Jon said.

AB turned, looking at Lil Jon intensely. "I saw you wheeling what looked like a fucking dying man today out in the yard. That who you talking about, squirt?"

"Yeah, yeah, that's him. Well, he want to meet you tomorrow. Said y'all could do some bizness."

AB moved close to Lil Jon, towering over him like a dark shadow. "How am I supposed to do bizness with a fucking dying man, squirt? From the looks of him today, it won't be long." AB laughed at Lil Jon as if he were a stupid young inmate trying to catch a bone from a big dog.

Lil Jon reached into his front pocket and tossed five Marlboro cigarettes at AB's feet. "My fucking dying friend's name is Sam Black, and he wants to meet you in the yard tomorrow half an hour before midday count. You want to meet or not? He was shanked in Jackson, and now he's been brought here to die. He was king last place he was in. You want to meet or not, I said!"

AB looked impressed. "All right, tell him I'll give him five minutes for these five cigarettes. He got more? Do you know?"

Lil Jon shrugged with his hands tucked in his front pockets, turned, and walked away. He spoke quietly as he half skipped out the door. "See you tomorrow at one. Just you—no friends invited!"

Chapter 26

Dee had cooked all day with a little help from Chester. She was pleased to see everyone around the table, enjoying the fruits of their labor. She still couldn't get over the heat and humidity on this little island. Poor Chester had looked as if he were frying over the hot stove, so she had encouraged him to take breaks.

"Um, Ms. Seela," said Chester, "I need to ask you a question."

"Yes, Chester? What is it?"

"Did Uncle Sam ask about me today?"

Seela was surprised at his question. She knew there'd been no mention of Chester that day. Sam had dozed for much of their visit. When he'd been awake, he'd been feverishly telling her about what had happened to him and delivering orders for the following Sunday. He'd also told many stories about the privately owned prison where he ran his drug ring and talked about how corrupt the prisons were, saying they were getting worse.

Seela smiled sweetly at Chester. "Yes, he did ask about you. I told him you were wearing some of his clothes, and I said how well they fit you. I told him you were learning how to cook also. He said to tell you that he loves you and always has."

Chester flashed his crooked smiled. "I know! He told me all the time when I see him at my pa's gas station, especially when he stayed out back when he was sick. He tell me a lot of things, Ms. Seela." Chester stared at Seela, wanting to say more, but he didn't.

"I'm so glad you knew the kind part of my brother, Chester. His addiction just overpowered him. It's such a shame that he's dying at such a young age. I do believe if he had not been shanked the first time, he wouldn't be dying this young. It's his disease that can't fight the infection. It's just horrible, you guys."

Everyone commiserated with Seela's message with a sad face. Joseph pushed his chair back and started to clear the dishes from the table. "I have to say once again, this was another fantastic meal at the Black family household. You ladies show enough know-how to cook up some grub. I'm going to clean this here kitchen in thanks to a wonderful meal and time well spent with everyone. I best be leaving shortly since I have a quick morning upon me." Joseph smiled at the three women, melting all of them in some way.

"I was hoping I could have a little time to talk to you about Sam today," said Seela as she handed him her plate.

"Sure, let me whip out some clean dishes for your beautiful Mamaw, and we can talk."

Seela blushed as Joseph spoke to her, but she tried to act cool about her emotions flowing over for him. After Joseph washed the dishes, Chester joined in to dry. They were cutting up with each other by the sink. Seela watched them closely, noticing how comfortable Joseph seemed with Chester, even after such a short time of knowing him, as well as with all of them in general.

Joseph walked Seela out to the back garden, where Chester had made a new seating area. Chester had hammered two of the rickety, broken chairs back together, and Dee had spray-painted them and strung twinkling white lights in the trees around the perimeter. It was a clear, beautiful night. The stars shined on Joseph and Seela.

"Seela, it's nice to sit out here with you alone. I feel our friendship is all about people, and I'm thinking if you are interested, maybe we sometimes could see each other without all these people." Joseph gestured toward Mamaw's house.

Seela couldn't believe the words she was hearing. They were exactly what she'd wanted to hear. At the same time, she was scared shitless. She had just broken the law for her brother, and she planned to do so every Sunday until he died.

Seela's voice quivered. "Joseph, I feel like I've known you longer than I have. I guess it's because of how well you know my brother. It means so much to me to have you watch after him in his dying days. I just want you to know that the feelings I have for you are not just about my brother. I recognize them, and I'm not sure how to deal with them at this moment. I will tell you that you pull my heartstrings, Joseph Quinton."

Seela then looked down until Joseph pulled her face up to his. He planted his thick, luscious lips, which Seela had long desired, against her puckered pink lips, stirring the excitement she craved. As soon as she felt Joseph's mouth touch hers, her heart raced. Feelings Seela had not experienced in a long time rushed through her body. He opened her mouth with his tongue, shooting euphoria through her groin. Joseph then kissed Seela's face softly while sneaking his way to her right ear. Seela caressed Joseph's arm, feeling his tight bicep muscles. His body felt good to her.

Suddenly, something crashed, making Seela and Joseph jump. There lay Chester on the ground, with a spilled garbage bag beside him. Seela sprang to help him up. "Chester, are you okay, honey?"

"Yes, ma'am. I didn't hurt anything. I tripped over something—maybe a rock."

Seela presumed that Chester had seen them kissing, thus the fall. She couldn't help but giggle. "Here—let me help you up and get you back in the house. We were just going in also. Mr. Joseph has an early start to his day tomorrow."

"Okay," said Chester as he wiped the dirt and grass off his knees. "See? No scratches!"

Joseph walked Chester and Seela into the house. "Hey, Chester! High five, my man. I'll see you soon?" Joseph held his hand up high for Chester to hit.

Chester hit Joseph's hand clumsily and smiled. "See you soon, Yosef! If you see Uncle Sam, you tell him I love him, because I do."

"You got it, my man. I will get the message to him tomorrow."

Joseph said good night to all the ladies with big hugs and kisses.

Seela slowly walked him down the driveway to his truck. Joseph got in his truck without giving Seela a good-night kiss. She wanted to feel his taut body once more.

Joseph smiled at Seela while looking into Mamaw's front window as he spoke. "I would love to start back up where we left off in the garden, but there is a little person watching out the window. I do believe he's waiting for you to come back in to see him. That boy loves you something fierce already. You've got that sweetness and beauty that any smart man would want. I'll call you tomorrow, and we will make a date. I can drive to your town where you live. And no interruptions."

Seela's heart sank with unquenched desire. "Okay, that sounds great. I would love for you to come to my town, but it's a three-hour drive. Plan to stay in my guest bedroom so that you don't drive so far in one day."

That was music to Joseph's ears. He smiled with a heart-melting look at Seela as he pulled out of the rocky drive. He stuck his head out the window, yelling back at Seela. "Go on in, Seela. I want to watch you in my rearview mirror while you walk toward your house, just like when you leave the prison."

Seela threw Joseph a kiss and found herself swaying her hips back and forth as she trotted back to the house. She spotted Chester standing behind the curtain, trying to be still and unseen. She snickered to herself. All she could think about was how Joseph's lips felt on her lips and skin. Every touch of his sent an electrical current straight through her navel. She was turned on.

Chapter 27

Seela woke up to the sound of Chester's snoring interlaced with her grandmother's the next morning. It sounded as if they were making a song together. She smiled but then reflected on what Chester had said before they went to sleep. He had asked her how it was possible for her to love both him and Joseph at the same time. His longing had cut Seela's heart to the core, and she had done her best to reassure him that she could love both of them in different ways. She hadn't had a clue how to address a child about love; she'd used her womanly instinct. In the end, he'd seemed satisfied as Seela tucked him in with as much nurturance as she could exhibit.

Seela walked down the hall toward freshly brewed coffee. Dee sat at the kitchen table, working on her laptop.

"Good morning! We probably need to head out early today. Our salon book is packed this week. I figure we should get back early so we can make sure our linens and salon are ready for our bustling week of women and hair." Dee leaned back in her chair. "You going to be able to get through all of this? You think you can keep it together this week without letting your clients know what you are going through?"

Seela looked at Dee with despair. "I will get through, Dee. If I feel a moment coming on, I will exit to my office and regroup."

Dee reached up to hug Seela around her small shoulders. Seela sat down and explained her conversation with Chester the night before. "Dee, he asked me a dozen questions about love and declared that he loved me 'more than Yosef.'"

At the mention of Yosef, Dee dribbled her coffee down her chin.

"Dee, don't laugh! Chester asked me if I was sure I loved him back."

Dee's smile turned to a quivering frown, for she understood Chester's emotions. The situation hit a little too close to home, as there had been times in her life when she hadn't felt loved. "I'm so sorry, Seela. I know that broke your heart. Chester is such a wonderful, loving soul. I see how much he loves you, and I know you love him already too."

"Yes," said Seela. "I explained to him last night the different languages of love. I think he understands. I will tell him every day that I love him so that he will know."

They sat for a while, enjoying the birds outside the window while they drank their morning coffee. Suddenly, Mavvie charged through the door. "Thank goodness you are still here, Seels. I need to sage you this morning before you leave for home. You picked a lot up yesterday in that awful prison. Sam is around some horrible energy, and I can't let you take that home with you."

Dee's eyes grew big. "Whoa," said Dee. "You guys talk some crazy stuff. I'm going to wake Mamaw. I'll see you two later."

Seela abandoned the rest of her coffee. "Let's step into the garden, Mavvie. I have Chester here with me. I need to get him home before Dee and I head back."

Mavvie lit her sage stick, and the smoke barreled all around her. "Yes, my love, that is great!" Mavvie pushed Seela's arms straight up in the air. She started the stick at the bottom of Seela's feet, swirling it around every inch of her body until she reached the top of Seela's head. She chanted her normal chants in broken French. The smoke flew through the wind as they stood watching it, as if they were witnessing the bad energy attached to Seela fly away into the beautiful blue sky.

Mavvie took a deep breath and exhaled heavily. "Do you feel better, my love?"

Seela's head faced up toward the sky with her eyes closed. She breathed in and said, "I feel so light but good, Mavvie." Mavvie then turned to run back to the house, leaving Seela standing there. "Wait— that's it?" Seela said.

"Yes, Seela. I need to see Chester now. He's in your bed, right?"

"I need to sage him, so let me do it before he wakes." Mavvie ran through the yard, holding her white dress up so she wouldn't trip on the flowing fabric that draped all around her.

Seela ran behind her. "Wait. I want to be in the room in case he wakes up, Mavvie. You could scare him with that smoking stick!"

They reached Seela's bedroom door, and Chester was sitting up on the side of the bed, smiling. "Good morning, Ms. Seela and Ms. Mavvie. I sleep good with you, Ms. Seela. It scared me when you weren't here when I woked up."

Seela started to approach Chester, but Mavvie stopped her. "Wait, Seels. Stop and stand right there. Chester, sweetheart, can Mavvie sprinkle you with my fairy stick before we go to the kitchen for a pancake breakfast? It's a special dust that will make you feel wonderful and cleanse your body. I just did it to your Seela, and she said she feels fabulous!"

Chester stood up beside the bed and poked his chest out like a proud rooster. "Okay," he said. "If Ms. Seela like it, then I do it too."

Mavvie pushed Chester's arms up while swirling the sage around him from his toes up to his head.

"It smells funny," Chester said while trying not to inhale the smoke.

Seela smiled, trying not to interfere. "It doesn't smell bad, Chester."

"No, just funny."

"Do you feel all right, Chester?"

"I do."

Mavvie finished at the top of his head and then gave Chester a big hug. "You are such a sweet, sweet soul, my baby. Now, let's go get your pancakes. I think your friend Dee is whipping up something delish for you." Chester and Mavvie walked down the hallway hand in hand.

Dee turned when she heard Chester. "My main man, Chester. Good morning! I heard you got to sleep with the princess last night!"

"Yep!" said Chester. "Ms. Seela snore."

Seela laughed. "I was going to say the same thing about you, Chester!"

Dee chuckled as she said, "Yes, I bet if Mavvie would have walked in last night, she would have heard a song of snoring mouth quartets between the four of us!"

Chester sat smiling, happy to be there with all of them. He never wanted his visits to end with Seela and her family. Seela's phone beeped as she got a text. Chester reached for her phone on the kitchen table and handed it to Seela. Seela looked at her phone and beamed.

"Is it Yosef, Ms. Seela?"

"Yes, it is, Chester. He just said to have a safe trip home today, and he looks forward to seeing me this week. He's driving up to my home to take me out on a real date, Chester."

"Can I come?" he said.

Seela didn't know how to reply. She desperately wanted alone time with Joseph.

Dee immediately saved Seela. "I've got an idea, Chester. Why don't you come back with us next Monday, and you can stay with us for the week? That way, you can see where Ms. Seela and I both live."

Chester shook his head. "I want to come with Yosef too."

"Well, I guess I can ask him if he wants company for the ride up. Then maybe Dee can sit with you while Joseph and I go out to dinner. Does that sound good, Chester?"

Chester ran to Seela and squeezed her tightly around her waist. "Yes, Ms. Seela, that sounds great!"

After Seela and Dee dropped Chester off at the gas station, Dee wasted no time in hitting Seela with a million questions about Joseph and what his touch was like.

Chapter 28

Sam busily worked his way through all the vultures, trying to collect a team of inmates who'd care for him in the fashion he was used to. Lil Jon mopped by Sam's room, peeping into the glass window. Sam saw him and pushed his buzzer to alert Big Sexy. She looked over to Sam's room. Sam mouthed for her to open his door. She shook her head while pushing his buzzer for Lil Jon to enter.

"Hey, man," said Lil Jon. "How'd you sleep last night? I snuck over and checked on you. Man, your ass was sitting straight up on the side of the bed, sound asleep. It 'bout scared me to death, thinking you were already dead. I stood and watched until I saw your chest move. Then I went on back to my bunk. Big Sexy wrapped around your finger, I see. She let me stand there until I was ready to go."

Sam smiled slightly as he sat up in his wheelchair. "I give her nothing but flattery and love, Lil Jon. A woman like her—that is all she wants. Sad she so big. She can't help it. You ever had a whole lot of lovin' from a woman like that, Lil Jon?"

Lil Jon turned and scanned Big Sexy. His eyes grew wide at the thought. He laughed while focusing on Sam again. "I have to say no, Sam, my man. I haven't. Not that I wouldn't, but I'm wondering if I would be able to breathe if she got on top of my scrawny black ass." They both laughed together.

Big Sexy headed toward them.

"Oh shit. You think she heard us, man?" Lil Jon said.

"Hell no! She just coming to give me dead meds!" Sam bellowed.

"Are you taking them, Sam? I thought you been saving and hiding them."

"Yes, she doesn't know. Just my caregiver, Nurse Brandy. She be the only one who knows what I'm doing."

Big Sexy walked through the heavy metal door to Sam's room. "Okay, I don't know what your plans are this morning, Sam. Lil Jon taking you to the shower or yard first?"

"Big Sexy, you know my ass doesn't do anything until I've shit, showered, and shaved. I've taken my shit, so now Lil Jon goin' take me to the shower and give me a nice shave. I'll wash my ole dog ass." They laughed together.

"Okay, here are your pills for this morning, and I assume you aren't going to eat that cheese sandwich on your table there?"

"Hell no, Big Sexy, you got to get me something else. You see my blown-up fucking self. If I eat that sandwich, it's going to make it worse. Get Mr. Williams to get me some fucking decent food. You guys already killing me slowly with all this morphine. At least I could have something that doesn't hurt my stomach for hours."

Big Sexy picked up the sandwich and asked if he wanted to give it to another dying inmate who would be thankful for it.

"Give it to whoever the hell you want, Big Sexy. You cook at home for your kids, Big Sexy?"

"Yes, Sam, I have to. We for sure can't afford to go out to eat."

"When you cook, you can bring leftovers in your lunch box for me. I'll get you some money sent to your house for exchange. That sound good, Big Sexy? You can then take your rug rats out to dinner. Deal?"

Big Sexy hesitated, knowing she would be jeopardizing her job if anyone found out. "Okay, what kind of food do you like, Sam? Or what do you think won't hurt you?"

"I don't know what won't hurt me, Big Sexy. You got a computer at home? Google my condition, and see what my fucking dying liver can handle."

Big Sexy stopped at Sam's door before pushing her clicker to let herself out. She didn't turn back to look at Sam. "I'll research your condition tonight. When I'm back at work the day after tomorrow, I will stock our minifridge with some baggies of food that you can have. Have Lil Jon heat it up for you. No one will really know; they will think it's my leftovers in the fridge."

Sam spoke in his gravelly voice. "You will have a money card in your mail by Friday, Big Sexy. Just write down your address, and I'll get it to you immediately. There will be extra money on it for the groceries you spend on me. We straight, Big Sexy? I know you good, and it's your lucky month to have met a fucking dying prisoner like me."

Big Sexy threw a hand up with an okay sign and walked out, leaving the metal door open so Lil Jon could take Sam to the showers. As they made their way down the hallway, Sam asked Lil Jon if he'd delivered his message to AB.

"Yea, man, he'll be out there waiting on you. I had to tell him who you were before you came here in order for him to agree to meet you. He said he didn't have time to do bizness with a dying man like you. As soon as I told him who you were, he agreed. He did ask if you had any more of the Marlboros I gave him."

Sam smiled without opening his mouth. "Okay, Lil Jon, that's all. I don't want you to ever deal with that man again. You got it? Don't go anywhere near him or his posse. You got it? You my man until I exit this hell of a shithole. If he even try to talk to you, I better be told. You hear me?"

Lil Jon agreed. He wasn't used to dealing with hard-core criminals, so this experience was scary and thrilling to him. "I know I'm your man, Sam. I know there is a reason you in my life right now. I wouldn't do anything to jeopardize our friendship either."

They reached the shower room. They heard inmates inside, cursing. Lil Jon stopped as if he didn't want to take Sam in there.

"What you stopping for, Lil Jon? Open the goddamn door. We may need to stop a fight."

Lil Jon stood still. "Sam, you're a dying man in a wheelchair, and I'm a scrawny-ass little guy. I don't think you and I are going to stop whatever is going on in there."

Sam yelled, "Open the fucking door, Lil Jon! We going in to shower. If whoever shit-for-nothings are in there got a problem, then you run for Big Sexy, and I'll take what they fucking got. I just hope they kill my goddamn self. I could give a shit!"

Lil Jon pushed the door open, and they saw AB and two other guys having a confrontation. Sam shouted as loudly as he could, "I'm fucking Sam Black, king of all kings in these prisons for over twenty years! Now I'm a fucking dying king in here. You all take a good look at what can happen to every fucking one of you." Sam reached for his blanket across his lap and pulled it back so they could see the stitches that ran from his rectum to his testicles, which were each the size of a grapefruit.

The inmates stood still in silence while Lil Jon stood holding on to Sam's wheelchair, thinking he might need to wheel him out fast, or maybe he was keeping Sam in front of him as his protector.

AB motioned for the other two inmates to leave the shower room. Sam spoke before AB.

"I've heard of you in Cottonwood and at Jackson. Matter of fact, I had a bunkmate in Cottonwood who knew you well. He was my main man there for a few years until I got sick. As a matter of fact, he still has my phone and is probably running my bizness as we speak. He doesn't even know about my shanking and where I am now. I can't talk, because as you see, my fucking junkie ass is on its way out of here. The only fucking thing I want now is to be comfortable while it happens. I want to do what gives me satisfaction while my blimp ass dies miserably inside this hellhole."

AB seemed to show empathy in his face as he stepped closer. Lil Jon clenched Sam's wheelchair handles tightly. "Man, this is a fucked-up situation. Once Lil Squirt here told me who you were, I did a little research. Made some calls from my bunk last night to find out your story. I am the leader king in here, and I will help you, Mr. Sam Black. You are one of me, and I'm your soldier on the yard. You got it! I'm in for life, so there isn't anything I need to worry about on messing up my sentence. So you just tell me what you want."

Sam smiled. "Those words are music to my ears, AB. I'm a heroin addict, so truthfully, that's all I love doing besides wheeling and dealing. So I figure since I can't do heroin in my dying days, I can get a high from wheeling and dealing in this fucking shithole."

AB listened to Sam while studying his rotting body. Sam looked like a living corpse already, but one that still had a highly functioning, crazy brain.

"Okay, this is what I see we can do," Sam said. "I got the goods to make you and me some money real quick. I'm stocked on Marlboros and bubble gum. Lil Jon and I will be out on the yard at one o'clock every day. You can get ten Marlboros from me every day, and you sell them for ten dollar apiece. The bubble gum goes for a dollar. I'll give you twenty pieces. We will split the profits, even though I'm providing the goods."

"Why?" replied AB.

Sam chuckled. "Because that's the way I am. I need something to feed my soul while I lay dying in that cinder block rat box of a room."

"Well then, all right. We got a deal, Sam Black. You want to wheel and deal for a little while, then let's do it. You want me to keep my mouth shut with other inmates in the other prisons about you being here?"

"Hell yeah, AB! You can't say anything to anyone, my man. My family could be affected by this. It's more serious than you know. I was in one of the worst privately owned state prisons here in Georgia. The guards and warden don't give a shit about an inmate. My boys down there on the inside could be tortured. I don't want you to get linked to me either. So Lil Jon is the only one I'll be seen with. All right? We will see you in the yard later today." Sam threw his hand up for a fist shake.

"Yeah, man. We straight." AB turned and walked out, leaving Sam and Lil Jon alone in the shower. While Lil Jon helped Sam shave and shower, they had no clue AB stood guard at the shower room door outside so no one could enter while Sam showered.

Lil Jon helped Sam get dressed in the new terry robe Joseph had brought him. He placed Sam's black toboggan hat on his head. Sam motioned for Lil Jon to step outside his room while he got in his locker to load up with cigarettes and bubble gum. When he'd finished, he motioned for Lil Jon to come back in to get him.

"All right, my man, let's get this party started."

They strolled down the hallway as if they were going to a party. Sam sang a Hall and Oates song that Lil Jon had never heard, but he was skipping to Sam's beat. They reached the yard door, and when they opened it, they saw at least twenty inmates staring at them. Lil Jon stopped and said, "Do you think these guys are nice, or did we walk out at the wrong time, Sam?"

The inmates parted, and there sat AB by himself on his usual table. The men scattered like mice when AB waved them away. Lil Jon wheeled Sam over beside AB's table and parked Sam's wheelchair beside AB. "You good, my man?" Lil Jon said. "I'm going to do my work duties, and I'll be back for you in an hour."

Sam gave him a thumbs-up. "Yeah, man, get your work done so you can take care of my dying ass. You didn't know you were getting more work duties when you met me, did you, boy?"

Lil Jon tapped Sam's hand. "Man, you ain't work to me. You give me life. I'll see you shortly." Lil Jon ran quickly out of the yard. Sam watched to make sure he didn't have any confrontations with anyone until he got through the metal door. The yard was not a good place to be. Too much could happen without guards seeing.

AB scanned the yard, telling Sam who each inmate was and what he was in for. Being in a state prison meant that most were serving long sentences. It was a dangerous prison, something Sam had never experienced. He might have been king in his little prison, but this was a different story. Sam figured if he were going to die there, he wanted to be king of the inmates before departing. Sam handily gave AB the cigarettes and bubble gum over the next hour as they sat together.

"The way I see it, AB, if we do this for the rest of the week until my supply gets low, we both should make two hundred forty dollars apiece for the next four days' work. You will send mine on a Green Dot card to an address that I will get to you this week. Whoever you have working for you on the outside, you get them to mail my money to the address I give you. We straight with that?"

"Yeah, man, we straight. You know, I got a phone if you want to borrow it sometimes. You tell me, and I'll get it to you for an evening if that will help you."

"Hell yeah, I had a fucking iPhone the past two years where I was. I even had a Facebook account. I do kind of miss talking to my peeps at night, even all the crazy-ass women who want to talk and hear bullshit from a prisoner like me." They laughed.

"Sam, I did hear from some guys down south that you one fearless, crazy motherfucker."

"Now that I've been killed and brought back to die here in this shithole, I'm triple fearless. There's nothing that scares me at this point."

AB sat listening to Sam, looking out at all of the incarcerated men walking around passing time and bullshitting in the yard. AB's heart and soul were saddened as he listened to Sam. Sam sat with his eyes closed and his head resting back against his wheelchair, soaking the sun up. He spoke without moving any part of his body.

"Hey, man, what time is it? I think I'm ready to lie down. My body is so weak, and I don't want to pass out here in this jungle yard. You think you can get me back inside?"

AB motioned for his main guy in the prison. A tall muscle machine of a guy walked toward Sam. AB said, "I want you to take Mr. Black here to his hall. His main guy still not back, and he's ready for a nap. You got it, Ken? When you get to the hall door, just push the button and walk back here. The nurse will come get Mr. Black at the door."

"Yeah, Big Sexy will come get me. Have you seen her?" asked Sam. "She is one whole lotta woman. That's why I call her Big Sexy. I'm working her. She'll be putty in my hand soon." Sam smiled a devilish grin.

Ken grasped the handles on Sam's wheelchair. "You ready to take it on in, Mr. Sam?"

"Yeah, man, let's do it. Throw Ken a Marl, AB. Don't worry. I got that one. You won't owe. Why? That's how I roll, man! Robin Hood was my nickname in the last prison I was in.

You all will see why by the time I'm gone from here. These motherfuckers think they got me here, feeding me morphine and trying to kill my ass off real quick. Well, that ain't happening! I'm not leaving here until I'm good and fucking ready."

As Ken pushed Sam back down the cold, shiny marble floors, Sam said, "What you in for, Ken? You in for life like your boss?"

"Hell no, man. I get out in five years. My sentence was twenty years to do ten. So I'm halfway there. When I get out, I'm walking a straight line. I have a son who was a baby when I got in trouble. It's been hard, but I'm pulling through. Let's just say I was with the wrong people when something bad happened, and I got caught up in it. I was young and dumb, thinking my friends were everything. My son will be eleven when I get out. I'm going to be a better person for him. He's my rock right now. It's what keeps me going and positive about life."

"Man, that's good to hear," Sam said weakly. "You stay straight and narrow when you leave this shithole of a prison. You take care of your boy."

Chapter 29

Only a few select clients knew what was going on in Seela's life. She felt it was better not to talk about it, so the week would not revolve around her brother's dying life in prison. Seela was beside herself with anticipation on Wednesday, knowing Joseph and Chester were driving up for the evening. Dee planned to spend the night at Seela's with Chester while Seela and Joseph went out for a romantic dinner.

Dee passed by Seela's styling chair and winked. "Seels, you best be getting home to get gussied up for your date tonight. What you think you are going to wear on this little date of yours? I feel nervous for you, like you are going on a blind date! It's like we don't even know Joseph, because y'all's relationship has been built on Sam and all of us."

"I know. It does feel like I'm meeting him for the first time. I'm excited for Chester to get to come also. He will like seeing where we live and work."

"Don't be surprised if Chester wants to stay here with you, Seels. I think Joseph is going to have a hard time getting him back in the car to go back home."

Seela headed out of the salon with a skip in her step. She felt joy that she hadn't felt in a long time. She tried hard not to think of Sam and his condition. When she arrived at her front porch, a beautiful bouquet of flowers sat by her door. It was so big that it covered her front door mat. The colors of the flowers made her heart fill with love. Seela reached down for the card. It said, "I hope these flowers make you smile, and I hope your smile continues until Chester and I reach you. You are the sunshine in both of our lives. Chester and Joseph."

Seela could barely pick up the arrangement because it was so heavy. She took it inside and sat the gorgeous bunch on her dining table. Seela stood back to admire the flowers while feeling loved. When she thought of Joseph, she felt heat rise up through her body. She shivered, trying to shake it off.

Seela stood in her closet for what seemed like an eternity, trying to figure out what to wear. She heard the doorbell and frantically ran out of her closet. She opened the door to Dee and pulled her inside. "Thank goodness you are here! I need you to help me pick out something to wear."

Dee gawked at Seela as if she had three heads. "Seels, wear your sexy black dress. You can't go wrong!"

Seela smirked at Dee. "You don't think it's too sexy, do you?"

"Hell no, Seels! Hurry—go put it on. Come out here and model it for me."

Seela ran into her bedroom, quickly stepped into the black dress, and threw on her black sling-back pumps. She ruffled her hair to tease it up until it was full and fluffy. She greeted Dee in her small, cozy living room. Dee stood up, giving Seela a cat whistle. "Dang, girl, you look hot! That Joseph is not going to know what to do. I don't think he's seen you dressed like this!"

"Heck no," said Seela. "I don't even think he's seen me with much makeup on. It's all off by the time I come out from visiting Sam. Do you think I'm too dressed up?" Seela looked into the large mirror hanging in her foyer. She turned as if modeling her dress for an audience.

"Girl, you look like a million bucks. Chester and Joseph are going to be surprised when they walk through your door."

On cue, the doorbell rang. Seela looked at Dee with wild eyes. "Is that them already? I thought Joseph said they would be here at six." Seela glanced at her watch. "They are a half hour early." Seela walked over to open the stained-glass door. There stood Chester with his crooked grin.

"Hey, Ms. Seela!" Chester froze at the sight of Seela. "Wow, you look bootiful, Ms. Seela. Yosef is parking his truck; he'll be right here." Chester handed Seela an old photograph. It was a picture of Sam and her when they were children. Seela stared at it in shock. It was from their tenth birthday party. She smiled, remembering the day.

"Where did you find this picture, Chester?"

"I've had it awhile," said Chester. "It was in Sam's wallet. He gave it to me one time when he was sick. He said I could put it in my wallet, and I did. I want you to have it. Okay?"

Tears pooled in Seela's beautiful green eyes. As Joseph approached the house, she wiped her face quickly, shoving the picture into her clutch on the foyer table. He smiled radiantly at her, deferring Seela's thoughts of Sam.

"Good evening, Ms. Seela. I must say, you are one beautiful sight for my eyes! It was well worth the drive, and I enjoyed having a copilot like this one." Joseph squeezed around Chester's neck before reaching to kiss Seela on her cheek. "You even smell delicious. Chester, what do you think of Ms. Seela tonight? She's one gorgeous lady, I must say."

"Um, she's the most prettiest woman I know," said Chester. "Can I see your house, Ms. Seela?"

"Oh yes, Chester! Come in, you two. I can't wait to show you my home." Seela reached around Chester's broad shoulders, leading him toward her kitchen, knowing that was his favorite room at her grandmother's house. Dee walked out the kitchen doorway with a pitcher of lemonade and glasses for everyone. She had Chester's favorite cookies on the tray also.

"Hey Chubby Chester, I've been getting ready for you tonight. We going to have a great date night ourselves. We'll walk down to the burger joint and then grab ice cream on the way home, and maybe if we aren't too tired, we'll watch a scary movie."

Chester grinned. "I like that. I like burgers too!"

Dee hugged Chester while winking at Joseph. "How was your drive up? Chester here keep you entertained, Mr. Joseph?"

"As a matter of fact, he did. He told me all kinds of stories. This here fellow is full of them!" Joseph patted Chester on his back, chuckling as if they had an inside secret now.

"What kind of stories, Chester?" said Seela. "Made-up ones or stories about you?"

Chester glanced at Joseph but quickly turned his head toward Seela. "Real stories, Ms. Seela. Some about me and some about my dad." Chester glanced at Joseph again. He hesitated and then said softly, "And some about Sam."

Seela grabbed both of Chester's hands, staring at his face. "Chester, I would love to hear stories about Sam. We will sit out at Mamaw's, and you can share some. Will that be okay?"

Chester looked sad, as if he didn't want to share with Seela what he had told Joseph. They weren't all good stories, because most of the times Chester had seen Sam, Sam had been sick from heroin. Sam stayed at his place when he needed a safe spot to get over his days of vomiting before he hit the streets again. Chester and Bill were his guards from the outside world until he was capable of taking care of himself again. Anxious to be alone with Joseph, Seela dropped the subject and hugged Chester good-bye.

Joseph and Seela strolled down the lit-up street, walking on a sidewalk overflowing with flowers reaching out from picket fences. Clairsville was a quaint town with a small population shaped by old southern money. Joseph held Seela's hand, squeezing it tightly as they walked. "How did you find this cute little town, Seela?"

Seela kept her eyes forward as she replied, "I felt I was led here by angels, Joseph. It's been a safe place for me ever since I left the island. I left years ago, driving to the first town that felt safe for me. I drove for three hours through many tiny towns, wondering if I should drive to the big city to start my adulthood life or stay with what I'm used to: a small town with big attitudes of love. That's what I get here in Clairsville. I was welcomed in the beginning, and it's only gotten better as I've grown with this town. We have a few great restaurants and a fabulous hair salon, which is opening a spectacular art gallery where southern local artists can display their talent. We just got a theater for plays and musicals, so I have to say, we are moving on up in Clairsville. I'm glad to be a part of it." Seela turned, facing Joseph. "I'm also glad I've met you, Joseph Quinton." She stood on her tiptoes and kissed his cheek.

"Ms. Seela, you can do better than that." Joseph bent down and cupped Seela's face with his large hands. He then kissed her soft pink lips as if she were a delicate rose. His tongue moved through her mouth as if they were making love right then. Seela's body trembled inside, with sparks shooting from places she had not felt since high school with her boyfriend, Johnny. She did not want Joseph to stop, but they were now standing outside the restaurant, probably being stared at by diners. They entered, holding hands. The hostess recognized Seela and greeted her with a big hug.

"I've been waiting on you," the hostess said with a thick southern accent. "I picked out the best table we have. Come this way." She escorted them through the narrow restaurant to the front corner by the window. Long velvet curtains hung so that no one could look in, but they could see the white lights twinkling over the street.

Joseph and Seela feasted and sat for hours, talking, laughing, and sharing their aspirations. Joseph romantically fed Seela food from his plate. She licked his fingers as she took the food from his hand. It was a magical evening for Seela. She felt as if she were on cloud nine the entire night. She didn't want the excitement to end. The restaurant turned the lights up, as if to let Joseph and Seela know they were closing down.

"I would love to see your salon, Seela, and, of course, the new gallery. Is it far from here?" Joseph said. Seela's face lit up in agreement.

They walked for several blocks in content silence. Joseph studied every business sign to catch a glimpse of Seela's name in lights. Then, at the end of the street, he saw a sign hanging with big, swirly letters bearing her name. He turned to Seela, grabbing her hand, and without hesitation, he pulled her toward her salon. He could barely contain his hunger for another kiss. As soon as Seela opened the salon door, the alarm beeped. She motioned for Joseph to step aside while she ran to her office to turn it off.

When she walked out of her office into the salon, Joseph was sitting in her styling chair. "I take it this is your chair, Seela?" He swiveled around to face the mirror.

Seela approached Joseph and leaned over on him, whispering, "Yes, it is, Joseph. How can you tell?"

He pointed to the vase at her station, which held two of the white flowers that remained from the flower arrangement he had sent. The card was propped beside it. He looked at Seela through the mirror and then reached up and around to pull her into his lap. Joseph swirled his tongue around Seela's ear and moved his way down her neck. His hands caressed her thighs and moved over to her buttocks. He squeezed her against him as if he wanted to suck her up into his body.

Seela's body rushed with hot lava shooting through every nerve ending. She felt like a rocket getting ready for takeoff, and if she got any more of Joseph's fuel, she would be in outer space before she knew it. She could feel her panties getting drenched as Joseph kissed and groped her curves, gyrating against her with his hard, muscular bulk. They kissed until Seela could feel her face becoming raw. She reluctantly pulled herself away. "Come, Joseph. Let me show you the salon." She didn't want him to see the gallery until it was complete. His mind was reeling with lust, so he didn't argue.

Dee walked out onto Seela's porch as Joseph and Seela came up the walkway. "I was just coming out to sit on the front porch and listen to some nightlife. I see I can mosey on down to my own little cottage now and listen as I walk."

"Yes, thank you, Dee, for hanging with Chester. Did you guys have fun?" Seela said.

Dee smiled at Seela and Joseph, sensing the electricity between them. "Did we!" said Dee. "Chester loved the fact that we can walk everywhere. We had a great burger, and then we went on down to Dippin' Dots and got two cups of ice cream. He didn't want to watch a scary movie. He said he didn't want to have bad dreams." Dee smiled, looking back through Seela's front door. "He's special—I'll tell you that."

Seela and Joseph walked onto the porch and hugged Dee. "Yes, he is," said Seela. "I'm so glad I met Chester. Now he's a new bright light in our lives."

Dee headed home, leaving Joseph and Seela alone on her porch. Seela asked Joseph if he wanted to sit outside with a nighttime toddy or if he was ready to turn in.

"All I want right now, Seela, is to be here with you. Can we sit in the living room with our nightcaps? How does that sound?"

Seela poured each of them a snifter and joined Joseph on the sofa. They toasted and sipped before Joseph cupped Seela's face again. "You make me feel like I've never felt before, Seela. It's scaring the shit out of me. I never thought I would have such strong feelings for anyone so quickly, let alone Sam Black's twin sister."

Seela took in the statement. "Joseph, you say that like you have a strong relationship with my brother. I'm nothing like my brother, although I love him dearly and would do anything for him. Are you worried about me being Sam's twin sister?"

"No, Seela. I don't look down on Sam. He has a disease that got pushed into our rotten, corrupt system. He just could never get out of the web he got into. My heart hurts for your brother."

Seela felt a sense of comfort come over her as she listened to Joseph. "I know, Joseph. His addiction is such a bad disease. I hate it so much. Knowing that there is nothing I can do to help him is killing me."

Joseph hugged Seela as they sat quietly on her sofa. Seela rested her head on his chest, which felt like the best pillow ever. As such, they fell asleep in each other's arms.

The next morning, Chester woke to find Seela's side of the bed untouched. He jumped out of bed, shouting for her. No one replied. Chester put his robe and slippers on carefully. He walked out into the living room, where Joseph and Seela were curled up.

Chapter 30

Chester had two fun-filled days with Dee and Seela at the salon. The clients fell in love with him, including Ms. Kathy. She even took him shopping and out for a root beer float. Ms. Kathy was happy to have some entertaining company with her for a change.

The mood was not as festive in Sam's bleak prison room. Joseph made it in to see Sam on Friday for a visit and was prepared to tell Sam about his time with Seela.

"Hey, my main man, Joseph Quinton." Sam's voice was considerably weaker. His stomach had gotten even bigger. His fingers were blown up like rubber gloves filled with air. Sam lifted his head forward to look straight at Joseph. "How was your visit up to my twin? Did you two have a good time? You better have been a fucking gentleman to my sis!" Sam chuckled, but it hurt his chest to laugh. He stretched his hand across his enormous stomach as if that would help him.

Joseph sat down in the chair next to Sam's locker. He rolled his eyes. "Man, your sister is one beautiful woman, Sam. Inside and out! I had a great date with Seela, and I don't know if you knew, but Chubby Chester rode with me. He ended up staying with Seela. He's coming back with her this weekend."

Sam sat quietly while listening to Joseph. "Is that right? Well, how was your ride with ole Chubby? What stories he have for you? Anything you didn't know already?" Sam looked serious.

"He said you were his uncle Sam and was pretty adamant about it. He mentioned taking care of you a lot when you were out running the streets on the island. He said you told him the truth about some things when you were sick. What is he talking about, Sam?"

"Yeah, man, that's the only place I could go where no one knew where I was while I got back on my fucking feet. I would run in heroin houses hard for days until I couldn't stand it anymore. Then I would go to old Bill Johnson's, where I knew it was safe. All I had to do was hand Bill my wallet when I came in the gas station and go out back. When I was ready to leave four or five days later, he would give it back to me with everything in order just how I gave it to him."

"Let's get to the point. Why is Bill Johnson so loyal to you, Sam?"

Sam's eyes turned wild. "You don't ask questions about anybody I know. You fucking hear me, Joseph Quinton? Your questions are only about what I've been fucking doing in here while locked up, not what I did on the outside. Those days are fucking gone, and so is my life!"

Joseph remained still, knowing he was dealing with a man at death's door. He didn't want to incite him any further.

"If you don't have anything else, Joseph, I'm ready for you to leave. I can't be getting upset. This fucking fluid on my lungs is smothering me. I need to focus on breathing right now." Sam turned his head away.

Joseph left in silence while Sam motioned for Big Sexy to take his place. Big Sexy opened Sam's door and ambled over to his bed. Her heavy body moved slowly, but somehow, Big Sexy looked as if she were walking fast. "Sam, let me fix your pillow. Your head is all jacked up."

Sam leaned forward as best as he could. "Big Sexy, you bring me some grub? I'm fucking starving. What did you find out that I can eat that won't hurt me so bad?"

Big Sexy frowned. "There's not a lot, Sam. I brought you some banana and some crackers. Meat is not your friend. Your body can't process much. You really don't need to be drinking much of anything because of all the fluid on your body. I feel horrible because I said I would cook for you, but there really isn't anything you can have."

"Fuck that shit, Big Sexy. I'm fucking dying. You cook me some spaghetti or bean burritos. I don't give a shit if I throw the shit back out my fucking mouth. It will taste good going down for a minute."

Big Sexy shifted nervously, as if she were getting in trouble with the teacher. "Okay, calm down, Sam. I'll bring you whatever you want me to cook for you, but you were the one who said to research your condition."

"Well, fuck that now." Sam looked discouraged at not getting something good to eat immediately. "Go get Mr. Williams, Big Sexy. Will you, please?"

"Okay, I'll send him in here." She shuffled away, determined to appease him next time.

Mr. Williams tapped twice on the glass. Sam turned his head, mouthing, "Come in." When Mr. Williams opened Sam's door, Sam tried to push his heavy body so that he could sit up better in his bed. Mr. Williams reached over to help him the best he could.

"I hear I've been summoned by you. What's up, Sam? You doing as best as you can?"

"Yes, best is right! I want you to go back to your office and order me a fucking pizza. These people are killing me with morphine and starving me with damn cold-ass cheese sandwiches. I'll get you money for it, and I'll pay double. Order me up a double ground beef with onions. You got it? Lil Jon will wheel me down to your office to eat it when you get it. I'll know when it's here, because I'll smell the fucking pie."

Mr. Williams shook his head, laughing at Sam. "You got any other requests, Sam? You seem to be on a roll with what you want."

Sam smiled back at Mr. Williams. "Just think of it as my last fucking supper!" The men laughed together.

"It may be after you eat it, Sam," Mr. Williams quipped while exiting the room to follow through with the pizza delivery.

Lil Jon soon stopped by Sam's room with his mop, and Big Sexy buzzed him in. "Hey, man, you all right? You don't look so good. You want me to get the oxygen mask for you?"

Sam's chest labored for breath. "No, I want you to get me out of this bed and wheel my fucking fat ass down to Mr. Williams's office. Leave me there for about fifteen minutes. Then come back and get me. When is the last time you had a fucking piece of Domino's pizza, Lil Jon?"

"Aw, man, it's been awhile! I thought I smelled it when I came down your hall."

"You sure as hell did, Lil Jon. You taking me to eat some right now in Mr. Williams's office. When you come back and get me, I'll bring you some back to my room. You got it? You like ground beef pizza?"

Lil Jon was amazed at what Sam got done while dying in prison. "Hell yeah. I can already taste it, Sam. You the fucking king—I tell you right now!" Lil Jon laughed the entire way down the hallway to Mr. Williams's office door.

Sam leaned forward in his wheelchair and knocked twice. Mr. Williams called him in, and Lil Jon pushed him into a tunnel of food aromas he had not smelled in a long time. "Let's eat!" Sam shouted while weakly wheeling himself over to Mr. Williams's desk, where the steaming pizza box sat.

Mr. Williams opened the box and threw Sam a napkin. "Here. Enjoy, but don't eat too much. I'm not ready for you to die because of me feeding you pizza."

Sam rolled his eyes as if he had gone to heaven already. "I haven't had something so fucking good in a long time, Mr. Williams. Don't worry if I die from this damn pizza. You'll know I felt like I was in heaven eating it! Because we both know those fucking gates are going to be closed when I leave this hell of a world I've been in."

Mr. Williams leaned back in his old office chair, looking hard at Sam. "What's your belief, Sam? You got one? The way you've lived your life, I don't see why you're worried where you're going next. None of us know where we're going when our time is up. I will tell you this: when you do die, there will be no more pain. That stops here. Your body is what feels pain on earth. Your soul does not. Now, to where that goes, I don't know. I suggest that while your body prepares to die, you prepare your soul for the next adventure. You do that, and you will be okay, Sam Black. I hate to see a man like you battle such a disease as you have all your life. Our system is not set up right for addicts like you. As long as you are in my care here, I'll do my best to make it as comfortable as I can. You understand what I'm saying, Sam?"

Sam continued to eat while processing every word. "We straight, Mr. Williams. It's all fucking good. Toss me a napkin so I can take a few pieces back to my cell." Sam wrapped up the pizza and put it in his lap, covering it with his prison gown. He gave Mr. Williams a thumbs-up with his open-fingered gloves on. "You the man!"

As soon as Sam turned the corner, Lil Jon popped out of a utility room with his mop. "Hey, Sam, I was just coming to get you. Man, that pizza smells damn good!"

As soon as Sam saw Big Sexy, he waved for her to unlock his room. Lil Jon reached around Sam, pushing the heavy door open. Sam yelled out the best he could, "Big Sexy, Lil Jon goin' to clean my floors and commode! Give him a few minutes in here." Big Sexy waved over her counter at Sam. His door locked behind them as soon as they were inside. Lil Jon helped Sam into his bed. It was getting harder and harder to lift Sam with all the fluid that had built up throughout his body.

"Lil Jon, I set the pizza on the tray when I stood up from my wheelchair. Fucking grab a piece of it now. Eat it while you stand over behind my locker. Big Sexy's not fucking paying attention. Besides, she'll think I got you cleaning my shitty toilet."

Sam looked over at Lil Jon as he ate a slice as if it were the first time he had tasted cake. He ate it so fast that Sam tossed him another piece before Big Sexy saw him. "This shit tastes so good. You've made my week! Whatever you want me to do, just ask," Lil Jon said.

Sam sat back in his bed with his eyes closed and a smile on his face. All he could think of was what Mr. Williams had said about his body and soul. Right now, feeding Lil Jon pizza made his soul feel good. Did that count? Big Sexy knocked on the glass. Lil Jon jumped down as if he were cleaning Sam's toilet, and Sam opened his eyes. "Damn, Big Sexy, you scared the living shit out of me."

She motioned for Lil Jon to exit, pointing to her watch.

"Oh yeah, Lil Jon, they getting ready to do count. You better get back to your room. Come by later before bed count tonight, okay? I may want a stroll out to the yard here on this floor. Maybe take a cig, and you can give me a couple puffs."

Lil Jon high-fived Sam and darted out. Big Sexy walked in, following the smell. "What you got up in here, Sam Black? It smells like Italian, if I would take a guess."

"Well, you win the fucking prize, Big Sexy. It's pizza. You want the last slice? I'll give it to your sweet little ass if you want it. Mr. Williams gave it to me."

Big Sexy shook her head in exasperation. "You never cease to amaze me, Sam. Now you getting Domino's pizza brought to you. I was making you spaghetti tonight, but it looks like you've moved on to others in here to get you food."

"Hell no! You bring me fucking spaghetti, Big Sexy. I can't wait to taste your cooking. Who the hell cares if it kills me? That's what they are trying to do anyway. They're killing me fucking miserably, letting me fucking drown in my own body fluid. Just fucking look at me. Lil Jon wrapped my legs up with gauze to keep the fluid from running down my fucking elephant legs."

Big Sexy stared. It was a horrible sight to look at. Her heart was breaking over Sam's condition. She had no control over any of it, but she could try to help make Sam as comfortable as she could without hurting her job. Big Sexy tucked the thin blanket around Sam's shivering body. Sam's lips were quivering as if he were standing in an icebox. Big Sexy picked his robe up from his wheelchair and stretched it across Sam's body before leaving.

Sam rested for an hour while Big Sexy kept an eye on him. The buzzer went off, startling Sam. When he turned his head to see if Lil Jon had returned, his eyes met Big Sexy's. She put her finger to her mouth to tell Sam not to speak. She pulled her iPhone out and placed it beside Sam's body. She then placed the earplugs in Sam's ears. She had the music set to Ludacris so Sam could hear his favorite songs. He rested his head on the nasty sponge of a pillow. Big Sexy pulled his toboggan down over his ears, concealing the earplugs.

"I'll be back in an hour. I can't let my phone die down, so that will be all the time you can listen today." Big Sexy turned at the door, winking at Sam as he listened to some of his favorite music.

Five minutes into listening, Sam realized he could use the phone to call someone right there from his own fucking bed. He chuckled at this connection to the outside but knew he would have to be careful with Big Sexy. Sam sat up so that he could see all the guards at their stations outside the glass wall. He then stopped the music and punched in *69 to block Big Sexy's number from the recipient's display.

He dialed Charlie's number quickly. "Hey, Charlie, it's Sam. Hey, babe! I can't talk loud or long, so listen quick."

Charlie was shocked at hearing Sam's weak voice. "Sam, where are you, and why haven't I heard from you? It's been over a month, and I thought you were dead."

"Well, you guessed right! I was dead, but they brought me back just to fucking kill me again. Listen, Charlie, I want you to know I thank you for everything you have done for me. Even when you got out, you stood by me and did what I told you to do. I know your life has been a lot easier with my help money-wise, with you helping me with my bizness in Cottonwood, but there is no more. They have given me sixty days to live, so I want you to keep all my money you have and get on your feet. No more buying purses or clothes, Charlie. You got to get out there and make a living for yourself. I know it's hard being transgender, but hell, go work at Walmart. Take the fucking wig off, Charlie.

"I know you love me, so you listen to me now. I'm headed out of this fucking hellhole of a world. I hate that you have to stay in it, but you do, so you need to walk the straight and narrow. Never give up on yourself, Charlie. Be who you really think you are. It's a cruel and crazy world out there. I hate that both our lives were screwed when we got here. I know you feel like a woman trapped in a man's body. I understand. That's why I watched over you in Cottonwood. I want you to do me a favor before I die." Sam paused and heard Charlie crying into the phone. He couldn't understand how someone born physically a man could sound so much like a woman.

"Please, Charlie, get yourself together. It will be all right. I need you to get three money cards. Send one for one hundred dollars to this address I'm going to give you. Address it to Ms. Williams. Then get two more cards, one for two hundred and fifty dollars and the other one for one thousand, okay? Send the two-hundred-fifty-dollar one to this address. Shit, I don't know her last name. Address it to the children. I mean write the word *children*. I may be asking for you to send to some other of my peeps who are helping me right now. After that, the rest is yours. You got it?"

Charlie stumbled on the other end of the line, not knowing what to say. She loved Sam but knew he used her for whatever he needed her to do outside his prison walls. Sam had even bought her a cute, fluffy white dog that Charlie had named after Sam.

"No one knows about you, Charlie, so you don't have to worry about any of my money you are holding. It's yours, okay? I know you did a lot for me. For the times I yelled at you in the past when I was at Cottonwood, I apologize, Charlie. I have to hang up now, but I'll call you again before my fucking dying ass goes on to the blue yonder, Charlie. Okay?"

Charlie held the receiver tightly to her ear. Tears flowed like a river as she now realized her relationship was all about business with Sam. She had fallen in love with a man who didn't even know how to love a person. Money and heroin were his true loves, as he'd once told her while she was locked up in Cottonwood, serving her short sentence as a man.

Big Sexy returned to Sam's room as he hurriedly deleted Charlie's phone number from her phone. "Did you like listening to the music, Sam?"

Sam smiled. "Yes, I did. Big Sexy, you be checking your mail at the end of the week. There will be a nice surprise for you and your children."

She smiled at Sam as she walked out of his room with her cell phone. "You are something else, Sam Black. I'm leaving your door open because I know Lil Jon is on his way to say good night to you."

"Yeah, he goin' to take me outside for a quick breath of air, okay?"

Big Sexy walked away, shaking her head and saying, "I know what you going to do, Sam."

Lil Jon entered the room with his little sidestep that he always did. "Hey, man, you feel like a ride to the small yard out here?"

"Hell yes. I got us two cigs in my pocket with a couple pieces of bubble gum to back it. Let's fucking blow this Popsicle stand."

Lil Jon wheeled Sam out to the yard, where only two inmates sat. They were sick inmates in for treatment from another prison. Lil Jon lit Sam's cigarette and handed it to him so he could take a drag. "You got it, Sam?"

"Yeah, man, if I just get the taste of this fucking cigarette, that's enough to satisfy my craving. You enjoy yours, Lil Jon." They sat in silence, taking in the flavor of a good Marlboro cigarette.

Sam snickered. "So Big Sexy brought her phone in my room and let me listen to some Luda today. Can you believe that shit? I already got her eatin' out of my fucking hands."

"Man, she care about you. Do you feel that way about me, man? I'm fucking in here watching you die and helping you every day in every way I can. Is that what you fucking think of me, Sam? You got me eating out of your fucking hands?"

"Whoa, whoa, Lil Jon. No way in hell I think that about you! You one of me! These guards in here are for shit. Yes, maybe Big Sexy feeling sad for me, but I'm still a fucking prisoner to her. She still, in the end, got to do her fucking job, and if that hurts me, so be it."

"I'm sorry for blowing up. I just hate watching you every day now. You getting worse, Sam. It's going to hurt me when you die. It's weighing on me right now."

Sam lightly smacked Lil Jon's hand. "I hate that you have to watch me die like this. I hate that my twin has to see me like this too. I never wanted it to be like this, but now look at me. Here I am in purgatory!"

"Is that what you think, Sam?"

"I don't know what I think, Lil Jon. Mr. Williams told me today that I needed to get right with my soul and quit worrying about where I'm going from here. I think he's right. Who the hell knows what happens to us when we die? I think I'll get my soul right before I die, and whatever happens beyond will happen."

"How you going to do that, Sam?"

"I'm going to sit up all my nights I have left, Lil Jon. I'm going to relive my past and ask whoever the fuck cares to accept my apologies. I may not get through it all, but I'm going to do my best and maybe change a few hearts in here before I die." Sam leaned back, looking up at the sky. "Lil Jon, do know the song 'Roll Out' by Ludacris?"

Lil Jon laughed. "Hell yeah, I love that song. You want me to sing it for you, Sam?"

"Fuck yeah, if you know it! I love it too."

Lil Jon stood up and walked around Sam as he rapped like Ludacris, throwing his arms out with emotion on certain words. Lil Jon sounded just like him, to Sam's amazement. Sam chimed in as if he were Lil Jon's backup. The other two inmates joined in with their "umps" and "awws."

After Lil Jon finished, Sam smiled his usual shit-eating grin. "Damn, my boy Lil Jon. That was some good stuff. If I didn't know it was you, I could have mistaken you for Luda."

Sam and Lil Jon headed back to Sam's room. "Don't lay me back," said Sam. "I want to sit on the side of the bed with my feet hanging off like they are now."

"Sam, what happens if you fall? These women in here can't lift you up. They will have to wait until morning for a male guard if you fall on the floor."

"I don't fucking care," said Sam. "My fat ass can just lay there and die."

Lil Jon walked out of Sam's room and looked back at him through the window, hoping Sam would get tired and lean back on his bed. Sam waved for Lil Jon to go back to his own room.

Sure enough, that night, Sam fell onto the floor as he drifted off to sleep. The noise was so loud it woke the whole floor up. Big Sexy and another guard ran to Sam's room. It took them three attempts to get Sam off the floor. He had hit his eye on the tray table leg as he went down. Because of his body's condition, the bleeding would not stop. Big Sexy wrapped his head with gauze to hold the bleeding. She sat with Sam until he drifted back to sleep.

Chapter 31

Joseph knocked on Sam's window, shocked to see Sam's head bandaged like a mummy. Joseph thought maybe Sam had gotten into a fight out in the yard. He automatically thought about informing Seela. "What the hell is on your head, Sam? What happened yesterday?"

"I fell off my bed last night and hit my fucking head."

"You want Seela to see you with that wrapped around your head tomorrow, or you want me to get you a better bandage job done?"

Sam couldn't argue with his suggestion. He didn't want to scare the shit out of Seela.

That Saturday evening, Joseph visited Seela at her grandmother's. He couldn't wait to see her; he'd been thinking all week about their date on Wednesday and about holding her all night on her sofa.

Seela and Chester walked outside to greet him as he pulled up in the long drive. Chester seemed to be as excited as Seela. He walked crookedly but quickly to Joseph's truck.

"Hey!" Chester said sharply. "You see Sam today?"

"As a matter of fact, I did, Chester. He told me to tell you hello."

Chester smiled with his half-broken smile and crossed eyes as he scanned Joseph for answers. Seela walked up to Joseph's truck and put her arm around Chester. "We've been waiting for you, Joseph. I think Chester was just as excited as me to see you!"

"Yep, I was waiting for you to get here. I wanted to tell you I want to see Sam. Yosef, will you take me to see him? I need to see Sam before he dies. I have a question to ask him."

Seela was surprised to hear this from Chester. "It's not that easy to see Sam, honey. They only allow family, Chester. Sam doesn't really want anyone to see him this way."

"I'm his family," said Chester. "I always take care of him when he sick. No one knows how to but me. He tell me everything. I love him, and he loves me, Ms. Seela. I need to see him."

Joseph saw Chester's determination and wanted to save Seela from the heartache. "Hold on, buddy. We will see what we can do. Don't be getting upset, okay? Mr. Joseph here has got pull, so I'll work some magic if you feel you need to see Sam that bad."

"I do," said Chester without hesitation. "Will you take me?"

"I'll see what I can do, Chester, okay?"

"Okay, Yosef. Thank you." Chester held his hand out for a shake.

Joseph grabbed him around the neck and gave him a big hug. "Anything for you, my main man!"

They made their way into Mamaw's house. Mamaw waited patiently at the kitchen table in her electric scooter. Mamaw studied Seela and Joseph. She could see the energy flowing all around them in a great way. She hadn't seen Seela so happy since she'd come back to the island.

Later that evening, after dinner, Seela and Joseph sat out back, holding hands, both wishing Chester's bedtime would arrive soon. Chester sat in an Adirondack chair across from them, making up silly questions to keep them in his conversation and company. Seela's breath would sink with her heart each time Joseph softly ran his fingers across the top of her hand. Their desires were not satiated that evening, as they felt like school kids waiting for alone time that never came. They set another date, eager to devour each other.

Seela watched Joseph's taillights until they disappeared into the darkness. When she opened the back kitchen door, the phone rang. She moved quickly to answer it, as it was almost eleven o'clock. "Hello?" said Seela into the old olive-green rotary phone.

Sam spoke with broken breath. "Seels, it's you. Oh, I'm so glad you answered the phone."

"Sam? How are you calling me? What has happened? Are you all right?"

"No, Seels. I'm not okay. I'm fucking dying. Listen to me. Tomorrow when you come, bring double the cigarettes and bubble gum, okay? Don't worry; Joseph's bringing you in. It will be okay. You got it?"

Seela felt discouraged. "Sam, how am I going to put all of that on me?"

Sam tried to keep calm so no one could see him talking on Big Sexy's phone. "Wear one of Mamaw's bras, Seela. It will be okay. No one will notice."

"How are you calling me, Sam?" Seela looked into the phone as if she could see him.

"You know that crazy Big Sexy, don't you?"

"Yes, Sam."

"She give me her phone to listen to music in my room with her headphones. So I wait until she not paying attention to my dying ass, and I make a few phone calls. I delete them before she get her phone back. Here she come! I gotta go, Sis. See you tomorrow." With that, Sam hung up the phone.

Seela stood still. How could Sam expect her to do all of this? Her heart beat faster as she contemplated smuggling even more items into the prison. Seela immediately grabbed her cell phone. She headed to the backyard to consult with Dee, who advised her to calm the hell down and carefully pack everything in her bra and along her waistline.

"This is what I would do, Seels: drink a tall vodka and orange juice on your way down. That will give you the courage to walk in calmly."

"I didn't think of that Dee. That's exactly what I'm going to do tomorrow."

Seela's fears diminished for the night, as all she could think about was having Joseph's beefy arms around her again soon.

Chapter 32

The next morning, Seela stood in the bathroom, cramming Marlboro cigarettes into her grandmother's bra, which was strapped around her small frame. She stood looking in the mirror, wondering if Joseph would notice her chest. Someone knocked on the door. "Yes? Chester, is that you?"

"Um, yes, Ms. Seela. I need to use the bathroom."

"Come on in. I'm finished in here. I'll go start breakfast for you and Mamaw. Okay?"

As Seela opened the door, Chester smiled brightly, happy to see her face upon waking up. "That sounds good, Ms. Seela. Can we have pancakes and sausage this morning?"

"Sure, Chester, I'll even let you mix the batter!"

Chester hurried into the bathroom so that he could get into the kitchen to help Seela. "I'll wear my apron too!"

Seela walked down the hallway with her huge chest popping out from her shirt. She started the sausage and then went to wake Mamaw. "Good morning, Mamaw. Are you ready to rise and shine with me and Chester?"

Mamaw rolled over toward Seela. Her eyes widened as she saw Seela standing before her. "Well, good morning, Seels. Why your boobs look so big this morning? That was the first thing I saw. I don't think I've ever seen you with boobies." Mamaw laughed as she tried to steady herself. "What that Sam have you bringing in to him today, Seels? I know he used to make your Mama do it. She would have to borrow one of my brassieres."

"That's exactly what he told me to do," said Seela. She rolled her eyes while throwing her hands in the air. "My damn twin knows how to manipulate all of us."

"It's okay, Seela. Sam loves that bubble gum, so it makes me happy to know you getting it to him. To hell with the law. It's damn bubble gum!"

"I know, Mamaw, but I am breaking the law, no matter how we see it. I'm just glad I have Joseph to escort me in."

"Me too," said Mamaw. "I do like that Joseph. You falling for him, aren't you? I see it when the two of you are together."

Seela smiled at her grandmother without saying a word.

Chester appeared at the bedroom door. "Um, Ms. Seela, I think the sausage needs to be turned. I was scared to do it, because Mamaw say I can't cook with grease. It may burn me."

"Yes, you are right, Chester. Let me go see about it." Seela ran down the hallway, past all the photographs that covered the walls from floor to ceiling.

Chester helped Mamaw to the kitchen. He gathered her medicine and applesauce. "Here, Mamaw. I got all your stuff for you."

Mamaw kissed Chester's hand. "You so sweet, honey, remembering all my morning stuff. We can't get this old engine of mine going today until you fuel it with all this garbage they have me taking."

"It's okay, Mamaw. I'll help you," Chester said. "I'll check your sugar for you." Chester looked over at Seela. "Mamaw taught me how to check her sugar and give her a shot. I know how, Ms. Seela." Chester smiled proudly, knowing he could take care of Mamaw if she needed him.

"I'm so proud of you, Chester. I don't like to give Mamaw a shot, so now if she needs someone to help, you can be the one."

While Chester and Mamaw sat at the kitchen table, eating their breakfast, Seela went into the den, where her grandfather's liquor cabinet remained. She opened the doors quietly so that her grandmother wouldn't hear her. She reached in to look for a bottle of vodka. The bottle was so old that the dust was half an inch thick. Seela blew the dust off before opening it. She poured a glass half full of vodka. Then she closed the old cabinet and walked into the kitchen, talking to Chester and Mamaw to keep them distracted while she filled her glass with orange juice.

"So, Chester, what is on your agenda for today while I'm gone to see Sam?"

"Um, I don't know, Ms. Seela." He looked over to Mamaw. "What do you want to do today, Mamaw?"

"How about you do some yard cleaning for me today? I'll observe and help as much as I can?"

"Sure, Mamaw. Um, Ms. Seela, we are going to do yard work today." Chester smiled, showing all of his teeth and raising his eyebrows in excitement. He liked to do whatever anyone wanted him to. He just loved being there with them.

Seela glanced at her watch. "Yikes, I need to get on the road. I'll be home this afternoon, and we will have dinner before I head home. Chester, I'll ask your dad if you can come home with me next week, okay? You may need to see about your dad and Mamaw this week."

"Okay," Chester said with a sad face.

Seela hugged Chester around the neck as she kissed him on the cheek. "I'll see you in a little while, Chester."

Chester stood in the driveway, watching Seela as she sped away. His heart always felt heavy when Seela left him. In such a short time, Chester had fallen in love with Seela in a special way.

Seela turned up Hall and Oates as loudly as she could crank her car stereo. She sang as she drank all the way down to the prison. Dee had been right: Seela felt loose, as if she had no cares in the world. She pulled into the prison parking lot a little too fast, causing her wheels to screech. When Seela stepped out onto the concrete parking lot, she felt as if she were stepping on clouds. "Damn," she whispered. "I'm freaking buzzed as hell. I've got to hold it together for Sam."

Seela walked loosely and quickly to the front gate. There stood a man she had never seen before. "Hi. Are you Ms. Seela Black?"

Seela's heart sank and began to beat in her stomach. All she could think was that somebody knew what she had packed against her body. "Yes, I'm Seela Black." She stayed still, waiting to be arrested.

"Hi. I'm your brother's counselor, Mr. Williams."

Seela sighed with relief. "Is he okay?"

"Yes, he's waiting for you upstairs. I was just leaving, and he told me you were on your way. I thought I would wait and meet Sam Black's twin sister. I'm doing my best to watch after him during his last days." Mr. Williams shook his head. "I have to say, Ms. Black, Sam is some character. He and I have a good relationship, and as he says all the time, I know what time it is with him." Mr. Williams patted Seela on her shoulder. "Go enjoy your visit with Sam. I believe Officer Quinton is on his way down right now to get you."

Seela smiled, thanking Mr. Williams for all he had done for her brother. He waved at Seela as he walked out the heavy metal door. Seela signed her papers and went in with a breeze. The vodka had given her just enough ease for these steps before Joseph opened the door to meet her.

"Good morning, sunshine! You sure are smiling big. You that happy to see me?"

Seela realized she might look a little tipsy. She tried to change her facial expression without Joseph noticing. "Of course I'm happy to see you. There was a strange man I didn't know when I first got here. It startled me for a moment, as I thought you were going to take me up to see Sam. It ended up being Sam's counselor, Mr. Williams. He was a really nice man. He seems to like Sam too."

"Oh yes, Sam's got everyone eating out of his hands in here. He's got some kind of magic for sure."

Seela walked down the hall with no cares in the world. Dee had been right: vodka was the trick for courage. Joseph reached Sam's hallway. "This is where I leave you, Seela. I'll be back at three, okay? You and Sam have a good visit. He's been waiting all week for you." Joseph smiled at Seela. He wanted to tell her he knew what she was bringing in, but he knew he couldn't. Seela looked up at Joseph to take in one more memory of his gorgeous face until she saw him again at three.

Seela stopped at Sam's window before she tapped on the glass. His eyes were closed. His stomach was huge. His shoulders were as small as

Seela's. His feet stuck out from underneath the old, dingy prison sheet, and the bottoms of his feet were oozing with fluid. Her brother could no longer stand on his feet because of the pain. The buzzer went off, and Big Sexy motioned for her to hurry into the room.

"You ain't supposed to be out in the hallway without a guard escort, especially with the crazies we have on this floor today."

Sam saw Seela enter. "I'm so glad to see you! Why you smiling so big, Seels?"

Seela didn't want Sam to know she had been drinking. "Sam, I'm just happy to see you. Can't I smile about that?"

"Sure, Sis. Come over here and give me a hug." As Seela leaned down to hug Sam, he whispered, "Look to my right, and you will see where Lil Jon set up my toboggan over by my commode. Go stand over there, and dump everything you brought in into that hat. He'll come in a minute to mop my floor. He'll set the hat in my locker. You got me, Sis?"

Seela leaned back up to stand straight. She looked over at the toboggan without moving her head. "I see it," she said under her breath. Liquored up, Seela had no fear, and at one point, it seemed thrilling to be sneaking cigarettes and bubble gum into Sam's toboggan. Seela walked over to Sam's commode as if she wanted to flush it for him. When she reached for the handle, she dumped the cigarettes into Sam's toboggan. Ten ziplock bags held two packs each. Sam watched the guards and nurses through the window to ensure they weren't paying attention.

"It's okay, Seels. Go ahead—get the rest out of your pants. These fucking shit-for-nothing guards aren't paying attention to us. They all wrapped up watching goddamn football play-offs."

She finished her duty and sat down in the cold metal chair that awaited her every Sunday. "How was this week, Sam? Anything happen you want to tell me about? Why is your head bandaged like that?"

"I fucking fell off my bed this week, Seels. I can't lie down at night. I feel like I'm fucking drowning with all this fluid around my lungs. Goddamn, I think they going to let me fucking drown in my own fluid if the morphine doesn't get me first."

"I thought you haven't been taking the pills?"

"I have to take some, Seels. I'm in fucking pain! I just don't take fucking four a day like they want me to. Soon, if I don't die, I'm sure they'll just start shooting me up with it. What a fucking way for me to die—getting high like I have always loved!"

Seela's eyes filled with tears in the manic haze of being intoxicated. She no longer felt accomplished at all she had smuggled in. She wiped her face before Sam saw her. "Sam, I forgot to tell you. I have the CDs you wanted me to bring to you." She leaned forward to reach for them in the back of her pants.

"Be careful, Sis. Let me see who's looking first."

"Oh!" she exclaimed. She had gotten so comfortable that she had almost forgotten about the guards watching them. "How are you going to play them, Sam?"

"You see that room over there, where some of the inmates are sitting, watching the ball game? We have a CD-DVD player over there, and once a week, they play a movie for us. I plan on sitting over there with Big Sexy's headphones, listening to these CDs. She'll do it because I've greased her wallet, you see. She got about four kids, Seels. She don't make jack shit working in here. Yesterday she got two hundred fifty dollars in the mail from me. She going to get more as long as she help me be as comfortable as I can."

"Sam, how in the world did you send her money? I don't understand."

"You don't need to understand, Seels. It's my bizness in here. You got it? You just bring my goodies, Seels. What I make in here before I die, I'm giving back to the ones who need it and the ones who help me. You see? I got to clean up my soul, and in this short time, there ain't no way in hell it's possible, but I'm going to do my damnedest to make my soul feel right before I die. I got some stuff I need to clear up and some fucking shit I need to share with you, Sis."

Seela couldn't read between his crazy lines, especially with the buzz she had going on at that point.

"First, Seels, let's get this money situation handled before my brain gets way out there. My ammonia levels are already rising. It will soon take over my brain, and I won't be able to function, so I need to get all my bizness taken care of. You listening? You look like you are in a daze, Seels."

Seela shook her head as if to clear the fog. "I am, Sam. I hate hearing all of this. I feel like I still need to fight to get you home so that when you do go through this horrible part before you die, you are not alone but with your family. It doesn't matter to us; you would never be a burden."

Sam shook his head. "I wish I could come home to you guys, but Mom and Mamaw couldn't handle it."

"I don't care what you say, Sam. I'm contacting Johnny to see if he knows an attorney on the island who can help me get you home. This is crazy, you dying here like this!"

"When is the last time you saw Johnny? Was it when you left the island seventeen years ago, pregnant with his child?"

Seela sat in shock. She hadn't heard those words since the day she'd given their baby up for adoption.

Chapter 33

"Sam, I can't believe those words just came out of your mouth! How did you know? You were locked up when all of that happened. I didn't think anyone knew but Johnny," said Seela, feeling her face on fire and her hands shaking.

Sam stared at Seela and rolled his eyes. "Well, surprise! I knew the day that baby was delivered, Seels. Have you forgotten who I am? Your fuckin' twin! You may not know it, but all my life, I've watched over you, Seela. You the only thing that mattered to me in life. That's why I stayed away from your home—I knew I was nothing but a junkie and didn't want to hurt your heart with my fucking junkie-ass self."

Seela sat in disbelief. She had thought all these years that her secret was safe with her ex-boyfriend. All the shame and guilt she'd felt while driving away from the facility where she'd given birth flooded back.

"Seela, don't faint on me. I can't pick your ass up. Even when I'm locked up, I got people working for me on the outside. You see, this is how it's always worked for me. I always start a bizness in here, be it gambling on sports or hustling—whatever I can convince these guards to bring in to me. I give them a cut, and we in bizness. That give me money to do my bizness in the outside world."

Seela felt as if she were going to vomit up the booze she had consumed. She didn't want to talk about her past anymore. "Hey, Sam, I was listening to the Hall and Oates CD on the way down here. I forgot how much I love them. What's your favorite song of theirs?"

"I love 'Sara Smile,'" Sam said. Seela began to sing it, and Sam chimed in. They sang for a couple of minutes before Sam stopped.

"Damn, Seels, you sound good." Sam formed the nicest smile she had seen on him yet. It was almost angelic. "You sing to Joseph, Seela? You know, I think that man falling hard for you. I never seen Joseph look the way he do when I mention your name. You know, he a great guy, and I wouldn't mind you dating him."

"Listen to you, Sam Black. You are acting as if you are my father and not my twin! I'll have you know I think he is a very nice man. As a matter of fact, we are all smitten with Joseph. Even Chester!"

"Chester?" replied Sam, raising an eyebrow. "He been hanging out with you a lot?"

"Yes, I feel so close to him already. His mother died when he was very young. I think he misses that attention from a woman. I feel so bad for him sometimes, Sam."

"Don't you worry about Chubby Chester. He know nothing but love, Seels. Even the way his life been, he happy no matter what. That's the great thing about Down's syndrome. After I was running hard in a heroin house, Chubs would take care of me when I was sick and throwing my guts out for days. As soon as I got better, off I went again, leaving him sad. But as soon as I came back for help, that boy was waiting with nothing but love to help me." Sam smiled, staring off into space. "Nothing but love! Chester still driving his three-wheeler I got him?"

Seela shook her head and giggled, thinking of Chester wheeling up dust.

"Every time I left him, be it back to the big house or just to run the streets, I would give him a gift. I always made it big too, Seels. That boy call me Uncle Sam!"

"I know," said Seela. "He truly believes you are his uncle. He showed me a picture in the gas station that you gave him of Uncle Sam saying, 'I want you!' He thinks because that sign has the words *Uncle Sam* written on it that you are his uncle. I tried to explain to him, but it was too hard, so I don't care at this point if Chester believes whatever he wants."

Sam agreed. "Oh, and speaking of Chubs, how about you take one of those burritos over on my tray and get Big Sexy to heat it up for me?

All this talking has got me hungry. Whatever you do, walk straight out to Big Sexy. Don't turn and look back at me. You hear?"

Seela nodded and proceeded out Sam's door. As she stepped toward the station, she heard a man screaming and knocking on the glass wall of his room. She turned, froze at the sight, and then screamed, dropping Sam's burrito to the floor. The man was standing on his bed with his pants down, slamming his gigantic penis back and forth against the glass wall.

Startled by Seela's screams, Sam tried to wheel himself out of his tiny prison room. His wheelchair got stuck against his bed rail, and he didn't have the strength to dislodge it. "I'm coming to shove that black dick of yours down your goddamn throat! Then I'm going to watch it come out your black ass and wrap it around your fucking neck and hang you. You hear me, you goddamn fucking animal? How dare you do this to my twin? I'm fucking going to kill you, you crazy motherfucker."

Big Sexy ran over with a folding white screen and placed it in front of the inmate's glass wall. She grabbed Seela, pushed her into Sam's room, and shut Sam's door before he could get out. Sam's face was bloodred as he continued to yell at the exposed inmate. "You better be removed from this floor, or you won't make it through the night, motherfucker! You done messed with the wrong fuckin' person."

Seela tried to calm Sam down, but nothing seemed to work.

Big Sexy returned with Sam's heated food and a dose of morphine. "Calm down, Sam. I'm having the crazy guy put in the hole where he came from. He ain't faking us out anymore. There ain't nothing wrong with that man but crazy!"

Sam soon relaxed. Seela sat with him for another hour while both of them shared more stories of the afterlife and discussed whether anyone really knew what was beyond life on earth. At exactly three o'clock, Joseph tapped on Sam's window while opening the door with his large brass key ring. He popped his head in. "Are you ready, Ms. Black? I'm here to escort you out to your car. I hear we had a commotion today."

"A fucking nightmare for my twin to see is more like it, Joseph! If they hadn't put him in the hole, my dying ass would be over choking his black ass tonight."

Seela stood up and gave Sam a kiss. She lingered, looking down at him.

"Go on, Seels," he said. "Get on out of here before I cry. I can't be doing that in here. The king doesn't cry." Sam winked at Seela with tears in his eyes.

Seela wiped his eyes and caressed his wrinkled, tired face. "Yes, kings don't cry, do they? Leave that to me, Sam, your little princess."

Sam yelled to Joseph, "Get my twin a tissue! She getting all sappy on me over here."

As Joseph walked Seela out, he apologized for what she had encountered.

"It's okay. I think it was more traumatizing for Sam to know what I was shown," Seela said. "I'll be okay, but please check on Sam after I leave."

Only minutes after watching Seela leave the grounds safely, Joseph spotted Sam in the prison yard with his toboggan covering his ears and a blanket across his lap. Joseph shook his head at the sight of Sam already out in the yard in his wheelchair, sharing a cigarette with another inmate.

Joseph headed down to Mr. Williams's office and knocked. "Hey, man, you in?"

"Yes, come on in, Officer Quinton," Mr. Williams called out.

Joseph entered and sat down in the chair, facing Mr. Williams. "That Sam Black never ceases to amaze me. He's in his room near death with Seela before she leaves. As soon as she's gone, I see him in the yard, hustling." They both sighed. "I don't know what all he had Seela bringing in today. I'm thinking just like last time, Marlboros and bubble gum."

"You think she knows you know she's bringing all that shit in, Joseph?"

"Hell no! I can't let her know. I don't even say anything to Sam. It's not like he's dealing drugs in the yard. If hustling a few cigarettes makes him happy before he dies, so be it. I need him alive a little while longer. I need a few more nuggets of information from him. These private prisons are so corrupt. It can be a big money-making business and is going to get out of hand with all these criminals. We will end up with the prisoners taking over if it continues to get worse. Sam has all the information I need. I have to talk to him in morning times, though. I can tell his ammonia level starts peaking after four or so in the afternoon. It can get crazy with him after that. I'm checking on out of here and will see you tomorrow. I've got a dinner to get to."

Joseph hugged Chester upon arriving at Mamaw's house that evening. "Chester, how are you today? You get some yard work done for Mamaw?"

Chester pointed over to an area covered with a pile of old brush. It had been burned down to nothing but smoking ash. "This week, I'm going to make that a flower garden. That's what Mamaw says she wants. She said she wants to put Edward's and Sam's ashes there. I'm going to help her make them tombstones too!" Chester exclaimed proudly.

Joseph patted Chester on the shoulder as they walked into the house. "I think that will be spectacular, Chester. I know it will be beautiful when you are done."

"Hey there, Joseph!" Mamaw beamed as if she had seen a movie star walk through her back kitchen door. Chester stood beside Joseph, grinning as a lottery winner would. "Did you tell Joseph about our garden we are going to make?" Mamaw said.

"Yes, ma'am, I did," said Chester. "I told Yosef we are going to make them tombstones too."

Seela looked confused about what they were talking about. "What tombstones?"

Mamaw paused and chose her words. "Chester and I cleaned out all the weeds and old brush that was piled out there in the side front yard. We are going to get some dirt and mulch next. Then we going to make us a gorgeous flower garden that we can sit in. Maybe have a bird feeder or two. We going to make a sanctuary for your granddaddy and

Sam, Seels. We can spread some of their ashes there together so we can visit them anytime we want."

Seela looked back and forth from Mamaw to Chester with a mixture of emotions. They almost seemed happy to talk about death and tombstones, which infuriated her. Then she realized they were just bonding, and these were imminent circumstances; her brother's death was unstoppable. No one could do anything at that point but plant a resting place on the grounds of people who loved Sam. Seela walked over to her grandmother and knelt beside her. "Mamaw, that sounds like a great idea. I know Mavvie will like it too. Have you guys seen her today?"

Mamaw replied, "I thought I saw her go down to your mom's place today."

Seela sighed. "I'm going to try to talk to her before I leave for home."

"Cat and Mavvie been talking lately," Mamaw told Seela like an informant. "I see Mavvie going in her house. When your mom does come out, it's brief. She always seems to be painting or cleaning her brushes. I don't know what your crazy mom up to, Seels."

Chester spoke up. "I saw her this week." Seela was surprised that Chester hadn't told her.

"Yep, I did."

"Did you go down to her house?" asked Seela.

"No, ma'am. She talked out her window to me when I was working in the yard."

"What did she say to you, Chester?" asked Seela.

"She asked if I was Chester from the gas station, and I told her yes, ma'am, I was. I told her I met you at my pa's station, and you let me come visit you here with Mamaw."

"What else did she say, Chester?"

"Um, I don't remember. She didn't talk long to me before she closed her window."

Sensing Chester's discomfort, Seela dropped the subject. Besides, she wanted nothing more than to be held by Joseph after the whammy that Sam had dropped on her. She couldn't get over how much power Sam held while dying, even while helplessly locked away all this time. And Sam knew about her giving a baby up for adoption. It was too much.

Seela and Joseph enjoyed their time together, holding on to every second that evening. Neither of them wanted the evening to end. Seela asked Joseph to follow Chester off the island back to his house. They were all in the driveway, exchanging good-byes, when Mavvie ran from Cat's house.

"Hi, Mavvie," Seela said. "I wondered where you have been. I haven't seen much of you this weekend."

"How is Sam?" asked Mavvie.

"He's just getting worse, Mavvie. It's so sad to watch him die like this."

Mavvie squeezed her hands. "You will be okay, Seels. You have a lot to go through these next few weeks. You be strong, and I promise you there is going to be the brightest light ever after all of this is over. Your life will be wonderful. I promise. This seems so horrible right now, but I tell you, once you go through this small bit of misery, big love will come after." Mavvie threw her hands in the air. "It's the yin of the yang, my sweets! Now, go say good-bye to your mom before she goes to bed."

Seela watched Chester drive off with Joseph close behind before focusing on Catherine.

Chapter 34

Seela skipped down to her mom's cottage surrounded by the strong scent of turpentine. Glass mason jars were spread over the porch, holding a variety of paintbrushes and soaking the oil paints Cat had been using on her canvases. Cat's music played loudly. It sounded as if she were listening to Creedence Clearwater Revival. Seela knocked on her mother's heavy wooden door. Cat did not hear Seela's knock. Seela knocked harder.

Cat stopped painting and sat still. She thought she had heard something, but the music and her painting were the only things in her head.

Seela spoke up. "Mom, I know you are in there, and I need you to talk to me. Please, will you at least come outside for a minute? It's about Sam."

Cat set the brush on her palette while turning her antiquated boom box off. Cat opened the door, revealing herself to Seela. "What is going on with Sam? He hasn't died, has he?"

"No, Mom, he hasn't, but it won't be long. He wants to talk to you, so tomorrow listen for his call. He says it's important that he speak with you. Do you know what's so important, Mom? I know he wants to talk to you, but there seems to be more to it. He seems like he's worried about something else. Do you know what that could be?"

"Seels, you just keep to your business of what you have to do. Your brother got too much for you to ever understand." Cat reached her head out a little farther for Seela to see. "Seela, I'm glad you are here and seeing about Sam. I've been so sick with my illness that I don't know what would have happened to him if you had not come. I know Sam is happy having you with him in his last dying days. You take care of him the best you can, Seels. He needs his twin."

Seela's heart sank at her mother's deadpan voice. Cat's heart seemed cold, as if she knew everything that was going to happen.

"Mom, can we at least sit and talk? I've been here for a while now, and you haven't even given me a chance to explain why I left the island eighteen years ago. It wasn't you; it was where my life was headed, and I needed to get away from Johnny. He broke my heart, Mama. I felt like Sam and I were branded as half breeds, and I wasn't going to live my life in judgment on this island. Plus, Sam was always off the chart with his addiction already. I just couldn't handle it. Can't you understand what I had to do?" Tears welled in Seela's eyes.

"I do understand what you are saying, Seela. I will see you tomorrow, okay?" With that, Cat said good night to Seela and shut her door. Seela stood in amazement at how brief the encounter had been. She heard Cat turn the boom box back on to the highest volume that she could. Taking in the music that Sam loved, Seela slumped down in a chair on her mother's porch. She cried uncontrollably, wanting more time with her mother and brother.

Meanwhile, Sam had another rough night. Fluid smothered his lungs, and his stomach ballooned even bigger overnight. He couldn't lie down, so he sat sideways on the side of his bed. He figured out how to raise the top part and leaned against it. Lil Jon had placed pillows and foam all around, so if Sam fell, he would not hit the hard floor. Big Sexy appeared at Sam's window. She mouthed to Sam that she would bring him some music to listen to soon. Feeling horrible, Sam raised his hand, trying to acknowledge her. Some days were better for Sam than others. This was not a good day. His breath was short, and he could feel more pain in his abdomen.

Big Sexy returned with her cell phone. She tried to position Sam so that he could lie there with the headphones in his ears with his toboggan on so no one would notice. She slid the phone under the sheet beside Sam's swollen body.

"What else you need, honey? You lookin' pretty pale right now, especially next to my black ass!"

Sam chuckled slightly. "Yeah, Big Sexy, go get me a shot of morphine. I've got bad pain in my stomach area. It's my fucking liver! This shit food I've been putting in my fucking body!"

Big Sexy returned quickly with a syringe full for Sam. "Turn over a little, and let me pop you in the butt, Sam. This will take that pain right away."

Sam could barely turn his big body. He was now like a beached whale stuck in the sand. Big Sexy helped by putting her body against his to hold him over so she could administer the shot. "There you go, Sam. Listen to the music, and you'll probably go to la-la land. I'm locking you in for now. No going out of here today. They say there was a gang murder last night on H wing."

Sam gasped. "What? H Wing?" He looked puzzled because he knew that was next to AB's wing. "You know anything about it? If you don't, then find out, Big Sexy! I got you—you know Green Dot cards coming your way. Go find out what's happening. Damn, now that you done shot me up, my ass is going to candy land, and shit like this fucking happening. You should have told me first!"

She shook her head. "I ain't watching your sick, weak, dying ass fret about somebody else's stupid shit up in here. Listen to the music playlist I made you. I think you'll enjoy it."

"Okay, okay, Big Sexy. Lock my fucking door, and get on out of here then. Let me listen before I pass out." As soon as Big Sexy stepped out of the room, he stopped the music and dialed his mom's number.

Cat's phone rang, showing a blocked number. She almost didn't answer but then picked up, saying nothing.

Sam's voice cracked. "Mom, that you?"

Cat smiled into her phone upon hearing Sam's broken voice. "Sam, I'm so glad I answered the phone. I almost didn't, seeing it was a blocked caller."

"I don't have long to talk, Mom. I love ya, Mom. You know what time it is for me, don't you? I'm going to check on out of this tortured world I've struggled in all my life. It's time. I've done some bad shit, and I've been asking for forgiveness these past few weeks. I've been going back on all my crap. I feel like I'm in fucking purgatory right now." Sam looked sad as tears formed. "I got it, Mom. My soul going to be pure when I leave this fucking world. You hear me? There will be no more pain for me. The only thing I'm leaving here with is my soul. I'm getting it right. I'll call you tomorrow same time, okay? I can't talk anymore. Wait—you still painting?"

Despite Cat being such a cold-spirited woman, Sam could crush her emotions with just the sound of his voice, which spelled death. She tried to reply clearly. "Yes, Sam. I've done quite a few. It's the only thing that keeps my mind off of everything—my cancer and now you. I didn't ever think we both would be dying at the same time."

"Have you told Mamaw about your illness, Mom?"

"They all know little, and that's the way I'm keeping it. You don't say anything either, Sam. You hear me?"

Sam stared ahead and paused before saying, "We straight, Mom. We partners, you and me. I love you."

"I love you too, Sam. Yes, we partners. I've been taping all your money I got where you told me. Charlie sent what she had too."

"Good, good. I'll call you tomorrow, so answer when you see a blocked caller, okay?"

"I'll be waiting, Sam. I love you." They both hung up.

Sam contemplated whom to call before Big Sexy returned. He dialed Charlie's number. It rang four times before she answered softly.

"Charlie, it's Sam."

Charlie perked up at hearing Sam's voice. "Hey, Sam! How are you calling now? Did you get a phone in there too?"

"No, I didn't get a damn phone. I'm fucking dying, Charlie. Now, listen. I got this nurse who lets me listen to music on her iPhone. She doesn't know I'm calling you; that's why the number comes up as a blocked caller. I know I was insensitive the last time I called you. My mind ain't right anymore with all this ammonia going to my brain and the morphine they give me. I want to tell you thank you for all you did for me out there, running a lot of my bizness. I tried to take good care of you while you helped me. I know it's hard hearing I'm fucking dying. I can't believe it either, but it's getting ready to happen." Sam paused to muster more breath before speaking again. "I tell you one goddamn thing: it's going to be when I'm ready, Charlie."

Charlie looked into her phone with a heartbroken face. Sam was ripping her heart out, and he couldn't have cared less. His emotions were matter-of-fact.

"Charlie, you still there?"

"Yes, Sam. I'm here." Since the last call, she had vowed to finish Sam's business until he passed, and that would be the end of this crazy world she had been in with him since she'd met him in the awful privately owned prison. "Sam, whatever you want me to do, you just tell me, okay?"

"That's just what I wanted to hear, Charlie. I got a few more things I need you to do, but don't worry; you'll get enough money to pay your bills for a couple months until you find a job. We good?"

"Yes, Sam. Whatever I can do," Charlie answered as if she were Sam's soldier. He had made her home beautiful with elegant furnishings. She had every designer purse constructed since meeting Sam Black two years ago. Would her world end when Sam died? She wondered.

"I gotta run. I'll call you tomorrow with what I'll be sending to you this week, okay?"

"All right, Sam. I'll be here." Charlie sat in astonishment, thinking about the past two years of love she'd given Sam—all for nothing except the material things she now had. She had aspired to share her home with Sam someday, but instead, she would never see him again. The realization crushed her heart into pieces. She didn't know if anyone would accept her, as Sam Black had.

Sam erased his calls from Big Sexy's phone and toggled to the playlist. The song "Let It Be" began to play. Sam sang out loud as he felt the words penetrate his brain. Tears rolled down his face as he felt the power of every word. Sam whispered, "Speaking words of wisdom, let it be."

Chapter 35

Lil Jon walked up to Sam's window with his mop and stood watching Sam sing and cry. Lil Jon asked Big Sexy what kind of music she had Sam listening to.

She smiled. "The kind that touches his heart, Lil Jon. Go see about him for me, okay? I'm backed up here, giving meds out right now."

Lil Jon tapped on Sam's window while Big Sexy buzzed him in. Sam pulled the earbuds out and said, "Hey, my main man. I've been waiting on you. What the hell is going on out there? Big Sexy say there was a gang murder in H wing."

Lil Jon mopped all around Sam's bed as he talked. "Yeah, man, it's bad. We on lockdown right now. No one allowed out of their rooms except for chow time. It's been hell out there. Thank hell I'm on my way out of here and they got me on this work detail. Otherwise, my little fucking black ass be holed up in my room too. That shit make my brain go crazy, Sam. I ain't good at being locked in small rooms."

Sam snickered. "Well, look here at my fucking ass, dying in a locked-up room. I guess you couldn't handle this either, huh? You know, after being shanked and not safe out in hall wings with other caged crazy inmates, I feel kind of safe being locked in here, Lil Jon. Ain't no fucking crazy-ass inmate getting me now.

"We going to have to reroute on these Marlboros then, Lil Jon. The way I see it, we got five packs of twenty cigs. We on lockdown, so the price going double. That means four hundred dollars a pack, Lil Jon. That mean we keep a pack, we sell four packs, and we'll make sixteen hundred dollars. Goddamn straight, Lil Jon. Let's holler for our dollars we about to make."

Lil Jon laughed in amazement that Sam, lying there dying in pain, wanted to wheel and deal. "How we going to do that with everyone on lockdown, Sam?"

Sam smiled his Lucifer grin. "I'm going to tell you how it's done when we have lockdowns, Lil Jon. You got a key to the janitorial supply room, don't you?" Lil Jon nodded. "This is what you going to do. Get a word to King AB, and tell him we got Marls for twenty dollars apiece. He'll get the word out. These caged vultures, after a few days of lockdown, will be dying for a cig. They can smoke on one for days, Lil Jon. They'll get their women, wives, or moms to send the fucking money for that one fucking Marlboro. I've been there, Lil Jon, so I fucking know how good one drag is when you been holed up for days with four fucking walls caving in on you. Go into the janitor's room, and you get this deodorizer in a white jar. It's this thick blue jelly-looking stuff. It will eat any odor up in one fucking second—that shit so powerful. You bring me a jar in here, okay? I'm going to try it out first before you give it out. Let AB know about it. Let's get this store opened up, Lil Jon."

Lil Jon mopped his way out of Sam's room and headed to the H wing. He passed a janitorial door and popped his head in. He quickly tried to assess where the deodorizer might be located. He zoomed in on what seemed to be it. He grabbed a couple jars and shoved them into his jumper pockets.

When Lil Jon mopped into wing H, he saw AB sitting on a table in the common area. The hallways in this wing looked like chicken-wire cages lined in a row and stacked high on top of each other.

"Hey, man, how come you not in your room?" Lil Jon said.

AB looked over at Lil Jon. "I got word you were coming to see me, Lil Jon."

Lil Jon looked mystified. He didn't know how AB could have gotten this information so quickly or who had let him be outside of his room. Lil Jon didn't know that Sam had instructed Big Sexy to radio the guard in H wing and get word to AB that Lil Jon was mopping down to him.

"Sam hasn't explained to you what king is in here, Lil Jon? After all, Sam was king in the last place, and from what I hear, a big one," said AB. "You get special privileges when you king of the caged animals. I got pull with the guards here. I make their jobs easier, Lil Jon. You got that?"

Lil Jon agreed. This world was new to him, and he couldn't wait to be free from it.

"So what news you got for me? What's ole Sam up to over there besides dying?" AB asked.

Lil Jon mopped while he talked nervously. "He want me to let you know he got Marls for twenty dollars apiece. He say you know these guys will pay it if lockdown stay on through this week. He says he'll even give the blue shot you put in your toilet that eats the smoke while you smoke it in your room. He's going to try it this afternoon to see how it work."

AB contemplated what he was hearing while looking down the hallway for anyone coming their way. "What's in it for me, Lil Squirt?"

"Sam says he'll split three ways our profit. We got one pack we will split, and then we will sell the other four."

"Oh," said AB. "We got that many?" His brain started making calculations. "You tell Sam we in bizness. Let's do it. Lil Jon, you cool with me. Listen here: you deal only with me. You don't talk to any one of these blood-sucking prisoners in here, no matter what they say to you. You hear me? You listen to Sam. You got it?" AB popped Lil Jon on his shoulder. "This floor here is full of murderers. They don't care about their life, let alone yours."

"I got you, AB. I don't even like coming in here. Can't we meet out in the hall somewhere? Get back to Sam with your order count and where you want to meet me. I'll see you then." Lil Jon threw his hand up for a high shake. "I gotta get back to my wing."

Lil Jon headed back down the quiet hallway to his wing. He decided that before bed count, he would swing back by to see Sam one last time before he was locked in for the night. When he reached Sam's room, he saw that Sam had fallen asleep while sitting sideways. His mouth was open, and his lips were cracked and shriveled up like a raisin. Lil Jon stood for a second before getting Big Sexy to buzz him in. He needed to see Sam's chest move. He feared that he might have died already. Then Sam took a deep breath and coughed. Lil Jon's heart skipped in excitement at seeing Sam move. Big Sexy buzzed Lil Jon in. Sam woke to the sound of the metal door opening.

"Sam, something told me to come check on you. Let me get you set up here. We got to get this figured out. You going to fall on the floor again. Big Sexy's the only one here tonight, and with us on lockdown, your ass would just have to lay there."

Sam was drugged with his nightly cocktail. He could hardly move. It was like his days of being strung out on heroin. He whispered, "I can't fucking move, you little shit. I'm flying so fucking high right now. Why you have to bring your little fucking black ass in here and interrupt my high? I was fishing. I was about to catch the biggest fucking catfish you ever seen, Lil Jon. It would have fed me and you for days."

"Yeah," said Lil Jon. "When you probably tried to reel it in, you would be falling off this fucking bed, Sam. It's a good thing I came in. I got an idea. I'll be right back."

Lil Jon ran to the utility closet. He remembered seeing an old chair in the closet where he'd found the blue stuff, and it had seemed to be like a wheelchair. Sure enough, when he opened the closet, he found an old wooden chair that reclined. It had a high back and a headrest. He wheeled it back to Sam's room.

Big Sexy joined them. "What in the hell do you have here, Lil Jon? Better yet, where did you get it?"

"I found it in a closet when I was looking for floor cleaner this week. It's going to be Sam's bed now, okay? Help me get him in it."

Sam mumbled incoherently. That afternoon, out of boredom, along with the morphine, Sam had taken a few pills from the stash of pills he had collected. Lil Jon took the foam padding from under Sam's legs and put it in the seat of the chair. He placed a towel over the ensemble and put a pillow on the back to make it soft for Sam's broken skin. He then covered the chair with a clean white sheet he had brought from the laundry room. The chair looked nice and neat for Sam to get in.

Big Sexy and Lil Jon lifted at least three times before they could get Sam's limp body under theirs. They turned and plopped him back down like a dead person. Sam's head hit the padded headrest, which Lil Jon had wrapped with hand towels. Sam moved to get comfortable in the chair with his glazed eyes looking out to his side. He threw his hand out to Lil Jon. Sam's legs were wrapped with gauze to the tops of his knees to keep the fluid from seeping out everywhere. His calves ached terribly, so Lil Jon propped pillows under each leg. They left Sam to fall back to sleep in his medicated high.

Big Sexy and Lil John exited the room, feeling better about the rest of the night. Lil Jon glanced back at Sam through the glass window. He looked as if he were sitting on a puffy marshmallow. It made Lil Jon feel better that he had made Sam's life a little more comfortable. Sam fell into a deep sleep in the comfort of his new death-row wheelchair. His dreams went deep into the memory of when he'd first met Charlie. He'd saved her from being raped by the crazy caged inmates on a daily basis. Charlie was in love with a man who would never be with her as a couple, but her dreams of Sam satisfied her enough. Once she'd been released, she'd vowed to do whatever Sam wanted to repay him for saving her during her incarceration in a men's prison as a transgender woman.

The next morning, Lil Jon skipped as quickly as he could to Sam's room with his mop. Sam was sitting up, as if he had been waiting for Lil Jon for hours. "Hey, my main man! I feel so good this morning. Can you believe I actually fucking slept some last night? I talked Big Sexy into letting you take me in the shower this morning. I told her I sweated so bad last night on my roller-coaster high I was on. Whew. It was a good one, I have to say."

Lil Jon laughed. "Yeah, man. You were flying fucking high for sure. It's a good thing you're locked up in this room when you like that. You couldn't fend for yourself for nothing in the world. Did you catch us any catfish? I think I dreamed about eating them last night."

"Damn, Lil Jon, I caught so many fucking fish last night. Even some fine, voluptuously shaped two-legged fish. Sometimes dreaming is all you got, and it can be the best you have."

"You got that straight, Sam. That's all I got right now until I get out of here. I got dreams! I can't wait to look out a clear window and see bright sunshine in the morning."

"Boy, you stay on the straight and narrow when you get out of here. You hear me? No reason you should ever step back in one of these pits of fire-burning hell, looking out a blurred glass window, ever again," barked Sam.

Lil Jon stood with his hands in his pockets, as if Sam were scolding him. "I'm straight, Sam. I promise with my word I ain't coming back. I'm going to walk the straight line and see about my baby boy."

Lil Jon realized he had the blue jelly Sam wanted. He pulled it out of his pocket and quickly dropped it into Sam's trash can. "There's your blue stuff you wanted, Sam. Did you hear from AB how much he want today and where I'm supposed to meet him? I told him I didn't want to go in H wing. It's freaky in there."

Sam laughed. "I'm glad you afraid, Lil Jon. That show me you don't want this life."

"Hell no, I don't," said Lil Jon.

"When we go to the shower, AB is getting an escort there too. So don't you worry. You aren't touching anything. You just be my chauffer today. I got to protect your little tattooed ass. I'm going to give him all of these fucking Marlboros and trust he'll pay me at the end of the week. He and I on the same team, so he's good for his word."

Lil Jon looked confused. "If you don't mind me asking, Sam, how does AB pay you if y'all locked up in here?"

Sam chuckled at Lil Jon's lack of experience in the prison world. "I'll tell you a little story on how our mafia world works in here, my son. First of all, there is never any cash passed around in here. It's all done with bank cards and Green Dot cards, reloadable credit cards. All we do is swap numbers back and forth. We then transfer off the cards to secret checking accounts on the outside. You just always have to have someone you can trust on the outside to manage your money. We kings in here run a bizness, you see, with guards and sometimes wardens. It's according to how corrupt a prison it is. It's been my world my whole life. It gives me a rush, gambling with whatever I got in here, even my life."

Lil Jon now understood the process, knowing that all he wanted was his cut on a Green Dot card. The thought of securing a little money for when he got out comforted him. He was forever thankful to have met Sam, his own Robin Hood. He felt strong love for Sam.

"Okay, let's get this show on the road. I'm loaded with the Marls. Give me a jar of that jelly. I'll give it to AB too. He can divvy that shit out. Can you push this chair, Lil Jon? It sure is some goddamn heavy old wood. Where in the hell did you find it? It looks like a killing chair. Don't you think?"

"I didn't even think about that. You think that what it is? Holy fucking shit! I didn't mean to put you in a death-row chair."

They laughed nervously as Lil Jon pushed Sam out of his room. Sam waved to Big Sexy. He motioned that he would be back, pointing to his watch. He then pointed to his ears to let her know he wanted her phone later to listen to music. Big Sexy waved at them, placing her fingers to her mouth for them to be quiet down the hall. Sam gave her the bird, chuckling.

"Fuck everyone in here. Fuck the killers too for getting us on this fucking lockdown. I tell you one thing: I need some fresh air, and if I don't get it soon, I feel like it won't be long before my dying ass checks on out. I'm going to be one pissed motherfucker if they don't let my twin in to see me this Sunday. I'm calling today and having her bring in eight packs this Sunday. Think about how much money that is. Hell, I may keep the price at twenty dollars a Marlboro. We goin' to get them hooked this week on the flava! Who wants that shitty bugle, when you can have a tasty Marlboro? I heard from AB they be unrolling them and making four tiny cigs out of one. We got 'em now, son! Make us holler for our dollars!" Sam held his hand up and back for Lil Jon to slap.

"You do the math yet, Lil Jon? That's fucking twenty-eight hundred dollars for us to split. You need to find someone you trust on the outside to set up a bank card or Green Dot card. Get them to give you the number on the card, and I'll get my girl to load your money on your card.

Then you transfer it off as soon as it gets on there to another account no one knows. You got me? I'm getting ready to make you a little bank to have for when you get out, son. You always remember Uncle Sam."

Lil Jon smiled as he reached in front of Sam for the bathroom door. "I like that. Uncle Sam. You do feel like my unc for sure."

When Lil Jon wheeled Sam into the shower, AB was already standing in a stall.

"Is that you, my brother?" asked Sam.

"Hell yeah." AB opened the stall door and stepped out. "Well, you looking a lot better today, Sam. Where did you get the death-row chair? Man, I have to say, with all that padding and white shit wrapped around it, it look pretty damned comfortable. You like it?"

"Hell yeah," said Sam. "My boy here dug it out of a closet last night and wrapped it up, and I finally got a few hours of sleep last night, along with a hellacious high."

The three men laughed together. "Yeah, after seeing how high he was last night, it made me feel good knowing he is locked up tight in his room. Somebody could rob you blind, and you wouldn't care when you like that," said Lil Jon.

"Let 'em rob my fucking ass and kill it too. At least I'll go out flying fucking high, just the way I like it!" Sam pulled the four bags of cigarettes out and tossed them to AB. "Here is the blue jelly too. Just give each guy a dollop of this shit to keep in his locker. You drop a fucking tiny bit—and I mean tiny piece—in the toilet before you light your cig, and it will eat that fucking smoke right up. Now, tell them they have to blow into the fucking commode."

AB reached down and did a shoulder shake with Sam. "I got you. We straight until Friday, right? I'll get you numbers. You can transfer off your and Lil Squirt's money. You know, I got a phone if you want to take it sometime to your room and use it. Then Lil Jon can get it back to me."

"I got Big Sexy bringing her phone in for me to listen to music at night, and I use it to call my peeps. I don't think she have a clue, and if she does, I don't think she cares. I take care of her sweet ass, so she watch after me. Big Sexy like everything I do for her. You know how women are." Sam displayed his devilish grin. His eyebrows were shaped in an upside-down *V.* "Money for your honey make her holler for the dollar!" he yelled.

AB headed back to his wing, where the caged inmates were waiting patiently for their one and only Marlboro, which had enhanced their day since AB had started taking orders. That evening, all was calm and quiet in wing H. Inmates took turns burning the rerolled cigarettes they had made, sucking and tasting every draw as if it were their last. Some inmates moaned in pleasure after their first drag. It was amazing what little could soothe their bodies and give them a moment of happiness.

Sam lay in his death-row chair, which he called his Cadillac chair. Lil Jon had brought him more pillows to stuff under his arms. It was like a big, puffy rolling recliner.

Joseph popped up at Sam's window. He tapped twice with his keys. Sam weakly motioned for him to come in. Joseph stared at the concoction. "Who got you that chair? Mr. Williams?"

"Hell no! No one who fucking works in here care that much about my comfort. Lil Jon found this death-row chair stuffed in a closet somewhere and brought it to me. He fucking filled it up with padding and pillows, and now it's my fucking cloud to heaven."

Joseph could no longer hide his sadness at the situation.

"What's up with that face, Joseph? You look like Seela broke it off with you."

Joseph sighed. "I was just thinking how sad Seela is going to be when you pass. It's going to kill her."

"I know what it's going to fucking do to her! She's my fucking twin. I know her inside out, Joseph. I know her emotions and illnesses sometimes before she even feel them. Like I said before, she hangs on my fucking chain! You understand me? I'm going to get straight with her this next Sunday because I don't know how many I have left. Some days I feel like it is my last, when I can hardly catch a breath. Then today I wake up feeling like I could take a step if I could stand on these two elephant feet."

"What are you talking about 'getting straight with Seela,' Sam?"

"I mean I need to let her know some things about me and why I did them so she'll be straight with me when I pass. I want her to know everything, even if she hate me for a minute. Because that's all it would be is a minute if she did get mad at me. She can't get too mad at her fucking dying twin now, can she?"

Joseph tried not to show his concern. "I can't imagine Seela getting angry at you."

Sam made a sour face while glaring at Joseph.

"Chester is asking to come visit you. I talked to Mr. Williams about it today. When we get off prison lockdown, he agreed I could take you to the chow room and let you see Chester for an hour. Would you want to do that? He seems to be very eager to see you before you die."

Sam tried not to show emotion in his face for Chester. "Yeah, if the boy need to see me before I croak, I guess that be good. Lord knows, he's seen me many times near death after a week's run in heroin houses."

"Chester will be very grateful," said Joseph. "I guess we will let him visit you an hour before Seela comes in next Sunday if lockdown is cleared. That sound good?"

Sam nodded in agreement. "Hey, what's the scoop on who got killed, or what gang is it?"

"Now, Sam, do you think I'm going to tell you that? I'm trying to protect your ass. You think I'm going to give you some gossip? It's nothing for you to worry about."

Sam was on his mission to clear his soul by helping the three main people who were helping to keep him comfortable in his dying days. His plan was in place, so maybe it was best not to know of any more dangerous shit going on. "So you going up to see Seels this week?"

"As a matter of fact, I am, Sam. Tomorrow midday, I'll travel up. Anything you want me to tell her for you?"

Sam shook his head. "Just tell her I love her, and I'll see her Sunday if we aren't still on lockdown. Tell her to shoot behind the eight ball." Sam laughed.

"Seela shoots pool?"

"She used to with me when we were growing up. When we were

teens, we would go to the pool hall and hustle people. We'd come home with pockets full of crumpled one-dollar bills. We were a pair." Sam smiled as he reminisced about a great memory with his sister.

Joseph stood up from the metal chair, reaching gently over to shake Sam's hand. "I'll be back Thursday. Let's you and I have a name session, okay?"

"Sure, you better get it while you can. I may be checking out of Hotel California real soon."

Joseph stood at Sam's door and pointed his finger at Sam. "Don't you be doing anything like that right now, Sam. Like you said, you got a few things you still have to do."

"Get on out of here, Joseph. Go see my beautiful twin. I'll see you Thursday. I need to close my eyes now." Sam wanted Joseph to leave so he could light a Marlboro for just one puff before he fell asleep.

Sam threw a pinch of the blue jelly into his commode. He lit his cig with a match Lil Jon had tucked into his front gown pocket. He struck the match against the concrete wall and lit his delicious Marlboro. He took one drag. He held the smoke in as if he never wanted to let it out of his body. Sam rolled over as far as he could reach toward the commode and blew the smoke straight in. He sat back in his chair and closed his eyes. His thoughts raced, focusing on what had transpired that day and what he needed to accomplish before making his exit. Sam was determined to die on his own time, not the prison's. Sam smiled as he thought of Seela falling in love with Joseph and forming a new relationship with Chester. He knew her bond with Chester had given her another kind of love.

Chapter 36

The next day, Joseph drove up to Seela's with a cab full of flowers he had picked up at a nursery on the way. He had bought so many that one could barely see his head in his truck. When Joseph arrived in Clairsville, he stopped first at Seela's house to drop off a huge bouquet of white peonies on her front porch. He'd wrapped the flowers in white paper and a pink ribbon.

He then drove to Seela's salon. Joseph pulled to the curb in front of the salon. Seela saw his truck from inside, and the sight of him energized her like only intense attraction could. "Dee, Joseph's here!" Seela called out to the front desk while applying color on a client.

Dee jumped up and ran out the door with bells chiming as the door slammed shut. "Hey there, Joseph. How are you? Did you have a good trip up? You need some help with anything?"

Joseph walked to the passenger side of his truck. Dee noticed the cab full of flowers. Joseph pulled out two bouquets. He handed one to Dee, making her face flush pink. "These are for you, Dee."

"Why, thank you! They are beautiful." Dee smelled the beautiful bouquet.

"I hope you like them. Somehow, I thought you would like a colorful bunch—something happy feeling. What do you think? They make you feel happy, Dee?"

"Do they!" said Dee. "I got goosies, and you aren't even my boyfriend!" Dee grabbed Joseph's hand to escort him into the salon. "Come on in. Seela is just finishing up her last client. She's so excited to see you, Joseph."

When they walked into the salon, the noise halted as if someone had turned the volume button all the way down in one snap. All eyes turned toward Joseph and Dee.

"Ladies, this is Joseph Quinton. If you promise not to bite, I'm sure he'll come by and introduce himself personally," Dee said while Joseph basked in the flattery.

All the ladies laughed as each one reached her hand out for a shake. A few women lifted their hair dryers off of their heads so they could take in the handsome man holding a huge bouquet of white and yellow gerbera daisies.

Joseph handed them to Seela while giving her a kiss on the cheek. "These are for you, beautiful lady. They are from Chester. He said you like gerbera daisies. He taught me something I didn't know about you." Joseph winked, aware of all the eyes on them.

Her heart fluttered. "These are so beautiful, Joseph. I do love gerbera daisies. They are such a happy flower. Don't you think?" Seela stared at the flowers as if they were smiling at her.

Joseph turned to all the ladies waiting patiently to meet him. He spoke to the salon filled with smiling faces like a star about to perform onstage. "Hi, ladies. I'm Joseph. I hope that Seela has mentioned my name to you all. Now you can put a face with that name. I'm quite fond of your hairstylist, so hopefully you will see more of my mug of a face if she will let me visit more often. I just love your little town. It's a very welcoming, quaint place, I have to say. Now that you know who I am, I'm going to step up front and let Seela finish her work." Joseph smiled brightly and made his way to the waiting area. As soon as he sat down, a client plopped down beside him.

"Well, it sure is nice to meet you, Mr. Joseph. We have heard so much about you and have seen all the flowers that seem to pop up every week. My name is Ms. Kathy."

Joseph shook her hand, amused. "Oh yes, Ms. Kathy. I've heard nothing but wonderful things about you."

"Same here," said Ms. Kathy. "You are more handsome than described by Seela and Dee. I can see why Seela is so smitten with you!"

Ms. Kathy squeezed closer to Joseph, smiling flirtatiously. Joseph chuckled. He sat for a while, enjoying the scene and being the center of attention as the only man in the shop. Dee then asked him to keep her company while she did the daily checkout. They howled the entire time like lifelong friends until Seela finished up.

"Hey, guys, what's so funny?"

"We were just laughing about the women in your salon. I felt like a movie star! Have they never seen a man before?" Joseph said.

"It's just that now you won't get to be labeled the old maid of the town, Seela," quipped Dee.

Joseph continued to laugh.

Seela frowned at them. "That's not nice to say that about me!"

"Seels, you know it's the truth. Don't get me wrong. Joseph is one handsome fellow, but truth be told, these ladies in this town just want you to be happy and in love, not all alone doing hair."

Seela smiled at Joseph. "Sorry if it was overwhelming with all of my ladies. They just love me and want the best for me." Joseph responded by holding her close.

Dee rushed the pair of lovebirds out so she could finish the books. Joseph followed Seela to her house. As she walked up the sidewalk to her porch, she spotted the peonies standing tall in white paper. "Joseph! More flowers? You didn't have to." Seela picked them up, smiling as she pressed her face into the soft petals.

"Those are from me. Like I said, Chester wanted you to have gerbera daisies. He even gave me money to buy his."

"I love them, Joseph. I'm going to put them in a pretty vase. Come on in, and make yourself comfortable. I put clean sheets on the guest bed, so you can put your bag in there. If you want to take a shower, I put towels, soap, and shampoo in there for you too."

Joseph walked toward her guest room, wishing it were Seela's room. "You are quite a host, Seels. I think I will take a shower, if you don't mind. I would like to be fresh and clean for you this evening. Where are we going tonight? You said it's a secret, but what attire?"

"It's casual. Wear comfortable shoes also."

"Great! My kind of date—casual and comfortable."

While Joseph showered, Seela stood by his bedroom door, fantasizing about their evening. Seela wondered if he had left his door open on purpose. She could smell his soap, which let off a manly wood scent. When she heard the faucet turn, Seela ran to the kitchen. She started pulling fruit and cheese out as if she had been in there the whole time, preparing a snack before their fun-filled night.

Seela yelled, "I have cold beer or wine if you would like! I made us a snack before we go out. I'm sure you have to be a little hungry after that drive."

Joseph stepped out of the guest bedroom door with a towel tied around his chiseled waist. She could smell his body from fifteen feet away, and the scent made her delirious with desire. She wanted to jump on Joseph and forget the plans for the evening. She wanted to frolic in her bed with him and love him for the next eighteen hours he would be there. Seela gained her composure while focusing on his face.

"If you would like a drink before we go out, I can make you one, Joseph."

"Whatever you are drinking will work for me."

Joseph walked slowly back to the guest room, leaving Seela to watch and desire. He dressed in jeans and a button-down shirt with the sleeves slightly rolled up. He took her breath away as he sat down in a chair on her screened porch, where she had placed their refreshments. Joseph surveyed Seela's small backyard, which was manicured like a fresh set of nails done on a weekly basis. Creatures scattered everywhere in the grass and flowers. "It's really beautiful and peaceful out here, Seela. It feels nice."

They sat together, enjoying Seela's peaceful porch. Time passed quickly. Seela jumped up while looking at her watch. "I have to hurry and get ready, Joseph. I'll be right back."

Seela stepped out into the foyer from her bedroom, dressed in cowboy boots and a flowery, flowing, short dress. Her hair cascaded down her shoulders, taking Joseph's breath away. He had not seen Seela with her hair down many times. While visiting the prison, she always wore it pulled back and didn't wear makeup, per Sam's orders. "Wow, Seels! You look breathtaking. You should have told me you like cowboy boots. I would have brought mine."

Seela beamed as she heard Joseph's words. "You have cowboy boots, Joseph?"

"Yes, ma'am. What—you don't think a black man can own a pair of cowboy boots? I am from the South!"

They laughed as Joseph reached for Seela, pulling her close to his tight, chiseled body. He pushed her hair away from her face. His hand on her face made her body quiver with excitement. Joseph placed his lips on Seela's. He pushed his tongue through her mouth as if to attach and not let go. Seela's body pulsated, quivering with excitement.

Seela hesitantly pulled away after a minute of kissing feverishly. She sneakily checked her watch. "Joseph, we probably should be going. We don't want to be late for the show!"

"What kind of show are we going to see?"

"A country music concert. There are a few local southern groups playing at our music hall tonight, so I got us tickets. I hope you like to dance!" Seela grabbed her keys to lock her house. "We will walk. The music hall is just one street over."

When they arrived, Seela stopped and pulled Joseph to the side of the building. She motioned for him to kiss her one last time before they entered a roomful of people curious whom Seela Black was with. She pulled away, saying, "I hope you are ready for this. Can you two-step or shag?"

"Oh, Seela, you are in for a run for your money tonight. Dancing is my side job. You didn't know?"

Seela was pleased.

The music, a blend of country and beach, thundered through the hall while couples two-stepped excitedly. Joseph pulled Seela out to the floor immediately.

Seela was delighted Joseph could shag. "It's a South Carolina thing, Seels. It's kind of bred into me."

They shuffled to the floor. They looked as if they had been dancing together for years. Joseph knew when to swing Seela out, and their footwork followed one another as if they had practiced many times before this evening. Guests stood watching them dance as if they were in a competition. Seela's face beamed with happiness as she and Joseph danced the night away. Her hair was soaking wet by the time they finished their evening.

Seela and Joseph strolled leisurely back to her house. Seela didn't want the night to end, but the hours seemed to be running into minutes with Joseph there with her. When they got to her house, Joseph asked for Seela's keys. He opened the door and stood back for Seela to walk in before him. Joseph shut the door, fastening the locks behind him quickly. Before Seela could take a breath, Joseph's lips were attached to hers.

His hands ran over Seela's body fiercely, trying to feel every inch of her. Seela's curves melted into his Joseph's hard body. The touch was electrifying for the two lovers. Joseph picked Seela up and carried her to her bedroom. They fell together onto the bed. Seela's mind raced with excitement and fear. Joseph unbuttoned the front of Seela's dress as she caressed his toned forearms. He paused and whispered, "I'll stop if you want."

Seela caressed his gorgeous face, not saying a word. Joseph carefully unbuttoned each button as if it were a delicate flower. His lips kissed Seela's chest. He moved his mouth across her breasts, making her quiver. She couldn't remember feeling such electricity.

Joseph sat up with his legs straddled over Seela's torso. He unbuttoned his shirt and threw it across the room to Seela's chair. He glistened in the moonlight that flickered in from Seela's bedroom window. Seela's eyes were mesmerized at Joseph sitting on top of her. She had dreamed of this moment but hadn't known it would be tonight. Joseph leaned down and pulled Seela's dress down off her body. She lay there in her lace bra and silk panties, which also glistened in the moonlight. Her skin looked pretty to Joseph. It was like the color of milk and honey combined. Joseph stared for a moment before ravishing Seela's body with kisses as fast as he could. He felt as if he were the happiest person on earth to be there with her in this moment.

"Seela, I've dreamed of being with you. You are so beautiful. Tell me if I'm moving too fast. I can't seem to control myself with you."

Seela couldn't speak. No more words were needed. They rolled around, ravaging each other's body all night. Seela let Joseph explore every inch of her body as if she were a new creature on earth. She felt free as he massaged parts of her body that she hadn't even known she had sensory responses to.

After both climaxed with force, they held each other tightly. Seela was tucked under Joseph's arm as she rubbed her fingers across his bulging chest muscles. She looked up at Joseph and saw that his eyes were shut; he had finally fallen asleep. Seela closed her eyes, snuggling into Joseph, not wanting the moment to ever end.

Chapter 37

Joseph woke to Seela's empty bedside. She brought him a steaming cup of coffee, but all he wanted was her body again.

"I was hoping for you, Seela, instead of coffee." When he tried to pull her into bed, she set the coffee down on the dresser.

"Okay, lie back down, and close your eyes, Joseph!" As he complied, Seela jumped into her bed, spooning close to Joseph's back. She wanted to please him.

Joseph chuckled, yawned, stretched his arms up, and turned to Seela. He squeezed her body while placing his mouth on her ear. "Good morning, my love. This is more like what I had in mind."

Seela smiled as she felt Joseph's hard body against her backside. He rubbed against her body, slowly grinding into her. Joseph had a way of igniting her fire instantly and keeping the flame burning. He was now rock hard, and she intended to appease him. *To hell with breakfast*, she thought. Instead, they made love for what seemed like hours.

Seela breathlessly rolled over after the longest orgasm she'd ever had. "Oh shit!" she said when she noticed the time. "I'm supposed to be at the salon in thirty minutes." She kissed Joseph on his lips. "That was fantastic. It will keep me fantasizing even more now." As he took in Seela's face with his eyes, she knew she was in love with Officer Joseph Quinton.

Seela almost glided into her salon, giddy with happiness, which her clients had not seen before. The day zoomed by with her head in the clouds, replaying every minute of the night before. At the end of the day, the contractor from the art gallery waited for Seela to check out his team's progress. He was a little nervous because loose fixtures and pipes were not concealed before they entered the space. Seela's lovemaking fog served the contractor well. She didn't notice any loose ends while walking through the gallery.

"Ma'am, I'm glad you're happy," he said.

"Happy? I love it!" she shouted as if from a rooftop. "I know now my opening will be postponed due to my brother's illness, but at least it will give me time to get artwork in here. What do you think, Dee? You like the brick walls they preserved?"

"Seela, it's beautiful! I can't wait to see the finished space." Dee kissed Seela on the cheek while Henry, the contractor, turned away, eager to get back to work.

As Dee and Seela locked up the salon, Dee suggested cooking together. Seela agreed—not before getting in a call with her new man, however.

Seela ran into her house, wanting to get everything ready for Dee so she could sit and talk with Joseph on her screened porch. She chopped vegetables and wrapped them in foil. She opened a bottle of wine and placed it on a tray with glasses and cheese. She found herself singing all the while until Joseph called.

"Well, hello," Seela said seductively. "I just finished with my to-dos before your call. Perfect timing."

"Did you have a lot of to-do items, beautiful? I hope I didn't leave you much to do when you got home."

"Of course not. Dee is coming over this evening, so I wanted to get the food ready before your call. She won't be here for another hour. I thought that would give us time to talk."

"I've missed you today," Joseph said quickly. "You've been on my mind all day. It actually made me a little stupid at work."

Seela reeled, knowing their feelings were mutual. "Did you see Sam today, Joseph?"

"I looked in on him, and he was knocked out. He's looking worse, Seela. I want you to know before you see him this next Sunday. His stomach is getting bigger, and his lungs are getting weaker. His lips are very dry and cracked. Do you know what he needs, Seela? Read between my lines like you do with Sam. By the way, I forgot to relay a message from him earlier this week. He said for you to shoot behind the eight ball."

"What in the world does that mean?" she said, mostly to herself, thinking she didn't want to read between lines or speak in code any longer.

"I don't know, Seela. That's what he said for me to tell you."

"Maybe it was morphine crazy talk. Let me know if you figure it out."

Seela and Joseph talked for an hour before Dee let herself in with her key. She found Seela curled up on the sofa swing on her screened-in porch, talking on the phone. Dee watched Seela from the kitchen door, happy to see her dear friend in love. Dee then tapped on the back door to the porch, startling Seela. Seela motioned for Dee to join her and said a long good-bye to Joseph. Dee poured wine and munched on cheese before talking. Happiness spewed out of Seela. They smiled at one another.

"Well? Speak, woman! How was your evening?" Dee finally bellowed.

Seela leaned back on the swing, staring at the beaded board ceiling. "Dee, we made love, and it was the most unbelievable feeling and experience I think I've ever had. Joseph made it so beautiful. I could feel the sparks of energy flowing all around us. It was so amazing! I can't get it off my mind, Dee. Joseph said the same thing. He said our time together made him stupid at work."

Dee giggled. "Girl, look what you done thrown on that man. How he going to work up in that prison with his head all messed up with your sweetness?"

They talked about love and sex over the first bottle of wine before realizing how hungry they were. Seela cooked the chicken and vegetables on the grill.

"Dang, Seels, I got a buzz from that wine!" They laughed and tussled like little girls playing.

"It's okay, Dee. Go open another bottle, and stay here tonight. Girls' sleepover! Yeah!"

Dee wasted no time in opening another bottle of wine. "Let's have some fun. I mean, it won't be like the fun you had last night, but I guarantee I can make us laugh."

Dee and Seela sat out back in her beautifully lit yard while grilling the food. Seela talked about Joseph and then sometimes switched to Sam while Dee took all the information in. Then Seela remembered Sam's message. "Shoot behind the eight ball. What do you think he meant by that?" They pondered several meanings.

"Seela, I got it!" Dee said. "He wants eight packs of cigarettes instead of five. Isn't that how many you took him the last time?"

"Dee, you are right! I bet that is exactly what he's talking about. I'll buy eight packs this week before we head down."

Chapter 38

Mutually hungover, the two women pulled down Mamaw's dusty driveway. Just as Joseph had promised, he and Chester stood there, waiting on their arrival.

The women made their way out of the car as Chester pointed to Mamaw's front yard. "I finished Mamaw's flower garden." The yard now had ferns and flowers planted perfectly everywhere, and two large rocks sat in the center. "Those are Edward's and Sam's rocks. I carved their names on them by myself," said Chester. "Next week, I'm going to help get Mamaw a swing to sit next to the rocks."

Seela's heart filled with a mixture of emotions. "Is that what she wants, Chester?"

"Yes, ma'am, she does."

"We will shop for one tomorrow and surprise her this weekend with it, okay?" Seela said.

"Okay," said Chester. "I like that!"

They went into the house as a group. Mamaw was excited to see everyone at her kitchen table again. She hated all the lonely days shut off from the world beyond reality TV shows.

Sam could barely breathe. His breathing was getting worse every day, and he hadn't been able to get outside for fresh air all week because of the lockdown. His anger had gotten the best of him a few times while he helplessly rotted away. Even Lil Jon had been locked in his hall more than usual. Sam felt as if he were spiraling downward rapidly, but he still had a lot to do before giving up this hell of a nasty world he had made for himself.

Big Sexy let herself into Sam's room and repositioned his body for more comfort. "You want to listen to some music?"

Sam weakly agreed, not caring how she moved him. She retrieved a piece of gum from his locker, knowing he had been chewing on the same one all day. He spit the old one into her gloved hand. She put the earphones in his ears and turned the music on. He gave her a thumbs-up.

As soon as Big Sexy exited, Sam dialed Charlie, who answered right away this time.

"Sam, is that you?"

"Yes, it's me." His voice was almost unrecognizable. "You all right, Charlie?"

She knew she didn't have much time to talk before he would have to hang up, so she held back her tears. "Yes, I've been waiting to hear from you. I can't believe this has happened to you, Sam. I don't know what to do or say. I've done everything you asked me to. I sent all your money I was holding to your mother except for what you told me to keep. I want you to know I did everything you told me to, Sam. I always have because I loved you. I will always love you, Sam."

"I know, Charlie, but it's all over now. I'm gone soon. You need to get out of fairy-tale land with me and figure out what you are going to do now. Get out, and get a fucking job. Hold on to that money I sent you. Keep it for emergencies. You got it? You'll be okay, Charlie. I'm glad I had you in my life. You hear me?"

At these words, Charlie's heart sank. Maybe he did love her after all, she surmised. Charlie couldn't hold back the tears any longer. Her eye makeup ran dark all the way to her neck.

Sam continued with hardly a breath. "Charlie, I'll be calling you this week for one more favor before I die, okay? There will be something in it for you too. Tuck it away for later. Don't go spend it on a purse or shoes. You hear me?" Sam choked as he forced more words. "Charlie, we made good partners. Thanks for keeping your word with me and doing whatever I asked of you. You help me with this last favor, okay?"

"Yes, Sam, whatever you want me to do. After everything you have done for me—"

"I already gave you my nurse's address from in here, and I'll be sending a card number for you to transfer money on for my guy Lil Jon in here, who has been taking care of me. If it weren't for him, I don't know what I would have done, Charlie. I'm making a few thou with what my twin bringing in with Marlboros. I'll get back with the money split and the card numbers. You got it, Charlie?"

"I got it," she replied.

With that, Sam hung up and dialed his mother's number.

Cat also answered right away, knowing this could be the last time she would hear her son's voice.

"Mom," Sam said with broken breath.

"My Sam, I've been worried about you all week. Chester told me you were still on lockdown. They feeding you and letting you get out and get some sun? I know that makes you feel better with sunlight on your face."

Sam coughed. "Yes, Mom, you know how much I love that sun shining down on my face. Soon it will all the time. I know because I saw it when I died the first time, when I was fishing with Dad and Granddaddy. I dream about sun all the time."

Cat's heart shattered as she listened to her dying son. She mourned for the way he had lived his life.

"Mom, I'm telling Seela everything next time I see her. I need to leave this world knowing that my twin knows who I really am and what I've done. I'm fixing my soul right now in these last few days of dying hell right here on earth. When I decide to leave this earth, everyone will know it. I won't be that piece-of-shit state prisoner lying in a pool of blood with no one caring. You got me, Mom? I know what I got to do. I sit up every night with it all torturing me in my head. I'm going through purgatory right now for all the fucking shit I did in my past. It's fucking burning hell right now for me, Mom." Sam's face twisted in pain.

Cat started to cry uncontrollably, knowing there was nothing she could do for Sam. With her cancer, she was equally weak. At the sound of his mother's tears, Sam sobbed also.

"Mom, I love you, and I'm sorry for everything I put you through. You hear me? I hate it all. How could you still love me for what I put you through?"

Cat wiped her large brown eyes. "Oh, Sam, I could never stop loving you. You are my son. No matter what you have done in your lifetime, I will love you to the end. You understand me? As we always said, you and me are a team."

Sam hung on to his mother's words before his breathing became too labored to talk further. "I love you, Mom. I need to go before Big Sexy catch me. I need to get a shot anyway. I'm so tired."

Cat hung up, curled up in her old bucket chair, and cried until she fell asleep.

Big Sexy soon brought Sam a shot of morphine. He couldn't feel it soon enough. "Give it to me, Big Sexy! I need sleep. Do you know if I'm going to see my twin Sunday?"

"I don't know, Sam. They still haven't lifted the lockdown. I don't know what's going on. It all seems strange to me. I've never known them to keep it for this long. I hear there are some strange stories going around."

"Like what?" said Sam.

"I will inform you of anything I find out." Big Sexy lifted Sam, reaching for her phone from his side. "Did you remember to delete your numbers? Don't think I'm a fool. I just want you to know I got your number, and you know mine, so as you say, we are straight, Sam Black!" Big Sexy almost kissed Sam's forehead but realized she shouldn't. "Sam, I'll check on you later and see if you get some rest. I'm here all night." She tucked Sam's sheets around his swollen legs, which were stretched out on the wooden chair Lil Jon had padded, and fixed his toboggan.

When Big Sexy exited, she watched Sam through the window. She could see Sam was drifting away faster, yet his brain could still be as sharp as a tack. In all her years of working in the prison, she had never displayed feelings for a dying inmate. Sam touched her in a different way.

That night, Lil Jon snuck over to see how Sam was doing. He stood at his window, staring for as long as Big Sexy would let him. At one point, Sam started coughing uncontrollably. Both Big Sexy and Lil Jon ran to his side to help get him comfortable. Lil Jon propped Sam up with pillows and wiped his sweat with a warm cloth.

"I knew I needed to come over here to check on you, man. You okay? You need any meds from your stash in your locker?"

Sam held two fingers up, and Lil Jon fed him the pills while Big Sexy went off to get another blanket.

"Anything else, Unc?" asked Lil Jon.

Sam smiled with a crooked smile at hearing Lil Jon call him Uncle Sam but said nothing.

"I'll be back in the morning. I get mopping duties for four hours tomorrow, so I'll be around to see you. Let me know if Big Sexy let me take you to the showers. At least wipe you down with a warm cloth. I know you like that, especially if Seela gets to come see you." Lil Jon tapped Sam's hand as it lay on the chair arm, swollen like a puffed dead fish. "Hope those pills help you sleep, man."

Chapter 39

Chester was cooking breakfast with Dee when Seela woke to her alarm. She had slept peacefully the entire night since Chester had slept on the sofa. Seela walked into the kitchen to the smell of bacon frying and coffee brewing in the old percolator. "Good morning, everyone. You guys are up early."

"Yep!" said Chester. "I already made my bed up, Ms. Seela." Chester pointed to the sofa in the den as he smiled, showing all his little teeth.

"That's great, Chester. I see you are helping Dee cook too."

"Yep, I'm making biscuits. Mamaw showed me how."

"Wow," said Seela. "That's an art. I'm proud of you, Chester!" Seela hugged Chester while observing what he was doing.

"Don't worry, Seels. Chester got this. He's made them a few times, he said. Chester said Mamaw get him to make them for her for dinner." Dee winked at Seela. "I think Mamaw got a good thing going on with teaching Chester how to cook."

"Yep," said Chester. "I like to cook."

Seela's phone rang. It was Sam. "Good morning, Seels. It's twin."

"Sam? How are you calling me?" Seela replied with Chester and Dee eyeing her.

"I can't talk long. I'm in Mr. Williams's office. He letting me use his phone. I'm going to be able to see you tomorrow for three hours. Bring up lots of hamburgers. I'm starving in here. You got me? Joseph told you my message about staying behind the eight ball? You getting a special visit. This shithole still on lockdown. Tell Chubs I'll have to wait and see if I can see him next week. Tell the boy Uncle Sam loves him. You hear me?" Sam talked rapidly so as to get everything in.

"I got it, Sam. I'll be there, and I can't wait to see you."

"Seels, I love you and hope you heard all my messages. Please do what I ask of you."

When he hung up with Seela, Sam instructed Mr. Williams to dial his mom's number, but Mr. Williams hesitated. Sam said, "You got to give me one more call, man. I need to talk to my mom now. It will just be a minute."

Sighing, Mr. Williams dialed the number and handed Sam his phone. "Make it quick, Sam. I don't need you jeopardizing my job."

Sam smirked. "Fuck everyone in here! They wouldn't fire you. They just trying to kill me. That's all they want me to do is fucking die! I know what fucking time it is, Mr. Williams. I know they told you to watch me until I die." Sam smiled. He had hardly any teeth in his mouth now due to the morphine.

Cat answered her phone as soon as the prison number displayed. "Sam, baby, is that you?"

"Yes, Mom. It's me. You doing okay today? You taking your meds? I don't want you in pain now."

"Oh, honey, I'm surviving. I haven't gone out of this little shack of my house in a few days. I been weak from my meds, and I'm trying to finish these paintings for Seels."

"Did you tell her, Mom? Did you tell her about your paintings?"

"No, Sam, I didn't yet. I want to wait until I get all your money taped in the back of the paintings. Isn't that what you wanted me to do?"

"Shhh, Mom. Yeah, yeah, you got it. Just don't say it out loud!"

"I'm almost done, Sam. I'm getting so weak, but I promise you it will be done before you or I leave this place. I love you, Son, and I pray for us to be together hand in hand soon."

"I love you too, Mom. I'm sorry I've been in so much trouble. I hope you understand who Sam Black really is and was when I'm gone."

"I know one goddamn thing, Sam Black. You are my son, and I love you no matter what."

They both sat holding their phones to their heads, hoping to feel a little more of each other. Sam wiped his tears away, not wanting Mr. Williams to see him crying.

"I'll call you tomorrow, Mom. You look out for this number or the other."

"Okay," Cat said. "I'll be here waiting."

"Mom, one more thing. If you need help with your paintings, just get Chubby to help you. That boy will keep a secret. He's the best at it. You tell him not to say anything, and I promise you he won't. I love you."

Cat held the phone and stared at the paintings, which were her best creations by far.

Seela pulled Dee aside while Chester plated the food. "You were right. I think he wants eight packs. I'm also going to take him filet mignon. He's never tasted filet mignon, and he's starving to death. I'm cooking it and taking it in. Don't you think I can do it?"

Dee gasped. "I don't see why not. You've smuggled in worse things already!"

That day, Seela shopped for all her goodies for Sam and vodka for her courage juice. She also took Dee and Chester to find Mamaw a swing for her new flower garden. Chester had done so much work in the yard that it looked like a different property.

While they were shopping at the local hardware store, suddenly, Seela heard Johnny's voice. She couldn't believe her ears. She looked at Dee, putting her finger to her mouth to indicate for her to be silent. Seela quietly made her way to the front of the store, as if wanting to sneak out undetected.

Chester walked by, yelling loudly for Seela. As soon as Seela turned the corner, she bumped into Johnny, whom she had not seen since she had left the island. She'd never wanted to see his face again. Everyone in town knew Chester's voice because he worked at the local gas station and was Bill Johnson's son. *Dammit, Chester,* Seela thought as she and Johnny stood face-to-face.

"Well, I'll just be damned. Seela Black!" Johnny shouted in amazement at Seela's beauty, noting that nothing had changed about her in so long.

Chester stepped forward, putting out his hand to shake Johnny's. "Hi, Johnny," said Chester. "Do you know Ms. Seela?"

"Yes, I do, Chubby! She and I were high school sweeties back in the day," Johnny said boastfully. His stomach now hung over his jeans, perhaps from too much beer. "Are you here visiting your mom?" he asked Seela. "I hear she's been sick for a while. My mother-in-law gossips about everyone on the island."

"And your wife, Meshell, too," said Chester. "She like to gossip."

"Chester, that wasn't nice to say," snapped Seela.

"I'm just saying what Mamaw said."

Johnny laughed. "Yes, Chubby, I guess the apple doesn't fall far from the tree."

Seela looked at Johnny as if she wanted to ask him a question, but then she turned to walk away. "Nice to see you," she said, and she pushed Chester toward the door.

Dee was outside in the hardware store's garden, looking at outdoor swings. She waved at Seela and Chester. "Hey, guys, check these out. They have a lot of swings."

As soon as Dee saw Seela's face, she knew something was wrong. "You okay? You look like you just saw a ghost!"

"I think I just did."

"Why is Mr. Johnny a ghost, Ms. Seela? He said he was your high school sweetie. Is that why?" asked Chester.

"I haven't seen him since then, Chester, so yes, it was like seeing a ghost. It's a figure of speech."

Dee recalled the name. "Isn't he the one you wanted to ask for help to get Sam released?"

"Yes. It just wasn't the place to bring it up. I've seen him now, so I'll get his contact info and give him a call."

Just then, she heard Johnny calling her name across the parking lot. He was standing by his shiny new pickup truck. "Do you guys need help? I got a truck. You buying that swing you sitting in?"

Dee guessed the man was Johnny by the look on Seela's face. She stepped out of the flowers she was standing in and approached him. She held her hand out to shake his. "Hi. I'm Seela's friend Dee. We do have access to a truck, but if you are offering right now, I believe we may take you up on it. We need to get it to her Mamaw's."

"Mamaw! I wouldn't mind seeing that lovely woman. I would be glad to help y'all. Besides, she never leaves her house and never allows anyone on her property. How did I get so fortunate today?" Johnny whistled.

Dee laughed, thinking of Mamaw's shotgun. It probably never had a bullet loaded in it.

Johnny helped the hardware man load the swing into his pickup truck and burned rubber out of the parking lot as he headed to Mamaw's.

Dee was clearly amused. "Seela, he's a character. I don't see you with someone like him, though. Especially after seeing you with Mr. Joseph."

Chester leaned forward to speak to Seela. "Um, Ms. Seela? Was Mr. Johnny your boyfriend in high school? I know his wife, Ms. Meshell. She's nice to me when she come by the gas station."

"Yes, Chester. Johnny and I did date some in school, but it was so long ago. I can't even remember our time together anymore."

They pulled into the driveway and quickly spotted Mamaw out by her garden, admiring what she and Chester had accomplished. Johnny pulled over and eagerly hopped out of his truck to greet her.

"It's been forever since I've seen you, but you're still as beautiful as ever." Johnny leaned down in front of Mamaw in her chair, hugging her around her neck.

Mamaw looked surprised at this turn of events. She touched his hand. "Well, I'll be. If it ain't that pistol of a handsome boy I knew so long ago. How you been, son? Married, I hear, and with some children?"

Johnny nodded. "Yes, ma'am, I have three children now."

"Well, what brings you out here on my property today?" Mamaw squinted at Johnny but then noticed the swing in his truck. "Is that for my beautiful garden Chester has helped me make these past few weeks?"

"As a matter of fact, it is, Mamaw," Johnny said. "I can still call you Mamaw, can't I?"

"Why, of course you can, Johnny. You've known me since you were a little boy. I wouldn't have it any other way."

Seela noticed that Johnny's boyish grin had not changed. He had always had a childlike face.

"Let's get this swing in your garden, Mamaw," said Seela. She turned to Chester, motioning for him to help Johnny unload it.

Dee ran over to Johnny's truck. "Here—let me help. I may be a woman, but I am as strong as an ox. Come on, Chester. You can help too. Mamaw, where you thinking this pretty ole swing is supposed to be in your garden you have going here?" Dee threw her hand out as she stood in the back of Johnny's truck, looking out at the strategically placed flowers.

Mamaw pointed to a bare spot surrounded by broken pieces of slate spread out. "Right there! I got it all ready for my beautiful swing, Dee."

The way the rocks had been turned cast an inviting effect. The new garden had purpose and power, along with beauty and magic. Mavvie might have had something to do with it during the night in order to make it a perfect praying place. Mamaw had had Chester hang wired mason jars with tea lights, so if one sat out there in the evening, the flames would light up like fireflies in the night. The garden was just the right size and was filled with all the flowers that were special to Mamaw. She had visions of flowers blooming all year long.

Seela watched Johnny and Chester place the swing in the garden. She stood staring, having a flashback to her and Johnny's childhood. Seela thought about how crazy she and Johnny had been for each other. Before Johnny left, he looked as if he wanted to embrace Seela, but she kept her distance. She wanted him to leave as quickly as possible, so she instructed Dee and Chester to go inside and start getting ready for dinner. She and Mamaw said their thanks and good-byes to Johnny.

"Let's sit here a moment, Mamaw, and pray together, okay?" Seela said softly. She leaned her head down on her grandmother's shoulder.

"Yes, honey. I think that's a great idea. Let's pray for Sam. Let us pray he's not in pain and soon will be at peace."

Within a few minutes, Mavvie appeared, hiding behind a bush, watching the women pray. She stood with her stick as the white cloth flew high in the wind. Mavvie silently joined them in prayer. Seela opened her eyes, jumping in surprise to see Mavvie standing there. Mavvie's head was wrapped in a white turban that matched the white cloth tied to the stick flying beside her. She looked like an angel who had appeared before them. Mamaw jumped when Seela yelled, and she opened her eyes to see her sister.

"Damn, Mavs. Why you want to scare us like that?"

"I didn't want to interrupt your praying." Mavvie smiled, waving her flag around them as if she were sweeping the spirits around them away. "I came up to hear about Sam. I have felt him a lot today, and I know you are going to see him tomorrow, Seels. You have to be strong for him. He is going to be very weak. I feel it won't be much longer. You pray with him tomorrow."

Seela began to cry. "I will, Mavvie. I too feel it's getting close."

Mamaw reached for her scooter and motioned for Seela to help her to her chair. "I can't be sad right now. I've cried enough these past few weeks, ladies. Let's go fry some chicken in honor of Sam. That's his favorite, so that's why I thought we would have it tonight. Chester has been a godsend, Seela. He does keep my spirits up when they get down. Just look all around. It seems to be getting prettier and prettier out here."

The three women looked out onto the sacred property. "I do love it here, Mamaw. I have some great childhood memories that fill my soul with goodness," said Seela. Mamaw and Mavvie concurred as they admired the new landscape.

They headed into the house to find Chester covered in flour except for the whites of his eyes and his puffy bright red lips shining through. Mamaw wheeled over to the stove. "Okay, Chester, let's teach you how to make fried chicken!"

Seela ran outside as soon as she heard Joseph's truck. Joseph jumped out of his truck and scooped Seela up like a five-pound sack of potatoes. He lifted her off the ground with his muscular arms, pulling her into his body.

They kissed for what seemed like minutes. Seela felt like a tiny creature cradled in his arms. Joseph carried her sideways in his arms down the driveway.

"I'm not letting you go, Seela. I've missed you every day since I left you Thursday morning. I see why Sam talks about you the way he does. Like he says, you are a bright, shining diamond."

"Is that what Sam said about me, Joseph?" She giggled at the thought of her brother calling her a diamond.

Joseph smiled at how taken he had become so effortlessly. They walked into Mamaw's kitchen. The smell of fried chicken popping in the fryer filled the air.

"Hey, Yosef," said Chester. "I'm learning how to fry chicken like Mamaw do it." He raised his eyebrows up and down, grinning with his tongs in his mitted hand. Flour was sprinkled all over him.

"Hey, man, that's great. It smells some kind of good up in here now," said Joseph. "I can't wait to taste your cooking, Chester!"

Mamaw sat at the end of the kitchen table in her scooter, mixing the mashed potatoes in a metal bowl. "Come over here, and give me a hug, Joseph. I've missed you this week!"

Joseph scurried over and hugged Mamaw with his broad arms. "I think I'll just have to come visit you during the week, Mamaw. I can't have you missing me, now, can I?"

Mamaw looked as if she were blushing as Joseph doted over her. He was such a handsome man that anyone would have felt the same way.

Seela and Joseph sat down at the kitchen table, watching the others feverishly cook in Mamaw's kitchen. Mamaw scooped the bowl naked, trying to get every morsel of potatoes out into the casserole dish. She reached into the bowl with her fingers for the last bit. Joseph laughed at Mamaw as she licked the potatoes off of her fingers and then put them back into the bowl for more. She slung the potatoes from her fingers into the casserole.

Seela gasped and grabbed the metal mixing bowl from her grandmother. "Oh good Lord, Mamaw! You can't lick your fingers and then put food on them and put them in the dish again. That's cross-contamination!"

"Screw contamination, Seels. It's just me. It's not like I'm some stranger!"

Seela shook her head while Joseph chuckled in amusement. Seela put the potato casserole in the oven.

"Yep," said Chester innocently. "Mamaw always do that when she's mixing in the bowl. I've seen her."

"Chester, don't be telling stuff on me. You and me a team, aren't we?"

"Yep, we are," said Chester, smiling crookedly while winking at Mamaw.

After dinner, everyone retreated to the garden to share favorite childhood memories. Chester sat quietly, listening to everyone. He tried to remember a favorite childhood memory but couldn't seem to get it out for everyone to hear. Then he spoke up, interrupting Dee's recollection. "Um, I remember a good story one time of Sam and me."

Seela sat up in attention when Chester spoke.

"Um, one time, Sam and me were just hanging out when he wanted company. He told me how he saved me as a baby. Yep, he said he saved me. That's why he love me so much. He said he would never let anything happen to me, because he knew I loved him no matter what he did, good or bad."

Chester stared off into the distance and then smiled at everyone. "He told me a big secret one time. I never told it to anyone. It's mine and Sam's secret."

"What is the secret about, Chester?" said Seela.

Chester paused, as if he had already said too much. "I'll ask Sam if I can share it with you when I see him on my visit, Ms. Seela. I promised to keep it in here." Chester pointed to his heart.

Mystery enveloped the group as Chester stuck to his promise to

Sam. Seela wanted to hear more but didn't press the matter. She noticed Joseph was deep in thought.

"I see you got Mamaw her swing she wanted. Did the store deliver it?" he said.

Dee sipped her wine, looking away, waiting for Seela to answer. Seela hesitated before replying. "No, not delivery from the store, but delivery from my high school boyfriend, Johnny. I ran into him at the hardware store. He offered to help."

"Was that weird for you?" asked Joseph. "I mean, was it a bad breakup back then?"

"No, Joseph, it wasn't bad. Johnny broke up with me. His loss, right?" Seela giggled nervously and kissed him on the cheek.

"You are absolutely right, Seela. A big loss for that Johnny, but what a gain for me," he said happily. As everyone smiled at the star-crossed lovers, Joseph made his statement even more definitive by adding, "Seela Black, you are my bright and shining star, and I hope I never get to stop looking at you."

Chester spoke afterward. "Yes, you are my star too, Ms. Seela."

They all toasted with their glasses.

Chapter 40

The next morning, Dee woke to the smell of steak cooking. She put on her robe and house slippers as fast as she could. "That Seela—she really goin' to do it. Damn, I don't know how she's going to pull this one off," Dee muttered.

Dee walked into Mamaw's outdated pine-walled kitchen, smelling the delicious cut of filet that Seela had bought for Sam. "Seels, it sure is smelling good in here. It smells like a hot Saturday night date instead of a Sunday morning breakfast."

Seela had music playing softly as she drank a courage juice cocktail of orange juice and vodka. "I'm almost ready to head out, Dee. Will you cook Chester and Mamaw breakfast this morning when they wake?"

"I can't believe they haven't woken up with this delicious smell you got cooking up in here right now. How do you plan on keeping the filet mignon vapor from seeping out from your behind?"

Seela had the plan nailed to every detail. "I'm going to wrap it in five layers of Saran Wrap and then brown paper I have already cut from this lunch bag here. Then I'll wrap it in foil, and when I get there, I'll take the foil off before going inside."

Dee shook her head in amazement. "You got this all figured out, don't you? At least you have Joseph taking you in, so that helps. I wonder if he knows you bringing all this shit in."

"I don't think so. But he loves me. And I love him too!" Seela said.

"Girl, I know you do. I ain't never seen you like this. I know the timing is not right, but no one knows when love will come knocking on your heart."

"Joseph is coming to my house tonight, Dee. We will leave today soon after my visit with Sam, okay?"

"That's all good with me. I'll take Chester to the beach today while you're gone. We will go to your favorite spot and say a little prayer for Sam."

Seela loaded herself up with cigarettes, bubble gum, and her brother's favorite candy, Laffy Taffy. Seela had her routine down and wasted no time in heading out to deliver her goodies to her dying twin brother.

Seela drove down the highway, listening to songs that reminded her of Sam and their childhood and drinking from her large tumbler of courage juice. She danced in her seat as she sang happily to the songs, not realizing how intoxicated she was getting. She hadn't eaten, so the vodka was going to her head quickly.

Seela pulled into the prison parking lot aggressively and loosely. Scanning the parking lot, she got the steak out and removed the foil. She placed it in the back of her pants, down in between her panties and jeans.

As she hurried down the wire-fence walkway, Seela felt the effects of her courage juice kick in. She heard her feet hitting the pavement but could not feel them. There was a little swagger about her. Confidence was Seela's main game. She strutted with her head high and no worries. It was amazing how well the cocktail worked.

The guard slid the window open after making Seela wait for a few minutes outside. "Who you here to see, ma'am? Did you fill out the form on the clipboard?"

Seela handed her the filled-out form. She knew the lady could see her through the glass. Seela also knew she had a special visit that day. The prison was still on lockdown for a double murder from the week before. The victims were still unknown to almost everyone.

A few minutes later, the loud metal door opened. The guard opened the window and told Seela to walk through the metal detector. "When you go through the second door, wait there, and an officer will be down to get you."

For a minute, Seela feared that her escort would not be Joseph, since the officer didn't say his name. She started to get nervous, thinking about the filet. Then the main prison door flew open, and Joseph appeared. Her heart leaped as she took a few deep breaths while keeping eye contact with him.

"Well, hello, Ms. Black. Let me escort you up to Mr. Sam Black's room. He's waiting for you. He had his pal Lil Jon clean him up and give him a nice shave. I stopped by and saw him earlier. It's strange—he pops up like toast the day you come to visit him."

Seela listened to Joseph, gaining strength from the man who had just declared his love for her. She looked straight ahead without saying a word. When they turned the corner to the elevator, the filet slid down into the crotch of Seela's jeans. As she took each step, she could hear the Saran Wrap move. She walked deliberately slower so Joseph could get a few steps ahead and not hear her legs crunching with plastic wrap.

Joseph stopped and turned to look straight at Seela. "Are you okay? You look like something is wrong."

"Oh no, Joseph. Nothing is wrong. I was just thinking of you and me tonight," she said. She knew that would detour any other thought in Joseph's mind.

He smiled sweetly. "I can't get you off my mind either. You go on in, and have a great visit with Sam, okay? I'll be back at three."

Seela winked at Joseph, hoping no camera or person saw her. Her equilibrium was officially off now, and things began to blur. Seela walked through the double locked doors that kept Sam safe from all the bad riffraff infesting the rest of the prison. The filet continued to fall down her pants. Big Sexy greeted Seela, smiling largely as she buzzed Sam's door to let her in.

Seela looked at Sam through the glass. He was sitting in his rigged death-row chair. He looked like a dead man who had already been embalmed. Seela's heart sank when she saw him. There she stood, drunk, looking at her dying brother in a caged prison room. She dismissed any emotion and rushed to his side.

Sam smiled slightly while holding his arm out to hug Seela. "Hey, Sis, I've been waiting on you. You seem so happy to see me too."

"I am, Sam. I'm so glad they let me have a special visit today. I don't know what I would have done if they hadn't let me come see you. What if you'd died while you all were on lockdown, and I hadn't been able to see you? That would have killed me worse, Sam."

"Don't you fucking worry, Sis. I'll tell you one goddamn thing: they will let me see you once a week until I do kick on out of this hellhole. They all know what's being covered up here with ole warden having me shanked. They fucking can't wait for my sick ass to check on out of here so they can sweep all my shit and shenanigans with that corrupt so-called privately owned prison off the fucking porch! No one going to let this story out, Seels. Too many politics involved all around, Sis.

"I've had many nights in here being tortured in my brain with everything I've done. Then I think of how I fucking got here. The last stint I had in that private prison did me in. I was sent to a drug addict's incarcerated heaven. It was so fucking corrupt with every fucking person who worked there. It took me getting a few ass beatings from the guards and warden, but within a year, I was the king, dealing the drugs and doing whatever I wanted as long as I was dealing out their drugs. I had my own posse that guarded me like the fucking president has guarding his black ass."

Sam started to choke from talking like rapid fire. Fluid smothered his lungs. "I think of how I only had a four-year sentence, and if I hadn't been sent to a prison that was so corrupt, I probably would not be here dying, Sis. I wouldn't have gotten so sick if I hadn't had access to the drugs I was doing. With my Hep C, I could have had a longer life. Who knows? Maybe I'd have stayed straight if I had been sent to the right place. Now look. I'm fucking forty-six years old, dying in a shithole of a cinder block room."

Tears welled up in Seela's eyes. Sam was now repeating the same phrases and messages, she noticed. The clock could not be turned back. Suddenly, she realized she hadn't taken out the stuff she had smuggled in. "Today you get to eat filet mignon." Seela stood, turning her back to Sam. "You reach in the back of my pants. There is a baggie. When you feel it, pull it out, and I'll stand here watching Big Sexy at the desk."

Sam reached quickly down Seela's pants. He'd never in his life tasted filet mignon. "Damn, Sis, it's about slid down to your crotch! Filet of crotch." They both laughed as Sam had his hand down Seela's jeans, scrambling for the steak. He grabbed the gourmet steak gift and pulled it out into his lap. "Seels, I can smell it. It smells so good. Go ahead and sit back down. Big Sexy ain't going to mess with us. She's my friend now. You know that." Sam displayed his devilish grin.

He bit into the steak as if it were birthday cake. "This is so fucking good. So this is what filet taste like? Now I know why everybody says it's the best. It's like butter in your mouth, Seels. It's still warm too! How did you do that, Sis?"

Seela smiled, watching her brother have filet mignon for the first time in his life. "That's red meat, and your body will probably reject it. I was thinking maybe you could give some to Lil Jon."

Sam stopped chewing. "Yeah, hell, I didn't think about my consequences in eating this, Sis. You are right. My body probably won't even take it on through!" Sam set the rest of the steak on his tray, covering it with his hat. "Aw, hell, Sis, we in trouble now."

"What do you mean? What's going on?"

"I can assure you my stomach will explode in the next hour, and you locked in here with me with nowhere to go when it happens. Now, ain't that some shit, Sis?" They both laughed hysterically, risking drawing attention because of how loud they were.

"Maybe it won't happen until after I leave, Sam. Let's not worry about it right now. I want to visit with you while I can." By now, Seela's alcohol-induced buzz had evened out. "Have you been singing, Sam? You know how that makes you feel good inside."

"Yeah, Sis, let's sing a little tune." Sam started "Sara Smile," and Seela chimed in. She harmonized with him. He continued and then slowly got softer. Seela sang over Sam. He listened to her sweet voice with his eyes closed. Seela realized he was listening to her and enjoying hearing her sing. His smile was sublime. She started "Amazing Grace."

Sam winced with chills at one point when Seela hit a high note. "Damn, Seels, you trying to send me on up to the fucking gates of heaven right now? That's some beautiful shit right there!"

Seela smiled, knowing she had made him feel good.

"After all this beautiful singing, I think I have to throw up. Hurry—help me get my head over toward the commode."

Seela quickly helped Sam. He started to vomit profusely. The filet mignon shot out of his mouth like a fire hydrant hose turned on full blast. It was still in full chunks but covered with stomach bile and blood. Sam yelled each time the vomit shot out. Big Sexy saw what was happening and ran to Sam's door. When she walked in and saw the steak in the toilet, she turned to Seela and made a sour face before rushing out.

"Fuck her," said Sam. "She won't say anything, Seels. Don't worry, okay? You good. You hear me? I'm 'bout checked out of this shithole anyway." Then Lil Jon entered Sam's room with his mop, and Sam said, "Hey, man, get your ass in here. You are just in time. I have vomit on my floors. As a matter of fact, get some cleaner before you come in." Sam threw orders to Lil Jon as if he were his slave.

Lil Jon returned in no time with a bottle of cleaner, holding his mop and bucket. He immediately sprayed the cleaner on the floor, asking no questions.

"Lil Jon, Sis brought me a fucking filet mignon today, and it's your lucky day too! I only ate a few bites, and as you see, my stomach gave it right back to me. So when you start out of here, grab that baggie under my hat right there on my tray. You got it? Slip into a cleaning closet, and enjoy the fucking shit out of it, boy. It's some good fucking beef!"

Then Sam realized that the rest of his goodies were still tucked against Seela's body.

Joseph met with Mr. Williams while Seela visited Sam.

"How's that patient of yours? I see you got his sister a visit!" exclaimed Mr. Williams.

"That wasn't hard. I just called and told them it was Sam Black who wanted a private visit today. Believe me, they didn't hesitate to give it to him. I really don't think the system thought he would survive this long." Joseph chuckled.

"I know," said Mr. Williams. "That man wheels his janky-ass wheelchair down here every day to use my phone to call his mom and sometimes somebody else that he whispers orders to. He had his mom send my wife flowers the other day. Can you believe that fucking shit? A damn prisoner sending flowers to my house!"

"And may I ask why he sent flowers to your wife?" said Joseph.

"Sam told me he wanted to thank me for allowing him to use my phone. He knew I couldn't afford to surprise my wife with flowers, so he did it for me. That man is something else. A dying prisoner thinking about me and my wife!"

The men reflected on Sam and what might happen next. "I tell you one thing," said Joseph. "I'll never forget this experience with Sam Black. He has taught me a lot. Oh, wait—that's not it for today. Wait until you hear this shit! You know how that man has Seela bringing in his bubble gum and cigarettes for trades? Today she brought in steak, I believe. I could smell the shit permeating from her behind. I could hear the plastic wrap moving as she walked down the hallway with me. I had to leave her at the front door and let her walk in by herself. I just wanted to crack up laughing but had to hold my composure!"

Mr. Williams gasped. "Steak? That man is so sick he can hardly hold anything down. He was in here yesterday, talking about steak on the phone. I didn't hear him ask her for it, though."

"You didn't have to, Mr. Williams. Those twins have their own communication with riddles and codes. I've figured that out already."

Joseph kept this in mind when he went to retrieve Seela. He knocked on the window and then let himself in as Big Sexy studied his muscular body.

"Did you guys have a good visit? Your time is up, Ms. Seela."

Sam grinned at Joseph. "You know damn fucking well we had a good visit, Joseph. You make sure she gets to come back next week if I make it through."

Seela ran to Sam's side. "Don't say anything like that, Sam. I can't bear the thought of not seeing you next week."

Sam reached for Seela's hand and kissed it with his dry, cracked lips. "I love you, Sis. I'm not going anywhere yet. I got a little more work to do. You give Mamaw a big hug and kiss for me. You tell her I love her. You got it? Tell Chubby I'll see him next week."

Seela stood looking down at her dying twin brother. "So you do want to see Chester next week? He said he wants to ask you about a secret you told him. He said he would ask you if he can tell me the secret. What's he talking about, Sam?"

"That boy not all there, Seels. He gets things confused sometimes. It's probably something stupid I told him when I was fucked-up high. No telling!"

Joseph and Seela said good-bye to Sam. Seela stood outside his window, looking in once more. Sam waved for her to go on and mouthed that he loved her. Had it not been for having Joseph by her side and knowing she would be in his arms that night, Seela would have lost it. Sam looked worse than any descriptive picture from a medical dictionary.

Sam knew this, but he had more business to conduct in this godforsaken place. He packed himself with all of the Marlboros Seela had brought, except for a few for himself and Lil Jon. He put his toboggan on and waited for Lil Jon to come wheel him down to meet AB, but not before Big Sexy snuck in to scold him for eating steak.

When Lil Jon showed up, Big Sexy had more to say. "You boys be safe on your stroll. You hear me? Word's already getting out in here what you be doing, Sam. I don't need to find you laid out in one of these hallways!"

"Who the fuck cares if you do, Big Sexy? It just means less time I'm tortured here in this hellhole of a place. I've been fucking killed once, so who the fuck cares if it happens again? This time, just let me bleed!"

Lil Jon ran up behind Sam's chair and started to push him out of his room. "Come on, man. Let's go get some sunshine. It's nice out there."

Lil Jon had a skip when he walked down the hall with Sam. "Hey, Unc! Sing me a song, why don't you? You strong enough?"

"I'll try, son. You know the song 'Have You Ever Seen the Rain?' by Creedence?"

Sam proceeded to sing, and Lil Jon was touched to the core. He vowed to get some of that Creedence shit when he got out.

Sam inhaled deeply as soon as his face hit the outdoor air. "This is what I'm talking about, Lil Jon. You think when I die, it will feel as good as this fucking sun shining down on my face? If it is, I can take it! I got a feeling it ain't going to be much longer, my man. My brain is starting to fade now. I'm getting where I don't care anymore, not like when I first got here and worried for days about everyone and everything. If I make it through next week, I have to tell my twin something I never thought I would. I did something seventeen years ago that I think she may never forgive me for. But how can she disown her dying twin at this point?"

"Why do you have to tell her if you are dying anyway? Take it to your grave, man. No one will know." Lil Jon stood in front of Sam. "Why do it now?"

"Because it could change people's lives when it comes out. You got me? This is what I got to do. It's the right thing, and that's what I've been trying to do with the ones I love and care for before my ass dies the second time around. I feel maybe that's why I was sent back."

Lil Jon swung his arm down to high-five Sam. "Hey, man, you do what you got to do. It's your conscience."

The metal door opened, and AB walked out into the yard. He waved to Sam and Lil Jon as he looked all around the buildings surrounding the small yard. He sat on a bench alongside Sam. "Hey, man, you still kicking, I see. When you thinking you've had enough of this shit in here? Why don't you close your eyes, take a hot shot, and check on out? That's what I would have done already."

Sam listened to AB closely. "AB, my man, you and I got different stories. I've decided to finish my own. I'm not going to let these corrupt motherfuckers who are part of what they call the judicial system do it!

When I get done with what I have to do, I'll take myself right on out. It's my game now."

Sam pulled his toboggan off and set it in his lap. "Lil Jon, I want you to lean down like you helping me get situated in my death-row chair." The men snickered. "Then you pick up my toboggan and toss it on the table. AB, you casually reach for the Marls. We got fucking eight packs today. I took out half a pack for Lil Jon and myself. You keep the rest of that pack, and we got seven to sell. I already did the math, so we should make twenty-eight hundred dollars, and split two ways this week. You guys got me? I don't need a fucking cut no more. This is for you guys."

AB was astonished. "Man, you straight with that? Your brain high from morphine? You just had your sister jeopardize her life only to give this to us?"

"Well, I will tell you, there was no way in hell she was getting caught, so no, I didn't jeopardize her life. I would never do that to her. My twin everything to me! Now, listen. You send Lil Jon his take to that card number he gave you as soon as you get everything sold. I know you will have no problem, right, AB?"

AB balled his fist to pump Sam's. "You know I got it, Sam. We both can't thank you enough for what you've done for us in this short time. You are king in my eyes, man."

Sam smiled while leaning his head back on his pillow. The sun shined down on his leathery, tired skin. "That's what I wanted to hear, AB. You let everyone in here know when I die this time around. You hear me? You all light your lighters and sing me a song as I enter the blue skies of yonder. Hell, I can't say *heaven*, because I don't know if they let my kind in!"

Once the men finished their business for the day, Lil Jon wheeled Sam back to his room. He could tell Sam was exhausted from all the excitement of his sister's visit and their dealings in the yard. Lil John went into Sam's locker as Sam settled in for sleep. "You want two pills tonight?" Sam nodded, and Lil Jon handed him a piece of Laffy Taffy with the pills. "There you go. It's banana, your favorite."

Sam opened his mouth for Lil Jon to place the two pills on his tongue, followed by the candy. Lil Jon headed to his cell while Sam sat chewing the taffy with the few teeth he had left. The strong doses of morphine had caused eight of his teeth to fall out in the past month. Had he not been on the brink of death, he knew this would have scared the fuck out of him. The shit was more powerful than any heroin he had ridden on, at least in his deteriorating mind.

Big Sexy felt the need to visit with Sam as he was drifting off. She sat in the chair beside him. "Is there anything you want me to do for you, Sam? My shift is over in an hour, and I want you to be as comfortable as you can until I get back tomorrow at two."

"As a matter of fact, I need you to write something for me. I got pen and paper over there." He pointed to his locker. Sam was so high now from the morphine that he wasn't even thinking of all the candy and bubble gum stored in his locker.

Big Sexy opened his locker and yelled, "Damn, Sam Black! I ain't never seen so much bubble gum in a prison in my entire career of working in one. What in the hell are we going to do with all of this shit when you do pass?"

Sam didn't care and didn't reply. "I need you to write! You take that candy, and give it to Lil Jon when I die. You hear me? Fuck this place! You think I'm worried?"

"Okay, okay, calm yourself. What is it you want me to write?"

"Get the paper out, and I'll fucking tell you. It's to be written for Officer Quinton."

Big Sexy sat in the chair next to Sam. "Okay," she said. "Give it to me, Sam."

He chose his words carefully, as he didn't have much time before nodding off. "I, Sam Black, was shanked at Jacks State Penitentiary. It was ordered by the warden at Cottonwood. I was the drug mafia king in his prison. I dealt whatever was delivered to me. I fucking made thousands of dollars for me, the fucking guards, and the warden. Once I got too sick to deal, the warden just left me there in my bunk to die. He knew he couldn't let me go anywhere. My fucking ass was pumped full of God knows what. How could a fucking prisoner from a goddamn

privately owned prison go to the hospital with his body full of every
street drug there was? Once I did get to the hospital, those fuckers knew
what time it was."

Sam looked over at Big Sexy, who wrote feverishly. Her heart ached,
but she tried not to show it. "So that's when my sick ass got sent to Jacks
State Prison from the hospital. That is, once they got me pumped full
of antibiotics and tapped my stomach. I could barely stand up, but they
still sent me there.. Then ole warden heard what was going on and knew
I wouldn't be coming back to Cottonwood, so he got the word to Jacks
State Prison to shank my fucking dying ass. Big Sexy, can you believe
it? I wish they would have just left me in my pool of blood, dying in that
hellhole. If I'd had just one more minute, I'd be fishing."

Sam smiled, thinking of what he'd seen when he was out from the
shanking. "I wonder if I'll see them again, Big Sexy."

"Who, Sam? Who will you see again?"

"My dad and granddaddy. We were fishing and drinking wine. It
was so wonderful, Big Sexy. I dream about it all the time now."

"Well, I'm sure you will see them again, Sam. I'm sure they are
waiting right now for your ass, wondering where you are."

"Let's finish this letter. Now, I'm going to take this information to
my grave with me. Joseph Quinton, if you love my twin, you will read
and destroy this letter. Take all this information, and hold it close to
your heart. This investigation is over. No one will know the truth except
you and my twin. Let her tell the story one day. If you tell it, it will ruin
your relationship with Seela. I don't want that to happen. I want you to
watch after my twin and love her unconditionally. My life and all this
bullshit is over!" Sam reached over with his weak arm. "Here, Big Sexy.
Let me put my John Hancock on that fucking letter." Sam signed the
bottom of the paper and then tried to fold it.

Big Sexy stood up, reaching for the letter. "Give it to me. I'll put it
in an envelope for you." Big Sexy took the letter to her station, sealed
it in an envelope, and brought it back to Sam. "Where would you like
for me to put it, Sam?"

Sam pointed to his locker. "Lock it up in there. I'll give it to Joseph when I'm ready. This here between you and me. You got it, Big Sexy?"

She smiled and replied, "I'm with you, Sam Black. Even when you leave me, I'll be with you." Big Sexy blew Sam a kiss as she shuffled out of his room.

Chapter 41

Seela stirred her sauce feverishly, waiting for Joseph to arrive that evening after seeing Sam. She had driven home like Mario Andretti trying to win his last race. She had quickly spruced up her house and pulled frozen homemade sauce out of her freezer. All of a sudden, she heard Joseph's truck pull up in front of her house. Seela wiped her hands and ran to her front door. She could not get to his truck fast enough. They kissed as if it had been weeks since they'd seen each other. Joseph and Seela held hands as they walked into Seela's home, which smelled like a mixture of garlic and irresistible tomato sauce.

Seela glanced into the oven to check on the pasta dish. When she stood up from the oven, she felt Joseph at her back. Before she could turn around, Joseph picked her up off the floor. He carried Seela to her bed, carefully placed her on her white spread, and nestled in next to her. They passionately kissed for what seemed like an hour. If the sparks between them had been visible, Seela's room would have been lit up like the Fourth of July.

Seela sat up. "Oh no, Joseph! The oven—it's still on, and my pasta dish is probably burned by now."

Joseph smiled proudly. "It's not burned. I turned the oven off when I picked you up."

Seela hit Joseph's arm lightly. "Joseph Quinton, were you being sneaky in my house?"

"I guess so, if that's what it took to get you here with me."

Seela sighed with pleasure. "Well, are you ready to have dinner with me? All of this kissing has got me hungry."

Joseph chuckled. "You bet. I was starving when I got here, but holding and kissing you takes precedence over pasta any day."

Seela and Joseph ate at the backyard table and remained there for hours into the evening. After dinner, Joseph cleaned the dishes while Seela prepared her bedroom. When Joseph entered the room, Seela had candles lit all around the room. Wonderful smells filled the air. He had fantasized about this evening all week. Seela stepped out of the bathroom with a silky white gown draped on her slender body. Her long brown hair flowed around her shoulders. She smiled seductively as she approached him with calculated steps.

Joseph studied her, capturing her in his mind as if snapping a picture to hold in his brain for later thoughts. He touched her cheek as he ran his fingers over her neck. He pulled Seela's face to his. They kissed until they fell onto the bed. Seela and Joseph made love as if it were the first time for both of them. They moved slowly with each other, caressing and loving one another for hours until they clung together in blissful sleep.

The next morning, Seela woke to Joseph lying beside her, sleeping soundly. She quietly got out of bed and returned to Joseph with a hot cup of coffee. He laid his eyes on her. "Good morning, handsome. Did you sleep well?" she cooed.

"Did I ever! Probably the best sleep I've had in a long time, Seela. Definitely the best time I've ever had was last night with you."

Seela rested her head on her pillow. "All of this has been so wonderful for me, Joseph. I haven't had feelings or emotions like this ever. I had forgotten what being in love feels like. Ever since Sam got sick, my feelings have been so down. I almost feel guilty feeling these wonderful emotions I'm having right now."

He rolled over, squeezing her tightly. "Your brother wouldn't want it any other way, Seela. Sam loves you so much. He just wants you to be happy. Like he says, he doesn't want anyone crying over him."

"I know," said Seela. "I know he wants nothing but happiness for me. I still can't bear the thought of him dying. Will you see him tonight when you go back?"

"If you want me to go see him, I will. I wasn't planning on seeing him until tomorrow, but I can make a pop-up visit if you would like."

"I feel he's close to death," said Seela. "My mind and heart are heavy with him right now. Will you please check on him and let me know his condition? I need to see him this Sunday. Chester also needs to see Sam. I don't know what he wants to ask Sam, but it seems important to Chester. Sam has to hang on a little longer."

"I'll call you after I visit with Sam this afternoon and give you a report on your twin. He hasn't let me forget that you are his diamond that hangs from his chain."

Sam was busy that afternoon, getting a little yard time and then having Lil Jon drop him off at Mr. Williams's office to make a few phone calls and maybe eat some pizza with him. Mr. Williams had to quickly let Sam in and leave him to check on another inmate. He handed Sam his phone while motioning with his finger to his mouth to be quiet. Sam looked around Mr. Williams's office before calling his mom. The room was bare and held nothing of worth in Sam's dying mind. He then dialed his mother's number.

Catherine answered the phone quickly. "Sam, honey, is that you?"

"Yes, Mom. How you doing today? You been on my mind constantly. Joseph said you never leave your house. Have you got all your paintings done and sealed up? Did you hide everything like I told you, Mom?"

Catherine's hands shook. "Yes, Son, I got everything done just like you told me. It's all sealed, so no one will know. I feel very weak now but am happy we will be together soon. I'm trying to hold on for you, Sam, but don't know how much longer I can. This cancer has eaten me up, and now pain pills aren't working."

"Mom, I'm so sorry you are in pain. I'm going to send some of my morphine tabs with Seels when she comes this week. She'll give them to you. I hide them in my locker, so I got a pretty good stash."

"No need! I'm about ready to check out myself. I feel my time has been spent."

"Mom, will you at least talk to Seels before you think you are near the end? She needs to hear that you love her. I know she got Mamaw, but still, you are her mother, and I know she loves you."

Catherine crumpled into tears. "I will talk to her, Sam. I do love Seela as much as I do you. She's been gone for so long. I feel like she doesn't want to talk to me. She is here for you."

"That's not true, Mom. She said you wouldn't let her in."

"I couldn't, Sam. I had all my paintings out, and I couldn't let her see what I was doing with them. I was just going by your orders!"

"Okay, Mom, don't get upset! It's all right. I understand now. Listen, ole Willie is gone to get a pizza for us. He said we going to have a pizza party. I'm going to call you later to check on you, Mom. I guess this pizza will be my last supper of something good I like."

Catherine smiled. "I'm so glad Mr. Williams is so nice to you, Sam. It comforts my soul, knowing that you at least have some good people watching after you."

"Yes, Mom. It's how it's supposed to be. I've figured that much out. I was sent back for a reason. I know now why I didn't walk off with Granddaddy out of that fishing boat. A lot has happened in these past ten weeks. I had a lot of shit I needed to clean up and take care of before I die. I've about done it. Even finding love for Seela. Now, ain't that some good fucking shit?"

Cat took in this new information, knowing she would never see her daughter get married. "I'm happy for Seela too. I don't know this man, but you do, and if you approve, then I know Seels is getting a good man. It comforts my heart."

Joseph appeared, and Sam kissed into the phone before saying goodbye to his mother.

"Sam, you ready? We're going to take a ride to the break room."

Joseph pushed Sam down the cold cinder block hallway slowly, as if he were stalling with Sam. "Did you have a good conversation with your mom?"

"Yes, I did, Joseph. She real sick, in case you didn't know. She's eat up with cancer. I don't think Seels or my grandmother know how bad it is. She kept it a secret for a long time."

Joseph stopped Sam's wheelchair and walked in front of Sam to face him. "You mean to tell me that Seela is going to lose you and her mom at the same time?"

"Yes, that's what I fucking mean to tell you, Joseph."

Joseph stood in shock, trying to grasp what Sam had just told him. "I guess you and your mom have all this shit planned out, Sam. Is this what you call a fucking plan in your life? Do you realize what this is going to do to Seela?"

This was the first time Sam had heard Joseph become incensed. He was taken aback a little. "Yes, I fucking realize what it is going to do! It's my goddamn twin we are talking about. I feel every fucking emotion she does. Haven't you got that by now?" Sam's chest started to shake as he cried out. "I hurt so fucking bad thinking about what I've done in my life and how it is going to hurt my twin's heart and almost break it, Joseph. The only thing that I can hold on to now is that she has your love. That's huge to me, Joseph. I'm glad she knows and loves Chubby Chester now too."

Joseph looked confused. "What does all this have to do with Chester?"

"Seela needs all the love she can get once I'm gone. She'll get it from the two of you, Joseph. You two will fill her heart when it becomes empty when I die! You hear me?"

Sam sat with his head held down. "I'm fucking close to dying. It's almost time. Spirits coming to me all the time, calling me. I got to hold on a little longer and see Seels one more time. I have a few more stories to tell her, and then you can close the fucking book on Sam Black."

Joseph proceeded to wheel Sam in silence. He now knew he had to stay by Seela's side no matter what, given her mother's situation.

Lil Jon sat at the break table, smiling as if it were Christmas morning, as if he were waiting on Santa.

"Whew wee, Lil Jon. We getting ready to have us some pepperoni pizza. It pays off to hang out with the fucking dying big dog. Don't it?" Sam quipped as Joseph wheeled him to the table.

Big Sexy walked by and saw the group of men laughing and eating pizza. She stopped and poked her head in the door. "Now, how come I wasn't invited to this party y'all got going on up in here? Sam, I thought I was your babe. Why you holding out on me with hot pizza?"

"Big Sexy, come on over here, and get yourself some pie. You know I was going to bring you some back when I came to my room. Shit, you the only babe I got! You're my ray of sunshine that keeps me going every day, Big Sexy."

Sam reached up to embrace Big Sexy as she walked over. "Give me a hug, Big Sexy. Nobody in here going to say anything. I want to feel your sweetness wrap around me and give me a charge of all that goodness you have in your heart and soul."

Big Sexy complied this time. "I love you, Sam Black," she whispered. "You always remember that. You hear me? I know when you are gone from this hellhole, you'll fly high, and I'll have you always watching over me."

Joseph, Lil Jon, and Mr. Williams had tears in their eyes. Each one turned away so the others wouldn't see, though Lil Jon was more obvious, wiping his eyes with his sleeve. "Unc, I can't take all this kind of talk. I'm going to my room for a while, okay? I'll come check on you before count this evening and sit with you. Thanks for the pizza, Mr. Williams."

"No problem. We are just thankful you watch after Sam here. I know he appreciates you too."

Sam winked at Lil Jon. "He knows how I feel, and don't any of you worry. When I'm long gone and Lil Jon gets to go home, he will be rewarded for what all he did for me. I got that shit taken care of." Sam held his hand up in a fist to hit Lil Jon's. "We straight always, man."

Lil Jon tapped Sam's fist with his. "Yeah, man, we always straight. I love ya, Unc."

Lil Jon skipped down the hall toward his wing. AB was exiting the shower room with his towel and shower bag. "Hey, squirt! You coming from seeing Sam? How's he doing today? I didn't see y'all come out to the yard."

"He's not good, AB. I don't know how much longer he's going to have. He looked really bad today. I'm going back later to sit with him as long as Big Sexy will let me. You want me to tell Sam anything?"

AB reached into his shower bag. "Here—give him this paper. It has the card number for him to get your and his parts of profits from the Marls. You know if his twin bringing in more?"

Lil Jon stuffed the paper in his pocket. "Yeah, man, she's coming. I'm sure she'll be loaded—that is, if Sam makes it until then. I'm telling you—he's going down fast."

"I hate to hear that, Lil Jon. I know it's going to be hard on you when he does pass. You've had almost three months with him. Hasn't it been?"

"Yeah, it seems longer than that. I feel like he's my pops, and I got to take care of him until he dies. I don't think I've ever had such heartache. It's worse than when they locked me up for a few years. I'm kind of glad now because had I not met Sam Black, I may have never changed who I am and my walk in life. Somehow, he has made me love my soul, and I will be forever grateful for that. I will always do good by my son until the day I die."

AB nodded in agreement. "Yeah, I hear you, squirt. He's touched my heart also. I think about him all the time now. It seems to consume my brain. What a sad situation, and these motherfuckers think they have covered Sam's shanking all up. I know Sam Black, and I know this story will eventually come out some way."

Chapter 42

Seela woke up to bright sunshine cascading through her bedroom window. She had forgotten to close the blinds behind her sheer curtains the night before. She stayed still, feeling the bright beam of sun land on her face. Sam came to Seela's mind quickly. She knew how much he loved the sun, particularly now, as he had little to look forward to each day. Her cell phone rang suddenly with an unknown number showing up on her caller ID.

"Hey, twin," Sam said with a gravelly voice. He was sitting at Mr. Williams's desk. "I couldn't sleep, so I went ahead and got up early. Lil Jon already shaved me and helped me get a hot shower. You still sleeping, Sis? I know it's early."

"I was just thinking of you right before you called." She wondered where he was calling her from this time, but she didn't bother to ask those questions any longer. He obviously didn't function like other prisoners whose amenities had been stripped away.

"I know, twin. That's why I'm calling you. I felt your thoughts like sun shining bright down on my face. It just appeared so bright, and all I could think of was you. I love ya, twin."

Seela sat straight up in amazement. "Sam, I was just lying in my bed, letting the sun shine down on my face. I forgot to pull my blinds last night. The sun made me think of you, Sam! Do you think that was some kind of sign for us?"

"Holy fucking shit, Seels. I hope it's not my day to exit this shithole of a place. I got a few more things I need to clear up before then. You coming Sunday, right?"

"Yes, I'll be in your room, waiting for you when you come back from visiting Chester."

"Okay, great, Sis. I guess Joseph got everything set up. You love him yet?"

Seela hesitated and then said, "Yes, I do, Sam. I have fallen in love with Joseph. Do you approve of my choice?"

Sam smiled. "Hell fucking yeah, I approve. He's one good, solid man, Seels. I'm glad you two met. Promise me one thing, Seels. Okay?"

"Yes, Sam, what is it?"

"Let that man love you hard! You hear me? You deserve it. And one more thing, Seels. It's about Chester. Love him hard! I have loved him since he was a baby, and now you take that on, and continue it for me. I know how much Chubby loves you already."

"Don't worry, Sam. I'm going to treasure and love both of these men. I realize what love I've been missing all these years."

"Okay, Sis, I'll look forward to our visit. I got a lot to share this Sunday. You bring my usual order, okay, Seels?"

"I've already loaded up on cigarettes this week. I just need to get you some bubble gum."

"I love you, Sis, and I'll see you Sunday." Sam kissed his fingers and tossed them out to the air. "Catch it, Seels. I just threw my kiss out to you."

On the other end of the line, Seela reached into the air and grasped her hand. "I caught it, Sam! I'm placing it on my cheek right now."

"Maybe you should close that one up in a mason jar, Seels," Sam joked.

"Maybe I will," said Seela, desperate for more time with her brother.

As Seela drove down to her grandmother's, she called Chester's father. When Bill answered, Seela wasted no time in prying for information.

"I just want to chat about Sam and Chester's relationship," she said. "My brother told me that he has loved Chester since he was a baby. How is that?"

"You know I've known your family a long time, Seela. When Chester was a baby, Sam was out clean for a short time. He frequented my gas station and did some construction work for me. I believe that's when he got so attached to Chester. Sam seemed to be fascinated with Chester's Down's syndrome. They just became buddies. Chester loves your brother fiercely."

Seela thought about this for a moment, and the picture still didn't seem complete. She didn't think Bill had any further information, though. "Well, that explains it. Is it all right if Chester stays the weekend with us, Bill?"

"Sure, but he's already beaten you to that question. Chester left this morning with his Xbox and suitcase. He's with your mamaw, I'm sure, right now."

Chapter 43

Seela's weekend was filled with entertaining Chester and Joseph. They spent quite a bit of time at the ocean. They even persuaded Mamaw to go with them to the Shrimp Shack to listen to the beach music. When they explored the beach where Seela and Sam used to play, they made a pact to spread Sam's ashes there when the time came.

Early Sunday morning, Seela made herself a vodka with orange juice. She drank it while she got dressed and loaded herself up with the goodies Sam had ordered. She went into Chester's room, where he was sleeping. He was snoring obnoxiously loudly. Seela shook his shoulder slightly while speaking his name. "Chester, it's time for you to wake up. It's your day to see Sam."

Chester opened his eyes and instantly smiled at Seela. "Good morning, Ms. Seela. I'm so excited."

"You best be getting up and getting dressed. We have to leave soon. I'll fix you a bowl of cereal, okay?"

"Yes, Ms. Seela. I like Frosted Flakes. Mamaw got me some."

"Frosted Flakes it is."

Seela made herself a large cocktail while making Chester's cereal. She sat with Chester while he ate his breakfast. She sipped her orange juice as if there were no alcohol in it.

Seela and Chester quietly left the house without waking Mamaw. Seela played her music loudly, bouncing up and down to the beat as she continued to get intoxicated with Chester riding alongside her. Every once in a while, he looked at Seela and smiled.

Seela drove into the prison lot, turning the curve a little too fast, causing her tires to squeal. "Oh shit!" She chuckled and scanned the parking lot to see if anyone had seen her.

"Um, Ms. Seela?" said Chester.

"Yes, honey. I'm sorry if I scared you pulling in. I didn't realize how fast I was driving."

Chester grinned. "You drove fast the whole way here, Ms. Seela."

Seela smiled. "I guess I'm just excited to see Sam today, like you, Chester."

Seela walked Chester up to the tall barbed-wire gate. "Now, Chester, don't be afraid when they take you in, okay? You will be taken to a visiting room, where they will bring Sam down to see you for a short visit. He's very weak, so he won't be able to stay long."

"I know," said Chester. "I've seen him sick a lot, Ms. Seela."

"I know you have, but it's different now."

"I'll be strong for Sam. I love him."

Seela rubbed her hand along Chester's face. "I know you do, honey, and I know he loves you too."

The gate door opened, causing Seela to jump. "Well, I guess Joseph is coming to get you. Walk to that door, and the guard will let you in. You should see Joseph there waiting for you. I'm going to sit in my car while you have your visit. I'll come in afterward, and Joseph will take you back to Mamaw's house."

Chester nodded in compliance. Seela watched him until he was no longer in her sight. She walked back to her car and continued to drink her cocktail.

Joseph high-fived Chester as soon as he saw him. "Hey, Chester. You ready to see Sam?"

"Yes, sir, I am," said Chester. "I couldn't sleep last night, because I was so excited."

Joseph put his arm around Chester's shoulders. "Let's get you to the visiting room so you can see your favorite person."

Sam was waiting in the visiting room in his death-row wheelchair, trying to catch his breath. The fluid had built up so much around Sam's lungs that he was constantly gasping for air.

Joseph opened the door as Chester pushed around him to get to Sam. He ran over and knelt down beside him. "Hey, Uncle Sam. I couldn't wait to see you today. I'm sorry you are dying in here. Ms. Seela said she was trying to get you home, but they aren't letting you come."

Sam reached his hand out for Chester. "Hold my hand, Chubs. I've missed you too. You look good. Seela got you all fixed up. She cut your hair like that?"

"Yes, sir, she did. Mamaw gave me some of your clothes to wear too." Chester pulled on his shirt. "This one yours too, Sam." Chester smiled, raising his eyebrows up and down.

"It looks good on you. I hear you've become a part-time resident with my mamaw. How she doing, Chubby?"

"She is good, Sam. We went to the Shrimp Shack the other night. She danced in her wheelchair to the band. I love seeing her happy."

Sam smiled at the thought. "I'm so glad, Chubs. She needs a little fun time with all this shit happening right now. You understand that I'm dying right now, don't you, Chubs?"

Chester nodded and started to cry. "Ms. Seela and I went to you and her special place at the beach Friday. She showed me where you two played and caught sea creatures. I told her you told me about the place before. Can we spread your ashes there when you die, Sam?"

Sam shook his head in frustration. "Who said I wanted to be cremated, Chubs? I kind of got a scared feeling of being thrown in fucking fire. What if a part of me is still alive? Who said I wanted to be cremated anyway?"

Chester shrugged. "I don't know. I just heard Ms. Seela talk about it with Mamaw." Sam and Chester sat in silence while Sam regained his breath. Chester then looked Sam squarely in the face and asked, "Why didn't you tell Ms. Seela she's my mom?"

Sam's eyes popped open with new life. He tried to move up in his chair, but he was too weak. He threw his hand over his forehead, rubbing his face.

"She is my mom, right?" Chester said. "You told me a long time ago when you were at our house. Do you remember?"

Sam knew he had, but he'd hoped Chester was too young to remember. "Chubby, did you say anything to Seels about this?"

"No, sir. I made a promise to you I would keep it to myself. I always keep my promises. Why haven't you told her?" Chester was visibly upset now.

"I was going to do it today, Chubs. I am telling her everything today. Who's taking you home from here, Chubs?"

"Um, Yosef is. After he brings Ms. Seela to your room."

"Okay, well, it's going to be a hard afternoon for Seels. I'm fucking getting ready to download all my shit I've hid from her all our lives— some good and some bad. She'll be fine with you, Chester. You'll finally have your mom, Chubs!" At that, Sam and Chester both cried softly. "It's going to be okay, Chubby. Seels will never leave you again. As soon as you walk out of this place today, your life has changed for the better. I'll tell Seels how I got the Johnsons to adopt you and how I've watched over you all these years to make sure you were okay. I've already called old man Bill and told him what to expect. You can see him whenever you want, but he fucking knows you are going to be with my twin from now on, where you are fucking supposed to be."

Chester could barely contain his delight. At the same time, he loved his adopted father. It was all complicated for him to process next to Sam, who now looked like a mummy in his young eyes. Still, he loved him just the same.

"Chubs, listen to me. You the only real love I've had all these years since Seels left me on the island. Even when I was doped out, you still was the one who took care of me and gave me love to get strong again. I hate it that I was a fucking junkie all my life, Chubs! I've laid here for eleven weeks, miserably dying, and I've had all this time to reflect on my fucking shit of a life I made for myself. All I wanted was money and drugs, two things that ruin your life, and you can take neither one with you. The needle was my love and savior, and now I've come here to die and find out that only God is my savior. I've repented over and over about my decisions in life and how I threw it all away."

Chester could only nod, trying to take in the message.

"I just hope they let me in so I can be with my family who await me above. I'm hoping the things I've done in the past three months will help. Hell, you never know! Maybe I got some brownie points, Chubs. I'm ready to go fishing with my pops and granddaddy."

Chester said, "I love you, Uncle Sam. I'll always remember our times together."

Sam reached for Chester's hand. "They getting ready to come get me and take me upstairs, Chubs. Just remember, Seela is going to be upset this afternoon but not at you. Let her have time by herself. She is going to have a lot to process, okay? Do you understand?"

"I do," said Chester. He stood up without saying another word.

Lil Jon knocked and popped his head in. "Hey, Unc, I need to take you back upstairs now. You good?"

"Lil Jon, come in here, and meet my nephew."

Lil Jon held his hand out to shake Chester's hand. "Nice to meet you, man. You favor your uncle."

"Why do you call him Unc?" said Chester. "Is he your uncle too?"

Sam and Lil Jon chuckled. Chester's serious face did not waver. "He's not my real uncle," said Lil Jon, "but he sure feels like it. This man has touched my heart since he been in here. I would do anything for him."

"Me too," said Chester. "I love him. He is my real uncle." Chester leaned down and kissed Sam on his forehead, making Sam tear up again.

"Remember, Chubs, I'll always be with you. I'll watch over you until the day you come to be with me in the great blue yonder."

Chester walked out with them, holding Sam's hand. Joseph came around the corner and stopped suddenly. "Whoa, wait a minute. Chester can't be out walking freely without a guard escort."

Sam said weakly, "He's not. You're fucking here now."

"All right, Sam. You go on up to your room, and I'll take Chester out and bring Seela in to visit. I'm going to take Chester home, so Seela will be escorted out by another officer."

Sam stopped his wheelchair. "You aren't going to be here to escort her out today, Joseph?"

"No, I thought since I was taking Chester home, I would just stay and wait to see Seela at your mamaw's after your visit today."

"Well, it may not be good that you are there when she gets home today. I'm going to tell Seela some stuff that may upset her pretty bad. I don't want Seels taking anything out on you. She is going to need time to process a few things. Maybe you can take Chubs out somewhere this afternoon."

Joseph sighed, fearful of the storm stirring. "Sure, Sam. Is she going to be all right?"

"Fuck yeah, she'll be all right. She told me she loves you, man. That's not going to fucking change from what I tell her. She's just going to be in a little shock for a moment after hearing some of my shit and shenanigans. I know my twin. She'll just need a little time by herself."

"Okay, I'll take Chester out this afternoon. I'm sure Seela will call us when she's ready."

"Yeah, man. That sounds like a good idea. Come here, Chubs. Let me give you some of me right now. This is it." Sam held his arms out.

Sam pulled Chester's head down to him tightly, whispering in his ear, "My life is ending, but yours is just getting started, Chubs. You take care of Seels. You hear me?"

Chester could only cry. Joseph gently pulled him away. Chester looked back at Sam all the way down the hallway with tears flowing down his face. Joseph and Chester walked out to Seela's car. She had now consumed three courage juice cocktails. She tried to summon her composure when she saw Joseph and Chester. She walked over to Chester with a loose swagger and carefully placed her arm around him. "How was your visit with Sam, honey? How was Sam?"

"Good," said Chester. "We had a good visit. I'm going to miss Uncle Sam. It makes me sad, Ms. Seela."

"Honey, I know. It's sad for all of us. Soon he won't suffer anymore."

"Yeah," said Chester. "He's been sick a long time."

Seela and Joseph put Chester in Joseph's truck, locked the door, and instructed him not to open it for anyone except Joseph. As she walked away, Chester knew that in a matter of minutes, Seela would know that he was her son.

Seela walked briskly with Joseph to Sam's hallway, forgetting all about the contraband on her body. Between the courage juice and the distraction with Chester, all her nervousness had gone away.

"Well, here is where I'll leave you, Seels. I'll see you when you get home, okay? Have a good visit with Sam." Joseph pushed the button to make the double metal doors open. Seela only responded with a wink. These steps had become so routine that she glided right through.

Upon seeing Seela, Sam asked, "Where's Joseph? I have something for him."

Seela turned quickly, yelling at Joseph to come back. Joseph turned around and ran back quickly, assuming something was wrong with Sam. Instead, Sam sat smiling at Joseph as he entered his room. Sam handed him an envelope and commanded, "Read it after you've left this property."

Seela was swimming in curiosity but then noticed that her brother was gasping for air. "Can't they give you some oxygen?" she asked while rushing to his side.

Sam chuckled. "They don't have to do anything, Seels. I'm a dying prisoner they want dead. They for sure not going to make my fucking dying-ass self comfortable. This is it. I'm at the end. My body so tired of fighting to stay alive." His tears melted her heart. They cried together.

"I can't take this, Sam! I'm trying to get you released to come home and be with us when it happens. This is breaking all of our hearts. I don't care how hard it is for us to take care of you. We can do it. I will even call Johnny to see if he will help me. He never left this crazy island; he's bound to know someone. If I can get you home to Mamaw's, Chester and Joseph will help me."

"Stop it! Stop this nonsense now!" Sam shouted, making her pull back in alarm. "I been telling you for weeks there is nothing else to do but let me go here. The pain in my body is killing me. I can't breathe. I feel like I'm drowning underwater sometimes. Look how fucking big my legs and ankles are, Seels. I feel like if you tap them, they will explode. I feel like I've been in purgatory, but now I've been saved. I'm not afraid to die, Seels. It's okay now. I've learned a lot these past eleven weeks. I really think I was brought back to finish my life out. I would have gone straight to hell, Sis. God's waiting on me now with all our family. Come lay with me. I'm fucking freezing to death." Sam shivered while weakly patting the side of his bed.

Seela lay down beside Sam. In a matter of minutes, Big Sexy ran toward Sam's glass door. She motioned for Seela to get up out of the bed.

Sam shot Big Sexy the bird with his weak middle finger. "Fuck the prison rules. I'm fucking dying and checking on out of here. You let my twin lie here with me. Her body is so warm that it's heating my fucking freezing dying ass up."

Crying uncontrollably, Seela crossed her arm over Sam's swollen body. She snuggled up to him, as she had when they were kids curled up together in bed.

"Sis, I've rotted here now for almost three months, alone in the dark at night with all these green lights of respiratory equipment to keep me alive. There are things in life that I've realized I never knew before. All the money I've made in these prisons—I can take none of it with me. The only thing that has strengthened me these past weeks is love. I've given and built love. That is the only thing that will accompany me when I leave this shithole. I've learned that love has no limits and will be the only thing that travels with me. So, Sis, go have love with Joseph. Love your family and Chubby Chester. Make wonderful memories. That's the only thing that you will be taking with you when you leave earth. You hear me, Sis?" Neither Sam nor Seela could contain their emotions.

"Go where you want to go in life, Seels. Everything is in your heart and soul. Strive to reach whatever the hell you want. You hear me? I'm going to be watching you." Sam wiped his tears with his right sleeve and caught his breath for a bit before continuing. "I got some things to tell you, Sis. I got to get clean with you so I can watch after you with a clear conscience."

Seela sat up. "Sam, what are you talking about? What things have you done that I don't know about? I've known your past with drugs and burglaries. It's all over now. I love you no matter what. You are my twin."

"Listen to me. You know when you left the island and gave your baby up for adoption in that little town north of here?"

Seela sighed. "Yes, Sam. That was a long time ago. You know I couldn't keep the baby. I was just eighteen years old, and Johnny never would have let anyone know he loved a mixed breed, as we were called back then. I could have never given a baby the right home, when I was leaving mine with nothing."

Seela watched Sam's chest pump hard as he struggled to breathe. "It's okay, Seels," he said. "Your baby is fine. I had you followed when you left. I couldn't let you give your baby to some stranger. So I did something no one knows about but me. I found the Johnsons and found out his wife couldn't have children. I had them adopt your baby. I wanted to be able to see my blood grow up, Seels."

Seela leaped from the bed and stared at Sam. "Chester!" she cried. "He's mine?"

"Yes, Chester is yours, and he knows it. That's why he wanted to come see me today. I told him a long time ago when I was drugged out, and evidently, I told him to keep the promise with me and not tell anyone. I'll be fucking damned if he hasn't kept this secret from you all this time you've been with him. He's yours for good. I already told ole man Bill this week. I told him since Chester's adopted mom passed, he needed to go on and let Chester be with you. He agreed as long as he and Chester can see each other."

Seela tried to pace, but she felt light-headed on her feet. She lay back down beside Sam. She'd had no clue she had birthed a Down's syndrome child, as she couldn't remember taking any diagnostic tests to indicate this. He was so special to her heart, and now she knew why. "Were you ever going to tell me, Sam, if this had not happened to you? Does Mom know?"

"No, she didn't know, Seels. I just told her this week. She said you going to be upset with me. I hope you understand what I did. You left me, Seels. Chester was a part of you, so I couldn't let him disappear like you did, Sis. Please let me know you aren't mad at me. I can die now, knowing I gave him back to you, Seels. That's a great feeling for me."

Seela lay there beside Sam in a ball of emotions. Big Sexy came in to see what all the hoopla was about, but Sam waved her away. She resolved to watch them from the nurses' station.

"Seela, there is something else."

"Sam, I don't think I can take any more. Are you trying to take me with you?" Seela said sarcastically.

"Listen up. It's important. Remember when I told you about the inmates shanking me and said that I thought it was an ordered hit on me? Well, it was, and the investigation started when I came out of the coma. They sent in DEA to secretly talk to me so they could find out about all the corruption in the privately owned prison down in Cottonwood. Hell, it's not just there. It's in all the prisons. They all have their own mafia world in there."

"Okay, well, what do I have to do with the DEA?" Seela asked impatiently.

"You are in love with him, Seels. You know that letter I gave Joseph earlier?"

"What? No," Seela whispered in shock. She immediately felt betrayed and confused. Was Joseph just playing her to get information, or was he really in love with her? The question flashed in her mind like a blinking sign. She didn't need to hear any more. Seela jumped off of Sam's bed. "You mean to tell me this has all been a setup? For Joseph to make a prison bust? You both kept this a secret from me?" Seela felt her heart being pulled out of her chest.

Sam tried raising his hand, but he was so weak that he couldn't. "Seels, please calm down. Joseph had no choice in not telling you. But I'll tell you one goddamn fucking thing: that man loves you deep, Seels. Don't screw this up because of my fucking bullshit. Neither one of us thought you two would fall in love. He's a great man, Seels. The letter I gave Joseph tells him to crash my story. I don't want him involved in something so ugly against me, your twin. My story will come out later. I want you to write it in a book one day, and then people will know the story. I want everyone to know that heroin destroys lives. People are dying on this shit every day, Sis. Back when I started using heroin, people said you may as well put a bullet to your brain. Nowadays, it's people just trying to kill their pain!"

Seela could not believe her ears. Her life had changed in a matter of minutes thanks to this information that her brother had bombarded her with in order to clear his own conscience before dying.

Then she realized she still had his shit concealed. "What do you want me to do with your stuff?" she asked numbly. "I don't even know why you had me bring it in today. You seem to be so weak. How can you get it to your friends if you can't even get out of bed now?"

"Don't worry, Sis. I got my ways. It's stock for me. Throw it all in my locker right now. Nobody around looking in here. Cover it with my hat."

Seela dumped all the cigarettes and candy into Sam's locker. She then sat back down and acted as if she knew nothing.

"Pull your chair close to me, Seels. I want to hold your hand. It's warm, and mine are freezing. There's one more thing I have to tell you, Sis." When he saw how distraught she was, he laughed nervously. "This is good shit! It's about my money I want you to have, but you have to listen on how you are going to get it."

Her brother had been a prisoner of the state for most of his adult life. She wondered how he could have money saved.

"Seels, Mom has it all right now, and she's getting it ready for you. It should be enough for you to pay down on a house on the island and get situated with Chester. I know in my heart you are coming back. Aren't you, Seels? Open you up a small salon down here, Sis, and let Dee take over your other one. I'm leaving enough for you to do both. Fuck these motherfuckers who are looking for my money too. They'll never find it. Warden will never know how I got all my money back. I may be dead soon, but the people I love will benefit from my mistakes, not him."

"Sam, how will I get the money? How much is it?"

"Seels, I can't think about how much it is. I can't even focus on the next second. It's enough to help you and Chester. Mom is sending all her artwork to your gallery. I got somebody coming to pick it up and deliver it all to your house. When it gets there, just you and Dee be there. I want you two to carefully unwrap Mom's paintings. Okay?"

Seela could only sigh and agree. "Why don't you want anyone else to be around?"

"The paintings are all special. You'll see. You are going to jump for joy when you open them. Showcase the art for your first gala. I know she did great paintings for you."

"I would love to do that. I know the canvas is where Mom paints everything bottled up inside. I will dedicate the show to her."

They sat in silence until Seela felt as if she were crawling to get out of her skin. He had slapped her with so much information. She needed time alone. Seela got up abruptly and kissed her brother on his cold, clammy forehead. He already felt as if life and blood were exiting his body. Seela could feel Sam's breath of death looming over him, so she decided to stay longer and watch him sleep.

Sam tried to say the right words to reassure her about her future, but he knew she did not want to hear any more. Big Sexy brought Sam another blanket without saying a word. Seela watched Sam's eyes close and tried to process what would happen once she walked out of the prison this time. She felt Joseph had betrayed her by not disclosing that he was investigating Sam's case and that he was DEA, not a prison guard. She wondered if he knew she was bringing in contraband too. Furthermore, now she was officially mother to a child with special needs. Her mind reeled for the next hour before an officer came to escort her out. At the sound of the buzzer, Sam opened his eyes.

"I love you, Seels. You hear me?"

"I love you too, my twin. If you pass before I get back here to see you again, go fly high, and be my red cardinal that watches after me. Come visit me, and let me know you are happy, Sam. Let me know you are watching over me and Chester."

At the sound of Seela and Chester being together, Sam rejoiced. He held Seela's hand weakly. "I'll always be watching over you. Every time you see that cardinal, throw a kiss up to me. Because that's where I'm going, Sis. Up! I think the good Lord is getting ready for a party!"

Seela kissed Sam several times before the estranged officer appeared at Sam's door. "I have to go now Sam. I'll be alright. I just need a little time to process everything you told me today. I love you, Sam."

"I love you my twin with all of my heart. I'm your cardinal from now on. You got it?"

"I got it Sam. I'll be watching for you, Seela said with a tearful voice."

The officer walked Seela down to the outside gate in silence. The fresh air seemed to only intensify her shock over what she had learned.

Once in the sanctuary of her car, Seela sat for some time with pressing questions. She wondered if Joseph knew about Chester. Her heart ached, knowing that Joseph had kept so much from her.

Chapter 44

Seela drove away from the prison, not knowing what direction she wanted to take. She knew she couldn't go back to Mamaw's just yet. She searched for her phone and called Dee, who sounded as bubbly as ever before Seela interrupted her.

"Dee, are you sitting down?"

When Dee confirmed that she was, Seela continued. "I never told you, but I gave a baby up for adoption when I was eighteen, before leaving the island. I just found out today that my baby is Chester. Sam has kept this secret all these years from all of us. My mother didn't even know."

"Holy shit! Chester is your son? It just seems impossible. Well, are you and Chester going to be together now? Are you ready to be a parent?"

"I get my son back, Dee! I knew the first time I met Chester there was something about him. I knew he was going to be in my life forever. It was the strangest feeling. He knew it too."

"Seela, it's not going to be easy to just become a mother overnight, what with the salon and the gallery, and what about his father? This is just unreal!" Dee could not believe what she was hearing.

"I am not going to abandon my son again, Dee. Bill knows everything. Apparently, Sam warned him and everybody else that today would be a tell-all marathon. There's more, Dee, but it's already taking everything out of me to drive safely. I will see you all soon, but I won't be back right away."

With these words, Dee was afraid that Seela would wreck or do something crazy. "Seela, don't you dare hang up on me yet. Please. I will come get you. Where are you?" She heard silence on the other end. She knew it would be fruitless to call her stubborn friend back.

In the meantime, Chester and Joseph finished cleaning the flower beds in Mamaw's yard. "How about you and I go get an ice cream? Does that sound good?" Joseph said. He was going crazy, wondering what Sam had shared with Seela and how she was doing.

"Yes, sir, Yosef. I love ice cream. I love chocolate." Chester shuffled down the driveway. "I'll go tell Mamaw we are going for ice cream."

Chester opened the carport door and yelled, "Mamaw, Yosef and I are going to get ice cream! You want us to bring you some back?" Chester winked at Joseph. "Mamaw like chocolate too."

Mamaw wheeled into the kitchen with her kitchen towel draped around her neck. "You boys go have fun. I don't need any ice cream. I've been cheating, eating those cake doughnuts Seela brought me. My sugar has to be high right now!"

Joseph opened his truck door and saw the envelope Sam had given him. He had forgotten to open it and read it. Chester had become his afternoon enjoyment.

"Hey, Chester, can we wait a minute so I can read this note from Sam?"

Joseph sat down in one of the freshly painted Adirondack chairs in the beautiful new garden Chester had made. Chester stood by Joseph's truck. He had a feeling he knew what was in the letter. As Joseph read Sam's letter, his face showed a number of emotions. At one point, he set the letter on his leg and just stared at it. Once he'd finished, he motioned for Chester to come over to him. Chester walked slowly, as if he were in trouble.

Joseph stood up and grabbed Chester before Chester could get to him. "Come here, son. Let me give you a hug." Joseph hugged and held on to Chester for what seemed to be an eternity. He then pushed Chester back so he could see his face before he spoke. "Did Sam tell Seela today about you, Chester?"

Chester nodded. "He said he was planning on telling her today even before I asked him why he hadn't told her yet. Ms. Seela is my mom, Yosef."

"I know. That's one of the surprises I just read in my letter here from Sam. How long have you known, Chester?"

"One time, Sam told me when he was staying with us. He was sick, throwing up for days, and I helped him get better. That's when he told me. He made me promise to keep it a secret. I don't think he remembered telling me. Will Ms. Seela be mad at him?"

"No, Chester, I don't think she can be mad at her dying twin brother, but she is going to have some strong emotions to deal with. From the sound of this letter, she learned a few more things that she didn't know."

"Like what?" asked Chester.

"Let's see what Seela tells us when we see her. Let's take a ride and go see the ocean, and then we will get some ice cream. Sound good?"

As they made their way down the driveway in Joseph's truck, they spotted Mavvie running to her house. She still had on all white for Sam. She stopped suddenly, waving at them to stop. "Where is Seela?" Mavvie shouted.

Joseph rolled his window down. "She should be coming home by now. Her visiting hours are up. You should see her soon, Mavvie. After today's visit, I'm sure you will be the first person she wants to see."

"I'll go get ready. I feel her presence right now, and she's not happy. Do you know what happened today?"

"No, ma'am, I don't. I do know Sam downloaded all his stuff on her today. She definitely has to be feeling a lot of emotions from her past." Joseph patted Chester's shoulder. "This one, for beginners."

Chester leaned forward and yelled, "Seela's my mom, Mavvie!" He grinned as big as he could.

Mavvie pulled her turban off of her head and threw it up into the air with her long hair flowing out behind her. Tears filled her eyes. "I knew it was so, Chester. I was waiting for Sam to tell us. I felt it the first time I met you. Welcome to the Black family!"

Chester could only continue grinning. "We going to get ice cream."

With that, Joseph waved and drove off, leaving Mavvie standing there, anxiously waiting for Seela.

Seela stopped at a liquor store by the prison and bought a bottle of cheap wine. She then drove, drinking from a Dixie cup all the while. She eventually pulled up to a favorite place she and Sam had shared as children. She drove as far as she could without driving onto the sand. Seela sat on her car's hood with the remaining swigs of her wine. She cussed and fussed to the sky, as if her angels were standing at attention while she scolded them for not foretelling the past three months. She argued with her angels about Joseph. If he had kept this secret of being undercover after they had fallen in love, what else could there be?

Seela lay on her car's hood until darkness set in, and then she headed to Mamaw's, knowing everyone would be worried about her by now.

Seela's phone rang, startling her, as she drove through the swampy roads. She saw that it was Joseph. She took a deep breath and answered. "Hello, Joseph. Are you at my grandmother's?"

"Yes, Seela. We all were getting worried. Thought you may be home by now. Is everything okay?"

"I am heading there now. Could you please tell Mamaw and Chester I will be home shortly? And then I need you to leave."

Seela's instruction stung like a bee. "I would like to see you. I need to discuss Sam's letter he gave me. It's really important."

"He discussed everything with me today, even the part you seem to have left out about your being DEA. I trusted you with my heart, Joseph. You lied to me, and now I don't know how I feel anymore."

Joseph's heart twisted into knots. He was madly in love with Seela— that was not a facade. "Seela, please let me explain everything. Sam and I didn't know it was going to turn out this way. He's the one who asked me to get his story so it wouldn't be just swept under the rug like a lot of things are in the prison system. Don't shut me out, Seela. I do love you and can promise I haven't lied to you about anything but my position in the prison."

"I suppose you knew about Chester too," said Seela.

"Whoa, wait a minute. Is that what you think? I just found out in my letter that Chester was your son. Hell, I didn't even know you had a child. Please let me talk to you. I need to see you. I love you. I love Chester too."

Seela took a deep breath. "Not tonight, Joseph. Please leave so I can come home and talk to Chester. I need to explain why I did what I did back then."

Joseph resolved to not press the matter right now. He needed to be patient. He knew she loved him.

Joseph delivered Seela's message to everyone and politely said he needed to turn in early. When he hugged Mamaw, she held on to him fiercely. When he embraced Chester, he didn't want to let go. They had all become family during this bizarre mix of both wonderful and tragic events.

Once Joseph was in his truck alone, his mind did somersaults. His investigation of the drug ring and Sam's shanking were now thrown out the window. He had no useful information to take back to headquarters. And what of his job now? Would he lose it because of a fouled investigation? And what about Seela, whom he loved fiercely? Would he lose her because of the concealment?

All of a sudden, Joseph felt as if a tornado had swept him up, mangled him, and spit him out all alone. Tears rolled down his face. Joseph wiped his face with an old crumpled napkin he found on his truck seat from Chester's ice cream. Joseph looked up to the dark, starry night. "Please, God, if you give me this one, I promise I will take care of Seela and Chester for the rest of my life."

Seela pulled up to Mavvie's house. Mavvie appeared in the doorway to welcome her with open arms as Seela ran into them. "Mavvie, it's been the worst day of my life. I couldn't wait to get here to see you. Please help me decipher what the heck is going on. I don't know if I can take it."

Mavvie rubbed Seela's forehead. "It's okay, my Seelie. This day had to come, and no, it wasn't your worst day of life. Remember that!" Mavvie's eyes bulged out.

Seela stopped crying. She wiped her tears and tried to speak with a normal voice, but the message tumbled out in a drunken haze. "What do you mean? You weren't there! You don't know what all Sam told me today. Or do you? Did you know about Chester?"

Mavvie chose her words carefully. "I've had strange feelings about Chester since the day he stepped on our property. My emotions always stirred strong when I got around him. I've been trying hard to figure it out. Then there was your apparent bond with him right away."

Seela proceeded to tell Mavvie how she'd given Chester up to an adoption agency and how Sam had persuaded the Johnsons to adopt him as a newborn. Mavvie did a few rituals on Seela before sending her home to her grandmother's to see Chester for the first time as her son.

On her way to Mamaw's, Seela noticed her mother's lights on. She approached her door and knocked once. "Mom, are you awake?"

When Cat didn't answer, Seela continued talking. "I saw Sam today, and he gave me a lot of information that I want to share with you. It won't be long now. Sam is ready to die."

Catherine was feverishly painting. She wore large headphones that drowned out any noise beyond the music. Seela resolved that she would return in the morning and force her way in if she had to.

Seela walked up to Mamaw's back door, hearing Chester's Xbox playing loudly. As soon as she entered, Chester threw his controller down onto the sofa, ran with his crooked feet to Seela, and threw his arms around her torso, squeezing as tightly as he could.

"Uncle Sam tell you, Ms. Seela?" Chester gazed at her with unconditional love.

"Yes, Chester, he did. Why didn't you tell me before if you knew? I can't believe you've held this in all this time."

"I couldn't tell you. I promised Uncle Sam a long time ago. That's why I had to see him before he dies."

Seela held on to Chester tightly. "I'm so sorry, honey. I did what I thought was the right thing at that time. I was just a kid."

"It's okay. I know. Uncle Sam told me that too. He said it was the right thing for you to do. He told me he would let me meet my real mom one day. I have you now. He said today I get to be with you always. Is that true?"

Seela stroked Chester's hair. "Yes, you never have to leave me again. We are all family. You have all of us. I'll even try to get you another visit to see Sam, since you are his blood."

"I would like that," said Chester.

Mamaw wheeled out from the bathroom. "Whew wee, don't anybody go back there for a while. You would think something crawled up in me and died. Whew, that's some powerful shit back there." Mamaw waved her hand back and forth in front of her face, cutting the heavy conversation with shared laughter.

"Mamaw, I'm sure you know by now about Chester?"

"Hell yeah, I know. Chester told me as soon as he got back from visiting Sam, but I'll tell you one thing, Seela: your brother kept that nugget to himself for all these years. I just can't believe he cheated me out of being able to have Chester in my life all this time."

"He couldn't, Mamaw. Think about it. He gave his word to the Johnsons. I'm just thankful now that he did it, because how would I have ever gotten Chester back? I see now that he did the only thing he knew to do."

"What do I call you now?" asked Chester.

"What do you want to call me? What did you call your adopted mom?"

"Mama," said Chester. "Can I call you Mama, Ms. Seels?"

"That sounds nice."

Mamaw wheeled over to Chester and took his hand. "Well, at least you don't have to change my name. I've always been your mamaw, and now more so since we are blood. You my great-grandchild, Chester. I just realized I'm a great-gran!"

They rejoiced in the moment.

"Can I call you Great-Gran?" asked Chester. "I like that."

"Sure, honey, you call me whatever you want."

"Why don't I cook us some dinner?" said Seela, feeling light-headed. She hadn't eaten a thing since early morning, before getting loaded with courage cocktails and, later, wine.

"Can we have hamburgers tonight with french fries?" Chester said.

"Let's see what we have in the fridge, Chester," Seela replied cautiously before taking inventory. "You are in luck. It looks like Great-Gran has all of that to fix."

Mamaw smiled and winked at Chester. "I guess we'll have a McDonald's kind of night then."

"Yep," said Chester. "I like McDonald's, but I like Mama's burgers better." He rubbed his tummy, thinking of homemade fries.

After dinner, Seela tucked Chester into the guest bed. She sat on the side of his bed, studying him, now knowing he was her son. She whispered, "I love you, Chester, and always have. You were so special to me the first time I met you, and now I know why." Seela smoothed Chester's blanket down around him and touched his face softly before quietly leaving the room. He watched her in true bliss.

Once tucked in her room, Seela called Dee, who was now safely at home, sipping on some cognac. She couldn't believe the news about Chester. Dee wondered how everything would play out with their lives in Clairsville, given the busy salon and the new gallery Seela had to manage. Dee answered her phone, saying, "Dare I even ask what else Sam's dying ass told you today?"

"Dee, Joseph's been undercover all this time! That man is as much a prison guard as I am an astronaut. He's been investigating the drug ring tied to Cottonwood and Sam's shanking. He never leaked a word, Dee. I don't know if I can trust or see him again." Seela could feel her face on fire with raw emotion. "You know how I am about trust, and I lost some of that with him today."

"Whoa, hold on, Seels. You can't be saying this right now. That man is a wonderful person. I'm sure he has explanations for everything he has done. You better give him a chance to talk to you about everything, girl. He loves you. Don't throw this beautiful love away! This is a serious investigation. He had to do what he had to do. It wasn't like a big, bad secret that would hurt or betray you. You need to look at this from all sides, not just yours, Seels."

Seela knew Dee was right, but exhaustion was setting in, and she couldn't think straight. "Dee, I desperately need sleep. I know the salon is in good hands this week. Tell all the ladies I miss them and will be back in the hair world soon. I love you, friend!"

The next day, Seela woke to the sound of coffee percolating. She wondered who had beat her to the machine. Seela tiptoed down the hall and peeped in on Chester, who was snoring loudly like a motorboat getting ready to take off from the dock. As she turned the corner into the kitchen, there sat Dee. She was reading the morning paper with her back to Seela.

"What is going on? When did you get here? I just talked to you last night! Am I dreaming?"

Dee jumped up. "Come here, girl. Let me hug you. You think I would leave you here to deal with all of this shit by yourself? You need me. I drove down after sipping on some cognac, and Mavvie let me in. I can't believe you didn't hear us giggling."

"Are you kidding me? After yesterday, I was out like a light! What about the salon? We just can't take all this time off and maintain—"

"Seela, get a grip. You're dealing with some real shit! Everybody in that town can wait a week for their hair." Dee went about pouring them coffee as Seela watched her in disbelief. Her life was chaotic; there was no more sense of normalcy.

Chester walked out into the kitchen in his pajamas with his hair disheveled. He beamed at the two women. "Dee, did Mama tell you what Sam told her yesterday?"

"Yes, Chester, she did. So I hear you coming to live with us?"

Chester stepped back, studying Seela's face. "Um, Mama? We aren't going to live here with Joseph?"

Seela was surprised to hear Chester ask that question. "Chester, I haven't thought of any of that yet. We have to make sure Sam rests in peace. Just knowing I have you now forever is the greatest feeling. I haven't even grasped the thought of where we will live."

"What about Joseph? Will he move with us to your house?"

Seela looked at Dee and then back at Chester.

"Joseph didn't do anything wrong," Chester said. "He loves us. He told me yesterday. I love him too. Don't you love him?"

"Yes, Chester, honey. I care for him deeply, but right now, my focus is Sam and you. Okay? Now, let's go surprise Mamaw with Dee being here. She's going to be so happy!"

They all snuck into Mamaw's bedroom, where Mamaw lay peacefully, snoring softly in rhythm, as if she were singing in her sleep. The three of them watched Mamaw as if she were a beautiful angel. Then Chester sneezed, startling Mamaw from her peaceful sleep. She jumped when she saw all of them standing at her bedroom door.

"Goddammit, this better not be some bad news about Sam, Seela. All y'all standing there like that about give me a heart attack. Dee! When did you get here? When I went to sleep last night, everyone was tucked in bed, sound asleep, and your gorgeous self wasn't here!"

Dee ran over to help Mamaw sit up on the side of her bed.

"Well," Mamaw said, "if it's a beautiful morning, then that means my grandson didn't pass last night while I was asleep. I dreamed about him all night. It gave me fits all night long. My heart feels heavy right now."

Dee sat beside Mamaw on her bed, rubbing her back. "You supposed to have those feelings, but I promise one day there will be a time when you realize that the heaviness you felt is gone. You will only have laughter and great feelings for that person. That's how it was when my mother passed when I was a child."

Mamaw lay her head on Dee's chest. "Aw, honey, I didn't know you lost your mom when you were a child. Did you know, Seela?"

"No, I didn't. Dee, why haven't you told me that before? You just said your mother was dead and had been for a while."

Dee looked over at Chester. "Chester and I have this in common. I wasn't raised by my mom either when I was little. I had foster parents, kind of like your adopted parents. Thank goodness they kept me until my father got out of prison and was able to get me back. That was one of the two best days of my life. The day I met Seels was the second best day."

Everyone stared at Dee for more information. Dee turned and stared out the window, pausing. She didn't want Seela to think she had betrayed her, as she believed Joseph had. "My father was in prison for ten years for manslaughter. He was a bad alcoholic. He got in a fight with a guy at a local bar one night. The guy he hit fell and hit his head on the corner of the pool table, which killed him. My father was so drunk he didn't even remember the fight or what it was about. He was sober for the rest of his life. When he was released early with good behavior and work studies, the first thing he did was find me. I promised him the day he died I would always be his bright and shining light down here when he looked down upon me. I know he and my mom are together, and I feel they orchestrated me meeting Seela. I'm sorry for not telling you the truth about my childhood sooner. I hope you don't feel you can't trust me now, Seela."

Seela realized that everyone was on high alert, knowing that she felt betrayed by Joseph. She had nothing but love for Dee as they embraced on Mamaw's bed, making them all topple over.

As Chester helped Mamaw sit up, she quipped, "Okay, now that we've all hugged and cried at the beginning of our morning, can someone help me to the potty? I feel everything moving inside, getting ready to exit. Seela, help me to the toilet!"

Dee and Chester ran out quickly, hoping no poop popped out of Mamaw before they could get out of her bedroom. "That was a close call, Chester. That's the last thing you want to smell before breakfast," Dee said. They chuckled together.

"Sometimes I do."

Dee laughed hysterically at Chester. "You are a hoot!"

Chester smiled at Dee, not knowing what a hoot was.

Chapter 45

Sam had a horrendous night and doubted he would make it to the following Sunday to see Seela one more time. He wanted to make sure she hadn't crashed her car or anything after hearing all the shit he had informed her of. It had now been a few days since their lengthy conversation.

Lil Jon popped up at Sam's door with his usual mop in hand. Big Sexy buzzed him in immediately. They knew the end was near, as Sam could not move at all. Lil Jon's eyes fill with tears as he stood there, looking at a man he had only known for three months. He loved him, and his heart was breaking from watching Sam die miserably. Big Sexy stood next to Lil Jon. "I hear the death rattle in his chest. I about spent the night in his room with him. I couldn't imagine him dying all by himself in here. He's holding on, I think, so he can see his sister one last time."

"Can I sit with him at night?" replied Lil Jon. "We don't have to let anyone know. I'll lie on the floor, and no one will know I'm in there. Please, Big Sexy. I would die if he died all alone. This is killin' me!"

"Okay, I'll see what I can do. You just keep your mouth shut. Don't say anything to anyone about Sam. You hear me?"

"Yes, ma'am." Lil Jon acted as if he were zipping his lips up. "I got you."

Big Sexy squeezed Sam's hand and then left to get back to other duties. Lil Jon wet a sponge at the tiny sink hanging on the wall next to Sam's toilet. He then wiped Sam's dry mouth inside and out. He unwrapped a piece of gum and placed it in Sam's mouth. Sam chewed it slowly, breaking the bubble gum down. He grabbed Lil Jon's hand, speaking with his weak, broken voice.

"Hey, man, you need to listen to me. I want you to take every cigarette I have out of my locker and put them in your pockets. Take them to AB. Let him sell them, and you two split the profits. Get them now while no one is looking in here. I'm watching everybody out there."

Lil Jon opened the locker and collected every cigarette as fast as he could stuff them in his overall pockets. "There are about four packs in here, Sam."

"That should bring you both in about eight hundred dollars apiece. That's my exit gift to the two of you. You've helped my last three months of life be easier to deal with while I fucking die here. Thanks for keeping me clean and my fucking hellhole of a cell here clean. Come over here, my boy. I need to hug you. I love ya."

Lil Jon bent down, embracing Sam and crying like a five-year-old. "I love you too, man. You gave me a love I've never felt before, Unc. You like the pop I never had. I'm going to miss you so much."

Sam pushed Lil Jon back so he could see his face. "Don't act stupid or do anything that could cause them to put you in lockdown when I pass. This place didn't put me here. They didn't do this to me. I did it to myself. You understand? Don't get angry with anyone in here. I'm ready to go on now. I've done the work I was sent back to do."

Lil Jon tapped his fist to Sam's. "We straight." He wiped the tears from his face. "Big Sexy going to let me sit with you tonight. She worried like me. We don't want you to be alone when you do leave this shithole. Who knows? If I'm with you, maybe I'll see you fly out the window."

"You better believe I'll tell you to watch my fucking angels take me right on out of here if you in here when the time comes." Sam reached for his oxygen mask. Lil Jon placed it over his face for him. Sam said through the mask, "Go meet AB out in the yard while you can. Get that shit off of you quick."

Lil Jon threw his thumb up. "I'll be back after count, and then I'm making a pallet on your floor tonight."

As Lil John exited, Big Sexy entered with her headphones. She turned her music on, adjusting it to Sam's ears. "I downloaded more of your favorites. Enjoy. Do you need a shot?"

Sam nodded. "Dope me up as much as you can. I'm done. I realized I started chasing money and drugs all at a very young age, when all I ever wanted was love. I know now that is the only thing you can take with you when you leave here, Big Sexy. Material things, money, sex, and drugs—none of that means anything in the end when you are lying in a fucking prison hospital bed, dying. Now I feel my soul is full. It's ready to transcend to the next world beyond this one."

Big Sexy cried with pain and joy. "Sam, that is so beautiful to hear. I know you are going to a great beyond from here. I'm so glad I got to know you. All the years I've worked in here, I've never gotten attached to an inmate. You were the first, Sam." She kissed Sam's hand after giving him a large dose of morphine.

As soon as she left, Sam called Charlie, who picked up right away. "This is my last time I'll talk to you Charlie. You live life to your dreams. You hear me? If you want to go be on fucking Broadway, go do it! Live life now. You don't get but one chance. Who cares if you feel like you got the wrong fucking body? Deal with it the best you can, and live for who you think you are. Don't fucking worry about what anybody thinks of you as a transgender woman. Be proud of who you are, and go out and live strong, Charlie. Promise me that!"

"I promise," whispered Charlie as she cried into the phone hysterically.

"One more thing. Forget about all the material things you think you need. I've been lying here, dying in this hospital bed, for the past three months. The number-one thing I learned while being kept locked up in this shithole of a prison is that none of that is important in your life. Your soul is the only thing you have when you are dying. Get your soul right, Charlie. All my love, Charlie," Sam said, and he didn't give her a chance to reply.

Charlie sat on her sofa, holding the phone to her chest while tears blotched her mascara. She would send the last money cards that she held on to for Sam to the addresses he had given her. There would be no more ties to that part of her life. Sam was right. She had to live strong and proud. It was time for Charlie to make something of her life and fill her soul.

Lil Jon went to the yard and saw AB sitting on his usual perch with a few inmates gathered around, shooting the daily bullshit of what they knew. AB motioned for them all to walk away. Lil Jon skipped up quickly to him.

"How is Sam doing?" asked AB. "You haven't brought him out in a week. What's up?"

"He's at the end, AB. It's like the fucking plug was pulled on him. He ready too. He asking for big shots of morphine now, when a month ago, he was hiding his pills from the nurses. It's breaking my heart watching him too, AB!" Lil Jon looked out into the yard, trying to steady his quivering voice.

AB tapped Lil Jon on the back, which was his version of an embrace. "It's his time. He been here long enough, being tortured like that for three months. I know you don't want to lose him in your life here, but he's got to go on. This here been his fucking hell. It's time he fly this coop and go be with whatever there fucking is beyond here."

Lil Jon scanned the yard. No one seemed to be paying attention to them. "Sam gave me four packs of Marls, and I have them in my pocket. He said you and I split the profit, which would be eight hundred dollars apiece. How you want me to give them to you?"

"Whoa, slow your roll, partner. Let me think about it a minute. I need to assess the yard. It's all about timing. Okay, you pretend you are tying your shoe, and pull out the cigs at the same time. Drop them by your shoe. Do it quickly now."

Lil Jon's heart was beating so fast that he felt as if it would beat out of his body. He leaned down quickly, throwing the cigarettes in between his two feet as he tied his shoe. AB laughed loudly, as if someone had said something funny. He then jumped from the table and bent over, still laughing as he snatched the baggie of cigarettes up from Lil Jon's feet. He stuffed them into his prison jumper so fast that no one noticed their quick exchange.

As promised, Lil Jon returned to Sam's room after count, holding a pillow and three blankets. With the headphones still on, Sam smiled at Lil Jon. Big Sexy scurried over to Lil Jon with a key to Sam's room. "Hurry, Lil Jon. Get in there, and get down on the floor. I don't want to see your head pop up unless something is happening to Sam, okay?"

"Yeah, yeah. You won't see me, Big Sexy."

Lil Jon ran in, tossing his pillow and two of the blankets onto the floor beside Sam's bed. He threw the other blanket over Sam's body. Big Sexy swished over to Sam and pulled the headphones off of his head gently. She left the men there, not knowing what they would all wake up to. Lil Jon tucked himself in as well as he could with what he had. "This floor is fucking hard down here. I don't care, though. I can handle it. I've definitely slept in worse situations, Sam."

Sam hung his hand down for Lil Jon to hold. Lil Jon held it while they both tried to sleep. The sound of the oxygen machine chimed in the background, which helped. Lil Jon could feel the death in Sam's hand. It was almost as if his soul were already lifting. Lil Jon felt as if he were holding the hand of Sam's corpse. Every once in a while, Lil Jon sat up to see Sam's heartbeat. A few times in the night, Sam yelled out the names of people Lil Jon had not heard of.

The next morning, when Big Sexy opened Sam's door, Lil Jon was curled up beside Sam in his bed, with his head at Sam's feet. Lil Jon's body was so small that he fit perfectly at the end of Sam's bed. Lil Jon jumped when he heard the door opening. "How long you been in Sam's bed, Lil Jon? It's a good thing I'm the only one working. You two could have gotten my fat ass fired."

Lil Jon skipped out the door quickly. "Don't worry, Big Sexy. There ain't nobody seen me. Besides, if they did, I don't believe nobody would do anything. As Sam always says, everybody in here know what time it is with him."

Chapter 46

That evening, Joseph called Seela several times. She didn't answer. Finally, he decided to drive over to her grandmother's house to see Seela face-to-face. He needed to declare his love for her. As soon as he turned into the driveway, Mavvie waved him down. Joseph pulled over, rolling his window down to speak to Mavvie. "Good morning, Mavvie."

"I knew you were coming, and I wanted to catch you before you see Seela. Will you drive me to my house? I would like a few words with you." Mavvie's words were calculated.

Mavvie hopped into the truck and stared ahead until they approached her house. "Please give me one second before you come in, and please take your shoes off at my front door. I'll motion when I'm ready, Joseph."

"Okay, no problem. I'll wait right here, Mavvie. Just let me know."

On the porch, Joseph unlaced his shoes and waited patiently. Mavvie opened the beautifully carved door, and smoke billowed out from behind her. She waved for Joseph to come inside.

Joseph hesitated, looking at all the smoke, but he noticed Mavvie holding one of her sage sticks, which Seela had told him about in the past.

"Hurry. I want to shut the door quickly," said Mavvie, so Joseph kicked his shoes off and stepped inside. "Please stand here." Mavvie waved her sage stick from Joseph's feet to the top of his head, chanting. Joseph stood still. "Okay, now go sit over there. Pick a seat." She watched to see which chair he would choose. He chose Seela's favorite purple chair.

"Are you comfortable, Joseph?" asked Mavvie as she made him hot tea.

"Very," said Joseph. He stared around in amazement at all the items Mavvie had collected over her lifetime. The place was like a mirage of her life, shaped by earthly treasures that only God could have made. He felt serene while sitting in her home, just as Seela had described.

"Mavvie, have you talked to Seela about us? I know I don't have to ask you about everything. I mean, I know you already know." Joseph was becoming agitated.

"You just need to give her some time to digest everything that has happened in the past few days. Let her breathe a little, and she will come back to you. Seela loves you."

Joseph took a deep breath. "You don't know how those words make me feel. I was beginning to wonder if I would ever see her again. She hasn't answered any of my calls."

"She's trying to get a grasp on learning that Chester is her son. She's thinking of you, Joseph. I know!" Mavvie held her hand out. "Come. Will you lie on my table? It will be most enjoyable. I promise."

Joseph hesitated and then complied. He had nothing to lose. He walked slowly to Mavvie's healing room, which glowed with candles and amethyst gemstones the size of car tires sparkling all around her room. As Joseph lay down on the table, Mavvie chanted in a French accent, saying words he couldn't understand. She told him to close his eyes and think of Seela. Beautiful thoughts came to Joseph's mind. He stayed still with his arms down by his sides. Mavvie waved a sweeping brush over Joseph. He felt a heavy feeling go through his body. His face changed to an expression of sadness. His eyes remained closed. Mavvie then shook her cloth bag over Joseph's body. Light powder sprinkled over him. He could smell a strange scent, but it was nice. It made him feel good.

Mavvie then touched his shoulder, squeezing two times. "You can sit up when you like now, but don't until you are ready. Take your time."

Joseph lay there for at least a minute, thinking about everything that had come up in his mind while he was on the table underneath

Mavvie's unbelievable special powers. He felt light now, as if all the negative thoughts of his relationship with Seela had been washed away.

"Joseph, I'm sorry to tell you that tonight is not the night for you to see Seela. Give her time. She will come to you. I promise. I know my niece. Now, there is something you need to do for me."

"Sure, anything, Mavvie. What is it?"

"I need to see Sam as soon as possible. Can you take me?"

"It's just not that easy. I'll have to pull some strings, and they say he is so weak now that it could be any minute when he passes. I'm really sorry."

Mavvie grabbed Joseph's hand. "It's not too late. You will get me in there tonight, Joseph. I have to see him before he dies. Let's go now."

Joseph could not believe his ears. Mavvie was convincing and demanding, but someone couldn't just visit a dying inmate at night.

"Just take me there, and I promise it will work out. You will get me in. It will happen. Just watch." She winked at him while grabbing his hand for them to head out the door.

"Okay, I guess we can try. I'm telling them you are his dying mother. You go along with whatever I say. Okay?" Joseph knew she would not take no for an answer, so he would have to do his damnedest to pull this one off.

"Whatever it takes. I need to see Sam tonight," Mavvie said with finality.

That afternoon, Dee had convinced Seela to go to the local nail salon to get a relaxing massage and pedicure with her. While sitting there, Seela heard Johnny's mother-in-law talking to the nail technician in the back of the salon. Seela snatched Dee's ball cap from her head and pulled it down over her face to disguise herself.

"What the heck, Seels? My hair all nappy today. Why you got to show it to everyone in here?" Dee said.

Seela shrank down in the large vibrating chair. "Johnny's mother-in-law is back there," she whispered. "I don't want her to see me."

Dee stretched her head forward and around Seela, looking to the back of the salon. There sat a large woman dressed in golf attire, wearing a visor on her head. Dee glanced back at Seela and mouthed, "I guess she would die if she knew ole Chubby Chester is Johnny's son?" Dee snickered, holding her hand over her mouth so no one would see.

"Shut up, Dee. Somebody may hear you. Everybody on this island knows Johnny's and Chester's names. I don't want them to ever know about Johnny being Chester's father. Chester is all mine. You hear me?"

Just then, the bell chimed as the front door swung open. In walked Johnny's wife, Michelle. She stormed back to where her mother and grandmother sat, getting their bimonthly pedicures. "I just knew it," Michelle spat. "I told you last week that I thought that Seela girl was back on the island. I hear she's at her grandmother's, staying and visiting her dying twin in prison. You would know that Sam Black would end up dying in there. He's never been nothing but a good-for-nothing junkie since he got out of high school!"

Seela sank even farther into her chair, pulling the ball cap farther down on her face, pretending to be napping. Dee's eyes were as big as her shiny toenails, which had just been manicured and freshly polished for the first time in years.

"Dee, don't say a word. They have no clue I'm in here, and they definitely don't know you. Let's just listen to what ole Johnny's wife has to say."

"I'm up for letting my polish dry overtime." Dee wiggled her feet out on the footrest of her chair. "Besides, I could use another one of those fifteen-minute neck massages. How about it, girl? Let me buy you one too." Dee winked at Seela.

They sat up front, getting their necks and arms massaged fiercely by women the size of peanuts with the strength of rhinos. Dee and Seela listened to Johnny's wife complain, moan, and say, "If I only had proof." She repeatedly shouted out to her nearly deaf grandmother sitting beside her mother, "I just ain't got no proof!" and "How do I get that?"

Seela knew when she heard the word *proof* that Michelle was probably referring to Chester. Seela wondered how many from the past knew what she hadn't known.

Seela motioned for Dee to leave. "I'll walk before you, Dee. You stay close behind me, so maybe no one will notice who I am."

"I got you, babe. Let's hit it. I'm tired of listening to her rants anyway."

Seela and Dee escaped unnoticed out of the salon and headed back to Mamaw's. They giggled about pulling off the concealment, but Seela worried about this woman causing trouble in the midst of her newfound relationship with Chester. When they arrived home, Chester was waiting patiently at the end of the drive, sitting on his three-wheeler, drinking iced tea from Mamaw's favorite Tupperware tumbler.

"Hey, Mama. I was waiting for you guys. Where did you go?"

"We went to the nail salon, Chester. I'm sorry. I should have asked you if you wanted to go."

Dee jumped out and showed Chester her painted toes. "Check these fresh babies out, Chubs! Nice, huh?"

"They are perdy, Ms. Dee. I don't think I want my toes painted, though." Chester twitched around with his arms, as if he thought they would force him to go.

"Oh no, Chester. You don't have to have your toes polished. They just clean your feet really good. It feels as if they take your skin socks off, and you feel like you have new feet. I'll take you sometime. I promise it feels good."

Chester smiled at the two of them contentedly, happy they were back in his presence.

Joseph drove as if he were in the Gumball Rally, watching every person and every turn as he and Mavvie made their way to the prison. He called Mr. Williams to ask him to honor another strange request regarding Sam Black. Like magic, Williams agreed to comply in a monotone voice. As they drove through the prison gates, Mavvie began taking deep breaths while closing her eyes.

"I would rather not look as we drive in, Joseph, if that's okay with you."

"Whatever you want to do, Mavvie. I'll tell you when we are there."

"Thank you, Joseph. It's better this way for me not to have this memory of driving in here."

After they drove through the gate and parked in Joseph's designated spot, he told Mavvie she could open her eyes. She inhaled deeply before doing so.

"It's okay, Joseph. I'm ready to go in now. I'm ready to see Sam. I need to do this for him and Seela."

Mr. Williams was nervously waiting at the front gate room, just as he'd said he would be. He escorted them in as if they were going to a coroner's room to identify a body.

Lil Jon was mopping Sam's floors, when Big Sexy stepped into his room. "I just got a buzz that Sam's mom is coming in right now. She'll be here in like one minute."

Sam turned his head in slow motion toward Big Sexy. "It's not my mom. I bet a dollar to a hundred it's my aunt Mavvie. I've been waiting on her. She been in my dreams all week. I knew she'd figure a way to get in here."

With urgency, Lil Jon mopped his way out of Sam's room.

Joseph walked Mavvie to Sam's double metal doors and pushed the buzzer to let them in. Mavvie jumped when she heard the loud noise.

"It's okay, Mavvie. Sam's room is on the right once you go through these doors. You will only have about thirty minutes with Sam. We really are sneaking you in."

Mavvie turned to go in the double metal doors. She could hear men's voices echoing, moaning in pain throughout the cold hallway. She approached Sam's window and stopped suddenly. She was shocked to see her nephew in such bad condition. Sam lay there in his bed with his eyes closed.

Big Sexy ran to Mavvie. "Well, hello. You must be Sam's mom, or are you his aunt? He said you would be his aunt coming in here, not his mom. He said he's been waiting on you."

"Yes, I'm his aunt Mavvie, and who are you?"

"I've been taking care of Sam while he's been here. Sam's right; you are like an angel before my presence. How come Sam didn't get the looks like you and his sister, Seela?" Big Sexy laughed sweetly as she opened Sam's door. "Look who you have coming to see you, Sam."

Sam turned his head slowly toward the door and grinned at Mavvie. "It's about goddamn time you got here, Mavvie. I don't think I'm fucking going to last much longer. We didn't know I was going to die like this, now, did we? Can you believe it, Mavvie? I threw my fucking life away for that shot of heroin. I lost my love of life, and now I figured it all out at the fucking end of my life. That's why God sent me back. Isn't it?"

Mavvie stood by Sam's side. She cupped his cold hand, squeezing it while tears rolled down her face. "It's okay, Sam. It is time you let go. Your work is done. Go fly now," Mavvie whispered in an angelic voice.

Sam closed his eyes. Mavvie prayed over Sam in her French Louisianan broken accent. She then placed her head on Sam's torso, crying out loud with Sam. "I love you, Sam, and so does all of your family. Go now, and be with your loved ones on the other side, Sam. They are waiting. It's okay."

Mavvie lifted her head up, feeling his soul transcending. It was as if once he saw Mavvie and heard her voice, he slipped into a coma. Mavvie sat beside Sam until Joseph came back for her an hour later.

"It won't be long, Joseph. His soul is lifting as we speak."

Joseph stared at Mavvie in shock. "You mean to tell me Sam is dying this minute?"

"He's been dying, Joseph. It's just his time now. Hurry and get me home, Joseph, so I can pray for him. I need to help Sam transcend out of this god-awful prison."

<hr />

Seela and Chester prepared for bed and then sat beside Chester's bed, praying together. Chester went first. *"Lord, help Uncle Sam. I don't want him to hurt no more. And thank you for giving me my mom. I love her. Amen."*

Seela lay beside Chester, trying not to cry out loud. Her body began to shake, but somehow, she pulled her emotions together to speak and say her prayers. *"My Lord and God and all my angels above, thank you for watching over my beautiful child until I could have him back in my life. I promise I will cherish Chester for the rest of my life. It's as if I'm losing a part of me right now, but at the same time, I'm getting a part of me back that has been gone for some time. Please allow Sam to enter the gates of heaven soon. I know he has suffered long enough here. He's ready to be with his family above. Dear God, if you are listening, please transcend my twin to your great blue yonder. I too am sending white light tonight. Amen."*

Seela kissed Chester good night. "I'll see you in the morning, my son. Sweet dreams."

"Um, Mama? What's white light? Why do you and Mavvie say that?"

Seela sat back down on Chester's bed. "You know how our bodies are made of energy?"

"Yes," said Chester. "Sorta."

"Well, you know when you close your eyes and you see darkness?"

"Yes," said Chester.

"When I close my eyes, I look for white light, not dark light. If you wait long enough after you close your eyes, you can find the white light, and you focus on it. That brings good energy around you. Some people never learn about white light. It's a great power to have."

"Can I have white light, Mama?"

"You can definitely try. Just close your eyes, and look for a bright light. It may take awhile, but stay focused. When I leave your room, just lie there, and see if you can see it. Okay?"

"Okay, I'm going to look for the white light," Chester said excitedly.

After Seela left Chester's room, he tried to see the white light until falling asleep.

Chapter 47

Lil Jon snuck down to Sam's room with his pillow and blanket in hand. Sam's room sounded better than Lil Jon's. The machines hooked up to Sam made enough noise to drown out the metal doors sliding open back and forth all night. This night was different from the last. Lil Jon slept peacefully for at least five hours beside Sam on the floor. Once he woke, he jumped straight up to see if Sam had passed.

"Hey, Pops, good morning. You okay?"

Sam didn't move or answer. Lil Jon touched his chest softly. He could feel his heartbeat. He leaned down to Sam's ear and whispered, "I love you, Pops. You changed my heart and my world. Now, go fishing!" Lil Jon kissed Sam's forehead as tears rolled down his cheeks. He knew this was probably the last time he would see Sam. He stood over him, staring and crying.

"I'm going to recite to you a poem, Unc. That sound good? I have a poem I looked up from one of my favorites, William Henley." Lil Jon started to read what he'd written on a small piece of paper. "Invictus" was the poem's title. His voice crackled as he read.

> *Out of the night that covers me,*
> *Black as the pit from pole to pole,*
> *I thank whatever gods may be*
> *For my unconquerable soul.*
> *In the fell clutch of circumstance,*
> *I have not winced nor cried aloud.*
> *Under the bludgeonings of chance*

My head is bloody, but unbowed.
Beyond this place of wrath and tears
Looms but the Horror of the shade,
And yet the menace of the years
Finds and shall find me unafraid.
It matters not how straight the gate,
How charged with punishments the scroll,
I am the master of my fate,
I am the captain of my soul.

Lil Jon closed his poem by kissing Sam on his forehead. "I love you, Unc. You changed my life. I'm going to show you I got this when I get out of here. I hope you listening to me. You changed my world."

Big Sexy opened Sam's door, and Lil Jon immediately wiped his face. "Don't worry," she said. "I saw you crying over your Mr. Sam. I know you love this man here." She touched Sam's leg. "I love him too, Lil Jon. He's done touched my heart like no one else ever has besides my children. He made me see me and my life. That's what he did."

They stood side by side, watching over Sam.

"You know what he said to me last night, Big Sexy? He told me to leave him lying in the bed if he died. He said he wanted to look down and see me beside him. He didn't want to be alone. I'm having a hard time leaving him. I don't want Sam to die alone in here."

"You go on and get in your room for count, and get your chores done. Then come on back to sit with Sam. Even when his sister here, you can sit outside his room."

"Really? You going to let me, Big Sexy?"

"Hurry! We already breakin' the rules up in here. Be quick, boy!"

At Big Sexy's command, Lil Jon skipped down the hall, knowing he could return to Sam's room under her watch. That night, he prepared his pallet beside Sam's bed as Sam slowly let go of his world. Lil Jon lay on the floor, listening hard for any movement. At times, he cried fiercely, hoping Sam heard him so that he would know Lil Jon loved him with all his heart and soul. Lil Jon sang Sam's favorite song out loud to him. He then talked about their first time meeting. He'd known immediately that Sam was a crazy motherfucker with the potential to be something other than a dying heroin junkie. He promised Sam that he would always take the straight and narrow. Sam's mouth was open as he drifted to the next place beyond. His heart was beating, but his body seemed empty. Lil Jon talked to Sam until he finally dozed off.

The next morning, Lil Jon woke to Big Sexy tapping on Sam's window with her keys. She mouthed for him to clean up his bed and get Sam wiped off from his nightly sweat. Sam's twin was on her way. Lil Jon tried to wake Sam, but he didn't want to move. He just grunted a low, gravelly sound in his chest.

"Hey, Unc. I got to get you sitting up a little. I want to wipe your face from all the sweat going on from that morphine pumping out your pores. It's smelling ripe up in here, my man." Lil Jon wiped his face and arms. "Big Sexy going to come in and brush what teeth you got too. I'm going to my room for count, and then I'll be back. Don't do anything until I get back. You hear me, Unc? I love you, man."

Seela woke to her alarm in a daze. She dressed quickly before anyone else in the house woke. She'd slept peacefully through the night. Things felt different. She walked down to her mom's house, trying not to get wet from the misty, light rain. Seela knocked a couple of times before Catherine came to her door.

"Who is it?"

"Good morning, Mama. Can we talk before I go see Sam this morning? I think he is at the end of his time now. He was really weak last Sunday."

"I know," said Catherine. She opened her door for Seela. "He hasn't called me in five days. It's just a matter of hours, I feel." Catherine's eyes looked as if she had been crying for days. "I don't know how much longer I have either, Seels. This cancer has gotten the best of me. It's all through my body, and it takes all I have to get out of bed these days. I'm sorry for not being there to help you. I'm sorry for everything!" Catherine held her arms out and said, "I hope you forgive me and understand one day." It was the first time Catherine had reached her arms out to Seela in the past three months Seela had been staying at Mamaw's.

Seela embraced her mother with an awkward hug. The feeling of her mother's arms around her body was foreign. Catherine stood back with her frail body to examine Seela. She smiled as she gently pushed Seela to the door. "Go see Sam now, Seela. Hurry. I know he's waiting.".

Seela almost choked on the fumes of oil paint and turpentine. She looked around but did not see any paintings.

"Okay, I'll come see you as soon as I get back. I know Sam will tell me to tell you he loves you, if he's able to speak to me."

"Yes," said Catherine. "I'll be waiting. I love you, Seela."

"I love you too, Mom." She threw her mother a kiss in the same fashion that the whole family did to one another.

Seela ran quickly back to her grandmother's carport. She tiptoed into the kitchen so that she wouldn't wake Chester or Mamaw. Seela packed her body with five packs of Marlboros while slurping her usual cocktail in preparation. She got out of the house without waking anyone.

It was a misty, dark morning as Seela drove on the twelfth Sunday to see her dying twin brother, Sam. She sipped on her morning courage cocktail of vodka and orange juice from a large tumbler. The radio blared Creedence Clearwater Revival, one of Sam's favorites, as Seela drove and thought about his life and how horrible it had been these last few months to watch Sam die while stuck in the crazy judicial prison system, which had caged him up like a wild animal. Through it all, she had discovered true love and connection with family she had left long ago.

Seela reflected on the past week. Her heart's emotions had been ripped out and then put back together as one great puzzle. Seela's speedometer was pressed all the way to the right as she drove fearlessly down the highway. "Oh shit! I'd better slow down, or else I'll never make it to see Sam," she said nervously.

As Seela crested over a small hill on the highway, black clouds stretched across the wide, luminous sky. In the blink of an eye, the clouds quickly started to separate into three sections of sunlit tunnels. The sun's rays parted the gloomy clouds as if beams of heaven were tugging Sam's soul up into sky. It was a glorious eternal sight through Seela's hazy, tearful eyes. She pulled over to the side of the highway and pressed her forehead against the windshield.

Seela prayed aloud. "Dear Lord, if this is a sign you are taking my twin brother from me today, please let his soul rise up to you and my family who are already in heaven. Please, Lord, let him go fishing again with Dad and Granddaddy. I know they have been waiting for him. Thank you, God, for sending him back to me. I've learned as much as Sam has learned in these twelve weeks." Seela looked up to the sky one more time before pulling back onto the highway. "When Sam makes it to you all, give me a sign, okay?" Seela smiled with tears rolling down her face as she drove on toward the state prison, gulping her vodka and orange juice cocktail.

When Seela reached the prison, she drove through the main gate with a relaxed but disturbed feeling. Suddenly, a large wolf crept out of the woods. It stopped in its tracks, staring at Seela as if it were telling her something. Its face was covered in blood. It had obviously just devoured another wild animal. Seela stared back in awe at the fearless wild creature. She had never seen a wolf in the wild before, let alone one of that size. The wolf turned away and ran off into the woods. Seela froze, not wanting to get out of the car, afraid of becoming the animal's dessert. She sat for at least five minutes in her car until she felt the wolf had gotten farther away.

Inside the prison, Lil Jon made his count hurriedly, finishing his work duties so he could get back to Sam. Big Sexy wiped Sam's face one more time while gently brushing what teeth Sam had left. She hummed "Amazing Grace" as she wiped Sam's face with a warm cloth. Sam's chest pumped up and down for air. She swabbed Sam's dry, cracked mouth. "Seela will be here in a few minutes, Sam. Hold on for her, okay?" she whispered into his ear. The room seemed to have calmed down to nothing but still air. Even the machines had quieted to just a tiny sound.

As Big Sexy was walking toward Sam's door, she heard a noise from him. She turned back quickly and saw Sam's open left hand draped down beside his bed. Big Sexy ran screaming into Sam's room. "Dear God, no! No, dear God. Sam." She pressed her head against his swollen body, hearing silence. She knew he had passed. She started crying uncontrollably over Sam's body, beating her fist into his chest. "No, Sam, I wasn't ready. I planned to tell you great stories today about me and sing to you one last time. Goddammit, Sam. I'm going to miss you so much." Big Sexy lay across Sam, crying with body and soul onto him one last time.

A few minutes passed as Big Sexy lay across Sam's lifeless form with her heart pounding onto his now-stiff body.

Lil Jon skipped down the hall with his usual swagger, anxiously trying to get to Sam's room. As soon as he got to Sam's window, he looked in before entering, as he always did. He saw Big Sexy lying across Sam's body. Lil Jon's knees buckled under him. He knew Sam had died. He fell to the floor, crying his heart out like a five-year-old boy. He hadn't gotten to be with Sam when he died. He didn't know if Sam had been alone. Lil Jon leaned against the wall with his faced cupped in his hands, crying the hardest he ever had in his entire life. Big Sexy walked out of Sam's room and fell down beside Lil Jon, holding him like a mother while they cried together.

Big Sexy and Lil Jon waited a few minutes before calling the guards. It was as if they were having their own memorial for Sam and didn't want anyone else to be a part of it. Lil Jon finally composed himself enough to walk to AB's hall to give him the news of Sam's passing.

Finally convinced the bloody wolf would not return, Seela walked to the front gate. As she reached the metal door, an unfamiliar face opened the window beside the door.

"Can I help you?"

"I'm here to see my brother, Sam Black. Officer Quinton usually escorts me in. Is he here?"

"Hold on a minute, ma'am. I'll have to call upstairs."

Seela stood outside in the misty rain, hoping Joseph would come for her. She knew that once she saw his face, everything would be okay.

The window flew open. "Come on through, ma'am, but Officer Quinton's not here anymore. Mr. Williams will be down in a few minutes to get you."

Seela's heart sank and started beating out of her stomach. What if Joseph had left and gone back up north on another mission? What had she done? Did he think she didn't want to be with him anymore? Crazy thoughts rushed through Seela's head. She forgot for a moment that she was waiting to see Sam.

The prison door opened, and Mr. Williams walked out with a somber expression. "Well, hello, Ms. Seela. It's a great pleasure to escort you up to see Sam this morning. I haven't been upstairs yet to my office, so I don't know his condition. You know he's near the end, don't you? We've been watching him real close and trying to keep him as comfortable as possible. Sam has made himself quite the posse in there."

"I thank all of you, Mr. Williams. Can I ask you where Officer Quinton went? The guard said he was no longer here."

"Yes, ma'am, I thought you would know that, Ms. Seela. His operation was dropped here. He left and moved on."

The two of them stepped into the elevator to ride up to Sam's room on the seventh floor. As they approached the third floor, Mr. Williams's walkie-talkie sounded. "Code red," it said over and over. Mr. Williams pushed the elevator button to stop. He pulled Seela off the elevator and told her they would have to go back out of the prison. "Ms. Seela, I hate to do this, but that code means someone's been killed. I have to get you on the outside of these walls quickly." They headed back down to the lobby, and Mr. Williams escorted Seela to a locked room.

Seela sat on a sofa, anxiously waiting for someone to get her. Her buzz was wearing off as she thought about Joseph and how she had probably screwed up the best thing in her life. Both he and her twin would be gone.

When Mr. Williams stepped off the elevator on the seventh floor, he saw Lil Jon at Sam's door, weeping. "Oh no! Hell no!" he bellowed. Tears filled his eyes.

Big Sexy turned to Mr. Williams and asked, "Is Sam's sister downstairs?"

Mr. Williams sighed. "Yes, ma'am, she is." He rubbed his forehead and stalled, not wanting to be the one to inform Seela of Sam's death.

"I'll do it," said Big Sexy. "Let me go tell her. The news will be better from me than you, woman to woman. Besides, she knows how much I loved Sam."

Big Sexy pushed Sam's eyelids shut. "I know you are free now, Mr. Sam Black. No more heartache or pain for you ever again."

Mr. Williams touched Sam's hand and said, "It was nice knowing you, Sam Black. You touched my heart." Tears filled his dark brown eyes and rolled down his sad face.

Seela was getting frustrated, thinking somebody had forgotten that she was locked in this room. She went to the tiny window on the door and peered down the hall. She saw Big Sexy come around the corner slowly with a flushed face, wiping her eyes with a tissue. Seela fell to the floor, crying hysterically. Big Sexy unlocked the door quickly as she heard Seela crying. Her big body sprawled over Seela, hugging her tightly.

"I'm so sorry, Seela. He just passed. Sam knew you were here. I had just cleaned his face and teeth. I told him you were coming up the elevator, and he peacefully went right after. I know how much Sam idolized and loved you, Seela. You were all he talked about. Sam was at peace when he died. I hope you know that."

Seela lay on the carpet, crying. She couldn't get control for what seemed to be ten or fifteen minutes. Big Sexy gave her tissues that she'd brought with her. As she gained composure, Seela sat with Big Sexy for at least thirty minutes. Big Sexy kept talking about Sam and all the great things he'd done for people. She told Seela that Sam had told her how he'd become king in prison and said that he was king in her heart now. She talked about how she'd gotten to know the real Sam Black and about all he had done for her in the last few months.

"I'm so sorry, Ms. Seela, but I have to escort you out of the prison now."

"I can't even see Sam's body?"

"Oh no! You are no longer allowed on the inside of these prison walls, Seela. Sam will be shipped to the local coroner's, and you can go see him there if you like."

Seela was too discombobulated to argue. She hugged Big Sexy at the front gate. "Please, let's stay in touch, Big Sexy. Dang! I can't be calling you Big Sexy. What's your real name?"

"It's Grace."

"Oh my goodness. Sam loved the name Grace. Did he know your real name?"

"Yes, he did, and he told me the same thing. I was humming 'Amazing Grace' to him right before he died."

"That makes me feel better, Grace. Will you walk to my car with me and get my business card so we can remain friends, Grace? I know Sam would love that."

"Yes, ma'am. I would love it too. I would like to meet Chubby—I mean Chester. Sam talked a lot about him too."

"Yes, he's great. Talk about someone who loved Sam. I'm going to hate telling him today."

Seela drove away in shock, talking and crying at the same time. "I'm so sorry, Sam, that I wasn't with you when you passed. If only I hadn't stopped to see Mom and if only I hadn't stopped on the side of the highway. Damn you, Seels. If only I had not waited in my car, watching the stupid-ass wolf. I would have been there with you, Sam. You wouldn't have been alone." Seela heaved. "I can't believe I've lost you for good, Sam, and I think I've lost Joseph too."

Despair washed over her. She passed the liquor store and turned her car around. The store didn't open for five more minutes, so she called Joseph while waiting. He didn't answer. She then called Dee, who was still in bed, sleeping in on a quiet Sunday morning.

Dee pulled her eye mask off, answering swiftly, knowing it was Seela. "Hey, honey, you just leave from seeing Sam?"

Seela could only cry.

"Oh no, I'm so sorry. Where are you? I'm coming to be with you right now." Dee jumped out of her bed and threw clothes on from the chair beside her bed. She started grabbing whatever clothes she could see and tossing them into an overnight bag.

Seela caught her breath and spoke. "Sam died when I got to the prison this morning, Dee. He knew I was there, but I hadn't made it to his room yet. It breaks my heart knowing he was by himself in that hellhole."

"You still didn't answer my question. Where are you?" Dee said.

"I'm just waiting for the liquor store to open, and then I'm going to be by myself today. I can't talk or see anyone right now, Dee. I hope you understand."

"I do, baby, but you can't be alone too long. You have to be there for your family. I'm headed down now. I'll go see about Chester, your mom, and Mamaw. Call me in a little while. I'll come to wherever you are if you want."

Seela knew there was no use debating the matter with Dee, as evidenced by the past. She rushed into the store, trying not to be recognized while buying liquor so early on a Sunday morning. She bought the most expensive bottle of champagne and two glasses.

Seela drove quickly but carefully, watching her mirrors to see if anyone was around. The roads were quiet this rainy morning. She drove to the shoreline where she and Sam had played together as children. A hurricane had washed it away many years ago, but Seela felt drawn to go there with her champagne. She pulled to the side of the road and sat in her car, looking out at the ocean, which was filled with big, crashing waves from the storm overnight. Seela popped her champagne and poured both glasses full. She set one glass on her dashboard. Seela picked up her glass and tapped it against the other one on her dash.

"Here's to you, Sam Black. I hope you are fishing right now. You were brought back to me for a reason from God, and I feel you did what you needed to do before reaching the great yonder of what's next. Fly high with your beautiful soul now. It's complete! I love you, my twin.

I'll see you again one day. You fly down and show me you're watching after me just like I asked, okay? I'll be watching for my red cardinal."

Seela cried hard, taking big gulps of the smooth champagne. Once she finished her glass, she reached for Sam's. Seela sat there for hours, watching the ocean and remembering the last few months. Her brother had died horribly, and she couldn't do anything about it. Once she could get control of her emotions, she started foraging through every compartment of her car, hoping to find just one hidden cigarette. Finally, she found a crumpled pack with three cigarettes in it. She lit one shakily and puffed on it as if she were starving for it. She took long, hard drags.

Dee zoomed into Mamaw's driveway, hoping to see Seela's car, but Seela wasn't there yet. Dee turned, looking back at Mavvie's house. She backed up and pulled her truck up to Mavvie's front porch. When she jumped out of the truck, Mavvie was already opening her door. Mavvie was wearing a beautiful blue dress. It was breathtaking.

"Mavvie, you look beautiful. That dress—the color is stunning on you!"

Mavvie smiled, speaking in her angelic voice. "This is the color Sam sees now, Dee. He's finally free. He did his work before he left this horrible world he made for himself here. Now it's over."

Dee stood there listening to Mavvie as if she were in a trance. It felt nice. Dee felt as if her emotions that had been all up in the air had been pulled back down, grouped together like a bunch of balloons, and put back into her now-calm body. "Mavvie, you make everything seem so great. I love that about you. How we going to tell the rest of them? Seela is off somewhere by herself, getting drunk. She said she couldn't talk or see anyone right now. Should we wait until she gets home?"

"Let's go to the house, Dee. We will do this. You can ask Catherine to come up to her mom's house, and we will tell them all together."

Dee shook her head. "I think you should tell them, Mavvie. You made it sound so nice to me. It should be from you."

"Yes, Dee. You just go get Catherine, please."

"Okay, but she's not so friendly sometimes. She may not answer me through the door."

"Tell her it's about Sam. She'll come," said Mavvie.

Dee hurried to Catherine's after she parked her truck on the side of the driveway to make room for Seela's car. Dee knocked on the door. "Good afternoon, Ms. Catherine. We were all wondering if you could come up to the house. We need to discuss Sam."

Dee waited for a response or for the door to open. She knocked louder. "Hey, Catherine, can you hear me? It's Dee, Seela's friend." Dee put her ear to the door but didn't hear any music or the television, as she normally did. She turned Catherine's doorknob, and the door opened.

Dee peeked her head into Catherine's little house. "Hello? Catherine? Are you sleeping?" She pushed the door open more so she could see into the front room, which was filled with junk and paint cans of all types. She took a few more steps until she reached Catherine's bedroom door. It was half open. She pushed it open slowly and saw Catherine lying on her side in her bed.

Dee walked over to Catherine, thinking she was dead also. Her eyes were shut. Dee touched her shoulder, causing Catherine to jump. Several bottles of pills spilled along the bedside table as they both scared each other.

Catherine looked as if she knew why Dee was in her bedroom. A tear rolled down her face as she spoke to Dee. "Sam is gone. Isn't he?"

Dee stood looking down at Cat and thinking how frail and weak she looked, as if she were almost dead. "Yes, Ms. Catherine. He passed this morning before Seela got to his room."

Catherine rolled her body away from Dee and spoke with a quivering voice. "Please leave me now. I need to be alone. Where is Seela?"

"She is on her way to Sam's and her favorite place to sit for a while. She too wants to be alone. Can I get you anything before I go see about Mamaw?"

"No, Dee. I don't want anything but to be by myself. Please leave now, and make sure my door is shut tightly."

Dee walked out quietly and closed the front door quietly but firmly behind her. When she got to Mamaw's house, she could hear Mamaw crying inside with Mavvie. Dee peeped into the living room window to see what Chester was doing. He was playing his Xbox as if nothing had happened. She wondered if he knew.

Dee opened the screen door and slightly smiled at Mamaw. "I'm so sorry for you, Mamaw. I know how much you loved Sam. At least he's not suffering anymore, and you have him to watch over you until you go to be with all your posse you got going on up there."

"Goddamn right! I'm ready to go too! Why is the good Lord keeping me here? I want to be with Edward and the rest of my family."

Chester walked into the kitchen with a frown. "You don't want to be here with me, Mamaw? I just got you as my great-gran."

"Aw, Chester, come over here, and give me a hug. That will make me feel better."

Chester smiled, glad to be wanted again, scurrying to his mamaw. Chester looked at Dee. "Where's Mama?"

"She will be here shortly. She needed to have a little time to herself, but I'm sure she'll be on her way home soon."

"I need to see her," Chester said. "I know she's sad right now, and I can make her feel better. I can tell her funny Sam stories that I know."

"I know she will love that, Chester. I'm going to call Seela now and tell her. I'll see if she's on her way here."

Dee dialed her number while walking down the hall to Seela's bedroom. Dee sighed with relief when Seela picked up. She had no idea how to tell her about finding her mother.

"Hey, Dee, I know I need to come home. I've cried my eyes out until I don't think I can make more tears. It will help me to be strong now for Mom, Mamaw, and Chester."

"Can you drive home, or have you had too much to drink? I can come get you."

"I'll be fine. Hell, I've been getting drunk while driving to the prison for the past twelve Sundays." They both chuckled through tears.

When Dee hung up and turned around, Mavvie caused her to jump.

She was standing behind her. "Why you want to scare me like that? You were so quiet, sneaking up on me."

"Where is Catherine? I knew she was sick, but I thought maybe something about Sam would get her up here."

"Mavvie, she's so sad in her bed. It was strange—her front door was unlocked. I found her lying in her bed." Dee's eyeballs were the size of silver dollars as she spoke. "It scared the shit out of me, Mavvie. I thought she was dead."

Mavvie grabbed Dee's hands. "Come. Let's go say a prayer, Dee. Run me to my house first to get some tools."

"Tools? What kind of tools are you talking about?" Dee asked.

"I need to make sure Sam's soul has lifted, and if it hasn't, I need to help it. Hurry. Let's go!"

Mavvie and Dee ran out of Mamaw's house, yelling to Mamaw and Chester that they would be back soon. They drove to Mavvie's, where Mavvie grabbed her bag of tools for the uplifting of Sam's soul.

As soon as Dee pulled up to Catherine's, Mavvie jumped from her truck. Mavvie lit her stick before entering Catherine's door. She waved it all around Dee, from her toes to the top of her head, and then repeated the ritual on herself. They entered the still house. Dee stood at the bedroom door, watching Mavvie run through her process of prayer while waving her stick and using her other tools. Tears filled Mavvie's eyes. She looked at Dee, speaking quietly. "Catherine will soon die of a broken heart, not her cancer. She loved her son, Sam, to death, and that's what she literally will do."

Dee started to cry. "That's so sad, Mavvie. I really haven't gotten to know Catherine. She would talk to me mostly through her door."

Mavvie looked in on Catherine and saw her sleeping peacefully. She then turned back to Dee and whispered softly, "We will come back later to check on her. Let's go see if Seelie is here."

As Mavvie and Dee walked out, Mavvie explained a little more to Dee about Catherine and her twins. "She and her children grew up together, Dee. She was only eighteen when she had her twins. She was just a baby herself. Sam grew up fast and ruled Catherine's life, and she let him. He was all she had. Seela lived mostly with her grandparents, and when she left the island at eighteen with no notice to them, it killed Catherine and Sam. I believe when you have such heartache as that, sometimes it can give you these horrible diseases that fester and grow inside of you. My sister could never see light; only darkness came to her. I have to get my sister to see white light. Then maybe she will be able to pass like she wants to when the time is right. I know she wants to be with her husband and family."

Seela pulled up as the ladies were walking up from Cat's house. They watched her as she jumped out of the car with an open bottle of champagne and a brown bag holding more bottles of champagne. She smiled with a half-drunk smirk at the two of them while raising the bottle in the air. "I bought more for us to celebrate Sam's freedom. Woohoo!"

Dee ran to Seela, reaching to help her with the bags.

"What are you two doing coming from Mom's house? Did you go tell her already?" Seela started to head to her mom's house with the open bottle of champagne. "I'm going down to have a toast with her!" She started sprinting before Dee grabbed her from behind.

"Wait, Seela!"

Seela stopped and stared back at Dee, who said, "Your mom said she wants to be alone for a little while. We think she may have taken something to help her sleep. We just checked on her."

Seela seemed erratic. "Let's go drink some champagne. We are going to celebrate life right now, not death. Let's all get dressed like Mavvie. It's time!"

The women ran up to Mamaw's house. Seela opened the back screen door, yelling to Chester and Mamaw, "Guys, let's get dressed up! It's time to celebrate life. We no longer have Sam here, but he's above us, giving us one more angel to watch over and protect us."

Mamaw wiped the tears from her face. "Yes, my Seels. You are right. That's exactly what Sam would want anyway. I'm going to put my best dress on right now." She turned her chair on and motored to the back of the house. "Somebody needs to tell Catherine to put her best dress on too!" Mamaw yelled out while riding her scooter down the hallway.

Chester was already in his room, changing into some of Sam's clothes hanging in the closet. Once they were all dressed, Seela popped the champagne and poured each one of them a glass. They sat in a circle out in Mamaw's new garden in their finest clothes. They all told funny stories about Sam and made toasts until the two bottles of champagne were gone. To their surprise, Catherine walked up to the flower garden in a beautiful pink dress. She didn't have many words but sat beside Seela, holding her hand with heavy tears puddled in her eyes. She was weak but did not want to miss this gathering, which was somewhat of a memorial for Sam.

After drinking all day, Seela was way too intoxicated. Dee helped her to her bedroom and into bed.

"Dee, I can't believe this fucking day." Seela was talking with her mouth half shut, so her words ran together. "Can you believe my fucking life? What the hell happened these past twelve weeks? I fell in love and lost him. I got my son back and lost my brother in the same week."

"Seels, we will have a better day tomorrow. You just lie down and go to sleep. I promise it will be a better day."

"I need to call Joseph, Dee."

"You are going to have to call him in the morning. You are way too drunk to talk to him tonight, and besides, you probably wouldn't remember it." Dee leaned down, closing Seela's eyes and kissing her cheek. "Go on now. Go to sleep." Dee lay there until she could hear Seela's soft snore. She kissed her lightly on her rose-petal cheek while saying good night. Dee left quietly from Seela's bed and went into Chester's room to check on him.

"Um, Ms. Dee, will you say my prayers with me? Mama Seela usually does it."

"Yes, Chester. I would love to say prayers with you," she replied, plopping her large body down beside him. "You want to go first?"

"Yes, ma'am, I'll go first. Dear God, I just want to say thank you for taking Sam today. He's been waiting for a long time, and now I know he's happy. I loved him with all my heart. I know he loved me too. He gave me my mama back, so, God, please take care of Sam for me because I can't anymore here. Amen."

Dee's eyes welled with tears as she tried to speak. "All I can say is, my God, whoever you are in that mighty kingdom we are supposed to go to, please, all of y'all up there, watch after us down here the next year while we all transcend into our new lives. I do believe we have it a lot harder here than anyone does up there. I send love to my family and friends who have passed and, most of all, to my higher power above. Amen."

"Um, Ms. Dee, what is higher power?"

"It's what I believe to be my God, Chester."

"Oh, okay," Chester said. "I'm going to sleep now."

Dee pulled Chester's door shut. She walked into the kitchen to find Mavvie and Mamaw sitting at the table in silence. "This has been one hell of a day," whispered Dee.

Mavvie rose from her seat. "I must go now and get some rest. Tomorrow will be another busy day."

Dee walked back out to the garden and sat under the clear sky. It was amazing how the sky had cleared after the storm. The stars beamed all over the black night. She pulled her phone out and looked up Joseph's number. She hesitated, wondering if she should call him to tell him about Sam. She selected his name on her phone, but as soon as she did, she pressed the button to hang up. "No, that's for Seela to do. I can't be in her business," Dee said to herself.

While Dee lay out under the stars in Mamaw's backyard, Seela awoke from a dream about Sam. She decided to dress and walk to Mavvie's house to soak in a hot salt bath in her outside tub and watch the beautiful, clear dark sky full of stars shining brightly. The stars could give her some answers to everything that had transpired in the past twelve weeks and also her life to come.

Seela snuck quietly past Chester's and Mamaw's doors as they both slept peacefully. She skipped quickly through the grass. Dew had already formed since the evening had set. As she approached Mavvie's backyard,

Seela heard music playing softly—the music Sam liked to listen to. His favorite Creedence Clearwater Revival song was playing. Seela crept quietly, expecting Mavvie to be in the salt tub where Seela planned to drown her sorrows from her day. Seela was surprised to find the tub filled with salt and steaming hot water. Tea-light candles were lit all around, making it look like heaven for Seela. There was a note beside the tub, sitting on a beautiful purple towel. It read,

> My beautiful Seels,
>
> Your time is now. You went through what you had to do, and now your life will start brand new. Trust in your family now. It will be okay. You did all the right things. Sam loves you deeply and will always be there for you. He is your twin. Enjoy your bath tonight! Learn tonight from the sky, and whatever shows up is what you were brought here to do. It's what is supposed to happen, my Seels. I love you.
>
> Aunt Mavvie.

Seela held the letter to her chest as she slipped her robe and gown down to the ground. She stepped into the deep tub filled with Mavvie's special blend of sea salt and surrounded by tea lights.

Seela sank into the salt bath, feeling relieved of her pains and the thoughts racing through her mind. The night was quiet. It was as if the nocturnal wildlife had gotten a memo to be silent and let Seela have her bath. All of sudden, she heard a loud bang. Seela jumped in surprise at seeing Cat standing in front of her in her bathrobe.

"Seela, I didn't know you were. I wouldn't have come. I'm sorry. I'll go home."

"No, Mama. Please don't leave! I'm so glad you're here. Do you come use Mavvie's hot tub often?"

"Ha! I haven't even seen Mavvie's place in five years at least. I didn't even know about this tub. I got a note on my door that said I should come to soak and have my last good-byes with Sam. That's why I'm here, Seela. Hell, I ain't got to get in that there tub to say good-bye to Sam. He knows how I loved him, and we said our good-byes before he ever left this god-awful world he lived through here."

"Mama, you need to know why I left here after high school. Getting pregnant with Johnny's child was the worst for me. I couldn't have my child be labeled a half breed on the island, as Sam and I were, let alone with Johnny and his family. I had to break the chain. It was so hard growing up here being biracial. I felt I was just carrying on what you did. I just couldn't live here and go through what you did with us. That's why I gave Chester up. That's why I left the island. I wanted more in life, Mama. I hope you forgive me and understand what I did."

Cat sat quietly listening to Seela as she talked and cried from Mavvie's metal tub. Tears filled Cat's eyes, as she knew what Seela was trying to say. All the memories from the past were heavy on her heart. She knew she hadn't been there to support Seela when Seela had needed her. Seela had had to act on her own emotions and feelings to survive the way she'd thought was right for her.

"Seela, I'm so sorry for what you went through. You never told any of us about your pregnancy. How could we help you? It was such a devastation when you left us with only a letter."

"I know, Mama. It was hard for me to leave like I did, but I felt it was the right decision for me. Your relationship with Sam was so close, and what he was going through at that time was so much on you. I felt I needed to break the chain in our family history. I felt I was keeping the drama and gossip going by getting pregnant with Johnny's child. I couldn't stand the thought of repeating what Sam and I went through as biracial kids on this island. That's why I gave Chester up. I hope you understand what I did." Seela sat in despair, waiting for her mother to respond. She knew Cat was heartbroken at losing her son and best friend. She understood why her mother had no desire to live any longer.

"Seels, I now understand what you did. Your brother loved you always and watched after you no matter what. He found a way to always see and know what you were doing. He always wrote me great letters about you. I knew he kept up and knew everything about you. I'll miss that. It doesn't matter. My time here is limited anyway. I'm just happy I have you now, Seels. You are as beautiful as you were when you left the island." Cat reached over and squeezed Seela's hand, which hung down from the metal tub, and she spoke the softest Seela had heard since she'd been on the island. "I love you with all my heart, Seels."

A tear rolled down Seela's cheek as she squeezed her mother's hand tightly. "I love you too, Mama, and I'm never leaving you again."

The two sat quietly, looking into the clear dark sky, gazing at all the beautiful stars that floated above them and wondering if Sam was watching them from above.

Chapter 48

One Year Later The Black family suffered another loss when Catherine passed away soon after Sam's death. In the time before she passed, Seela and Catherine shared loving moments and memories with each other. Chester even got to know Catherine better. She showed him how to paint with watercolors before her passing. After Catherine passed, they had a big ceremony with just the five of them, and they spread all three urns of ashes in Mamaw's special flower garden.

Lil Jon was out in the real world again. He kept his word to Sam about walking the straight and narrow. He was now working and taking care of his son and new wife. He landed a job at a newspaper plant, having learned printing during his three years in the prison system. On the one-year anniversary of Sam's death, Lil Jon chose to celebrate by listening to Creedence Clearwater Revival, chewing bubble gum, and grilling filet mignon under the bright sun in Sam's honor. His wife walked out to him with an envelope from the postal carrier. Lil Jon opened it and was surprised to find a note saying, "Stay straight, my man. I'm watching." The note contained a money card with a sticky note indicating that the amount on the card was $5,000. A smiley face had been drawn next to the amount.

Lil Jon jumped up and down with glee, hugging his wife and son. "Once again! Pops did it again!" He kissed the card and stuffed it into his shirt pocket, next to his heart. He looked up, holding two fingers to the sky. "I think about you every day, Pops. I love ya."

In another city on the same day, Mr. Williams and his wife rushed to the airport. They were celebrating Sam Black also. They were off to the Caribbean Islands for a long-awaited vacation courtesy of Sam, which Charlie had arranged per Sam's instructions. Mr. Williams had once told Sam that he and his wife could never afford a vacation. They always stayed home, working on their house and calling it a staycation. Sam had made sure Mr. Williams and his wife would get a real vacation, using the corrupt money the prisons had helped Sam make.

In the prison where Sam died, AB had a memorial for Sam that evening. AB was teaching young boys how to earn their GEDs now. The day before the one year anniversary of Sam's death, AB also received a money card for $5,000 in the mail. His note read,

> Hang in there, my man. Walk a straight line, love yourself to death, and it will all work out the way it's supposed to. This should be enough money to get you through until you get out of this fucking hellhole. Talk to me anytime, my man. I'm listening. It was signed The King!

AB smiled, and tears filled his dark eyes when he read Sam's note. He wrote Sam a note that evening and then burned it in his cell's metal sink. It read,

> Finally, I'm doing something that matters. Prison takes that away from you—the willpower to do something that actually matters to the world beyond our physical borders. This thankless job of teaching inmates for GED preparation is an honor knowing you are watching and, as you say, listening. I'll never forget you, my man, The King!

That evening, AB had all the inmates light a match before bedtime in honor of Sam.

The same day, Grace was at home with her children. She too was thinking of nothing but Sam. Grace made a cake in his honor. She and her two children gathered around her kitchen table while she lit the candles so they could blow them out.

"Wait," said Grace. "I would like to say something about why we are celebrating today."

"It's your friend Sam's birthday, Mama," her youngest girl said, grinning and waiting anxiously for a piece of cake.

"No, honey, it's not his birthday. It's the day God took him to be with him again. It's been one year since it happened, and in honor of knowing Mr. Sam Black, I will always remember him on this day. He touched my heart to the bottom, and because of Sam, I've changed my life. If it weren't for Sam Black, your mama wouldn't have gone back to school, where I'm now getting my nursing degree. Sam had money sent to me after he passed. I used it to go back to school. I do believe he was my angel from above."

"Wow, Mama. You didn't tell us that."

"I just did. Now, let's all make a wish and thank our Mr. Sam Black." The three of them took deep breaths and blew out the candles as they made their wishes.

One more celebration commenced in memory of Sam and Catherine Black: the grand opening of Seela's art gallery, which was stunning and filled with her mother's paintings. Seela had received them while she was still on the island, dealing with Sam's death and the lost love of Joseph.

She and Dee had done as Sam had asked her. The two of them had been alone when they'd opened the paintings wrapped with brown paper. They'd found envelopes taped to the backs of the paintings, marked with smiley faces and containing stacks of one hundred-dollar bills. He'd known Seela would use the money wisely and didn't need any instructions on what to do with it. Seela and Dee had laughed all afternoon as they unwrapped each painting. She realized all the trouble Catherine had gone through to not only insert the money into the pictures but also paint all the pictures per Sam's requests. Now the paintings were new fixtures for the grand opening of Seela's art gallery.

Seela and Chester walked out into the gallery from the back room, dressed to the nines, and greeted all the locals there to buy Catherine's art. The music of Van Morrison piped through the speakers in honor of Catherine, as that had been Catherine's music of choice to paint to. Dressed in a stunning white suit, Dee approached Seela, anxious to tell her about the visitor at the front door. Mamaw, with a red silk scarf tied around her neck, danced in her motorized wheelchair, happy to be a part of the evening.

Dee grabbed Seela's elbow. "You have a gentleman at the door who wants to purchase several paintings for his new house on the beach down south."

"I do? Who is it, Dee?"

"You need to go see, Seels. He's waiting at the door. He said he heard about your show but didn't have an invite or ticket to get in."

Seela raised her eyebrows in amazement and made her way through the crowd slowly, mumbling greetings and exchanging hugs. As soon as she could see the front door, her heart leaped. *Joseph*. There Joseph stood with his gorgeous smile, which she'd replayed over and over in her mind over the past year. Her eyes filled with tears as she ran into his open arms.

"Oh my God, it's you, Joseph. I didn't think you ever wanted to see me again. I can't believe you're here. Where have you been? I tried reaching you a few times, but you never answered."

"I'm so sorry, Seela. I had to leave the state and exit the program. I had to lay low for a year until the investigation was finally dropped. The DEA was not happy with me for dropping my story. I couldn't do that to you or Sam. I kept my word with him."

Seela couldn't believe Joseph was standing in front of her. "Chester is going to be so excited to see you, Joseph. Let me take you to him."

Joseph pulled Seela back. "Seela, I still love you." Joseph gazed at Seela, hoping she had not moved on in the past year that they had been apart.

Seela closed her eyes, kissing Joseph's luscious lips. "I never stopped thinking about you, and yes, I still love you. Come. Let's go surprise everybody! I can't believe you are here!"

As soon as Chester saw Joseph with Seela, he ran from the dessert table to hug him. "Yosef, I have missed you so much. Are you back now?"

"Yes, my man. I'm not letting you go either," Joseph whispered while hugging Chester tightly.

Mamaw wheeled her chair over to the table and gasped. "I could whip your heinie for leaving us, Joseph. Where in the hell did you go?" She grabbed Joseph's pant leg and said, "I'm holding on to you now."

"Don't worry, Mamaw. I'm not going anywhere. As a matter of fact, I bought a beach house almost walking distance from you."

Dee stopped in her tracks. "You weren't kidding about the beach house then?"

"No, ma'am. You can come visit. I'm hoping I can make Sam's wishes come true."

"What were Sam's wishes, Joseph?" asked Seela.

"I think he gave us all wishes, Seela. Even the ones he touched on the inside."

The grand opening of the gallery was a sensational hit, and Seela sold half of Catherine's paintings. At the end of the evening, Seela toasted her brother and mother while staring at Catherine's most vibrant painting: one of a cardinal against a black background. It hung on Seela's beloved brick wall in her gallery and was a painting she held dear to her heart. She would always keep it.

Seela glowed. She had Joseph back and knew they were all together now, just the way Sam would have wanted.

Six months later, Mamaw and Mavvie sat out in their beautiful landscaped garden, listening to the island's wildlife sing around them as they watched for their daily cardinal visit.

Seela feverishly typed on her laptop in the new house Joseph had purchased by the beach. After a few more sentences, she closed her screen, looking out the window at the ocean waves crashing back and forth. Suddenly, Joseph's hand touched her shoulder.

"Did you finish your brother's story, Seels? Are you done?" he said softly.

Seela stood up from her desk carefully, trying not to bump her five-months-pregnant belly. She looked over at Chester, who was sitting on the sofa, playing his Xbox. "Come, Chester. Let's all hug. I finished my book."

Chester threw his controller down and ran as quickly as he could to Seela and Joseph. They embraced as a family as Seela pointed to the open window that her desk faced. A bright red cardinal sat on a weeping willow tree limb, chirping its heart out. Seela looked lovingly at Joseph and Chester while touching her pregnant belly and said, "Now we have completed Sam's wishes."